W9-BNO-643

Praise for *Children of the Canyon*

"The music scene in Laurel Canyon in the '60s and '70s has been the subject of many books and drugged out tales. But nowhere have I seen the era and story told from the perspective of the children who were lucky/unlucky enough to be raised in this crazed environment. Until now...Kukoff has written an eye-opening novel filled with heart, humor, and insight. Pull up a chair, put on a Joni Mitchell album, and enjoy this little treasure."

—Ken Levine, Emmy award-winning writer/producer of *Cheers* and *TIME* magazine award-winning blogger

"This book's depths are treacherous and formidable. A debut novel you won't soon forget."

—Allison Burnett, author of *Undiscovered Gyrl*

"*Children of the Canyon* is relatable, funny, tragic, and page-turning. As a fellow writer, I adored and re-read the tapestry of wonderfully crafted, simply presented sentences that lurk above one's head well after the last page is flipped."

—Chip Jacobs, author of *Smogtown*

"This book is truly a classic of its time, a defining novel the likes of which certainly doesn't exist on the market. It will make you turn your own self inside-out and take stock of the pieces of yourself you forgot existed."

—Kate St. Clair, author of *Spelled*

"From the first sentence, I couldn't put this book down, and after lingering over the last sentence, I can't stop thinking about it. Everything about *Children of the Canyon* is unique, from the voice to the storyline to the surprising twists, turns, and observations. The amazing thing... is the way it can be laugh-out-loud funny one minute, and bring tears to your eyes the next—all the while illuminating truths about life that we all perceive but may not be able to so gracefully and astutely articulate."

—Lori Gottlieb, author of *Marry Him*

"David Kukoff was able to capture the true essence of a unique, unforgettable era while also telling a human tale of love and understanding of the self."

—Alice Carbone, host of award-winning *Coffee With Alice*

"Not since *The Catcher in the Rye* has a coming of age book struck such a resonating chord. It's relatable, magical, and moving. The themes of love, loss, the fragility of childhood, and the transition from the wonder years into adulthood will reverberate and linger long after the final page. *Children of the Canyon* has all the markings of becoming a literary classic."

—Tosha Michelle, host of *La Literati*

"A universal, and all too relatable tale of family boundaries, failing ideals, and the end of a counterculture done in by its own excesses and inability to gauge the shifting cultural landscape."

—Daniel Rosen, founder of Bookreels.com

CHILDREN
OF
THE CANYON

CHILDREN OF THE CANYON

BY DAVID KUKOFF

A VIREO BOOK · RARE BIRD BOOKS

THIS IS A GENUINE VIREO BOOK

V

A Vireo Book | Rare Bird Books
453 South Spring Street, Suite 531
Los Angeles, CA 90013
rarebirdbooks.com

Copyright © 2014 by David Kukoff

EXTENDED EDITION

All rights reserved, including the right to reproduce this book or portions thereof in any form whatsoever. For more information, address:
A Vireo Book | Rare Bird Books Subsidiary Rights Department, 453 South Spring Street, Suite 531, Los Angeles, CA 90013.

Originally published by

Set in Minion Pro
Printed in the United States
Distributed in the US by Publishers Group West.

10 9 8 7 6 5 4 3 2 1

Publisher's Cataloging-in-Publication data

Kukoff, David.
    Children of the canyon / by David Kukoff.
    p. cm.
    ISBN 978-1-940207-60-5

1. Coming of age—Fiction. 2. Laurel Canyon (Los Angeles, Calif.)—Fiction. 3. California—History—20th century—Fiction. 4. Rock music—California—Los Angeles—Fiction. 5. Popular culture—California—Los Angeles—Fiction. 6. Bildungsroman. I. Title.

PS3611 .U41 C35 2014
813.6—dc23

Then leaf subsides to leaf.
So Eden sank to grief,
So dawn goes down to day,
Nothing gold can stay.

Robert Frost

THE CIRCLE GAME

DAVID WATCHES SMILES.

He watches smiles because people are supposed to be happy when they smile. But the more he watches smiles, the more he thinks this isn't always true. People smile when they are angry, or sad, or just because, sometimes. You can't really tell unless you're inside their minds. This is where David thinks the missing half, the half that would make the smile a perfect circle, is hiding.

There are circles all over the cooperative where David goes to school. Most of them are bright smiley-face yellow stickers. The stickers and the smiles are supposed to make everyone happy, but all they make David do is think about unfinished circles and smiles that aren't really smiles, because they're always missing something.

David thinks about the people around him who all seem to be missing something, too. The gray-haired Indian woman who plays a guitar at the cooperative and sings to the kids seems to be missing something. The guy on TV who tries to sell you cars, while singing about his dog Spot that's really a cheetah, seems to be missing something, although in his case that something is probably an actual dog. Carole, David's mother, uses words she hears from the shrink, like psychic and soul child, to describe David but she smiles when she says them and David can tell she's missing something, too. David's father, Phil, seems to be missing something every time he comes out of his music studio and looks around as though he'd just stepped into bright sunlight. The three of them seem to be missing something whenever they eat meals together as a family, when Carole and Phil talk to David as if they're really talking to each other. David tries not to think about it because it makes him think about the other half of the circle in his mind, which makes him think things that don't make him smile at all.

Tonight David is sitting in the way-back of the car as Carole drives down the beach highway, the one below the mountain that rains rocks when it's dry out and mud when it rains. On warm days, the cooperative used to take the kids to the beach on field trips. All the parents had to agree on the trips because agreeing on the rules was the reason for having cooperatives in the first place. Carole and Phil didn't agree on sending David to the cooperative before they signed him up last year. He heard them fighting about it almost every night when he was trying to sleep. Carole used words that David didn't understand, and Phil growled a lot, but didn't really say much until it was too late to sign up for any place else. This was usually the way things went in their house: round in circles, without really ending anywhere.

The cooperative ended a month ago with an assembly on the painted benches that were always in a big semi-circle. Everyone sang and held hands as the children walked up to the stage one by one, but the children weren't mentioned by name. Singling anyone out was a big frowny-face at the cooperative because it didn't create cooperative kids.

David sees the beach up ahead and thinks about how the kids tumbled out of the van and ran around without having to agree on anything. All of them except David. He spent the time watching everything and trying to cram it all into his head because something told him that remembering these days would be important someday, when everything else was gone. This made sense, because even though the cooperative has been over for only a month, most of what happened there is already slipping out of his mind, the same way the squishy sand between the children's toes slipped away at the spot where the baby ocean waves met the beach.

David turns around and watches the headlights on the highway behind him as they draw closer. They look like the shapes on the television shows Carole puts him in front of on days when it gets to be too much and she can't take it anymore. Those days, like most days, David pays more attention to Carole's behavior than he pays to the shapes on the television. He watches as she paces around the house and he wonders what kind of music is playing inside her head to make her rub her hands together and hum through her nose. Phil is always talking about how the universe holds all kinds of invisible music that only certain people are able to hear. David wonders if this is like the game he used to play with at the cooperative, the one that has all the shapes in the universe—pointy star shapes, oval planet shapes, and circular moon shapes—and that played music when you put the right shape in the right place. But probably not; Phil says that musicians march to a different beat from everyone else, which is why he and the people he works with sleep at strange hours and eat with their hands, and why David has a hard time understanding them sometimes.

Sometimes Carole seems to hear what Phil is talking about, but most of the time she doesn't even pretend to listen to anything Phil says. That goes for David too, especially lately. He feels as though Carole is marching to a far different beat from anything Phil has ever heard.

Carole drives past the beach the cooperative used to go to, the one he loves, but the look on her face tells David he shouldn't ask why and they aren't stopping. Something is happening tonight and Carole is even more sad and hummy than usual. So David stares at the muddy cliffs along the highway and bounces up and down as the car goes over the bumps on the road.

Last year David taught himself to read from the signs on the highway sheds selling things like jewelry and body oils and organic food that makes you live longer. A lot of the grown-ups his parents know eat organic food and complain about how they don't like their lives. David once asked Carole why anyone would eat anything that gave him or her more of something they didn't like. She told him that most people lead with their hearts and not with their heads. This is one of the things he hopes will make sense someday.

The car continues past the roads that lead to the canyons, which Phil says are home to more coyotes than houses. David lives in a canyon closer to town, the one where the Bogeyman sneaked up the hill and killed a bunch of movie stars and rich people. The police still haven't caught the Bogeyman, and all the kids are scared, even though the parents said the Bogeyman only went after grown-ups who didn't live their lives the way grown-ups are supposed to.

Carole turns onto a dirt parking lot above the ocean, then lifts the gear stick and puts the car in park. Phil thinks it's lazy for a car to do all the gear shifting for you. He drives a red convertible that has a wooden knob and a rubber gearbox by the driver's seat and that stays in the garage with a black cover over it at night. David once asked Phil why he needed to cover the car if it's already in a garage and Phil said it kept the girls away. Kinda like a boy's clubhouse. He didn't know what Phil meant by that since he doesn't have a clubhouse and the only girl he knows lives on his block, is much older, and probably wouldn't want to go anywhere near a boy's clubhouse. Sometimes when David doesn't understand things, he wonders if he's marching to one of those beats Phil is always talking about, or if Phil is and just doesn't know it yet.

Carole turns off the engine. She and David get out of the car and walk down some steps to the beach where David hears the crashing sound of the waves. He also hears a guitar and a man singing a song they used to sing at the cooperative, a song about children and circles and games. David doesn't understand all the words but he thinks the song has something to do with growing up and knows it always makes the grown-ups sad whenever they hear the children singing it.

As they get closer to the sand, David and Carole see some people sitting around a fire. There's lots of smoke, but it isn't all coming from the fire. David sniffs and smells the same kinds of cigarettes Phil smokes that make him tired and smiley. Phil rarely sleeps and never smiles unless he smokes those cigarettes. Then he smiles a lot, and for no reason David can understand, because it's not as though anything has changed that would make him suddenly happy.

David doesn't like the way the smoke makes his lungs burn the way they do on days when the smog gets bad. Sometimes Carole drives David along the twisty street above the canyon and the air is so bad David can barely see the Valley below. Carole says that it would be the death of her to live in the Valley, which makes David wonder if someone could actually die from the air in the Valley. From what he's seen, it looks flat and gray and, even though it's just over the hill from where he lives, doesn't feel attached to any form of life he knows.

The man playing the guitar nods at Carole and smiles. "Is he here yet?"

Carole shakes her head.

"Would you like to get started anyway?" asks the man.

Carole looks at the people around the fire, then turns back to the man with the guitar.

"Can we give him a few more minutes?"

The man with the guitar nods and smiles again. David has the feeling he smiles a lot because he spends time with people who need to be around someone who smiles a lot, and that he's so used to it, he does it without even thinking anymore.

"That he should be late tonight is perfect," says Carole. "Just perfect." Carole tries to laugh, but it sounds more as if a piece of food got stuck in her throat on the way down.

David decides to explore, so he walks over to an empty part of the beach where he spots some tide pools. He loves tide pools, because so many different creatures can find a way to get along in a small space without being able to think or smile, or think about smiling.

"Hi."

David looks up and sees a girl sitting on some rocks nearby. He thinks she's about his age, but he can never tell with girls because sometimes they play games that make them seem older.

"Would you like to come over here and sit with me?"

David walks over and sits down next to her.

"Why are you out here all by yourself?" he asks.

"I live here."

"On the beach?"

"Nope. Up there."

She points to a big house above that looks like one of those lighthouses David has seen in paintings, only this house doesn't have a single light on.

"Why aren't you up there now?" asks David.

"I like it better down here."

David wonders if the lights are out in her house more than they're on. "Don't your parents care if you're out on the beach this late?"

"You mean my parent? I live with my mother. My father's gone."

"Dead?"

"No, just gone. And my mom's asleep. She drinks lots of wine at night then doesn't wake up until the next morning. Then she's cranky for the rest of the day unless she drinks the hair of the dog that bit her."

David has heard Phil and Carole talk about all kinds of strange things that people put into their bodies and he figures this must be one of them.

"What's your mother like?" asks the girl.

"She looks at me a lot and tells me how much she loves me. But she doesn't really seem happy about it. She says that's why she named me David."

"Why?"

"Because it's supposed to mean 'beloved.'"

"How can your parents name you something like that before they even know you?"

David doesn't know how to answer this, so he doesn't say anything. The girl picks up a stick and starts drawing a shape in the sand.

"What's your sign?" she asks.

"The one on the street where I live?"

"Your astrological sign. It's an animal or creature in the stars in the sky and the month you were born. I'm an Aquarius, which is an air sign. I'm everywhere in the universe but you can't always see me."

"How do I find my sign?"

"When were you born?"

"February 21st."

"You're a Pisces. A water sign."

"What does that mean?"

"It means you feel things real deep."

David feels sad that more kids don't talk the way she talks.

"So where do you live?" she asks, rubbing her goose-pimply arms.

"In the canyon above the pink hotel."

"Isn't that where that guy killed all those rich people and movie stars?"

"I think so." He doesn't want to tell her it's practically all he thinks about at night when he's in bed, especially when he hears the coyotes outside, which always sound closer to the house than Phil says they actually are.

"My mom says something's wrong with this city and we have to get out before it's too late."

"Too late for what?"

"I don't know."

The moon is brighter than usual and it lights up the girl's face. David likes looking at her face, and right now he doesn't care if he just sits here all night without going back to the grown-ups and their smoke and their smiles that mean lots of things, but almost never happiness.

David hears the man with the guitar say something, then he starts playing the circle song again.

"What's going on?" asks the girl.

"I don't know."

"Aren't you with them?"

"I came here with my mom."

"Where's your dad?"

"Late."

"Want to go back over there?"

David is silent. The girl stops drawing in the sand and stands up.

"Come on. I'll go with you."

David and the girl walk back over to the grown-ups, who are all standing and holding hands around the fire. Just like the children at the cooperative used to do before they all went home for the day. Phil is there too, but he's standing with a different group of grown-ups, across the fire from Carole.

The man with the guitar says something, then Carole and Phil each hold up one of their hands. They stand like that for a moment, then speak in the same kind of chanting voices as those shaved-head people at the airports who wear robes and have white, painted squigglys on their noses.

"We dissolve our union…
We relinquish our souls to Mother Earth…
We are free once again.
Free…"

"What are they talking about?" asks the girl.

"I don't know," says David, but he does know he is watching something that will change how everything works from now on.

Phil and Carole take off their wedding rings and throw them into the fire. Then they turn and start heading toward the ocean. The other grown-ups follow Carole and Phil, most of them taking off their shoes as they do and some of them taking off other clothing as well. Soon they are all playing around in the ocean the way the kids used to on their field trips with the cooperative, only now there are no grown-ups to watch and make sure nothing bad happens to them.

David and the girl walk back over to the tide pools and sit down. The girl picks up her stick and starts drawing in the sand again.

"I think my parents just got divorced," says David softly.

"You'll get used to it," says the girl, but she sounds as though she knows what she's talking about, which makes him feel a little better.

She finishes drawing her shape in the sand and shows it to David.

"Why did you draw a circle?" he asks.

She shrugs and throws the stick into the bushes, then slides onto her stomach.

"Let's play our own circle game," she says, putting her finger at the bottom of the circle.

"How?"

"Simple. Take your finger like this…"

She takes David's finger and puts it next to hers.

"Now trace it all the way up to the top of the circle. Go up on the left side and I'll do the same thing on the right side."

"What's the point?"

"To see if we meet at the top and right in the middle."

"What does it mean if we do?"

"I'll tell you later. Now lie down and close your eyes."

David slides onto his stomach and waits for her to close her eyes before closing his own. He doesn't know if he should move his finger fast or slow, or if she wants their fingers to meet at the top or not, or if he should even want them to. He remembers what Phil said about marching to your own beat, then he stops thinking and slowly starts moving his finger up the circle.

They hear a scream from the water. David and the girl open their eyes and look over at the ocean, where Carole is standing in the water with her arms raised high above her head.

"I'm free!" She spins around and around until she collapses into the water and the crashing sound of the waves finally drowns out her voice.

David and the girl turn their eyes back to the sand. Their fingers are touching at the top of the circle.

"Right in the middle," the girl says quietly.

David swallows. "So what do we win?"

"Each other's souls."

"What do you mean?"

"A circle's a perfect shape. So is the soul. If you find someone who can trace the outline of a circle the exact same way, then that person and you will be together."

"For how long?"

"Forever."

"There's no such thing as forever," says David. His lip starts to quiver. "People die and there's the Bogeyman and people get divorced, too."

"There is too such a thing as forever. If you think there is."

"What if I don't?"

"Then I'll think it enough for both of us."

She shivers, but neither of them wants to go over to the fire, so David moves closer and puts his jacket around her.

"Thanks," she says, putting her head on his shoulder. "I'm so tired I could fall asleep."

"Go ahead," says David.

"No way. That's how a baby is made. A boy and girl go to sleep together. When they wake up, the girl's pregnant."

"Did your mom tell you that, too?"

"No. That's just science. In books and everything."

"You better stay awake then. Because I don't want a baby."

"Not even someday?"

"Nope."

The girl moves closer.

"I don't want a baby, either," she says.

"I thought all girls wanted babies. That's why they play with dolls."

"Not me. I just want things to stay like this."

David wonders if maybe there might be such a thing as forever after all. "Me, too," he says.

"Let's wish for it then. Close your eyes."

"Again?"

"Yeah. You gotta close your eyes before you do anything special."

David closes his eyes.

"Now wish," she says.

David and the girl are both quiet for a moment. He counts to twenty then opens his eyes.

Hers are already open.

They turn to each other at the same time and she kisses him quickly on the lips.

Something inside David's chest feels like it flipped over and it takes him a second to catch his breath.

"Why'd you do that?" he asks.

"Sealed with a kiss. That's how you make something yours."

He thinks about it, then shrugs.

"Okay," he says softly.

"Topanga…" A woman's voice calls out from above.

"Looks like my mom woke up," says the girl. She wiggles out of his jacket and stands up.

"Your name is Topanga? Like that canyon my mom always drives by?"

"We lived there when I was born. My mom used to call it the Garden of Eden. Now she says the canyons are Mother Nature's bad children that she destroys with fire and floods."

Topanga starts to walk up the stairs leading up to the bluffs. David watches her for a moment then he grabs her stick and runs over to the dying fire. He pokes the stick around until he finds the rings, then slides the stick through the rings, pulls them out, and dunks them in the wet sand. By the time he's finished, Topanga is halfway up the staircase.

"Topanga…"

David digs the rings out from the cold wet sand and runs as fast as he can over to the staircase.

"Wait!"

Topanga turns around as David catches up to her. He takes the smaller ring out of his pocket and places it in her hand, then closes her fingers around the hot wet circle.

"There."

Topanga smiles, then turns around and heads back up the staircase and disappears into the long, wild grass at the top of the bluffs.

On his way back, David thinks about her smile. He is only six years old, but he can't remember another smile that made him smile so much just thinking about it. He wonders if maybe someday he'll meet her again and if she'll make him smile the way he does now, and if his smile will connect to hers and form the kind of perfect circle she was talking about. Maybe when he's grown up, he'll think everything will look different from how it does now, but a circle will remain the same. And then maybe he won't ever have to wonder about smiles and happiness and if anything really lasts forever.

COYOTES

THE FIRST HOWL WAKES David in the middle of the night. He lies in bed as his eyes go from his mind's dreamy shadows to the pitch-black of his room. His eyes don't have that sandpaper feeling he has whenever he wakes up before he's ready, a feeling he's used to ever since the night Carole sat on his bed a few weeks ago and told him she was leaving.

She sang him a song about a jet plane and tried to make him feel better, the way a person is always supposed to feel better whenever someone shares a song with them, but it only made him feel worse. Most nights he wakes up a lot before morning without knowing why.

He climbs out of his bed with the built-in drawers underneath that hold his sheets, opens his door, and walks down the hallway, his toes squishing in the shaggy brown carpet as he does. He passes the drawings of naked women and the painting with Phil's face in purple and black and goes to the living room. The big fish tank in the rock-covered walls makes wavy blue shapes that dance on the floor in front of him.

He looks through the sliding glass doors that lead to the steam-covered pool, at the hillside that disappears into the canyon. Usually that's where all the howls come from, but tonight the hillside doesn't seem to be stirring. David is about to go back to bed when he notices that one of the sliding glass doors is open and the windy brush-smell coming in is causing the curtains to flap around like ghosts.

CLANG!

The noise comes from behind him.

David turns around and follows the dancing aquarium lights into the middle of the living room, where he sees an enormous shape sitting on the bench in front of the piano. David isn't sure whether to go back to his bedroom or just scream as loudly as he can. Then he realizes that if the shape wanted to hurt anyone, it probably wouldn't be sitting quietly on a piano bench in the middle of the living room.

CLANG!!!

The piano keys bang again, this time louder than before, and David realizes that whatever this shape is, it's trying to play the piano.

The lights go on.

Phil is standing in the hallway in a bathrobe. A woman David has never seen before stands behind Phil, wearing something shiny and see-through in the light from the hallway behind her.

"Ben…"

Phil is speaking to the shape at the piano. In the light, David sees that the shape is big and fat and hairy and doesn't budge at the sound of Phil's voice.

"Ben."

Ben looks up and stares straight ahead with eyes that look as though they're trying to be somewhere other than here.

"It's covered with sand," he says.

Phil sits down next to Ben as the woman runs down the hallway to the bedroom Phil used to share with Carole.

"What's covered with sand?"

"My piano."

"That's because you put it in a sandbox."

"What?"

"Your piano. It's in a sandbox. In your living room. That's why it's covered with sand."

"That's got nothing to do with it."

"That's got everything to do with it. That's one of the reasons this record's taking so long."

Ben points a finger in Phil's face. "No, man, you don't get it. I'm talking about sand. Like sleep. Like quicksand. It's not reality here, it's metaphysics and metaphor."

CLANG!!!

"Sand!"

CLANG!!!

"Mr. Sandman. That's what my old man used to make me call him. Know why?"

"No," says Phil, even though David has the feeling he probably does know why.

"Because he said he'd put me into the big sleep if I ever showed him anything but complete fear and submission."

CLANG!!!

"That's what I'm talking about. Sand. The stuff you gotta bury your head in, just to make it through the day."

CLANG!!!

The final chord hangs in the air until it's replaced by the whistling sound of the hot wind coming in through the open glass door.

"Do you get it?"

"I get it," says Phil.

"DO YOU?"

Ben's eyes don't look faraway or angry anymore, only confused and sad. Phil squeezes Ben's shoulder the way he squeezes David's shoulder whenever David has nightmares.

"I get it."

Ben slumps back over the piano and holds his fingers over the keys. "I gotta use yours. Just 'til mine's safe to go back to."

"All right."

CLANG!!!

"But not now," says Phil.

"Right now."

"No," says Phil. "My kid's starting his first day of school tomorrow."

Ben looks up and notices David for the first time. "Hey..."

David takes a step back.

"Don't be afraid. There's nothing to be afraid of here." Ben stands up.

Phil puts his hand on Ben's shoulder again and tries to ease him back down to the piano bench. "Why don't you crash here tonight? I don't like the way you look."

"I've looked this way my whole life," says Ben. He smiles at David slowly, as though he's trying to remember how, then he disappears through the sliding glass doors.

✳

THE FIRST THING DAVID notices about his new school is that the children sit in rows instead of in a circle as they had at the cooperative. Also, there is a schedule on the wall that tells them what they will be working on every day, unlike the cooperative where they took a vote on most things.

"Scary, huh?" said Phil, when he walked David into the classroom. He'd said something about David getting used to it, but sitting in his seat, staring at the schedule, David feels like he's already used to it. It has times for everything, including recess, and David can't understand why knowing this would be scary.

The class begins with the Pledge of Allegiance and a few activities which are supposed to help the children remember each other's names. Then they go out onto the playground for recess. The warm winds are blowing which makes it hard to play tetherball and four square, so David sits with a kid named Jason in the lunch area, away from the giggling girls chasing the boys around the playground.

"Need a cootie shot?" asks Jason. He makes a crisscross shape with the second and third fingers of both hands and holds it out to David. He wears glasses and plaid pants that look perfectly creased, as if someone woke up early to press them for him.

"What for?"

"Girls. In case they kiss you."

David sticks his hand in his pocket and runs his fingers around the smooth circle of the ring he carries around with him.

"No, thanks," he says.

"Didn't get caught yet, huh? Me neither," says Jason proudly. They sit in silence and watch the boys and girls chase each other around the playground until the bell rings and the children head back to class.

David and Jason take their seats as their teacher, Mrs. Johnson, writes something on the blackboard. She has long hair and doesn't look old enough to be a Mrs., but is. She finishes writing, turns around, and smiles at the class.

"Who here has a pet?" she asks.

A lot of hands go up, including Jason's. David thinks about the fish in the living room, but they just swim around in circles and don't seem aware that someone else takes care of them, so he keeps his hand down.

"This Friday I want you to tell the class all about your pet. If you don't have one, I'd like you to tell us what kind of pet you'd like to have."

For the rest of the day the children listen to stories, dance to music, and do art projects that make David's fingertips crusty with glue. By the time class is dismissed, David still hasn't figured out what he wants to talk about for his pet report. He peels the glue off his fingers and waits until the others have left the classroom, then he walks over to Mrs. Johnson.

"I don't have a pet."

"That's okay," says Mrs. Johnson, giving him another smile.

"But I don't know what kind of pet I would have, either. If I did have one."

"Take the rest of the week to decide. Sometimes our lives end up giving us the answers to our questions without our having to think about them too much."

Phil's red convertible is parked outside by the classroom. David climbs in and tells Phil about the assignment.

"But you never wanted a pet," says Phil.

"I know, but we're still supposed to talk about one."

"That's called a hypothetical situation."

"A what?"

"A hypothetical situation is something that could be, instead of something that is. Right now, there are lots of people unhappy with the way things actually are. So they're trying to come up with hypothetical situations to make things better."

David thinks about this all the way home. Usually he thinks about how much he enjoys the wind blowing against his face, or wonders how anyone learns how to use the stick shift with the wooden knob. But today, the pet question and hypothetical situations are crusting all over his mind the way the glue did on his hands during art. He still doesn't have any answers when bedtime rolls around, so he closes his eyes and tries to find answers in the emptiness, but nothing comes to him except sleep.

✦

THE SECOND HOWL COMES the next night.

David is watching television in the study that doubles as a guest room when Phil's guests drink too much wine and can't drive home. The news on television is all about the capture of the Bogeyman and his family. The Bogeyman is short and smiles a lot and has carved a sign into his forehead that has something to do with killing Jews. Several girls in ponchos and scarves sit and cry on the sidewalk outside the jail where the Bogeyman is, and one of them talks about how the pigs may have captured their leader but nothing will ever break up their family. David wonders what makes this family so strong that it can never be broken up.

He turns off the television and stares at the postcard from Carole that came in the mail that morning. It is a picture of a group of people, all dressed in white robes, with uncombed hair all over their faces. Just like Ben. But David isn't thinking about Ben. He's thinking about Carole, who wrote that she misses David terribly but loves her new home.

"What does she mean, 'her new home'?" David asked Phil as he sat in the kitchen that morning smoking a cigarette.

"Carole's in an ashram."

"What's an ashram?"

"It's a place where people go to live together and study with someone who teaches them all the wise things he's learned about life," said Phil, in a way that sounded as though he didn't really mean it.

"Like the Bogeyman did with his family?"

"Something like that."

"Why does Ben have sand in his piano?"

Phil sighed, stubbed out his cigarette, and ran his hand through his hair.

"Ben grew up on the beach. It was his favorite place in the world. Then he became famous singing songs about the beach with his band."

"What happened to them?"

"They broke up."

"Like divorced?"

"Well, they were all family. Two brothers and a cousin. So yeah. Kind of. Now Ben's got a big mess in his head which he's trying to untangle by capturing what he once had."

"With sand?"

"That. And music."

"Does it help like that? Music?"

"For some people it's the only thing that helps."

Phil stood up and shuffled down the hallway toward his studio. David wanted to ask him when Carole would come back but he was scared that Phil would say something like "when she hears the music." Sometimes when Phil talks, David understands most of the words themselves, but not what they mean all put together. Whenever this happens, David does his best to cram it into his brain and store it there, one word at a time, so that one day he will be able to assemble them in a way that will make sense to him.

David puts down Carole's postcard and walks over to the living room where he hears loud voices. One voice seems louder than the rest and sounds like those songs at the cooperative where the leader would sing first and then the children would repeat. The only difference is these voices belong to grown-ups.

"Oh, there you are."

David looks over at the doorway where he sees the woman who was with Phil the night before. This is the third day in a row she's been at the house. Her name is Hallie and she's from a small town somewhere. She used to go to college but doesn't anymore, and she has a nice smile that's different from most of Phil's friends' smiles. Mostly because she doesn't use one, except when she's asking for something.

"Looking for Dad?" Hallie has heard David call Phil by his name several times but doesn't seem to notice or care. "He's in the living room. Wanna check out something that's gonna blow your little mind?"

Hallie leads David over to the living room where some grownups are listening to a black man with huge round hair that bobs up and down every time he speaks.

"That's Brother Louie Coleman," whispers Hallie.

David sometimes watches a cartoon about three ducks, who are also brothers, named Huey, Duey, and Louie, but David has the impression that this Brother Louie is nothing like that brother Louie. For one thing, his teeth are in neat white rows and look as if they could eat the duck brothers without even cooking them first.

"The lumpenproletariat," says Brother Louie. "That's what I'm talking about, people."

The grownups nod. They pay the same kind of attention to Brother Louie that David's classmates pay to Mrs. Johnson, but the grownups drink wine instead of fruit punch and don't have to come up with an answer to a hypothetical situation about a pet.

Brother Louie walks over to the fish tank and stands in front of it. The tank's lighting creates a fuzzy blue halo around Brother Louie's head.

"The lumpenproletariat was Karl Marx's word for the waste product of society. Every dog must have its everyday but everyday people ain't the point of this country."

"Hear hear," says a grownup woman whose clothing seems made of beads and little more.

"Now Marx didn't think the lumpen was worth nothin' but a lump of black coal. Well, this here lump of black Coleman is telling you that Marx was off the mark."

Some of the grownups clap loudly while a few others stick their fingers between their teeth and whistle.

"Now my brothers and sisters up north are stirring the pot. We're tightening up. We're taking our act on the road and coming down here to rain a dark as night shit-storm on the propaganda that's been teaching our children's minds the wrong kind of division. The kind that puts the rich on the inside, and everyone else in the outhouse. We need brothers and sisters to turn society's divisions inside out and upside down. Teach these old, everyday dogs some new goddamn tricks."

The grownups applaud as Phil walks over to Brother Louie and puts his arm around him.

"Isn't he amazing?" asks Hallie, staring right at Brother Louie.

David didn't understand anything Brother Louie was talking about, but since the grownups seem to feel the same way about Brother Louie as David feels about Mrs. Johnson, he nods and says nothing.

✦

"Is that your mother?" asks Jason.

"Who?"

"The woman who brought you to school."

David and Jason are sitting in the lunch area, eating each other's lunches. Jason heard something about people who don't eat meat out of their love for animals, so because he has a dog and a hamster, he traded his roast beef sandwich for David's peanut butter sandwich. Phil slept late after being up all night in the studio, so Hallie made David's lunch that morning.

Phil told her that David loved peanut butter, but peanut butter makes David think of Carole, who used to make it for him every day. David didn't want to say anything because Hallie looked as though she really enjoyed making his lunch. The other night David saw her reading a book by someone named Dr. Spock. He mentions this to Jason after telling him the woman who drives him to school isn't his mother. He doesn't tell Jason that his mother prefers to be called Carole and lives in an ashram with people who don't cut the hair on their heads or anywhere else on their bodies.

"Isn't Dr. Spock some spaceman on TV with funny ears?"

"I think so. But I think he also writes books about how to understand kids better."

Jason takes a bite of his sandwich as David watches the girls chase the boys around the lunch area. The boys don't look like they're running too fast, but somehow they do just enough to keep from being caught.

"Does the woman who takes you to school have any kids?" asks Jason.

"No."

"Then why do you think she's reading that book?"

David shrugs.

"Maybe she wants you to be her kid," says Jason.

David decides to change the subject. "So which one of your pets are you gonna talk about tomorrow?"

"My goldfish."

"How come?"

"I guess I feel sorry for him."

"Why?"

"Everyone loves dogs and hamsters. But goldfish are just here to get swallowed up by snakes and fraternity guys. At least that's what my dad said when I won him with a ping-pong ball."

Jason crumples the wax paper from the sandwich into a ball and throws it toward the garbage can. He misses it by about ten feet. David wonders if Jason's dad was the one who won the fish with the ping-pong ball and if Jason sits at the table during recess and lunch to hide from sports as well as girls.

"How about you?" asks Jason when he returns to the table.

"I don't know yet."

"When are you gonna figure it out?"

"Hopefully before tomorrow."

They watch as a girl named Maya finally catches up with one of the boys and kisses him right on the lips. The boy drops to the ground, playing dead, while the other girls laugh and jump up and down.

✦

THE THIRD HOWL COMES at a time of night when David has never been awake before. The noise is so loud that he sits up quickly in bed. The other howls sounded long and thin and faraway, but this one is nearby and sounds as if it came from right outside.

It also sounds as if it came from a person.

David tiptoes down the hallway, past the yellow light peeking out from under the locked door of Phil's studio, and into the living room. Nobody is sitting at the piano this time and no one is standing in the living room talking to grownups, either. He is about to return to his bedroom when he spots a blue light outside.

David walks over to the sliding glass doors and notices that they are open a crack. He wants to think about it. He wants to turn around and go back to sleep. But then he remembers what Ben told him, so he sucks in his breath and opens the glass doors a little wider and takes a step outside.

The Jacuzzi by the pool is on. Its jets are making soft whining noises and bubbles are pouring out and popping at the surface, leaving trails of white foam behind. David's eyes follow the trails of white foam over to Brother Louie who is sitting in the Jacuzzi. Tonight his hair is completely still and his eyes are closed.

"Mmm, that's right," he says to no one David can see. His left arm stretches out along the edge of the Jacuzzi, his right arm inside and underneath the water. He seems to be pushing a dark ball of hair up and down in front of him.

David sucks in his breath. Brother Louie turns, sees David, and stares at him for a moment. Then he smiles another one of those smiles where his teeth look as if they could eat the three duck brothers.

"Hey, little man. Wanna get a taste of what it's like to be a grownup?"

David takes a step backward.

"Don't be scared. Ain't nothin' to be scared of."

There is a splashing sound, then a head pops up from under the water. David looks closer and sees that the head belongs to Hallie. David sees Hallie's face in the moonlight. And even though he does not know exactly what is going on and has no idea what this man is talking about, he does know one thing.

She is scared. Very scared.

David turns around, runs back inside the house, closes the sliding glass doors, and locks them behind him. Then he runs down the hallway to his room and jumps under the covers where it's warm and dark and safe.

✦

DAVID SWALLOWS WHEN HE hears Mrs. Johnson call his name. He walks slowly up to the front of the classroom and tells his classmates that he doesn't have a pet but if he did, he would like to have a pet coyote. When his speech is finished, there is silence until Mrs. Johnson clears her throat.

"David, a coyote isn't a pet."

"I know. But I'd still like to have one as a pet, anyway."

"I'm afraid that's not possible. Coyotes are wild animals— they cannot be tamed and turned into pets. But thank you for your report."

David spends the rest of the morning doodling and counting the minutes on the clock until the class breaks for lunch. He hopes Jason likes American cheese because that's what Phil gave him that morning. They had to rush to get to school on time because Hallie had disappeared in the middle of the night.

✦

THE FOURTH HOWL COMES on a night when the moon lights up the sky, but this time David doesn't wake up. He is dreaming that he and Carole are running on a hill together, only Carole prefers it when David calls her Mom. And in his dream there is nothing to be afraid of; no families with Bogeymen, or people with long white robes or shiny white teeth. And even though David can tell somewhere deep inside that it's only a dream, that it's just one of those hypothetical situations Phil told him about, there are coyotes. Dozens of them, maybe hundreds, running wild and free, with him and his Mom. And the best part is that they let him feed them right out of his hand, the way it always should be with pets.

THE WAR AT HOME

ABASEBALL FALLS FROM THE cloudless blue sky. It is simply following the laws of gravity, David thinks, as he remembers the special he and Phil watched on public television the other night. What goes up must come down. It must obey the laws of Mother Nature if it is to live in peace and harmony on her green earth.

The ball lands with a soft *thwack* in the leather glove of a tough-looking boy. David has seen this boy as well as the others who play baseball on the cul-de-sac at the end of his block, but he has never thought about joining them. The way they play baseball, the confidence with which they run and catch and throw, makes him think they don't feel the same way he does inside, that someone is watching him all the time from somewhere, just waiting for him to trip over his own two feet and land flat on his face.

David stands underneath the cul-de-sac's street sign, Azure Place. The boys call it Azure Stadium and have painted sloppy-looking bases around the street. First base is by the tin mailbox someone tried to blow up with a firecracker last Halloween. Second base is at the dead end of the block, but the base is hard to see because it's covered with tire stains from all the drivers who hit the curb while turning around. Third base is by the patch of dead grass in front of the house that hasn't seen paint in years. Home is the manhole where the cul-de-sac begins.

One of the boys, a second-grader named Harris with arms that have new scrapes on them every week, can hit a baseball farther than any other boy in the neighborhood—maybe, from what David has heard, the entire city. He has broken at least one window, second stories included, in every house on the block, and the other boys follow him everywhere, even places they probably shouldn't. David has watched them disappear into the trees on the hillside without mentioning poison oak, or rattlesnakes, or the Bogeyman, whose family supposedly still lives out there somewhere. One neighbor, an older father who always drives his black Lincoln too fast down the block, threatened to fill Harris's legs with buckshot if he ever caught him or the others anywhere near his property, but Harris didn't flinch, even when the man was two inches away from his face.

Harris steps to the manhole, takes a practice swing, and crouches in a batting stance.

"Eh, batt-ah batt-ah. Eh, batt-ah batt-ah…suh-wing, battah!"

The boys in the cement outfield are chanting, trying to break Harris's concentration so he will swing under the ball and pop up, or swing over the ball and hit a grounder. Anything that will keep them from having to confront one of the headhunting missiles from Harris's bat. But Harris's attention is on one thing only, and that one thing, incoming, small and bullet-like as it looks to others, probably looks as big as a beach ball to Harris.

CRACK!

The ball rockets toward the outfielders, who watch helplessly as it sails over their heads and lands behind a neighbor's fence. One of the outfielders scrambles over the fence, grabs the ball, then hops back over and throws the ball toward home, but his throw is off-target and doesn't get there until well after Harris has stepped onto the manhole cover. The ball skips past the catcher, rolls down the block, and comes to a stop right near David.

"Little help?"

David looks over to see Harris standing between him and the catcher.

"You. Wanna give us back our ball?"

It doesn't sound like a question, even though it is. David picks up the ball and throws it as hard as he can over to where Harris is standing. The ball needs a couple of bounces to get there but David's aim is true and Harris looks impressed.

"Come here."

David walks over to Harris, trying not to look as if he's too eager to join them.

"Where do you live?"

David points to his house right as his thirteen-year-old next-door neighbor, Katie, runs out of her front door. She turns and yells something behind her, then stands on her front stoop as though she's waiting for a response, but there's nothing from inside but silence.

"She babysits for me sometimes," says David to Harris, as Katie storms down the hill past the boys. All of them stare at her, the way David has noticed older boys stare at girls when they're not just thinking about playing tricks on them.

"Pretty bad over there?" asks Harris, nodding at Katie's house. Katie's father is the one who drives the black Lincoln, the one who yelled at Harris.

"Sometimes. We hear a lot of yelling."

Harris turns back to the other boys, puts two fingers between his teeth, and whistles like those Army sergeants on the old movies Phil watches sometimes when he isn't in the studio.

"I'm thirsty. Who wants to take a break and head down the hill?"

The other boys run over to their bikes and skateboards. David can't believe that someone just two years older than he is can whistle, and immediately ten other boys are in formation and ready to move.

Harris turns to David. "Where are your wheels?"

David stares at him.

"Your bike? Skateboard? Gotta have a set of wheels. How else you gonna get around?"

David has never heard anyone talk about getting around on their own without checking with their parents. It excites him more than it scares him, and it scares him more than a little bit.

"My dad usually takes me."

A few of the boys laugh, but Harris raises his hand and they stop immediately.

"Your old man's the guy who drives that red convertible?"

David nods.

"Nice," says Harris, nodding. He points to his own bicycle, a red Schwinn with a banana seat and black racing stripes up and down the sides.

"You can ride on my handlebars today. But from now on, you're gonna need some wheels if you're gonna hang out with us. Got it?"

David nods, trying to hide his excitement at the idea of there being a "from now on." Harris climbs onto his bike and clamps his hands tightly on the black grips at the sides of his handlebars.

"Hop on."

David lifts himself up onto the metal crossbar and sits down as Harris kicks the pedals, then takes off down the hill. The wind rushes past David's ears as Harris navigates the canyon's twists and turns, making David's eyeballs tear up and his lips feel dry. For the first time in his life, he understands why Phil decided to keep the red convertible, even though Carole was always calling it a death trap.

"Lean back!" yells Harris.

David feels the bike turn to the right, then start to slow down as they glide into the parking lot of the market where everyone in the canyon goes for groceries. Last year the owner sold the place to a boat person from Vietnam. The boat person never smiles or makes conversation with any of the customers, who don't seem to like him any more than he seems to like them. When David asked Phil about him, Phil said people called him a boat person because he and his family escaped the war in Vietnam, on boats they made themselves. David asked why someone would want to come to a country to treat people so badly and be treated so badly right back. Phil said something about a chicken and an egg, and a pot and a black kettle, which made no sense to David. What did make sense to David was that whatever had happened to that man in his country must have been pretty bad to make him never like anyone, no matter who they were.

Harris skids to a stop next to the other bikes and skateboards that are already leaning against the wall of the store. As the other kids push and shove their way inside, Harris turns to David.

"We need a pack of cigarettes."

"What do you need a pack of cigarettes for?"

"Never mind that. Problem is, I don't have any money."

"So how are you going to get them?"

"I'm not. You are. It's part of your initiation."

David has been up late at night and has heard Phil's coughing fits, but the last thing he wants to do right now is admit that the second-to-last thing he wants to do right now is learn to smoke.

"The owner won't sell me cigarettes."

"Well, you're not exactly going to buy them from him. Understand?"

"Then who am I going to buy them from?"

The other kids are coming out of the store with red and purple juice from their popsicles dripping down the sides of their mouths. Harris squeezes David's shoulder gently but firmly.

"Like I said, you're not exactly gonna buy them."

David swallows hard and nods. His stomach feels like his hands and feet do when they fall asleep, only a million times worse as he enters the store.

The owner sits behind the counter, listening to a foreign language news program on a small transistor radio. He doesn't look up as David walks through the aisles, past the boxes of ramen noodles and instant rice, past the magazines with pictures of soldiers on the covers, and over to the racks of cigarettes lined up against the back wall.

David glances up at the fish-eye mirror in the top corner of the store and sees that the owner's eyes are on the radio. David tries to keep his hand steady as he grabs the closest pack of cigarettes, jams it far down into his pocket, and slowly moves toward the store's exit.

"Hey…"

David freezes. He wants to run but his legs won't move.

"What you have in your pocket?"

David shrugs.

"Maybe you no hear me. I ask you, what you have in your pocket?"

David slowly pulls his hand out of his pocket with the pack of cigarettes clenched tightly in his fist.

The owner looks outside where the rest of the boys are on their skateboards and bikes, watching Harris pop a wheelie. The owner turns back to David and gestures to the cigarettes.

"Those for you?"

David nods.

The owner chuckles and shakes his head.

"No. Those no for you."

He points over to Harris whose bike hits a bump in the parking lot and flips over, sending Harris flying into a patch of ivy off to the side. Harris stands up, rubbing a cherry-sized bruise on his elbow.

"Those no for him, either."

"He said they were."

"No. No for him. But I know why he want them." The owner gestures toward the door. "Go."

David stares at the owner, not sure whether or not to believe him.

"Take them. America is land of free, no?"

David nods.

"So take them. Go."

David runs out of the store and over to Harris, who is back up on his bike. David jumps onto the handlebars and they peel out of the parking lot, spraying dirt and gravel everywhere. They're halfway up the hill before David has a chance to catch his breath.

"You get 'em?" asks Harris.

David nods.

"Let me see."

David reaches into his pocket and pulls out the pack of cigarettes. He notices it's a different brand from the one Phil smokes, which you can't buy in just any store. These cigarettes look cheap, like they'll somehow kill you quicker and meaner than the other ones will, even though the white warning label on the side says the same thing it says on Phil's cigarettes.

"You got a hard pack," says Harris.

"Is that bad?"

"It's good. Soft pack cigarettes get all bent out of shape, when you sit on 'em."

Harris's house is made of reddish wood and glass and is almost hidden from the street by rows of tall plants and bushes. One of the kids, a long-faced boy named Lon who looks like he's smirking every time David sees him, follows David and Harris into the driveway, but Harris wheels his bike in front of him.

"Thought I'd say 'hi' to Keith. He hasn't seen me in a while," says Lon.

"He'll get over it," says Harris, motioning for David to follow him inside.

David looks over at Lon, who shakes his head and skates out of Harris's driveway, the *clackety-clack-clack* of his wheels echoing off the walls of the canyon as he makes his way back down the hill.

Harris's house has stone floors and wood beams and a cluster of plants that rises up like a pair of battling snakes toward the glass ceiling.

"You there?" The voice is weak and sounds as though it belongs to someone older.

Harris and David clamber down a winding metal staircase that leads to a large room below. Sitting in a wheelchair in front of a television is a bearded, long-haired man. He is older than Harris, but isn't old; maybe a teenager, maybe in his twenties. He wears a green army jacket with a faded logo, with one sleeve rolled up higher than the other. David spots what looks like bloody razor stubble marks all over the lower part of his arm.

David also realizes the man has no legs.

"Got my cancer sticks?" The man holds out his hand, his eyes not budging from the television as he does.

Harris takes out the cigarettes and hands them to the man, who rips open the pack and sticks one in his mouth. He pulls a lighter out of his jacket and lights the cigarette, then sucks in and blows a long cloud of smoke at Harris and David.

Harris coughs. "David, this is my brother, Keith."

"Half-brother," says Keith, smiling at David in a way that makes the hair on David's neck stand up.

"We've got different fathers," says Harris.

"Yeah, but that's only *half* the reason I'm his *half* brother," says Keith with a chuckle as he gestures toward his legs.

"Nice to meet you, Keith," says David, not knowing what else to say.

"Call me Charlie."

"Keith—"

"I'm serious," says Keith, no longer smiling. "I want your friend here to call me Charlie."

Keith turns to David.

"You *can* pronounce the name Charlie, right?"

David nods.

"Then say it," says Keith. "Let me hear you say, 'Nice to meet you, Charlie.'"

"Nice to meet you, Charlie."

"Happy now?" says Harris.

"Always," says Keith, smiling again. "I'm just a happy-go-lucky guy."

Keith turns back to the television. A game show is on where people have to guess the price of items other people buy in department stores, and whoever comes closest wins the items.

"See that?" asks Keith. "Free enterprise. Open market capitalism. It's worth a pair of legs, wouldn't you say?"

David nods.

"Yeah. Like either of you punks would know," says Keith with a sneer.

"Keith," says Harris, but Keith blows a big cloud of smoke into Harris's face and turns to David.

"You a ballplayer? Big on the national pastime?"

"I'm not very good," says David.

"Yeah, me neither. So we got that in common."

Keith snaps his fingers at Harris, who walks over to the television and changes the channel. A man with a large head is interviewing a man with an even larger head, and what's left of Keith's body seems to relax a bit.

He takes another drag of his cigarette and holds it up. "These from the gook?" he asks.

Harris and David stare at Keith, who sighs. "The smokes. Where'd you get 'em?"

"David here took them from the market at the bottom of the hill."

"So you pinched 'em from the gook. Nice work there, David here."

Keith inhales and holds the smoke inside for a long time before exhaling. "Fucker and his fellow yellows torpedoed my torso. Least he can do is keep me flush with cancer sticks. Finish what he started, only nice and slow this time."

Keith closes his eyes and leans back. He stays like that for a little bit before he starts snoring, his cigarette still hanging from his lips.

Harris spots an open beer can near where Keith is sitting. He pulls the cigarette out of Keith's mouth and drops it in the beer can where it lands with a sizzling sound.

"Sounds like a dud," mutters Harris.

"What's that?" asks David.

"Duds. Firecrackers that don't light. Like on the Fourth of July? That was always his favorite holiday."

Harris stares at Keith, a sad expression creeping down from his eyes to the corners of his mouth. Then the sadness stops and he looks like the outside Harris again, the one who breaks windows and rides fearlessly down the hill, against the wind, to steal cigarettes from the enemy.

✳

LATER THAT NIGHT DAVID asks Phil why Keith wanted to be called Charlie.

"Charlie was the name of the group of soldiers that did awful things in Vietnam."

"Is that why the boat man and Keith hate each other so much?"

"How do you know so much about Harris and his older brother?"

"I played baseball with Harris. Then we went over to his house after we stopped off at the market," says David, leaving out the part about the cigarettes.

"I think the boat man and Keith hate the idea of each other more than anything."

"Is that why the war is going on? Because people hate each other's ideas?"

"Sometimes it's a lot simpler than that. Sometimes all it boils down to is one country acting bigger than it is, then getting itself into a big mess. Then getting itself into an even bigger mess trying to get itself out of the first mess, which wouldn't have even happened had it simply known its place in the world."

Phil takes a drag of his cigarette, but blows it in the opposite direction from where David is sitting. "I don't want you hanging out with that guy."

"Harris?"

"Him, too, but I guess there's not much I can do about that. The one you need to try to avoid is that brother of his."

"Why?"

"Because he's wounded."

"You mean his legs?"

"His legs are the least of it. He doesn't understand things."

"Like what?"

"Like Mann was right. You can never go home again."

"Who was Mann?"

Phil stubs out his cigarette.

"Someone boys should never learn from."

✦

SOMETHING HAS CHANGED AT school, too. The playground is no longer a place where Jason and David can swap sandwiches and compare their homes and avoid the girls. Now that Harris and his group have accepted him, David is expected to sit with them and play their sports and be a part of whatever else they decide to be a part of.

One day Lon snatched a Captain Kangaroo lunchbox from a short kid with crusted snot around his nose. Lon then started a game of keep-away that lasted the entire lunch period. David liked the short kid and thought it was cruel to take away his lunch, but he still tossed the lunchbox over to Harris when it came his way.

Jason, who was eating by himself, watched the whole thing and shook his head, but David couldn't do anything about it.

Jason was last year's friend, and even though David missed his company and knew that Jason would never do something like this to him or anyone else, David now understood what Phil meant when he was talking about that Mann guy.

After school one day, Harris invites David over to his house. The two of them close the door to Harris's room and sing along to a loud band that comes from England. Harris and David pretend to be the band, destroying their instruments at the end of the show. In the middle of a sweaty drum solo, Harris's mother pokes her head in to tell them she put a frozen pizza in the oven for Keith and that Harris should go check on it. Then she pushes her hair up and dances with them before she leaves.

David likes the way she dances, free and loose with a lot of arm swinging up and down. It reminds him of the way Carole used to dance around the house sometimes, when she thought no one was watching her. Harris complains that she leaves him with Keith a lot and that she might as well leave him alone. When he says this, it makes David think that Harris doesn't understand what it truly feels like to feel completely alone in your own house.

Fifteen minutes later, Harris is kicking around some pillows, pretending they are part of his drum set, when both he and David smell something burning.

"Keith's pizza…" says Harris.

Harris throws the door open and runs down the rainbow-carpeted steps, two at a time, as David tries his best to keep up. They burst into the kitchen just in time to see Keith in his wheelchair, crouched over the oven. The smoke from Keith's cigarette blends in with the smoke from the charred pizza, and the smell makes David's nose tingle and his insides churn.

"Thought Mom told you to keep an eye on this," says Keith.

Harris shrugs.

Keith takes the pizza out of the oven and wheels himself over to the kitchen table. He slides the pizza off the tinfoil and onto a plate his mother has set out for him, along with a fork, a knife, and an open can of beer. He takes a bite of the pizza. Black crumbs go flying all over his lap.

"How is it?" asks Harris.

Keith makes a face.

"Is it *bad* bad? Or just bad?"

Keith swallows, then gestures at the black-and-blue mark on Harris's elbow from his failed wheelie in the market's parking lot the other day. "How's that bruise? *Bad* bad? Or just bad?"

"Bad."

"Come here."

Harris walks over to Keith.

"Let me see."

Harris holds up his elbow. Keith grabs it and thrusts it right into the steaming hot pizza.

"Now it's *bad* bad."

Harris pulls his elbow back. David has never seen him look like this before, as though he is going to cry. His lip quivers and his eyes look wet, but then he sees David staring at him and his face twitches, then freezes, and his eyes go cold.

"What are you looking at?"

David turns his gaze away and nods at the front door. "The guys are probably waiting."

Harris walks into the living room and grabs his glove. David stays behind, still staring at Keith who takes another bite of his pizza. Then he turns to David with his mouth full of burnt black crumbs.

"Enjoy the national pastime, kid. And tell all your comrades that Charlie sent you."

✛

THE SCORE IS TIED when David steps up to the plate. Harris is pitching, and his first pitch almost knocks David down. David stands up and stares at Harris, who doesn't look sad or angry the way he looked in his house an hour ago.

"Ready?" he asks.

David steps back in the batter's box. Something he has never felt before is racing through his temples, traveling from his head down into his stomach. He likes competition, liked beating Jason in the chess games they used to play during recess and lunch, loves beating Phil at cards even when he suspects Phil is letting him win, but this feels different. No matter what, Jason, and especially Phil, never looked like their lives absolutely depended on beating David.

He clutches the bat tighter, choking up the way he's seen Harris do when he's down in the count and his at-bat's very survival is at stake.

Harris winds up again.

David lifts the bat back.

"Eh battah battah, eh battah battah…"

This time the pitch is right over the plate, daring to be hit.

"Suh-wing, battah!"

David swings the bat across the plate, harder than he ever has before. There is a loud cracking sound, then the ball goes soaring into the space between the left fielder and the center fielder. David is almost too surprised to run at first but then he does, fast, toward first base.

Jason…

The ball rolls toward the curb then bounces over the left fielder's glove as he leans down to grab it. David touches first base and runs toward second as fast as he can.

Keith...

The ball takes a few more bounces toward the house of the man who threatened to shoot Harris. It rolls, then stops right between two of the pickets of his fence. David rounds second base and heads for third.

Harris...

Lon, who's playing center field and not smirking for once, gets to the ball before the left fielder does. Lon picks up the ball and throws it to the shortstop, who runs toward Lon to meet his cutoff throw.

Purple-faced and feeling like his breath is stabbing his lungs, David makes a wide swing around third base and makes a dash for...

"Home!" scream Harris's teammates.

The relay throw from the shortstop sails over the head of the catcher.

Home...

The manhole is close...now closer...

Harris, who is backing up the catcher, catches the ball on one hop. The catcher calls for Harris to throw him the ball.

Home...

But Harris doesn't throw the ball to the catcher. Instead, he pushes the catcher aside and runs over toward the manhole.

Home...

David is ten feet away...now five...now he looks up and sees...

Harris.

On the manhole.

With the ball in his glove and his shoulder down.

The collision is brief and painful as David runs right into Harris. David has momentum, which, according to that TV special, is like Mother Nature's gravity sideways. But Harris has age and size and determination, and in the end, Mann and Phil are as right as right can be and David goes down.

And out.

When his eyes finally open and his head clears some of the fuzziness away, the first person he sees is Harris, who offers David his hand.

"No hard feelings?"

But just like that first day, it doesn't sound like a question, and David stays put.

Harris lowers his head a little bit. He isn't looking at David anymore, but David can see a glimmer of the same expression he had on his face when Keith dunked his arm in the burnt pizza.

"No hard feelings?"

Now it sounds like a question.

David smiles. "No hard feelings," he says.

"I'm late for dinner," says one of the kids, checking his watch.

"Score's still tied," says Lon, smirking at David. "We gonna finish this thing or what?"

All eyes turn to Harris, who thinks about it for a moment. Then he shakes his head. "He scored. We're finished here."

David clambers to his feet as Harris, then Lon, then the others, follow the sound of the voices—women's voices, mothers' voices—ringing through the air, calling their boys home for dinner.

COSTUMES

DAVID SITS ON A couch in the waiting room, playing with a row of silver balls hanging from a metal rod. Every time he swings a ball down from one side, a ball from the other side pops up, then comes back down and slams against the row of balls, which starts the whole process over again from the beginning. David watches as the two outside balls go back and forth, back and forth, while the central balls of the contraption don't move, no matter how hard they're hit.

Phil has been in the other room talking to Doctor Martin for almost an hour, according to the white clock on the wall. They speak in the quiet voices grownups use when they're worried about children, but don't want them to know, even though Doctor Martin's door is not closed all the way. They're here because Phil got a call from David's principal, who told Phil the school was concerned about David.

"Like how?" asked Phil, holding the phone with the same clenched grip he used when he spoke to the suits at the record companies who he sometimes referred to as "squares."

"Apparently he was wandering around the classroom while the teacher was reading a story to the kids," said the principal.

"Maybe he didn't like the story."

"There's more. A few days later he tried to check a book out of the school library."

"What's wrong with that?"

"We don't push the idea of kids reading solo until fourth grade."

Phil said goodbye and hung up the phone.

For the next two days, David watched Phil make lots of phone calls and smoke lots of cigarettes. When he wasn't on the phone or smoking, he was muttering about having to do this all on his own. Carole had been at the ashram for almost two years, and the last thing David heard Phil say before making the call to Doctor Martin was that if she ever came back, maybe he could get a two-for-one special.

David is frustrated with the contraption; no matter how much he fiddles with it, he can't figure out a way to make the balls in the middle do anything except sit there while the balls on the outside get all the action. He stands up, walks past a sculpture dripping water from a bamboo shoot onto some slime-covered rocks, and over to Doctor Martin's door.

"Anxiety?"

"That's right. Because he wanted to check a book out of the library."

"And they've never called before? To discuss any of his other behavior?"

"Like what?"

"Anything antisocial or disruptive that would make him stand out from his peers."

"My kid? Not a chance," says Phil, half-proudly, half-something else David can't quite identify.

David looks in through the door and watches as Doctor Martin starts to tap his fingers together.

"Is he wetting his bed?"

"No."

"Any nightmares? Restless sleep? Violent thoughts or actions, either toward you or himself?"

Phil shakes his head.

Doctor Martin continues to tap his fingers together, then he shrugs. "He's bored. Put him in a different school."

Phil leans back. His chair is plastic and has an orange-colored seat cushion, which makes a soft squeaking sound as he shifts back and forth. He runs his hand through his hair, which, David notices for the first time, has a few gray spots in it.

"I don't know. I'm as progressive as the next guy but I also don't want him bused into some ghetto for Chrissake..."

"That's if you go with the public school option."

Doctor Martin opens his desk and starts rummaging through it. "The good news about busing, ironically, is that several excellent private schools have recently opened up. Quite a few parents feel the exact same way you do. And I have one school in mind that I think would be an excellent fit for your son."

Doctor Martin takes a card out of his desk and hands it to Phil. "Give Rose in Dr. Melman's office a call and tell them about our conversation. I'm sure they'll be more than happy to meet with you."

Doctor Martin looks up and sees David standing in the hallway. He gives David a smile that doesn't look like any smile David has ever seen before and makes him feel a little bit uncomfortable. But this man is trying to help him and David doesn't want to be rude. He smiles back, quickly, then turns and walks over to give the contraption with the metal balls another shot.

✦

"YOU'RE GOING *WHERE?*"

The kids are playing baseball on a smoggy day, the kind that's on the nightly news after David's lungs are already aching from a day outside. Harris is standing by the manhole, at bat, while David is playing catcher as usual.

David doesn't like playing catcher because he hates fetching the ball when it rolls behind him and he hates the way the squatting position makes his knees hurt and he really, really hates being knocked over every time there's a close play at home. But whenever he gets upset about it, he thinks about an episode of *Mutual of Omaha's Wild Kingdom* that talked about protective coloration, which animals use to blend in with their surroundings so they're safe from attacks from bigger animals. And David figures that the catcher's gear—helmet, mask, chest guard, shin plates—protects him in the same way. It isn't very colorful, but it does seem like the only thing that allows him to blend in with his surroundings.

"Some special school," David says, but the second the words come out of his mouth, he regrets it.

"Special how? Like Special Olympics?" yells Lon from centerfield. Lon never used to pay any attention to David until he started spending time at Harris's house. Now it seems like Lon goes out of his way to insult David every chance he gets—in school, on the way home from school, and especially during baseball games. But he hasn't picked an actual fight with David, at least not yet, because this would probably mean having to deal with Harris.

Sometimes protective coloration only goes so far, thinks David as he glances at Lon, then back over at Harris. Sometimes a person needs good, uncolored, actual protection.

"All I know is that I'm supposed to show up there on Monday," says David.

David leaves out the part about the IQ test, which he took in the lobby and which had a lot of questions that seemed almost too easy. He also doesn't tell Lon that he overheard the principal tell Phil how this school was renowned for giving structure to kids with wandering minds. The principal said this with a smile that made it feel like he knew something David and Phil didn't.

And then there's the uniform. David especially makes a point not to talk about the uniform that he will have to wear to school every day from now on. He got a good look at it when he and Phil toured the campus, and it seemed stiff and uncomfortable and like it definitely discouraged wandering of any sort.

"So what are you gonna be learning at this new school?" asks Harris.

David shrugs.

"No one told you?"

"Well, the principal did say something about pre-algebraic equations and introductory anthropology and choosing between Latinate or Germanic languages. But a lot of that's not until we reach the upper grades."

The other kids just stare at David, which makes him think he should probably pretend not to know the answer to questions like these in future.

The night before school starts, Phil walks into David's bedroom as he's trying on the uniform's blue jacket, white collared shirt, and gray pants. The jacket and shirt fit fine, but the rough material of the gray pants makes the top part of David's legs itch.

"What's wrong?" asks Phil as he watches David scratching.

"The pants. They're itchy."

"Want me to find some cream or something?"

David thinks about sitting in the bathroom of his new school rubbing cream onto his legs. His next thought is that if anyone ever caught him doing that, the itching would be the least of his problems.

"Every other kid has to wear these pants, too. I'm sure the itching goes away the more you wear them."

Phil stares at the patch on the blue jacket. It has a lot of stitching with letters in a foreign language and a picture of something that looks like a sword.

"You sure you want to do this?"

David wants to say no. He isn't sure he wants to wear a uniform every day. He isn't sure he wants to go to a school where everyone already knows everyone else. He isn't sure he wants to wake up a half-hour earlier every morning because that's how long it takes to drive to the new school. He can already tell that Phil doesn't like this part, either. Phil also doesn't like how much the new school costs, which makes David feel like he'd better like it, or that it should at least answer the questions about him that, until two weeks ago, he didn't even know he needed to ask. But something about the uniform makes David think he shouldn't be asking any questions at all, let alone trying to answer any big ones.

"I'm sure," he says.

"All right then," says Phil. "Get some sleep."

*

THAT NIGHT, DAVID WAKES up from a dream where his brain wandered away from a pack of other brains. All the other brains were colored gray, just like the illustrations in the science books the old school never wanted him to read. In David's dream, his brain was colored bright red and just wanted to go somewhere to read and be left alone. David wakes up hungry and thirsty, so he gets out of bed and goes into the kitchen where he sees Phil smoking a cigarette and drinking green tea.

"Is it bad to have a wandering mind?" he asks Phil.

"Of course not. It's a good thing."

"What's so good about it?"

"A wandering mind makes you creative. A wandering mind makes you want to explore all the exciting, different things that are going on inside of you."

"Then what did that principal mean?"

"I don't really know. I'm hoping you'll be able to tell me in a few weeks."

David walks over to the pantry, opens it, and starts making himself a peanut butter sandwich.

"Carole has a mind that makes her want to wander," says David. "And she's been gone for two years now."

Phil stubs out his cigarette.

"What made you think about her now?"

David shows Phil the postcard he got that day from Carole, the one he didn't tell Phil about when the mail came because Phil was in the studio with the door closed. In the postcard, Carole is sitting in a semi-circle with a group of other people in the ashram. All of the people in the picture are wearing white robes and smiling—warm smiles, different smiles from the ones on the faces of Doctor Martin and the new principal—that make them look similar, if not exactly the same.

Phil stares at the postcard for a long time. Then he puts it down and turns to face David. "Who said that? About her mind?

"You did once."

"That's not what I was talking about. Not exactly," Phil adds.

"When will she be back?"

"I don't know," says Phil.

"Will she be back?"

"I don't know," says Phil, softer this time.

✦

IT IS TWENTY PAST ten and David is almost finished with his worksheet.

He looks around at the students sitting in the five neat rows. All of them are dressed in their uniforms and doing their work without looking up at the clock on the wall. David has been in his new school for less than an hour and already he has looked up at the clock four times.

When he arrived that morning, the teacher took him to the front of the classroom and introduced him to the other students. They'd repeated his name and mumbled a greeting that sounded like something they used to greet every other new student in the exact same way. At the old school, the students and their teacher would get together and rehearse a new song or a reading for every new student. They would include something about where the new student was from, or about his or her hobbies. But David also remembers how the new students were also usually the target of a lunchtime game of smear the queer—a game with a ball, a dog pile, and a lot of black-and-blue bruises—which were the outdoor part of the new student's indoor welcome.

David finishes the last problem on his worksheet then stands up and takes it over to his pretty, blonde-haired teacher, Miss Basinger. Singer in the bay, he thinks, a nice picture in his mind that goes well with the sweet smile she gives him every time he brings her another finished worksheet. He wishes she would talk more, but he has heard that talk is cheap and, as Phil reminded him that morning, this school most definitely is not. Awards in glass frames fill the school's lobby, making it obvious what kind of place this is, even to a person who couldn't read. Reading, according to the pamphlets lined neatly on the coffee table, is something the children at this school all learn to do at a very young age, without anyone ever pushing it on them, solo or otherwise.

At recess, the kids play handball and chess and are more than willing to include David in their activities. Some ask him questions about his old school, about what he was learning, and what brought him to this place. Almost all of them started school somewhere else, only to wind up here when it became clear they didn't fit in with all the other kids.

"That's one thing they all have in common," David tells Phil on the way home after his first day.

"What?"

"Not being able to fit in."

Phil laughs the way he does when David says something that he didn't mean to be funny but that Phil enjoys, anyway.

David carpools to school now because of how far away it is and because of the hours Phil works these days. One afternoon, Phil arranges for the carpool to drop David off at Harris's house. Brother Louie is in town, and he and Phil are going to the homes of important supporters of the cause.

David has no idea what the cause is, but from what he has managed to overhear, it has something to do with the military, the police, and oppressed people of color. Although, as David heard one of Phil's musicians mutter one time, it's clear that "oppressed people of color" apparently does not include the brown-skinned Mexicans who work in the homes of the cause's supporters. What's also clear is that Phil has no desire for Brother Louie to see his fellow-cause-supporter's son marching around in a white shirt, a navy blazer, and a pair of gray slacks. Slacks that, ever since David began wearing them, have made the tops of his legs break out into splotchy red marks that itch no matter how hard he scratches.

David steps into Harris's room to make a quick change into his regular clothes but Harris is nowhere in sight. Instead, Lon and a few of the other kids are tossing Harris's football back and forth.

"How are the Special Olympics going?" asks Lon.

"Where's Harris?"

"Making sure his brother doesn't shit skid marks all over his underpants."

Lon nods at David's jacket. "Nice blazer. Mind if I check it out?"

"You want to see it?"

Lon smirks at the other kids, then turns back to David. "No, dumbass. I want to try it on."

David hands his jacket to Lon, who pulls it over his bony shoulders and holds his arms out like one of those plastic mannequins in department stores.

"What do you think? Should I give retard school a shot?"

The other kids laugh.

David feels his face reddening. "Give it back."

"What if I want it for myself? Maybe I'll just keep it. And then you'll never be able to go back to your special school with all your special new buddies."

David is silent.

Lon walks slowly over to David and stands a few inches away from his face. "Which would be a shame. Because even if you lived right here in this room, even if you looked exactly like Harris, acted exactly like Harris, even if you looked just like the rest of us and still went to our school, you'd still be special old you."

The other kids don't say a word, but David can feel their silent support for Lon, which makes the tips of his ears burn. As much as he hates wearing the catcher's gear, he realizes that right now he would give anything to be able to hide his burning red face behind a protective mask.

"Leave him alone."

The voice doesn't belong to Harris. It is much deeper and is full of anger, the kind only heard in the voices of people who know for a fact that something or someone is wrong. The boys turn to see Keith sitting in the doorway in his wheelchair.

"I wasn't—"

"Yeah. You were."

Keith stares around the room at the boys, who all drop their eyes the minute Keith's meet theirs. Including Lon, whose smirk is finally gone.

He turns around and tosses David's jacket back to him. "Let's go play ball."

Keith waits until they're down the hall and he hears the front door slam. Then he turns back to David and nods at the jacket.

"Wear it well," he says, patting the faded name on the green jacket on his own chest, then he turns and wheels himself back down the hallway.

✦

DAVID IS STANDING ON the playground, tired of watching the same games of four square and handball during recess, so he suggests they play smear the queer.

"Sounds violent," says one of the boys.

"And mean," says one of the girls, folding her hands across her chest.

The kids go back to their game, but David senses he's not exactly welcome anymore. He's about to go over to the lunch tables when he spots something off to the side.

Someone, actually.

Carole is standing on the other side of the chain-link fence that separates the school from the parking lot.

David walks slowly over to the fence without saying a word and stares at Carole. She looks thinner, and isn't wearing the robe she wore in the pictures. Something else is gone from the pictures, too: the smile she had on her face when she was with all the happy-looking, similar-but-not-the-same, ashram people.

"Hi," she says.

David cups his hand over his eyes to shield them from the sun's reflection on the painted white lines of the parking lot. Carole wraps her arms around her shoulders. "Nice uniform."

"It itches. I've got a rash."

"Want me to have a look at it?"

"Here?"

Carole laughs. "No. I mean later."

David pulls his jacket tightly around his chest. Out of the corner of his eye, he can see the other kids have stopped playing their games and are all staring at him.

"I used to wear a uniform, too," says Carole. "It was white. Everyone else wore them, too. Only we didn't exactly call it a uniform."

"I know. I saw your postcard."

Carole stares up into the sky, as though she's looking for something, but all that's there is a cluster of pillowy white clouds. "Wanna go to Disneyland?"

"Right now?"

"Whenever you're finished with school."

"What about carpool?"

"I'll call Phil."

"I have homework."

"A lot?"

"Whatever I don't get finished in class. But I can do it in the car," he adds quickly when he sees her face fall.

"Or down there," she says. "I thought we'd spend the night in a hotel since tomorrow's Saturday."

David has never spent the night away from home before, but he sees how badly Carole wants to take him to Disneyland. Then he wonders if spending the night away from the home your mother no longer lives in, with your mother, counts as spending the night away from home.

"Okay," says David.

"Great. What time are you done with school?"

"Three-fifteen."

"That's later than the other school."

"We learn more here."

Carole smiles at David, then turns and walks back over to the cab waiting for her in the parking lot. It isn't until she's gone that David realizes her smile was the same kind of smile he saw on the face of Doctor Martin.

As he thinks about it, he realizes why it makes him so sad: it looked like the kind of smile that someone had to teach someone else how to do in the first place.

✦

BY THE TIME CAROLE rented a car and came back for David, it was rush hour and the freeway had filled with traffic.

"All part of the journey," Carole says as they sit in the car, inching along and listening to a radio report about an army officer named Calley, who had been found guilty of war crimes. Carole's eyes grow misty with tears when the discussion turns to the people killed by the American soldiers under orders from the officer.

The last time David and Carole were in a car together was two years ago, on the way home from the beach, and even after the divorce, she didn't have tears in her eyes like now. David remembers how he watched the headlights of the cars behind them from the way-back. Now he is sitting in the front seat of a rental car that smells as though no one has ever sat in it before.

He misses the way-back, and how he and the other kids launched themselves over the hump of the backseat whenever the cooperative took them on field trips. All the drivers of his new carpool are dads who wear suits because they are on their way to work, and all of them have four-door cars and demand that the kids wear their seatbelts without any exceptions. Even Phil makes everyone wear seatbelts when it's his turn to drive, only he doesn't wear suits because he thinks they're ruining the music business. But seatbelts and suits are the rules these days, and all David knows is that he liked Phil better and liked his own life better when there were fewer rules and more exceptions.

✦

"So what are you learning in school?"

Carole and David are sitting in the dark restaurant overlooking a Caribbean that smells like chlorine. Both of them are starving after waiting in long lines for e-ticket rides that felt faster and more exciting the last time David was at Disneyland.

He shrugs, remembering Harris's question and the looks he got from the other kids.

"All that money and you don't know?"

David wonders if Carole is just making conversation or if this means she'll be around to ask questions at parent-teacher conferences.

"Lots of stuff, I guess."

"Like?"

David has to think for a moment, has to send his mind through the mountains of pages in his workbook before remembering something that stuck with him after he'd turned in his worksheet.

"The Indians and Columbus."

Carole snorts. "Did they teach you that Columbus murdered lots of Indians?"

"They left that part out."

"Well, he did. Even though they were the indigenous people."

"Does indigenous mean something that belongs in the environment?"

"How did you know that?"

"I saw it on an episode of *Mutual of Omaha's Wild Kingdom*. They were talking about how indigenous creatures use something called protective coloration so they can blend in with their environment and not be noticed by predators."

Carole smiles and stares at David.

"What?"

"Nothing. I was just thinking you've learned a lot while I was gone."

"Maybe it's because of the new school."

"Maybe," says Carole.

David thinks about wandering minds and takes a sip of his juice. "What did you learn while you were gone?"

"Just one thing."

"In two years?"

"It's a pretty big thing. The kind of thing that takes a person two years to learn."

Carole takes a sip of wine, then another one, then continues. "I learned that there are no 'I's inside of us. Only many 'we's."

A boat splashes by their table, past a group of pirates who are yo-ho-ho-ing away in front of piles of painted, plundered treasure.

"I don't understand."

"You will, honey. Someday when you're finally comfortable in your own skin."

David suddenly starts scratching the rash on his legs.

"Don't scratch, honey."

David wants Carole to make it better. He hates the itching, hates the feel of the pants against his skin. Worst of all, he hates the feeling that none of the other kids have these kinds of problems.

"It itches."

"I know, but you'll only make it worse."

Carole goes back to eating her salad. David stirs the juice in his glass, covers one end of the straw with his index finger and pulls it up, capturing some of the juice inside the straw as he does. Then he releases his finger and drops the liquid back inside the glass as the boat from the ride glides past their dinner table.

"Carole?"

"Yes?"

"Are you ever gonna stop wandering?"

Carole thinks about it for a moment, then slowly shakes her head.

"I don't think so."

"Why not?"

"Because I'm not really sure if I'm indigenous to anywhere."

"What about here? You're from here."

Carole takes David's hand and gives it a gentle squeeze. "That doesn't mean I'm *of* here, honey."

They spend the rest of the night watching the parade that lights up the sky. Mickey and Minnie wave to the kids in the crowd until they disappear around the corner on Disney's spotless Main Street. When David turns to Carole, he notices another tear in her eye as she watches the characters passing by, one after the other, each in their own bright decorated costume.

When the parade is over, David and Carole take the monorail back to the hotel and get ready for bed. As David changes from his school shirt and gray pants into the Dumbo tee shirt and pajama shorts that Carole bought for him in the gift shop, he notices that the rash on the tops of his legs is much worse. He turns to tell Carole about it, but she is already fast asleep in the twin bed next to him.

✴

DAVID HEARS A LOUD groaning sound coming from outside their garden-floor window. He turns over to look at Carole but she is making the high-pitched whistling sound through her teeth she used to make whenever she was in a deep sleep. It was different from the one she used to make when she pretended to be asleep, which was low and through her nose and used mostly to keep Phil from talking to her.

David climbs out of bed and slides open the glass doors to the patio. Carole doesn't like elevators, so they are in a room on the first floor by the pool. For a moment, he wonders if it's a good idea to go outside by himself, but then he remembers that the officer who killed the indigenous people in Vietnam is in jail. So is the Bogeyman. They're both hundreds of miles from

Disneyland, which is the happiest place on earth. So, wearing only his tee shirt and pajama shorts, he steps over the ledge by the patio and follows the groaning sound past the big trees and rocky waterfall, past the snack bars and pinball machines, and around the corner into a concrete alley. There, on a loading dock, hidden from where the hotel keeps its guests, David sees something.

Costumes.

Loads and loads of costumes from every character he saw dancing in the parade, now floating in a line while lowered from the dock down a pulley and into a large metal bin. Standing at each end of the pulley are two Mexican men dressed in white laundry worker uniforms. They chatter in Spanish, joking and slapping each other on the shoulders as each costume makes its way past them into the bin.

One of the men spots David and whistles to the other one. The pulley groans to a stop as they turn to David.

"Hey, you."

David freezes as one of the men walks over to him.

"You lost or something?"

David backs up, but the man gestures to him. "Relax. I ain't gonna hurt you."

David remembers how a big part of protective coloration was how the animals learned to read the faces of the predators. He sees something in this man's eyes he didn't see in Lon's eyes, sees something in this man's smile he didn't see in Doctor Martin's smile, that he doesn't even see in Carole's smile. He takes a step forward as the man gestures to the costumes.

"Like 'em?"

David nods.

"Wanna try one on?" The man walks over to the rack of costumes on the pulley and pulls down Mickey's, then walks back over to David. He is about to hand the costume over until he sees the rash on David's legs.

"Aye, aye, aye. What is that?"

"A rash."

"How long you had it?"

"Ever since I started school."

"And no one there did nothing about it?"

"My school's nurse put some pink stuff on it with a cotton swab."

"Didn't help, huh?"

David shakes his head.

The man whistles over to his friend who hops up on the loading dock. The friend reaches into a bag tied around his waist, pulls out a small tube, and hands it to the first man, who turns and hands it to David.

"Rub some of this on it."

David takes the ointment and rubs some of it on the tops of his legs.

"We get the scratches all the time. From the starch in our uniforms. So stiff it's like they could get up and walk away all by themselves."

David nods at the ointment. "What is that stuff?"

"Special Mexican remedy. Can't buy it in stores. Gotta be a local, know what I'm saying?"

The man stands up and picks up the costume then turns and hands it to David.

"Won't the real Mickey mind?" asks David.

The man laughs, then turns to his friend and says something in Spanish. The friend laughs, too. David's ears turn red, but this time it's a different shade of red from when Lon teased him.

"Ain't no real Mickey," says the first man. "Every day a different dude gets to put on this costume."

He looks around, then leans in close. "Wanna hear a secret?"

David nods.

"Sometimes I put this thing on myself. Just to see what it's like. And you know what? The minute I disappear inside, all my troubles go away."

He tosses the costume to David. "Now go on. Get happy."

The costume is too big, but David sits down so he can pull it up without it falling all over him and zips it up. He puts on the Mickey head and realizes that the holes for the eyes are way above his own. But it's warm and soft and fuzzy inside, and he smiles as everything finally goes dark.

✦

THAT MONDAY MORNING, MISS Basinger tells David that the principal would like to see him.

"But I'm not finished with my worksheet."

"It can wait." David notices she isn't smiling when she says this.

The principal leads David into his office, closes the door, and sits down across from him, leaning in so that his hawk-looking face is barely a foot away from David's.

"I understand that you suggested a violent game in the playground the other day."

The principal points at David's uniform. "See that uniform? The minute you put that uniform on, you have an obligation to uphold this school's values. Games like that aren't welcome here. They fly in the face of everything we stand for. Understand?"

David nods.

"No. Do you understand?" asks the principal again, now leaning in even closer.

All of a sudden, David realizes something.

The tops of his legs no longer itch.

He looks up at the principal and smiles the kind of smile that he knows the principal needs to see right now.

"I understand."

"Good. I trust that we won't have this conversation again. Because you're a fine young man and we're thrilled to have you here. You're one more standout in a long line of achievers."

David walks back to his classroom where the rest of the children are standing by the door, ready to be excused for recess. As they march out to the playground, he slips into the back of the line, just another student, dressed just like everyone else, his wandering mind at rest and ready to do whatever it is it came here to do.

GOD IS DEAD

THE FIRST TIME GOD appears on the playground, most of the children are busy watching a rattlesnake on the other side of the chain-link construction fence. The school has decided to tear away most of the brush-covered hillside by the parking lot and put up a new building, but the rattlesnake doesn't know any of this. It coils and hisses and darts its head back and forth, from the children to the bulldozer beside the chain-link fence.

"He can hiss all he wants at that bulldozer. It'll still destroy his habitat. And him right along with it."

David turns around to see a brown-haired girl with big eyes named Ariel standing behind him. She's tall and thin and has bony arms that shoot up in class to answer questions most of the other kids haven't finished understanding yet.

"What are they building over there, anyway?" David asks her.

"A science and nature center. Which my mom says is the epitome of irony."

"How come your mom thinks that?"

"My mom's a scientist. It's her job to figure out the grand scheme of things."

"What does that mean?"

"It means that there's a delicate balance at the center of everything around us that explains the secrets of the universe."

Ariel nods to the snake. "A creature like that can't adapt to any other environment. Once it's been pushed out of its home, it's as good as dead."

David feels sad for the snake. He remembers learning last year how snakes shed their skins. He felt jealous that they could just drop everything that hurt them on the outside and start all over again. But he couldn't see the point if that new start could be brought to an end by a bulldozer, where the goal is to create a place that is supposed to be about you, but has no use for you.

David walks over to the lunch area, which is deserted except for a long-haired man in a robe that looks like it's made of rags. He sits in the spot where David usually sits every day for lunch. David looks around, but the assistants who usually patrol the lunch area are nowhere in sight. So David decides to sit down because the man seems harmless enough, and even if he isn't, the school has fences that Phil assured David are harder to get out of than they are to get into.

"You're sitting in my place," says David.

The man looks up at him with a smile, then slides down to the other end of the lunch table. "That is wonderful, child."

"What is?"

"That you know your place."

David sits down as the man goes back to watching the bulldozer on the other side of the fence.

"What's your name?" asks the man.

"David."

"One of my favorites. Means beloved."

"What's your name?"

"God."

"Where do you live?" David asks, not really knowing what else to say to someone who calls himself God and appears out of thin air.

"Everywhere."

David wants to ask him if he ever sees Topanga, who also told him she was everywhere, but right now he's more curious about why God is sitting in his lunch area, so he asks him that instead.

God turns and stares at David. "Don't you know?"

David shakes his head.

"That's too bad," says God.

"You won't tell me?"

"It's not *my* place."

David wants to ask God what he means by this, but the bell rings.

"Will you be here tomorrow?" asks David.

"I will be here until I no longer have to," says God with a smile.

On his way out to carpool that afternoon, David passes a group of parents who are trying to re-elect the President. Whenever Phil talks about the President, it's always in a loud voice, and mostly to supporters of the cause he and Brother Louie fight for. David wonders why some causes make people want to fight while other causes don't. For example, Phil's group is in an uproar about the President who is ruining the country, but everyone, including Phil, completely ignores the destruction of a part of the country that's right outside the school. They drop off their children and drive away as fast as they can, past the new construction site and on to the office buildings, where they turn into the squares who Phil says are ruining the country right along with the president. David has no idea what a square is, but he remembers Topanga's perfect circle and has decided that this is something he agrees with Phil on.

David sees God sitting in the lunch area again the next day. He has no idea if the God he reads about in Hebrew School needs food in order to survive, but this God has clearly chosen to sit in the lunch area two days in a row, so David offers him half his peanut butter sandwich.

"Bless you," says God.

"Achoo," says David, not knowing what else to say.

This makes God laugh, the Adam's apple in his throat bobbing up and down as he does.

"Why is it called that?" asks David, pointing. "The Adam's apple."

"So that man remembers not to be led into temptation. The throat is where man's voice lives. And if man can speak loud and clear in a voice that is all his own, if he can be true to that voice and not be tempted to follow others, then he will realize an Eden far beyond that which even Adam and Eve knew."

David looks out at the bulldozers, which are tearing away another chunk of the hillside by the parking lot.

"I still don't know why you're here."

"You gave it some thought?"

David nods.

"Did you ask your mother?"

"My mom's gone most of the time."

"Where does she go?"

"Everywhere. Kinda like you."

The night when Carole dropped David off after their trip to Disneyland, David asked her if she was going back to another ashram. She shook her head and said that she wasn't sure where she was going. What she didn't say, but what was clear to David, was that she was sure it wouldn't be here.

"And your father?"

"He spends most of his time in the studio helping musicians make their music."

"What kind of music?"

God seems very interested in this last question. It scares David a little because he remembers reading something about the Bogeyman being a musician who thought he was God, but whom no one took seriously. Every musician David has ever seen come in and out of his house is always doing something musical—tapping their hands or feet or whistling to themselves, even while surrounded by company—but God hasn't so much as hummed either time David has seen him. Plus he seems to listen to David, and not in the way most grownups listen, with their eyes on you but their ears and minds somewhere else.

"He works with a lot of people who are trying to find their own voices," says David. "But the companies that put out the records want the songs to be shorter so they can play them on the radio. My dad says it takes longer to make songs shorter and in the end, they're not as good that way. So he doesn't come out of his studio for days sometimes."

"And your father enjoys this?"

"I don't know if he enjoys it. But I guess if he has to cut out a whole bunch of important details, he wants to make sure he gets it right."

"Do you know what they say about details?"

David shakes his head.

"You'll find out soon enough."

The bell rings and David walks over to the line and stands behind Ariel.

"That was the same creepy guy you were talking to the other day, wasn't it?"

"He's not creepy."

"What do you know about him?"

"Not a lot."

"Do you know his name?"

"Yes."

"What is it?"

"God."

Ariel laughs. "God? That's what he calls himself?"

"He has a right to call himself anything he wants. It's a free country."

"So God is right here. In our lunch area."

"I think he's hungry. And it's not like you or any of the other girls offered him anything."

"That's 'cause we're not as gullible as you boys are. Even if God did exist, none of you would know him if he drove down Mount Sinai in a Mercedes with a personalized license plate."

David thinks about how many of the carpool fathers drive cars made by Mercedes. Phil says the squares who drive those cars are as hard as the cars' roofs, which, unlike his convertible, wouldn't go down no matter how hard you pushed.

"Did your mom tell you that, too?"

"My mom doesn't believe in God."

"Do you believe everything your mom believes in?"

Ariel folds her arms across her chest. David likes it when she does this and thinks it makes her look kind of pretty, even though he's sure she'd only find that more annoying.

"Okay, let's say you're right. Say he is what he calls himself. How come he's just sitting there, watching all those bulldozers tearing up one of his creations, and doing nothing about it?"

"Maybe it's all part of the grand scheme of things."

Ariel turns her back on him as the line starts moving forward. David turns around to look for God, but he isn't in the lunch area any more. David scans the playground, trying to figure out where God could have gone, but the noise from the bulldozers hurts his ears, so he turns around and follows the other kids back into class.

✦

THE SOUND OF THE doorbell wakes David.

He gets out of bed and tiptoes into the hallway where he sees Phil open the door to his studio and walk over to the front door.

The doorbell rings again.

"Hang on," mutters Phil. He rubs his eyes as though he's been sleeping, even though David can tell he hasn't. Sometimes Phil does sleep in the studio, but only in between sets and never for more than an hour or two at a time. David knows this because he sometimes sneaks into the studio when Phil is sleeping on the couch and covers him with a blanket. Years ago, Phil used to be the one to cover David. It was always Phil's job because Carole was usually either sleeping or not home. Whenever David asked where Carole was, Phil would say that she was out, or that she was singing backup for a man named Cecil. All David knew about Cecil was that he wrote songs that were too long and smart for the radio, and that he never once set foot in Phil's studio.

Phil trudges down the hallway, past a statue of a fat, squinting man that Phil calls the Buddha, which is supposed to make you feel more in tune with nature. Carole had taken all her possessions when she went to the ashram, but she had left the Buddha behind. Phil left it sitting in the middle of the hallway where it would be the first thing any visitor saw when entering the house.

Two men are standing under the pale light of the lamp that hangs outside when Phil opens the door. Both men have long hair, but one man's looks wet and freshly combed while the other's looks like it hasn't seen shampoo in weeks. The man with the combed hair smokes a cigarette, and something about the way he and Phil stare at each other makes David feel they used to know each other, but their friendship didn't end well.

"Been a while, Nicky," says Phil to the cigarette smoker.

Nicky nods, even though it doesn't sound as though Phil meant it as a greeting.

"Hop," Phil says to the other man. It takes a moment before David realizes this is the man's name, or whatever passes for it.

There is a moment of silence as they stare at each other in the shadows, waiting for someone to speak.

"Cecil's dead," says Nicky finally. His voice is low and even, as though he had been practicing what to say in the car on the way over.

Phil lets the news sink in. Somehow, he looks surprised and not surprised at the same time.

"When?"

"Few hours ago."

"Really sad," says Hop, the man with the unwashed, stringy-looking hair. His eyes bob about wildly when he speaks, and he flashes David a smile that makes him look like someone who eats children, but only because he's hungry and can't help himself.

Nicky turns to Phil and nods at David.

"Didn't realize you had your kid with you tonight."

"Tends to work that way when they're nine years old."

"Where's his old lady?"

"Not around," says Phil, but the words don't sound friendly or even polite the way they usually do whenever Phil tells other grownups about Carole. Which, David realizes, happens a lot when your mother has been gone on and off for three years.

Nicky smiles a wide, toothy smile at David, the kind of smile that makes him look like someone who also eats children, not because he's hungry but because he just thinks it might be fun to try something new for dinner.

"How ya doing, kid?"

David doesn't answer him. He doesn't like the way this guy pronounces the word kid, making it rhyme with the word weed. He doesn't like the way this guy blows smoke through his nose when he exhales from his cigarette. And he really doesn't like the way this guy asked about Carole and used words like "old lady" to describe her, words that David thinks only Phil should be allowed to use. Most of all, David doesn't like that it's the middle of the night and someone's dead and two weird men seem to feel that the news somehow couldn't wait until morning.

Phil places an arm around David's shoulders and stares at the two men.

"Like I said, I'm real sorry."

"Sorry or not, we've got some business to attend to," says Nicky.

"I'm kinda busy."

"You kinda made a promise."

"It's three in the morning, for crying out loud. And…" Phil nods over at David.

Nicky shrugs. "Bring him along," he says. "It's not exactly a school night."

"Best extracurricular education a kid could get," says Hop.

Phil looks as though he's run out of arguments. "What about the body?" he asks.

"What about it?"

"We talked about transportation. Whole point of our agreement."

Nicky's lip curls up in a weird grin that looks like a sneer. "Let's just say that part's spoken for."

Nicky gestures for Phil to follow him and Hop outside. David goes along without asking if it's okay or not.

"*Voilà*," says Nicky, gesturing to a large, black car parked in the driveway. David has seen cars like this with weird-shaped symbols traced along the back flank of their oversized trunks and that usually travel with their lights on in the middle of the afternoon.

"You're kidding," says Phil.

"No, I don't believe I am," snickers Nicky.

"He's...in back?"

"Right-ee-oh," says Hop. "Put him there myself. Pennies on the eyes, whole nine stinkin' yards."

Hop bounces over to the rear doors of the vehicle and, with the pride of someone showing off the birth of a new baby, swings them open.

"Hop aboard Hop's magic carpet ride," he cackles.

Phil stares at the grinning Hop, then at Nicky who shrugs and blows a stream of smoke through his nose. Then Phil turns to David. "Not a word of this to anyone."

Phil looks at David in a way he never has before, as though they're not just father and son anymore, but two people who know the kinds of things about each other that could be dangerous someday. David wonders if any of the kids in his carpool have these feelings about their fathers—that they're just hanging out with them, sharing things on the same level as friends. Then he realizes this can't be the case, because the other fathers wear suits to work and drive in cars with hard roofs that wouldn't have room for a dead body.

As they drive through the canyon, David stares at the narrow road that cuts through the hill on its way to the Valley.

The casket slides back and forth and makes a loud thumping sound whenever Nicky takes a turn too hard. Occasionally a twang accompanies the thump making it sounds as though someone is playing a musical instrument before he or she has had the first lesson.

Hop, who is sitting next to David, follows David's eyes to the backseat with his own wild eyes. "We put his axe in there with him," he says.

David has been around musicians long enough to know that axe means guitar. He figures a dead guitarist having his axe in his casket is nothing unusual.

Cecil's music is playing on the cassette deck up front. The songs are slow and sad, but mostly long—very long—and seem appropriate for the car and the mood inside it. Nicky finishes a cigarette, then rolls down the window and flicks it out.

"Careful. This is fire country," says Phil, who sits next to Nicky.

"Well, then by all means, fire away," says Nicky. He rolls the window down farther and takes a deep whiff of the hot air as it rushes into the hearse. "Just wanna suck it all in sometimes," he continues. "Pull in every sight, every scent in before it's too late. Know what I'm saying?"

"My son has allergies," says Phil.

Nicky glances at David in the rearview mirror. "Sorry kid," he says, rolling up the window.

Hop taps his fingers on his knee as he sings along to the music. "Can't say we didn't see it coming," he murmurs, his eyes closed. "Still it's sad. Real sad."

David doesn't feel sadness, or anything else really; the voice on the cassette sounds far away and the words describe feelings David hasn't had in years. Feelings like the one Nicky just mentioned, about wanting to suck it all in before it was too late, the way David used to on days when the cooperative went to the beach. The new school, which isn't so new anymore, is nothing like the cooperative, whose songs and field trips David remembers less and less with every worksheet he fills out.

David wonders if Topanga still lives in the house overlooking the ocean. The other night David dreamed he was sitting with his feet in a tide pool, watching a hermit crab climb over his toes, when all of a sudden he looked over to see Topanga standing next to him. She told David her mother was asleep on the couch like Sleeping Beauty, that it would be years before she woke up and when she finally did, Topanga would be long gone. Even though David knew you weren't supposed to think in dreams, that they were supposed to have their own logic that had nothing to do with reality, he found his dream self thinking that Carole was the one who'd been asleep for years. That maybe one day she would wake up and come back before it was too late, before the boy she left behind on the beach that night, almost four years ago, was gone forever, too. Instead, he was the one who had woken up, leaving his mother, Topanga, and the tide pool washed away as the dream slipped through his brain, the way the wet sand on the beach once did through his hands and feet.

The music ends and Nicky pops out the cassette and hands it to Phil. "Some of his best work."

Phil stares at the cassette, which has Cecil's name and a symbol that looks like an Egyptian hieroglyph scrawled on it.

"Any plans for the suits to release it?" asks Phil.

"Someone oughta," says Nicky. "Gotta admit, it'd be a hell of an angle. Dead genius and his posthumous masterpiece. Van Gogh with an ear…for music."

"I'm sure you know plenty of people who'd see it that way."

Nicky glances over at Phil's face as though he's not sure if Phil is joking or not, but Phil isn't smiling. "Lighten up. Little gallows humor, for Chrissake. But glad to hear you're not hurting so much you gotta compromise your integrity."

Hop leans back on his headrest and closes his lizard-squinty eyes. "Song really reminds me of chicks," he says.

"Why?"

"It's all sadness, all the time. Music's supposed to tame the soul of the wild beast. Thing is, you sing, they listen, you think you made a connection, then bam—they're gone."

Hop turns to David. "You got a girlfriend?"

David thinks about Topanga again, but shakes his head.

"That's good. Way too much sadness for someone so young, know what I'm saying? Got the rest of your life to go there."

"Leave him alone," says Phil from the front seat.

"Don't mean nothing by it. Just giving the kid some life lessons, that's all."

"Careful kid," says Nicky, looking back at David in the rearview mirror. "Hop here flunked out of life at a very early age."

"Why don't you keep your eyes on the road?" Hop fires back. "This sucker's a hell of a lot harder to maneuver than a Harley."

Hop turns back to David. "Another thing…don't drink, you hear me? And don't do drugs, no matter what visions or versions of *paradisio* their users and abusers promise await you."

"I'm only nine."

"Cecil started boozing at nine. Man was a spirited liver of life and had a liver filled with lifelong spirits as a result. Eight generations of pickled Mason Dixonites, who put the South in Southern Comfort, tends to do that to a manchild. Know what I'm saying?"

David doesn't understand anything Hop is saying, but he nods because he enjoys listening.

"But see, here's the thing; sooner or later, ain't a barrel of dark side of the moonshine big enough can fill a man's soul. Day of reckoning comes, you gotta be filled up, deep down inside, with you and only you. Catch my drift, windsurfer?"

"Jeez, Hop, would you give it a rest already?" says Nicky.

"Kid needs to know what's in store for him."

"He's got his old man for that. Plus you're giving me a headache. So if you shut your mouth from here to the tree, I promise I'll split my last button of Navajo Night Train with you."

David looks out the window and watches as the concrete barriers on the sides of the roads get lower and lower until they give way to open desert. Ariel once gave an oral report about the city, built on top of the desert by a bunch of men who stole water so they could create life where none was meant to exist. She said that what these men had created was a mirage of life that was really all about human death and the destruction of the natural habitat.

Another kid, whose parents made him wear a big cross around his neck, raised his hand and told Ariel that the men would get what was coming to them when they met their maker. Ariel told him to stick with what could be proven, but the kid listed story after story about floods, fires, and other natural disasters that won the class over to his side.

David went over to Ariel during recess that day and told her something he'd always heard Phil saying, that most people confuse belief with faith and that none of it had to do with knowledge. Ariel didn't say a word; she just folded her arms across her chest and looked away, but David was still glad he'd said it because later, when he passed some of the parents campaigning for the President, he felt like he'd at least tried to do his part.

Phil gestures to the casket in the backseat of the hearse, and David finds himself wondering if Cecil ever liked to launch himself over the hump of the way-back, the way David did years ago.

"We in any trouble over this?" asks Phil.

"Dunno. Could be."

Phil exhales slowly, the same way he does when David interrupts his recording sessions too many times in one day.

"Okay. Would you tell me how we *could* be in trouble over this?"

"Cecil's stepfather controls all of the old lady's money ever since the old lady checked into the happy house."

Old lady, thinks David, wondering why those words keep popping up with Nicky.

"Dude's pure evil," says Hop, now awake again.

Nicky glances in the rearview mirror at Hop. "You can't be pure and evil, Hop."

"Sure you can. The duality of man. The yin and the yang of life. Mother Nature's rage combined with Father Time's redemption."

"Go back to sleep or you're gonna be one peyote-hungry little boy.

Hop closes his eyes as Nicky turns back to Phil.

"Anyway, Cecil's stepfather wanted to have Cecil's body flown back home."

"How'd you convince him otherwise?"

"Well, see, that's where we hit a little snag in the gray area department. Some people might say we took a less confrontational route as far as convincing him was concerned."

"So the guy has no idea the casket got…?"

"Rerouted?"

"I was gonna say stolen."

"No. But he will."

"Sure. When he gets an ash-filled canister containing the remains of his late stepson."

"Relax."

"You want me to relax?"

"Yeah, I do. You made a promise. To Cecil—in front of God and everyone."

"Meaning?"

"Meaning even if your loyalty to your late old buddy's for shit, at least respect your pledge to the man upstairs."

The hearse takes a left turn down a dirt road, past a long row of shrubs that form a ring around the desert floor. The shrubs are stubbly with purple and green buds that stick out in every direction. David sees a large hill in the distance rising into the sky with one of the strange-looking trees, the largest one David can see, perched on top.

Nicky parks the hearse, reaches into the backseat, and taps Hop on the knee. "Wakey-wakey, eggs and bakey."

"We firestarting?" asks the still-sleepy Hop with a yawn that sounds like a grunt.

"Indeed. Time to pull the pins and needles out of your feet and give me a hand with our guest of honor."

The men get out of the hearse, open up the back, and pull out the casket. Nicky and Phil drag the casket up the dirt path that leads to the top of the hill while Hop and David trail behind as they walk through the trees.

"They're called Joshua trees," Hop explains. "Named after the prophet Joshua, 'cause they look like a guy raising his arms to God."

"I talked to God," says David. David has the feeling Hop is the type who might actually believe a kid who claims to have spoken with God.

"Oh, yeah? When?"

"Last week. At school."

"What'd you tell him?"

"Not much. Mostly I just shared my sandwich with him."

Hop laughs. "Sure it wasn't just some hungry bum trying to scavenge food off a gullible kid?"

David is silent.

"Just kidding. Hey, we all talk to God. But for some of us, he talks back. My man Cecil here actually *channeled* the man upstairs. Wrote these long unfiltered masterpieces, and everyone who heard 'em swore on their mother's grave that they felt more connected to the magical secrets of the universe afterward."

Hop shakes his head. "But in the end, nobody really listened. Mere friggin' mortals, we are."

Hop and David catch up to the spot where Nicky and Phil have placed the casket down on the ground. Nicky fumbles through his jacket pocket, then removes a can of liquid and a lighter. He squirts the liquid all over the casket as though he's getting ready for a barbecue, then flicks open the lighter.

He pauses and stares at the flame before turning to Phil. "Hey, kid. I'm sorry. For what went down between Cecil and your old lady. Long time coming on that one."

Phil stares straight ahead, not looking at Nicky. "You were my best friend, Nick."

"I know."

"You knew."

"What do you want me to say? She always liked creative types. You said so yourself. Plus these times we're living in, all these mixed messages can really mess with your mind. Make a man lose his way in the darkness."

David watches Phil's face as he stares at the casket of the dead man in front of him. Usually David can't tell what Phil is feeling, but tonight he looks sad. The kind of sad that's never really about just one thing but that sneaks up on you when you least expect it. And tonight David can tell that if Phil has never really felt sad about what happened between him and Carole, he is definitely feeling it now.

As one tear makes its way down Phil's cheek, then another, David feels he will never be able to look at Phil the same way again. He has seen something in Phil he was not meant to see, a something that must be grown into, but not experienced right now; maybe someday, but definitely not now. He thinks about his friends and their fathers with their hard cars with the hard roofs that nothing can penetrate. He realizes he envies them even more than he envied the snake shedding its skin, because whatever pain the snake feels on the outside can be taken off in its entirety, so a new inside can come out to enjoy the world's beauty. But he realizes that the world's beauty goes away, because the truth is that God just doesn't care about it. And this makes David saddest of all.

Phil wipes his face, then nods at the casket.

"Ready?" asks Nicky.

Phil nods.

"Then let there be light." Nicky tosses the lighter on the casket, and a large ball of flame bursts up into the sky.

David steps back and watches the fire as it burns the casket, the smell of charred wood filling the air all around.

"Too bad his songs were just too damn long," says Nicky.

"I guess what they say ain't true," says Hop. "That God's in the details."

"God is dead," says David softly.

The men turn and stare at him, but David just turns and walks back down the hill, past the giant Joshua tree at the top of the mountain with its branches stretched upward into the smoke-filled sky, and over to the dead-body-carrying car with the hard roof.

✢

LATER THAT NIGHT, AFTER Hop and Nicky have dropped them off and driven away, David asks Phil why he was ever friends with them.

"Hop's a mess, but he doesn't mean to be. He just doesn't know any other way."

"What about Nicky?"

"Nicky's a snake."

"Because of what he knew? About Carole?"

"Among other reasons."

"But you forgive him for it?"

"A snake can't help its nature. But even in nature, there's a place for snakes."

Phil turns to leave the room.

"Phil?"

Phil stops.

"I don't hate Cecil. I miss him."

"You didn't even know him."

"I know. But I still miss him."

Phil stares over at David's wall, where the only children's record he ever produced and went gold was put in a big frame. "Me, too."

✢

THE FOLLOWING MONDAY AT school, David looks for God again but doesn't see him anywhere. A janitor looks at him as though he's crazy when David asks if the janitor has seen a man in long white robes, calling himself God. The janitor goes back to work and David stares at the construction site for a long time, but for the life of him, he can't see any sign of life there.

When David gets home from school, he is about to make himself a peanut butter sandwich when he stops.

The Buddha is gone.

David looks around the house for it, but can't find it anywhere. And every time he passes where it used to be, he can't help but think that the hallway looks empty without it. But as with most things that used to be part of your life without you really ever knowing it, after a few days, he doesn't even notice it anymore.

✦

THE NIGHT THE PRESIDENT is re-elected, Phil holds an assembly in the living room of the house. Phil always says an assembly is different from a meeting because at a meeting people in suits try to become the American dream, while at an assembly people in turtlenecks try to become the American dream's nightmare.

Halfway through the assembly, the doorbell rings. David, who is sitting in his room with the door open, hears Phil excuse himself from his guests, then walk over to the front door and open it.

Two policemen are standing there.

"Evening," says one of them.

After some small talk—no, as much as they would like to come in for a cup of coffee, they're on duty right now—the policemen ask Phil about Cecil and if he knows anything about the disappearance of the coffin.

"We heard it was a couple of his friends," says one of the policemen.

"He'd been out of my life for a while," says Phil. "But of course, I was sad to hear about his death."

Phil says this as though he has been practicing, as though it is one of the pieces of music he makes his musicians play over and over in his studio, on the way to getting their creations figured out just right.

"If you hear any details, you'll let us know?" asks the second policeman.

Phil nods, but David knows there won't be any details coming because God is in the details.

And David finally knows where God is.

Phil closes the door and goes back to his guests, who continue to argue about the President and how they will endure another four years. Despite the muffled voices, David can tell that their owners are full of anger. They want to do whatever it takes to make sure that the new President won't lie to their faces, the way a snake would if it could talk.

David lies in bed, staring at the ceiling and wondering if God ever heard any of what goes on down below. And if so, whether sharing a sandwich with him made any difference at all in the grand scheme of things.

THE MYTH OF CREATION

PHIL IS PUTTING PILES of clothing into the green duffel bag on his bed. David doesn't say a word or make eye contact as the bag slowly fills with stacks of flowered shirts and colorful shorts that Phil rarely wears.

"Do they really need you there?" David says at last, even though this is just more of a way to fill the space between them than an actual question.

"Ben is threatening to destroy the album he's been working on for the past four years."

"What's it called?"

"*The Golden State.*"

"What's it about?"

"California, childhood, and everything in between."

"What does 'everything in between' mean?"

"Some artists have the gift of being able to look at all the empty spaces in the universe and fill them with sounds, shapes, and images. And Ben's album is filled with that gift."

"But is it any good?"

Phil pauses, as though no one has asked him this before and he hasn't bothered to ask himself, either.

"I don't know," he answers.

"You don't?"

"I don't know if that's even the right way to look at it. Good or bad."

"How, then?"

"I think there's a decent chance that what Ben is creating is something more than just music."

"So why doesn't he like it?"

"Because creations are the reasons people have headaches."

Phil zips the bag shut and hoists it over his shoulder.

"Katie will stay here with you tonight. After that…"

"Carole will be here," says David, finishing the part Phil clearly has trouble adding.

Carole is back in town and staying with friends. Phil offered her the house, but she refused until Phil mentioned that he would be spending the week with Ben in Malibu.

The front door swings open and Katie, the seventeen year-old neighbor who's always arguing with her parents, walks in, holding a small backpack. Phil gestures to take Katie's backpack for her, but she clenches it tightly in her hands.

"I can carry my own stuff."

"You know where everything is?"

"Everything I need, yeah."

"If you don't, your mom and dad are right next door."

"Like I said, everything I need."

Phil leaves. Katie throws her backpack down on the couch, then moves toward the bathroom, unbuttoning her blouse.

"I'm going to take a shower."

After a moment, David hears the sound of water running. He glances down the hall and realizes Katie has left the bathroom door open.

He sits down on the living room couch and turns on the TV, where Greg Brady has turned into a rock star named Johnny

Bravo. This version of a rock star looks and sounds nothing like the people who show up in Phil's studio, but then again the family Greg Brady comes from looks and sounds nothing like the families David knows either.

"Could you bring me a towel?" Katie is calling from the bathroom.

"Now?"

"I don't know where they are."

"In the cabinet outside the bathroom."

"I'm dripping wet. Think you could help me out here?"

David walks to the cabinet, takes out a towel, and goes into the bathroom.

The shower curtain is closed.

"Here."

He puts the towel on the toilet seat and is about to leave when the shower curtain opens and Katie, wet and naked, steps out.

"Thanks." She picks up the towel and starts drying off.

David swallows, but somehow, even with all this water around him, his throat is completely dry. He turns around and heads into the kitchen where he fills up a glass from the water dispenser. Aside from the *Playboy* magazines Lon steals from the liquor stores, David has never seen a naked girl before. And those pictures looked very different from what just stepped out of the shower.

A few minutes later Katie, wearing a short tee shirt and underwear, sits down on the loveseat across from David and nods at the TV.

"What's on?"

"The Brady Bunch."

Katie starts to rub her legs together. David is doing his best to pay attention to the television, but his mind can't seem to focus on Jan Brady's envy of her brother's groovy new lifestyle.

"Pervert."

David looks up. "What?"

"I called you a pervert."

"What's that?"

Katie smiles and reaches for the remote control that Phil just bought. "Do we have to watch this? 'Cause something much better is on." She doesn't wait for David to answer before she changes the channel.

A large sports dome appears, which surrounds a bright green tennis court. A group of shirtless men dressed like Roman warriors carry a woman in tennis clothing toward the center of the court. Then there is a roar from the crowd as a man, also wearing white tennis clothing, enters in a chariot pulled by four women. The man looks much older than the woman and the crowd cheers as the man and woman walk to opposite sides of the court and start to hit the ball back and forth.

"Why are they hitting it right to each other like that?" asks David.

"They're just getting warmed up. Believe me, you'll know when it's for keeps."

A funny feeling is swirling around in the pit of David's stomach. He tries to focus on the television, but instead he finds himself thinking about Topanga. He wonders if she's on a beach somewhere, if she remembers drawing the circle in the sand with him that night, if she'd kissed anyone since then, if they even kissed at all, or if his entire memory of her is just something he dreamed one night. The funny feeling in his stomach fades away and he finds himself able to focus back on the television, where the younger woman easily defeats the older man.

The crowd cheers, and Katie, who has been watching the entire match at the edge of her seat, raises her fist when the man's final shot lands in the net. "We won!" she yells.

"What did you win?" asks David.

"What?"

"You said we won. What did you win?"

Katie just stares at David as though he's stupid. And even though David knows he is not stupid, knows that he goes to a school for kids who are especially not stupid, somehow Katie's glare has its intended effect. The funny feeling comes back into his stomach and his throat becomes dry again as Katie pulls her hair over one side of her head and starts braiding it.

"Just go to bed."

David folds his arms across his chest. He's actually in the mood to go to bed, but isn't in the mood to be told to go to bed. Especially not by her.

"Make me."

Katie stares at David. Then she turns to the TV and starts rubbing her legs together again. She isn't looking at him, but David knows she's watching his every move. He isn't sure what she's doing but both of them are aware that she's won their battle. He stands up and heads down the hallway to his room.

"Oh, David?"

David stops and turns around.

"Sweet dreams," she says with a smile.

✦

"You saw her naked!" Lon is standing on the pitcher's mound, staring at David with his mouth wide open.

"She opened the shower curtain."

"So what did you do?" yells Harris, trotting over from the retaining wall at the end of the cul-de-sac. He's just hit a long home run and went to go find the ball, but is coming back empty-handed. The idea of losing their balls has taken on a double meaning of late and has been the subject of endless jokes among the boys on the block. Right now, all eyes are on David, who has somehow found himself the first one to set foot into the unfamiliar territory over the wall where balls are lost and no one is quite sure where to find them.

"I gave her a towel."

"WHAT!"

Lon and Harris now make their way over to David, as do the rest of the kids who sense that something more significant than a baseball game is on the line here.

"She asked for one."

Lon smirks. "That's not what she was asking for."

"Yes, it was. I heard her."

"You heard her, all right. But you weren't paying attention too closely. She wanted you to give it to her."

"I did give it to her."

"Not the towel, turdbrain. Your...thing."

Sometimes in school, David hears kids giggling about the subject of where they came from. Mostly they wonder how the man managed to keep from peeing once his thing was inside the woman. Ariel, the girl whose parents were scientists, once brought in a textbook with colorful illustrations, but it looked more like something you would see at the doctor's office and their teacher soon took it away. And the illustrations didn't make David feel anything like the funny feeling he got in his stomach when Katie rubbed her legs together on the couch.

"I hear that chick's easy. Gives it to pretty much anyone who asks."

This is one of the bigger kids talking, one who already has the beginnings of a mustache growing over his lip. The wispy hairs are settling in between the smattering of pimples around his mouth, and David can't imagine how this kid is ever going to shave without turning his face into a bloody mess.

"Where'd you hear that?" asks Harris.

"From my brother's friend. He went all the way with her. Said it was just like baseball, only with the body parts as bases. And she let my brother's friend hit a home run with her on his very first time at bat."

Lon turns to David. "Could be you, ballboy. Circling the bases instead of walking around with a towel and your pud in your hand."

"She's my babysitter."

"Doesn't mean anything."

"It means I'm not playing baseball or doing anything else with her that ends up making a baby."

The kids laugh. David doesn't know what he said that was so funny. He can't associate what they're talking about with what he felt when Topanga kissed him before she disappeared up the stairs. All he knows is that it felt different, even if he can no longer feel exactly what it felt like.

There's a loud honk of a car horn and Katie's father comes barreling around the corner. The boys scatter, except for David. He watches Katie's father get out of his car, take off his jacket, and loosen his tie.

Katie's father stops when he sees David staring at him. "What are you looking at?"

David knows only what he has heard about Katie's father, but what he has heard has not been good. Stories involving belts, fists, and alcohol. Plus, he's always in a suit.

"Nothing," says David.

Katie's father strides past the neat rows of white daisies that line his front walkway and storms inside his house, slamming the door behind him with a loud bang.

✦

DAVID SENSES SOMETHING DIFFERENT the minute he closes the door.

The house has a funny smell, although David remembers Phil saying something about having the cleaning lady come while he stayed at Ben's. But what David smells doesn't smell like cleaning products, and what he hears definitely sounds like humming.

Carole is home.

Her back is to David as she works in the kitchen where she used to cook. David watches as Carole hums and rubs her hands together and waits for something on the stove to be ready. And even though it's a familiar sight, he feels like a stranger in his own house.

Carole turns around and sees David. She runs over and hugs him without saying a word, her arms fumbling to find room to clasp behind his backpack. Then she steps back and stares at David with a wide, dazed-looking smile on her face.

"Let me look at you."

David is never quite sure why adults always ask this since they almost never ask permission for anything else, but he stands there and lets her look him up and down.

"You've grown so big."

"It's been a while."

There is an awkward silence, broken by a loud, whistling sound from something on the stove.

"Cooking something?" asks David.

"Just tea. Cooking is slavery."

She pours herself some hot water from the kettle on the stove and adds a tea bag.

"Where were you?" This time, David wants to add, but doesn't. Part of being ten years old, of having double-digit bragging rights, seems to be knowing when it's best not to speak.

"I had to go on a journey, honey. To figure out who I was."

"Why does 'where' have anything to do with 'who'?"

Carole takes a sip of her tea. "Sometimes you have to look far and wide to find where you come from. I know that might sound strange, but it's true."

"So what did you find?"

"I found that I come from a long line of men with long names that have been in the family as long as they can remember. I found that there are advantages and disadvantages to this. One advantage is that it gives me one kind of freedom. One disadvantage is that it takes away another kind of freedom."

David no longer understands what Carole is talking about, but one thing he has always known about her is the more he tries to understand her, the more confusing she becomes. So he sits quietly as Carole sips her tea.

"So what do you usually do around this time?" Carole asks after a while.

"Homework. After a snack."

Carole looks nervously over at the refrigerator.

"It's okay," says David. "I can make it myself."

"And your homework?"

"I know all my subjects pretty well."

"Thanks," says Carole with a yawn that sounds more like a sigh of relief. She stretches out her legs on the couch. "I'm bushed. Mind if I take a nap?"

"You can sleep on the bed. Dad had it made up for you."

Carole finishes her tea and stares out the window at the small trees that line the side yard. Her gaze lands on one tree at the center of the cluster.

"I planted that one myself. Still can't get over how the seeds from one tree can populate an entire row."

"It's called a parthenogenic birth," says David.

Carole turns to stare at him.

"Parthenogenic," David repeats. "Means only one parent was needed."

"Where did you learn that?"

"School. We were discussing Gaia, the earth mother. Gaia emerged from Chaos, then, in her sleep, gave birth to the rest of the universe. It's part of a myth. But I don't remember which one."

David turns to face Carole, but she's already snoring.

THE DOORBELL RINGS IN the middle of the night. David has grown up in the kind of house where this is not out of the ordinary, so it does little more than wake him, with a yawn, from an already unsatisfying sleep. He tiptoes out of his room to see Carole sitting on the couch, stroking the hair of a sobbing Katie, who lies with her head in Carole's lap. It's a position David can't remember ever having been in himself.

"How did it happen?" asks Carole.

"You don't know?"

"Of course I know, technically. What I want to know is how a beautiful, powerful young woman like you allowed it to happen."

Katie stares at Carole, the tears still clinging to her eyeballs as though unsure whether or not to fall. "I wanted to feel what you feel."

Carole stares at Katie with an expression unlike any David has ever seen before. Then she stands up. "Come on."

"What are you doing?"

"Something I never got a chance to do a long time ago. Back when things were different." Carole opens her handbag and tosses around some pens, hair clips, and half-opened packs of gum. She pulls out a folded piece of paper and a book and hands them both to Katie, who glances at the book's cover.

"*Fear of Flying*?"

"It will empower you. So you won't need what's on that piece of paper in the future, ever again."

Katie unfolds the piece of paper and stares at it.

"These people are friends of mine," says Carole "Call them tomorrow."

"And say what?"

"That you're glad the laws have changed. Make an appointment, then call me and tell me what time it is and I'll meet you there."

"What if I don't want to get rid of it?"

"You do. You're young, Katie. You don't need grown-up headaches."

"But—"

"And you don't know what, or how I feel. And you don't want to either."

Katie sniffles and wipes her nose with a tissue. "You won't tell my parents? 'Cause they're not exactly the most understanding people."

Carole shakes her head.

"Thanks," says Katie. She gets up and walks over to the door.

"I wish you were my mother," she says. Then she slips out so quietly it's almost as though she wasn't even there in the first place.

＊

THREE WEEKS LATER, DAVID and Phil are out in the yard trimming some trees, when Katie's father comes barging through the side gate.

"I need to talk to you," he says to Phil. Although it's a weekend, Katie's father is dressed in slacks and a dress shirt with the sleeves barely rolled up.

"About what?"

"About Katie. I don't want her babysitting your kid anymore."

Phil puts down his gardening tools and turns to face Katie's father.

"Bout a month ago she got in a spot of trouble. Didn't say a word to her mother or me, but somehow wound up over here."

"And?"

"The trouble got taken care of. Courtesy of your wife. Only reason I found out was I happened to overhear Katie talking about it on the phone."

"Ever think you might hear more if you overheard less?"

Katie's father marches right up to Phil so that he is standing face-to-face with him. "Now you listen to me. I don't need any of your progressive, Jewish nonsense about what a square I am."

"Being a member of the world's oldest religion has nothing to do with being progressive."

Katie's father blinks for a moment. "I give that girl everything, including a stable home. Which is more than I can say for what's going on around here."

"Can't argue with you there. Or here," says Phil.

David has heard his father do business enough times on the phone to understand that he will remain calm with Katie's father. The only time David has ever seen Phil lose his cool is when he talks to his musicians about the way they treat their creations.

Katie's father reaches into his pocket and pulls out the copy of *Fear of Flying* David saw Carole give to Katie.

"Ever hear of this book?

Phil nods. "Lot of people reading it nowadays."

"I found it on my wife's night table. Didn't think anything of it until I realized the woman who wrote it has absolutely no fear of flying whatsoever."

Katie's father glares at Phil. His angry bloodshot eyes change to a different shade of red, one that looks as though he would like to cry, but forgot how to somewhere along the way to where he is now.

"All this sex, battle of the sexes. Babies having babies, killing babies. Where the hell are we?"

"I'll be damned if I know," says Phil.

"You'll be damned no matter what. Something tells me we all will."

Katie's father turns and walks out through the open side door. Phil hands David a pair of shears and nods at the weeds at the base of the tree. "Gotta knock out those weeds, or before we know it the foundation will be in trouble."

David starts to pull the weeds. As he does, he looks up to see Katie's father standing, staring at the daisies on his front walkway, the book still in his hand. He raises the book and brings it down on the head of the one of the daisies, then does it again and again until every one has had its head knocked off.

Then, with the same angry stride he has when he gets out of his car every day after work, he steps over the crushed white petals of the dead plants and disappears inside where, behind closed doors, two women are waiting for him.

THE RUSTLER'S MOON

THE FACES OF THE people are blurry.

David stretches out his hand, but grabs only a fistful of water as the faces blur even more. A few bubbles escape from his mouth and rise to the surface. David leans back slowly so the water doesn't rush up his nose, then he stretches his arms out and stares up at the surface of the pool.

The faces start to come into focus. A few are familiar, but most aren't, and if any of the people notice the bubbles, they don't seem to care where they're coming from. David wishes he could lie here like this forever, floating and bubbling away.

Soon he feels the front of his head pulsing. He leans forward slowly, wriggling his arms to steady himself, then he kicks his feet off the bottom of the pool and glides up to the surface without making any ripples in the water, the way he used to when he was little and pretended that he was invisible. He pops his head out from the water and looks around.

Two women in small bikinis are dancing in front of a transistor radio. A few men in open Hawaiian shirts stand nearby, watching the women over lowered sunglasses. Most of the men at the party are older than most of the women and everyone seems to be holding plastic cups filled with colorful drinks, sliced fruit, and paper umbrellas.

Phil moves from person to person, smiling and patting everyone on the back, or backside, especially if it's one of the women. He's been patting backs and backsides and smiling like this for almost two days straight—the news on TV is all about how the President has been caught with his hand in the cookie jar, and Phil and his friends are in the mood to play.

David walks over to the pile of towels by the outdoor table. He sifts through the fluffier folded ones on the top and instead grabs an older, more threadbare towel from the bottom. It feels harsh against his skin as he dries off, but it also has the face of his favorite Saturday morning cartoon character on it and David finds this more comforting than the comfort from the softer towels.

"Bet the First Lady's packing the china by the end of the week," says one of the partygoers, taking a puff from one of the skunky-smelling cigarettes someone is passing round.

David wonders why Phil closes all the windows whenever there's an actual skunk in the neighborhood but doesn't do anything whenever anyone lights up something that smells just as bad and fills the air with cancerous fumes to boot.

"They'll just send him to some Club Fed," says another one of the partygoers as he takes the cigarette from the first partygoer and takes a puff.

"He's going down much harder than that," says the first partygoer. "Who's sympathetic at this point? Never thought I'd say this, but thank God for the system."

David pokes the towel into his ear and tries to pop a stubborn water bubble lodged inside. He tilts his head and hops up and down on one foot, the way his swimming teacher always told him to do whenever he got water stuck in his ear, but this only makes the water feel like it's sinking in deeper.

One of the two partygoers, the one who thanked God for the system, turns to David. "Hey, kid, think you could track down your old man for us? We're running a little low on wine."

David glances over to where Phil was circulating a minute ago, but he's not there anymore. David doesn't feel like running errands for these guys, but he's also hungry and wants to ask Phil if he can order pizza.

David finishes drying off and walks past some people kissing and drinking on the loungers by the pool. He opens the sliding glass doors and feels the air conditioning whoosh over his skin, making the hair on his arms stand up. Phil likes to keep the air conditioning on to protect all the musical instruments and studio equipment from the elements. David always wonders why cigarette and other kinds of smoke and spilled wine or beer don't count as elements, but he wouldn't dream of asking Phil.

"Close the door behind you?"

This comes from Ben, who is bent over the piano. Ever since Phil spent the week at Ben's house in Malibu, Ben has lost weight and no longer wears clothing that looks like it belongs on a bed. Four young women, all in bikini tops and sarongs, sit around the piano bench. Ben's eyes are closed and his hands hover over the piano keys.

"Aren't you gonna play something?" asks one of the girls.

Ben's eyes open. He glances around at the girls, then looks over at David. "Piano's gotta go."

He stands up and pushes the piano bench, which screeches as it slides across the floor, scattering the girls.

"Where?" asks David.

"Huh?"

"Where's the piano gotta go?" David has seen Phil interact with Ben enough times to know that the best approach is to talk to him as though he's making complete sense.

Ben thinks about it. Then he nods at the open sliding glass doors. "Pool." He places his hands on two of the piano's legs and pushes.

"The piano can't go in the pool."

"It can if you give me a hand."

"I think Phil likes it right where it is."

"But—"

"But it's his piano."

Ben stops pushing the piano and looks off to the side, as if he's processing the information David has just given him. Then, huffing and puffing, he carries the bench calmly over to the piano and plops himself back down.

"So what am I supposed to do?" he asks.

"Play some music, maybe?" says David.

Ben thinks about it. "Cool." He puts his hands on the keys and starts to play.

David has heard people talk about having their minds blown, and it always made him wonder how it could be a good thing to have your gray matter so overwhelmed that it feels like it's about to explode. But now, he immediately sees why Phil, who complains when he has to wait for more than five minutes for coffee, has so much patience with Ben.

"What's this?" whispers one of the girls.

"Something new."

"I love it."

Ben stops playing. He opens his eyes and stares at the girl. "You do?"

The girl nods.

"But…it's new."

"I know."

"And you still like it?"

"More than your old stuff."

Ben smiles at the girl, then lifts his hands off the piano keys.

"Why'd you stop?" asks a different girl, but Ben places a finger on her lips.

"Shhh," whispers Ben. "Let it linger."

"Do any of you know where Phil is?" asks David.

"I think he went down the hall," giggles one of the girls with a knowing wink at one of the others. David decides to forget about Phil and go to his bedroom instead to start his essay.

A few weeks ago, Phil enrolled David in one of the school's summer programs and David signed up for a class in silent films. He's writing an essay on a film they watched in class, about a private in the army who falls headfirst into a trench, gets amnesia, and thinks he's behind enemy lines. David enjoyed the movie and has been looking forward to writing his essay, but when he gets to his bedroom and opens the door, the lights are out. He hears three muffled voices and what sounds like several zippers closing.

"Knock next time, okay?" growls one of the voices.

David closes the door and turns around. Phil is standing shirtless in the hallway behind him.

"David…"

"Fourth time this week."

"I know. I'll have everyone out by the end of the weekend."

"You said that last weekend."

Phil lights up a cigarette and runs a hand through his hair. As much as David hates Phil's smoking, he is always impressed that Phil can do this move every time without singeing his sideburns.

"Look, we've all been through hell with this guy. You understand, right?"

It takes a few seconds before David realizes that Phil is talking about the soon-to-be-ex-President. But for all the living room lectures he's overheard, David still doesn't understand how Phil or any of his friends have been through hell with a President who doesn't mess up their backyards and mess around in their bedrooms.

"I guess."

"How's your assignment going?"

"Probably a lot better if I had access to it."

"End of the weekend. Promise," says Phil, then someone calls his name from the pool area and he's outside before David gets the chance to ask him what three people could possibly be doing in a bed together.

The backyard is even more crowded, so David goes out front to check the mail. The mailbox has so many items packed in it, they're poking through the tin slot. Phil has told David to ignore every envelope except the blue ones, which contain the checks from the company handling Phil's record royalties. The blue envelopes have been arriving less and less often, but there's no shortage of red envelopes that look like bills.

David takes out all the junk mail and puts it into a cardboard box so it can be recycled. This is a new thing Phil has read about, but after weeks of bottles, cans, and red-enveloped bills, the cardboard box is even more full than the mailbox. Whoever is in charge of taking it away either hasn't heard anything about it, or isn't concerned about the planet.

David is halfway to Harris's house before he remembers it's the day before the League Championship and Harris is taking team pictures. Harris hadn't wanted to play League ball, but the neighbors had grown tired of having their windows broken and complained to his mother. He donated his uniform to Goodwill the day he got it and instead wore concert tee shirts and his Cat Diesel Power hat to games. Nobody said anything about it, because he was promoted to Colt League after one week and still going long on sixteen-year-olds who could throw breaking pitches.

A month later, a local reporter wrote an article about Harris, saying that most boys grow into their physical frames and face a life sentence of limitations, a cage constructed from strands of DNA whose shortcomings would pull on their owners' heartstrings, until they finally went completely taut. But for Harris, the opposite would be true. He had joined an elite group who, upon diving into their gene pools, had discovered a bubbling fountain of youth—a gateway to fields with lights that crackled when huge, heavy switches were thrown to scouts schooled in the physics of a swing and the trajectory of a pitch, and to scientists who applied their skills, not to solving the mysteries of the physical universe, but instead to breaking down the physical mechanics that allowed a man to earn a lifetime of livelihood by playing a game meant for boys. Soon, everyone from coaches to spectators, even umpires, was telling Harris to get rid of the hitch in his swing, or position his feet differently in the outfield, or take longer leadoffs when he was on base. David reminded Harris that this was just what adults were like, but Harris reminded David that none of them were ever like that when talking about Keith, or school, or practically anything else for that matter.

David wanders over to the cul-de-sac and stands at the manhole that once served as home plate. It was always David's job to draw the baselines, but without Harris around, they'd had fewer and fewer games until they'd stopped entirely. David hadn't bothered to buy chalk and nobody had asked him about it; eventually last winter's rainstorms washed away what was left of the base paths down the gutters.

He stares out at the houses past the base paths, the ones that used to seem so far away whenever it was his turn to hit, but that Harris could reach with a one-handed swing. They look close enough now that David could probably hit them if he wanted to, which he doesn't; as much as he misses the idea of playing, the desire to actually do so seems as far away as the houses once did. He wonders if that's how it works when you get older, that everything that used to seem so far away finally comes close enough to touch, but at that point you don't want it anymore.

"Little game of hot potato?"

David turns around to see Lon standing behind him, tossing a baseball up and down. Lon tosses the ball over to David, who catches it.

"No thanks." David lobs the ball back at Lon, hoping he'll get the hint, but the second Lon catches the ball he fires it right back at David.

"Come on."

"I said, 'no thanks,'" says David. He fires the ball, but it goes flying past Lon and rolls down the hill. It comes to a stop by the boarded-up log cabin at the bend where the street intersects with the main canyon road.

Lon looks up at the sky. "Gonna be a full-on orange pie in the sky tonight. A Rustler's Moon. Know why they call it that?"

David shakes his head.

"Really? All that special education and you don't know a damn thing about your own neighborhood?" Lon is still smiling but he sounds serious, as though for once he isn't in on some joke he's about to play on someone else.

He puts his arm around David's shoulder. "Years ago this place was all countryside. One night, a few cattle rustlers stole part of some rancher's herd, then stopped here to crash on their way back home. They were just teenagers, but the rancher didn't care. He tracked them down here by the light of a big, orange moon and splattered the walls of the cabin with their brains and insides. Got all of them except one, who escaped."

Lon's grip tightens. "Here's the fun part. Every time a rustler's moon appears in the sky, legend has it the rancher's ghost comes back here, looking for the one who got away. So we've all taken turns staying there, just to see for ourselves."

"Did you ever do it?"

"Sure did."

"So what happened?"

Lon takes his arm off David's shoulder. He's not smiling anymore. "I definitely saw something. Can't really say what it was for sure. One who had the closest call though, was Harris."

"Harris?"

"Yeah. He went there by himself one night after Keith tried to jam one of the old lady's knitting needles into his ribs. Claimed he saw something. And that what he saw scared the crap out of him."

David tells Lon he can't imagine Harris, who faces everything from a war-scarred half-brother to headhunting opposing pitchers on a daily basis, being scared of anything.

"Doesn't really matter if Harris is scared. Bigger question is, are you?"

David shakes his head and straightaway wishes he could take it back.

"Good. Then we'll meet you back here at sunset with your sleeping bag."

David looks down the hill. He wants to retrieve the ball and sleep in his own bed tonight, but he can't see the ball anymore and these days he's not sure that his own bed is entirely his own either.

✦

NOTEBOOK.

Pen.

Sleeping bag.

David checks off the items on his list as he places them in his school backpack, which he's emptied except for the items he'll need for his essay.

Food.

Water.

Electric lantern.

David runs his canteen under the water faucet, then twists the lid and puts it into his backpack. He opens the refrigerator and looks around, but there's no apple juice. He closes the refrigerator door and goes to look for Phil. On his way through the living room, he spots a tuxedoed woman behind the bar, stabbing a sharp metal object into an enormous block of ice.

"Any apple juice back there?"

"Ran out. Why don't you go tell the owner?" says the woman without looking up.

"He's my dad."

The woman looks up at David. Her expression changes. "You running away?" she asks, nodding at his backpack.

"No."

"Might want to rethink that," she mutters before going back to the ice.

David slides the glass doors open and steps outside. The music is so loud it makes the front part of his skull feel as though it's rattling, the way it does when he rides a bike over rough pavement. Everyone is doing what they were doing earlier, only they're doing more of it, and there are more of them to boot.

"A President brought down by the people," says one of them, passing on a skunky-smelling cigarette.

"Only in everywhere but America, 'til now," says another, exhaling a long stream of smoke that goes right past David's face, making him cough.

"What did he ever do to any of you?" asks David.

The partygoers stop smoking and turn to stare at David. The guy holding the cigarette opens his arms wide.

"We are the people, little man."

David doesn't think that any of these people are the people. At least he hopes not. He thinks about asking them if they know where Phil is, but there's a scream and a splash and by the time David turns around, Ben is standing on top of the piano, which is in the middle of the pool and sinking fast. People are jumping up and down around the pool and yelling, and Ben is waving his hands like a conductor as the water covers his ankles, then his knees. David doesn't stay long enough to see if the water makes its way up to Ben's chest.

✦

Lon and some of the other kids are waiting for David, right where Lon said they would be.

"Seven forty-five," says Lon, pointing to his wristwatch. "Twelve hours from now, we'll come down there to get you."

David hitches up his backpack and is about to go down the hill when he hears the sound of footsteps slapping against the pavement.

"Wait up."

Harris is pushing his way through the other kids, not giving them a second look as he trots up to David's side. He's still wearing his Cat Diesel cap, but he also has on a baseball jersey that fits him perfectly, with his last name stitched on the back.

"Want company?" Harris asks.

"Sure."

As Lon and the others watch, mouths agape, David follows Harris down the hill toward the cabin's rear. The weight from his backpack forces him to lean back so he doesn't tumble face-first down the hill.

"Wanna pick up the pace?" says Harris.

"I haven't hiked down like this before."

"Me, neither."

Harris jumps over a toppled tree that's blocking the path, then disappears into the brush.

The front of the cabin overlooks the small road that leads to the door, but the other side of the cabin, which has a small window at the top, overlooks a steep ravine that drops about fifty feet down into a dark, tree-covered crevice. After a careful descent, David reaches the side of the cabin, which is built right up against the hillside, and puts down his backpack.

David yells for Harris, but there's no answer so he picks up his backpack and makes his way around to the front of the cabin. His feet make a cracking sound as they trample over the fallen leaves, which are several inches deep. He reaches the cabin's door, pushes it open, and looks around.

The cabin is smaller than it looks on the outside, just a small, box-shaped living room with a smaller loft area. There's a space next to the living room that probably used to be a kitchen, but all that's left are some rusted-looking wires. A thick rope with some knots hangs down from the loft area, which has a window that overlooks the ravine below the canyon. The window, not cleaned in years, has light streaming through it, but looks smeared and unclean.

"Boo."

David turns to see Harris standing behind him, holding some twine. "Brought this from home. To booby trap the outside, in case those assholes get any funny ideas about trying to scare us when the sun goes down."

Harris is bouncing up and down and smiling more than he usually does, and his hands and arms are moving as though someone's puppeteering them. David also notices that the twine is the only thing Harris has brought.

Harris throws himself against and out the back door, which gives way with more of a loud bang than the kind of haunted house creak David was expecting. David lays his sleeping bag down on the floor and takes out his essay from his backpack. It's not completely dark yet, but he decides to work by the light of the electric lantern, partly because it helps him see better and partly because he likes it. He's almost finished with his assignment when the door opens and Harris walks back inside, still holding the ball of twine.

"What's that?" asks Harris, nodding at David's notes.

"An essay."

"School doesn't start for another couple of weeks."

"It's for a summer class I'm taking."

Harris plops himself down next to David. "You have to go to summer school?"

"I don't have to. It's just for fun," says David, blowing away some eraser rubbings.

Harris leans back against the walls of the cabin and stares up at the ceiling. "Amazing that this place hasn't fallen apart, seeing as how no one takes care of it."

"Who owns it?"

"City. Least that's what Keith says. He says they've been dying to sell it to developers, but people like your old man keep blocking the way."

"Sounds like my old man all right."

"Least he gives a shit about something," says Harris, still staring at the ceiling.

David unscrews the cap from his canteen and takes a long gulp of water.

Harris gestures for it. "Can I get some of that?"

David screws the cap back on and tosses the canteen to Harris. Harris unscrews the lid and takes a few sips, as if he wasn't really that thirsty in the first place, then closes it up again.

He tosses it back to David, but it sails through David's arms and hits him in the chest.

"Sorry."

"Don't be. You've got a great arm."

"Yeah. I do have that going for me."

Harris tosses his ball of twine up and down, higher and higher, catching it each time without looking.

"How'd today go?" asks David.

"Good."

"Who was there?"

"My teammates."

"Anyone else?"

"Like who?" snaps Harris.

"I don't know. Like…anyone."

Harris flicks his wrist. The ball of twine goes sailing through one of the rafters in a perfect parabola, then lands with a neat *thwack* back in Harris's hands.

"That reporter," he finally says. "But it wasn't a big deal. And it's not like anyone else came," he adds.

"So how come you felt like spending the night here?"

"You want me to leave?"

"No, I just figured…I mean, don't you have a game tomorrow?"

"Not 'til late afternoon."

"But you already spent a night in this place."

"Yeah, so?"

"So Lon said you saw something that scared you. Why would you be back for another look?"

Harris throws the ball of twine up in the air again. This time it lands on one of the beams near the top of the roof and stays there.

"Don't tell me you believe those stories."

"Lon said he thought he saw something too."

"Lon says a lot of things."

David and Harris watch the orange and red light peeking through the window, as the sunset cascades down through the trees and bounces off the rock walls in the canyon.

"This one guy on my team, he doesn't throw or catch so well, either," says Harris.

"Why does he play?"

"Got me. Kid wears his pants all high above his ankles, like he's expecting a flood. But his old man's there for every game, clapping away like crazy every time the damn kid strikes out or drops an easy popup. Reminded me of your old man."

"In what way?"

"Just seems like he's always so into you whenever I see you guys together."

David wonders if he should tell Harris what his house looked like when he left, but just thinking about it makes his stomach hurt, even more than it has been all day from the thought of a full night in this place.

"I miss playing ball," says David.

"Me, too," says Harris softly, staring up at the ball of twine.

"But you're still playing."

Harris flips his Cat Diesel hat forward and hops up on his feet. "Let's make a clubhouse."

"What?"

"A clubhouse. Let's turn this place into a clubhouse."

"Like how?"

"I don't know. I just always wanted one."

Harris starts pacing around the cabin floor as if he's drawing up plans in his head for something only he can see. "We can bring a bunch of posters and baseball pennants. Maybe rig up a refrigerator over where those wires are. This guy on my team was going on about some place way out in the desert where his brother lives, how he's got his own electricity and everything."

"Maybe we could put up a sign outside that says 'no girls allowed,' too."

Harris turns around and glares at David. "The hell's that supposed to mean?"

David swallows; somehow stating the obvious suddenly seems a lot harder than it should be. "Aren't we too old to have a clubhouse?"

"Aren't we too old to be spending the night here in the first place? Why are you here if we're too old?"

"Lon dared me."

"Ah. So you're not too old to play dare or double dare, right?"

David's ears burn, which takes his mind off the nausea in his stomach. "Why are you here?" he fires back. "You already proved how tough you were."

Harris sits back down against the wall and turns his attention back to the ceiling and he and David don't say another word to each other.

✢

"WAKE UP…"

David's eyes flutter open. He's lying on top of his sleeping bag and Harris is standing over him, his own eyes open wider than David has ever seen them before.

"I...I saw something," stammers Harris.

"What?"

"I don't know. I was sitting here and all of a sudden something flew right by me. Get up."

Harris yanks David from his sleeping bag and drags him over to the ladder leading to the loft.

"It went up there," he says, pointing.

David squints up at the loft, but doesn't see anything.

"Maybe it was a bat."

"It was not a bat."

"What about a—"

"It was nothing I've ever seen before." Harris grips David's arm hard. "Did you hear me? Something I have never seen before went right by me and disappeared right up there."

David remembers Lon talking about Harris's fears and how at the time David had thought it was strange, how the horrors of Harris's home should have made him scared of nothing.

Unless, David realizes now, they've made him scared of everything.

"There!" screams Harris.

David looks up and sees...

Something.

At least he thinks so.

But before he's even sure of what he's seen, or if he saw anything at all, Harris is up the ladder and into the loft. And David is climbing up after him, but he's not nearly as fast and agile as Harris and part of him somewhere deep down inside is wondering, just wondering, if it's possible that Harris is right, that something that floats and wants some part of them is really up there, waiting…

And then the window is open.

And there's a scream.

And a thud.

And David is left alone, perched halfway between the floor and the ceiling, bathed in the dirty light of the big, orange moon pouring in through the open window.

✦

THE HOSPITAL WAITING ROOM has copies of the magazine David used to read in the office of his dentist, the one who had bubblegum-flavored fluoride that made David actually look forward to brushing his teeth. David used to like the magazine, too, but right now he has to fight the urge to turn all the copies over on their fronts so he doesn't have to look at them.

Phil sits next to David, his head hanging low, but David isn't sure if this is due to his concern about Harris or to the effects of the alcohol that's practically oozing out of his pores.

"You can see him now."

Phil and David look up to see a nurse looming over them.

"Just you," she says, pointing at David and giving Phil a nasty look.

As they make their way down the hall, David tells the nurse about the Rustler's Moon, about the thing Harris said he saw, and how he followed it up to the loft.

"But you saw it, too?"

"I think so."

"And you really believe it was some kind of ghost?"

"I don't know what to believe right now," says David.

The nurse stops in front of an open door and gestures inside. "His mother was just here," she says, a bit softer now.

Harris is lying on the bed with one of his legs up in a sling. Most of his head is covered in bandages, but he doesn't look as puffy and cut-up as he did when David discovered him lying on the hillside outside the cabin.

Harris turns his head and sees David, but says nothing. David looks at the machines in Harris's room. They all seem to be beeping okay, but if everything really were okay, Harris probably wouldn't be here in the first place.

"The nurse said your mom just left."

"Yeah. Had to go take care of her other crippled son."

David can barely bring himself to look at Harris's leg. "Will it be okay?"

"Not completely," says Harris. "It'll probably wind up being an inch shorter than the other one."

"What about…?"

Harris shakes his head, answering David's unfinished question.

David fights down the knot in this throat. He reaches into his pocket and takes out the piece of paper that's been sitting in there all night, the letter he'd found on the hillside next to Harris, that must have fallen out of Harris's pocket.

"What's that?" asks Harris, but David can tell from his expression that he already knows. "Read it to me."

David unfolds the letter and reads aloud. "'I know it's been a long time since I've seen you. You probably don't remember much about me, and to tell you the truth, I don't remember much about you either. I don't know what to say except as you probably figured out, I read about you in the paper. I'll be coming down to watch you in the Championship Game on

Sunday, and hope you get this letter before then so you'll know I'm coming.'"

David pauses before reading the last word. "'Dad.'"

David looks up at Harris, who is staring straight ahead. Harris has mentioned his father exactly once in all the years David has known him, and that was to tell David that he couldn't remember ever laying eyes on the man.

"Anyone else seen this?" asks Harris.

David shakes his head. He offers the letter to Harris, who puts up his hand.

"Chuck it."

David crumples the letter up and tosses it at the garbage can, but misses.

"You never could throw," says Harris, almost enviously.

"Is he still going to the game tomorrow?"

"He knows I'm laid up in here. Mom told him. Hours ago."

They sit in silence together, the way they did in the cabin before David fell asleep.

"I saw something, too," David finally says.

"You saw exactly what I saw," says Harris. He closes his eyes and this time it's his turn to sleep.

It's nearly six in the morning, but everyone on the radio is talking about how the new President pardoned the old one so he will not face any charges. Phil listens all the way home. Even when they pull into the driveway, it's not until David opens the door that Phil turns off the radio.

"Get the mail," says Phil as he gathers David's backpack out of the small trunk of the convertible.

David scoops the mail out of the mailbox and puts it under his arm.

"Do me a favor—take the recycling in, too, and throw it out." Phil opens the front door and disappears inside.

David picks up the recycling box, then pauses as he looks around at his street. The sun is poking over the rooftops and the street looks as empty as it feels and sounds. David takes the recycling carton through the backyard gate so he can throw it into the big trashcan by the pool. The backyard is as quiet as the front yard, the people all gone, leaving nothing but cans and bottles behind.

David passes by the piano lying at the bottom of the pool, and even though he never gave it much thought when it was sitting in his living room all those years, he feels sad knowing it will never be played, or played with again.

BOLSHEVIKS

THE FALL IS COMING...

A new academic year, the last in this school before David will go to a new school, one where there won't be any uniforms or girls or geniuses who skip grades the way other kids skip boxes in hopscotch.

The fall is here.

Keith is as cheerful as David has ever seen him, and even though Keith can't take credit for the troops storming the American embassy, or for the helicopters taking off with their tails between their legs, he acts like a whole person for the first time, as if he has something to do other than treat his brother like a prisoner of war.

"Finally..."

Keith says this word over and over, a word that for him is more about beginnings than endings. He's taking classes at the community college and actually apologized to Harris recently after running over his foot with his wheelchair. Even though he still isn't much in the big brother department, at least it's movement, as their shrink mother would say.

But there's movement in your arms and legs, and there's movement that shakes the ground under your feet, and this second kind of movement is what's going through David when he opens the front door one day and sees Carole standing there.

Carole has been gone longer than usual this time—two years in countries all over Eastern Europe. While she was in Russia, her letters became shorter and shorter and the envelopes always looked like they'd been opened and closed again. Then her letters started coming only every other month or so, and finally they stopped coming at all. But yesterday Carole had called from the airport in France to tell David she'd be by to pick him up the next day for a visit.

Now, as he looks at her face for the first time in two years, David can see that there has been movement there, too. The thin lines that used to crease her cheeks have traveled downward to her chin, and the edges of her mouth are tight and pinched and look like places where smiles go to hide. Her eyes travel back and forth, up and down—looking at everything, it seems, except David.

The two of them stand in silence because David isn't sure if she wants to come in and Carole doesn't seem to know, either.

"Want to go for a drive?" she eventually asks, as though the movement of a gas-fueled car firing away on all pistons is the only kind that will remove the discomfort caused by their current state of stasis.

On their way through the canyon, David notices that Carole is driving slower than she used to. She's been down the canyon's main road millions of times, knows it like the back of her bony, newly veiny hand, but she's looking out the window as if she's never been here before.

"That one's new," says Carole, looking at a house built into the side of a cliff with only four wooden stilts propping it up.

"They're everywhere now. Dad says they're actually more stable than most of the houses built directly into the ground."

"He would know all about stability," mutters Carole.

David goes back to the textbook he's brought along for the ride.

"What's that you're reading?" she asks.

"Math."

"You're reading math? In summer?"

"I'm trying to get a head start on the school year."

David and two of his friends, Robbie and Tim, split last year's math prize three ways and have a bet about who will be this year's top math student. Robbie is a Chinese kid with immigrant parents who smile only for the customers in their store, and even then just barely. They also seem to have figured out, without much input from Robbie, that Robbie wants to be a doctor when he grows up. Tim is tall and hunched-over and has long arms that are always jammed deep in his pockets. He looks and sounds like he should be at the top of the class in every subject, but somehow never is.

Phil has never been too hung up on grades and Tim's mom is divorced and out at bars every night, but Robbie's parents kept him indoors all summer and David has a feeling that math will be even more competitive and joyless this year than usual.

"What math are you in this year?" asks Carole.

"Algebra."

"Oh."

David has the feeling she doesn't know what to ask next. "I'm reading about constants and variables."

"Oh, yeah? How's that going?"

The truth is that it's the most confusing thing David has ever tried to learn. The letters and numbers bounce around for no reason and he always puts them in the wrong places, and no matter how many hours he spends with his new tutor, he still can't blow through the equations the way he used to.

"Fine," he says.

They drive over the hill into the Valley, which, according to David's teachers, used to be full of orange trees. David can't remember seeing any orange trees there, but he has seen lots of lemon trees. He wonders if that's how it works on this side of the hill, that sweet fruit turns into sour, wrinkly-looking things that make your mouth pucker.

Carole turns down a wide, tree-lined street that looks as though it can't make up its mind whether it wants to be a country road or a city boulevard.

"Where are we going?" David asks.

"My new home," says Carole.

Carole's apartment is in a two-story building shaped like a big U. The courtyard has a leaf-filled pool, some lounge chairs with butt indentations and missing straps, and a plastic grass lawn that crunches under David's feet. The staircase's railing is rusty and looks like it could give someone lead splinters, and the stairs are concrete and flecked with turquoise and purple-colored pebbles that aren't pretty, they just make the staircase slippery. David clutches onto the railing, wincing every time some of the black paint flakes off and stabs his skin.

Carole's apartment is dark and smells like a combination of cat pee and chlorine. There's a boxy living room with a fireplace that has an unused-looking plastic log, and a kitchen with a brownish-greenish countertop and two built-in barstools. The dining area has a card table and two folding chairs that don't look like they could support anyone playing cards, let alone eating.

"Where's all the furniture?" asks David.

"The rental company said they'd be here in two weeks. Couches, tables, beds, the works. Oh, and a few paintings to give the place some character."

"No TV?"

"Honey, I barely watch. Besides, it was much more expensive. This building only has cable and you have to subscribe."

Before Carole went to Russia, she used to tell David that money was only good for making bad choices in life, but now she just sounds upset about not having any.

"I'll show you something I do have," she says with a wink, as she walks over to the kitchen. She opens the refrigerator, where David sees a few apples, some white boxes, and a row of jars with blue tops that takes up an entire shelf.

"Peanut butter," she says, gesturing to the jars.

David nods.

"You do still eat peanut butter sandwiches?"

David nods.

"Still pretty much every day?"

David doesn't feel like nodding a third time, but he doesn't need to because Carole is already at the pantry, taking out two slices of bread.

"Remember the peanut butter song I used to sing to you when you were little?"

David remembers that she used to sing when he was little, but it usually sounded more as if she was singing to herself.

"There's a famous song that goes, 'Peanut, peanut butter… AND jelly.' Well, you always hated jelly—you stamped your feet any time I so much as looked at the jelly jar. So for your sandwiches I'd sing, 'Peanut, peanut butter…NO jelly.'"

Something shifts inside David's memory and all of a sudden he's smiling, and Carole is singing the song again and dancing as she spreads the peanut butter on the first slice of bread. She's just about to butter the second one when the phone rings. David hasn't noticed it because it's the same mustard-looking yellow as the wall. Plus it's one of those older models where you have to put your finger in it and dial, instead of tap on a number pad like all the new phones.

Carole rushes over to the receiver and snatches it from the cradle as if it were her oldest friend in the world. She listens for a moment, then says something in Russian and hangs up.

"I have to take care of something."

She grabs her keys and runs out the door, forgetting to close it behind her as she does. She also forgets to finish making David's sandwich, but by the time he notices, he isn't really hungry anymore.

＋

A WEEK LATER, IT's Phil's turn to drive David to the apartment. Carole called a few days before and asked David to spend the weekend; her furniture had finally arrived and she wanted him to spend the night in his new room. She told him to feel free to bring over anything he wanted in order to make the place feel like his.

David looked around while packing his bag, but couldn't imagine any other room being his. He didn't want to take any of the pieces of his life off his wall or desk, over to a building where nothing, even the pebble-filled concrete staircase, looked etched in stone. So he told Carole he had a lot of math to study and he really just wanted to bring his books and a change of clothing.

Robbie and Tim called the day before to see how many chapters he'd read over the summer. They were each nearly three-quarters of the way through the book and David had told them he was too, but the reality was he wasn't anywhere close and his stomach tensed up every time he thought about it.

"Got everything?" asks Phil as he pulls into Carole's parking lot.

David had checked his overnight bag twice before he left, but now he runs his hand along the back of the bag's canvas, just to make sure he feels the sharp edges of the bulky textbook. "Yeah."

Phil takes a drag of his cigarette and exhales some smoke into the gray air as he looks around.

"Never figured her for a Valley type," he says.

"Why not?"

"Don't know. Just seems so…flat around here." He stubs out his cigarette in the convertible's already full ashtray, then yanks down the parking brake.

"You happy?"

David shrugs.

"It's okay. You should be. Your mother is back."

Carole answers the door with a big smile on her face, but it looks forced, as if she's trying to pump it full of hot air hoping it doesn't burst. She leads David inside and gestures around at all the new furniture. The boxes, card tables, and folding chairs have been replaced by couches, lamps, and plants, and the walls are lined with oil paintings of seashores and flower-covered fields. And there's a TV, and it has a big subscription cable box on top.

Then David notices the other people.

A man and a woman with sunken, red-rimmed eyes, sit at the dining room table. Their skin is pale and they wear clothing David has never seen before, yet they're staring at David as they might a large animal in a petting zoo that may or may not bite. The woman holds a baby in her arms and the man is sitting practically on top of her and is speaking too softly for David to hear anything he's saying.

"Honey, I want you to introduce you to some friends of mine. This is Svetlana, Mikhail, and baby Tatiana. They're refuseniks. From Russia. They just got to America today."

David has heard of refuseniks, people who somehow find a way to make the Russian government let them leave for America. He's seen features on the news about Russian men with engineering degrees who now work here as cab drivers and busboys, which made Phil observe that this country now probably had six Einsteins who were busy mopping vomit off the floors of a college dormitory.

The phone rings and Carole runs to answer it, looking relieved to be in another part of the room. Mikhail and Svetlana are trying to give a bottle to the baby, who is crying and pushing it away.

"You are David, yes?" asks Svetlana in slow, but steady English.

David nods.

"I have heard a great deal about you. You were practically all your mother spoke about."

David wants to say that until five minutes ago he didn't know they even existed, and that until thirty seconds ago he didn't know his mother knew enough about him to fill an entire conversation, but he's sure something would get lost in the translation.

"Tell me, David, what do you know about Russia?" Svetlana continues, shifting the baby from one arm to the other.

"That it's really cold most of the time. And people have to pay a lot of money for blue jeans and gum. And you call each other 'comrade' and your country 'Mother Russia.'"

Svetlana smiles.

"Yes, we were called comrades. And the country they do call Mother Russia. As though we were all the same, all family. But there is big difference between comrades and family, no?"

Svetlana says something to Mikhail, who reaches into their bag and digs around. He finds a pacifier and puts it in the baby's mouth.

"Your mother is good woman," says Svetlana. "Because of her, we no longer pretend to be comrades with sons of Mother Russia who would sell our baby for bowl of soup."

The baby quiets down and now the only sound in the room is coming from the phone area, where Carole is laughing at something the person on the other end just said.

"I'm gonna go study now," says David. He hoists his bag over his shoulder and walks down the hall toward the second bedroom. Behind him, he hears Carole hang up the phone.

"David…"

She stops talking as David reaches the doorway of the second bedroom and sees a kid sitting on the bed. He's about David's age and looks like a shrunken version of Mikhail, but his eyes resemble Svetlana's and, at present, are focused on a TV three feet away from the bed.

Carole catches up to where David is staring at this stranger, sitting in the room he can't quite bring himself to call his, watching the second television in the apartment Carole claimed didn't need even one.

"This is Vladimir, honey. He's your age."

"Actually, I am two years younger. You are twelve, yes?" asks Vladimir.

David turns to Carole, not sure if it was Vladimir's age she didn't know or David's, but she averts her eyes and nods at the TV.

"What's that you're watching, Vladimir?" she asks.

"Western. I am fascinated by them. Do you ever watch these movies?"

"David's father used to like them when he was younger," says Carole with a sideways glance at David.

"Does your father still like them?" asks Vladimir.

David looks at the TV and realizes that the movie features an actor who used to play cowboys but is now Governor—or, as Phil says, "now plays Governor"—and is stepping down in a few months.

"I think he outgrew them," says David.

"Such simple tales of good guys and bad guys, only you sympathize with cowboys and Indians, oppressor against oppressed. It is funny they are called Westerns because these stories seem more appropriate for Eastern bloc."

"Vladimir's a math whiz, too," says Carole proudly.

David has heard that all the Russians are geniuses in math and that the ones who aren't work for the KGB.

"Your mother has informed me that you have been studying all summer," says Vladimir. "What math will you be taking this year?"

"Algebra,"

"I see."

"Are you taking Algebra, too?"

"I have already completed Algebra Two. As for Algebra One, I studied it several years ago, but I cannot remember when exactly. My father taught it to me. Perhaps I could take look at your—"

Vladimir coughs, deeply and violently, making sounds David has never before heard come out of a human.

"Are you okay?" asks Carole. She takes a step forward, but Vladimir puts his hand up.

"I am fine," he gasps. He removes an inhaler from his shirt pocket and takes a few puffs.

"They weren't supposed to be here until next week," whispers Carole as Vladimir catches his breath.

"Where am I supposed to sleep?" David whispers back.

"Well, Svetlana, Mikhail, and the baby are going to sleep in my room…"

Carole trails off, and as much trouble as David might be having with advanced math, he has no problem putting two and two together.

"And I'll be sleeping in the living room."

"I'll be on the other couch. Right next to you."

"At least there's a TV now."

Carole sighs.

"Honey, what few rights these people had were taken away from them the minute they protested. Mikhail spent three years in Siberia. Please try to understand."

David wants to understand. He wants to understand that he didn't even bother to bring any of his stuff over, that everything in his mother's life right now is rented and that renters, like beggars and kids, can't be choosers, but nothing is helping. Something inside is screaming at everything his brain is saying, burning up his throat and stuffing up his nose with hot, wet, angry tears that he's trying his best to…

"Oh, honey? There's one more thing."

✦

DAVID SITS IN THE front seat of Carole's car, staring out the window, as Vladimir gasps away in the back seat. Carole is squatting over him, fumbling with his inhaler. Vladimir is clearly uncomfortable and Carole clearly doesn't know what she's doing, but all David can think about is that they're going to be late for class on the first day of his last year in this school.

And as if that isn't bad enough, he's going to have this weird kid tagging along.

Carole had taken Vladimir to David's school to be tested, and five minutes after Vladimir had finished the test, which had only taken him five minutes in the first place, the school had enrolled him and waived the tuition costs.

David had watched Carole celebrate in the living room with Vladimir's parents, remembering how Phil had taken him for testing years ago and that Carole had only found out about her son's chart-topping IQ from a letter David had sent her at the ashram. David also remembers how Phil had read the evaluation report and said something about David taking after his mother. Now, as David sits in the front seat, watching Carole hover over Vladimir, he finds himself praying that Phil was wrong.

By the time David and Vladimir get to class, Robbie and Tim are already sitting next to each other. The teacher is a pretty, blonde-haired woman named Ms. Watson who used to be Miss Johansen before she got married, the same year women started appearing on TV with picket signs. David and Vladimir stand in the doorway as Ms. Watson finishes writing some math problems on the board, then she turns around and gives them both a big smile.

"Hello, David. Welcome back."

David mumbles a quick "Thank you" as Ms. Watson turns to Vladimir.

"And you must be Vladimir."

"That is name they gave me. And that folks at Ellis Island were kind enough not to take from me. And what is your name?"

Ms. Watson cocks her head slightly. "My name is Ms. Watson."

"Wonderful. It is pleasure to meet you, Miss Watson."

A few of the students snicker, but Ms. Watson continues smiling. "'Ms.' It rhymes with 'fizz.'"

Vladimir looks confused. He strokes his chin as though there were a long, white beard on it. "But…I did not see wedding ring on your finger."

More snickers.

Ms. Watson puts her chalk down and turns to face the class. "Vladimir and his family have had a long, difficult journey to this country. I hope that every one of you will do your part to welcome him to our classroom and teach him about our culture."

Ms. Watson turns back to David and Vladimir. "Vladimir, I took the liberty of saving you a seat next to your new friend here."

She nods at a couple of seats across the aisle from Robbie and Tim. David sits down and stares straight ahead, ignoring their smirks as Ms. Watson writes another problem on the board.

"As you were told at the end of last year, we will be introducing an entirely new approach to math. Up until now, math was about numbers that always stayed the same, no matter in what kind of equation they were placed."

Vladimir raises his hand. "Excuse me…Mizz Watson?"

"Yes, Vladimir?"

"While I commend you for not ending your sentences with prepositions, as do many of your fellow countrymen, I cannot help but suggest one fairly simple correction to what you just said."

Vladimir pauses. Nobody in the class, not even Ms. Watson, moves a muscle.

"Go on," says Ms. Watson.

"Whenever equations involve numbers, and only numbers, they fall under the category of arithmetic. The word math refers to study of everything else. Lattices, matrices, and my personal favorite, imaginary numbers."

Ms. Watson isn't smiling anymore. She points at two equations on the blackboard. "Thank you, Vladimir. Why don't you come up here and solve this equation…"

Ms. Watson looks right at David who flicks his eyes away quickly, but not quickly enough. "And David? Why don't you come up and solve the one next to it?"

David feels the tips of his ears get hot. He stands up and walks to the blackboard, avoiding Robbie's and Tim's eyes all the way there. Vladimir is nearly finished with his problem, his chalk making a *clack-clack-clack* sound as it taps furiously away on the blackboard.

David picks up a piece of chalk and stares at the equation. He can tell at a glance that it's nowhere near as hard as the one Vladimir's working on. In fact, it's exactly what he's been spending all his free time studying these past few weeks. But the more he looks at it, the more the hot blood in his ears seems to leak into his brain, making it feel spongy and dizzy.

Vladimir puts down his chalk and turns to face Ms. Watson, who stares at the blackboard without blinking.

"That was a problem I studied in graduate school," she says quietly.

Ms. Watson turns to David, then it's Vladimir's turn, then finally the rest of the class looks over at David, who is holding his piece of chalk, trying to push down the lumps in his throat and stomach that are making him feel like he's going to throw up and cry at the same time. He turns and stares at the equation and the numbers immediately blur.

"What are you waiting for?" asks Vladimir.

"Vladimir," says Ms. Watson.

"But it is so easy! Constant is right in front of his face."

David closes his eyes, hoping his eyelids will act like an eraser and wipe the blurry, swirling numbers away, turning them into something clean and obvious and easy to use. When he opens his eyes, Vladimir is standing right next to him.

"Would you like me to show you?"

The nausea in David's stomach pours up into his throat and, hand over his mouth, he runs out of the classroom and down the hallway to the boys' bathroom.

✦

IT USED TO BE so easy, thinks David, as he hunches over a toilet in a stall, wiping the last of the vomit from around his mouth. Back when it was all about numbers, when he could amaze the adults by quickly figuring out the tip in restaurants, or helping Phil with his music royalty percentages without a calculator. Real life stuff, not this junk with letters that move around all over the place every time you try to pin them down and figure out what they were doing there.

"You okay in there?" calls Tim from the doorway.

David wipes his mouth again and coughs the last traces of vomit into the toilet.

"Fine."

"Ms. Watson wanted me to check on you. It's time for recess."

"I know."

David hears some scuffling and dragging from the doorway, followed by Robbie's voice. "So what's all this crap about imaginary numbers?"

David looks up and sees Robbie and Tim, each with an arm around one of Vladimir's elbows as they drag him into the bathroom.

"It is really quite fascinating," replies Vladimir. "You simply substitute—"

"I didn't ask you to explain it to me," says Robbie, cutting him off.

Vladimir blinks. "I do not understand," he says.

"Then let me explain it to you."

Robbie nods at Tim, who grabs Vladimir by the neck, pulls him over to the toilet, and pushes his face into it, about an inch away from the water.

"I don't know what kind of commie crap they've been teaching you over there, about numbers that don't exist, but here in the free world, we deal in real numbers. And me, Tim, and your boy here, are the three top math students in this class. As it is, my parents aren't too keen on me splitting the honors, but if they find out some Russian kid's been hogging the spotlight, that would be bad news for me."

Robbie tightens his grip around Vladimir's neck.

"Which would be worse news for you. Got it?"

Vladimir's face is turning red. He starts gasping for breath and as he writhes around, there's a *clunk* as his inhaler falls out of his shirt pocket and lands on the bathroom floor. Tim picks it up and holds it in front of Vladimir's face.

"What's this?"

"My inhaler. I have asthma."

"You have it right now?" asks Robbie.

"Not at present, but—"

Robbie splashes some toilet water in Vladimir's face, then grabs the inhaler and holds it up to Vladimir's mouth.

"Take a puff."

Vladimir, gasping, takes the inhaler, cocks it, and sucks in deeply.

"Again."

Vladimir stares at Tim, who shrugs and turns away as Robbie tightens his grip further.

"You heard me."

Slowly, Vladimir cocks the inhaler again and takes another puff.

"Once more."

David doesn't know much about inhalers except there are chemicals involved. And that there's probably a reason why doctors write usage instructions on the label. But he doesn't say a word as Vladimir raises the inhaler to his mouth for the third time.

Click.

The inhaler is empty.

Robbie releases his grip on Vladimir, who wheezes and tries to stand up, but Tim plants a foot in his chest and shoves him back down to the floor of the bathroom.

"Ever study history, commie boy?" asks Robbie.

Vladimir nods, still gasping.

"Good. 'Cause from now on, your new name around here is Vlad the Inhaler. Only difference is, next time you open your mouth in class, you're gonna be the one whose head winds up on a spike."

Robbie grabs the inhaler from Vladimir's palm, tosses it into the toilet, and walks out with Tim right behind him.

Vladimir sits on the floor, huffing and puffing, then turns to face David. And what David sees there isn't a look of fear, or humiliation, or even anger. Instead, Vladimir looks as though he is puzzled by David, even feels sorry for him. Something about this makes David even more nauseous than before, so he gets up and runs out of the bathroom as fast as he can, before he winds up hunched over another toilet.

✦

THE DOORBELL RINGS.

David knows that Phil is not expecting company because Phil isn't home; he's over at Ben's home studio. David puts down his math homework and walks over to answer the door.

"Who is it?"

"Me," says Carole's voice.

David opens the door to see Carole standing on the doorstep next to Vladimir, who is staring at a group of ants by the doorway. Carole's car is idling in the driveway, with Vladimir's parents in the back seat, passing the baby back and forth.

"Vladimir's parents have an emergency with Tatiana. I'm taking them to the hospital and I need to leave Vladimir here with you."

David and Vladimir haven't spoken since the first day of school, two weeks ago. The day after the bathroom incident, Svetlana worked out an agreement with the school that allowed Vladimir to work independently during the class's math period. Now Robbie and Tim's only competition is each other and David doesn't have to listen to any more comments about his mother's choice of houseguests. Which hasn't included David lately, because he has avoided Carole's calls. Phil keeps reminding David that Carole is still his mother, but David also heard Phil remind Carole on the phone that she would travel halfway around the world to help some commie refugees, but couldn't be bothered to get a television for her own son.

"Okay," is all David says.

Carole gives David a hug that is mostly forearm and hand, then closes the door.

Vladimir steps inside and looks around, his eyes settling on the row of gold records that line the hallway.

"These records, they are made of pure gold? Or are gold-plated?"

"Plated."

"Why not real?"

"It's mostly symbolic."

"How many copies must be sold to earn gold status?"

"Half a million."

"And for full million?"

"Then it goes platinum."

"But they place gold records next to platinum. How is one to know this is intended to be read sequentially and not additively? That it is half million then million, not half million plus million?"

"I don't know. You hungry?"

"Do you happen to have roast beef?"

"My dad's a vegetarian. We've got tofu and some green sprout things."

Vladimir makes a face. "Even in Russia, I would not eat that. Why would anyone in America deprive themselves so?"

"He orders me a lot of pizza."

"I noticed peanut butter in your mother's apartment. Is this dietary staple for you? One of your constants?" he adds with a wink.

"You want a peanut butter sandwich?"

Vladimir strokes his chin, then nods at the television. "Perhaps later. May I watch television?"

David hands Vladimir the remote control. He and Vladimir sit down on the couch and watch the news, which is doing a live story about a house in South Central L.A. that the police are burning down.

"I heard about this," says Vladimir. "On radio in car. Some revolutionaries who kidnapped heiress. Have you been following?"

"You want that peanut butter sandwich now?"

"Please, allow me, and to make for you as well. It is least I can do."

Vladimir heads over to the kitchen when the doorbell rings again. "Is your father expecting company?"

David shakes his head, silently praying, for the first time in a long time, that it's Carole.

Vladimir disappears into the kitchen as David walks over to the front door and stares through the peephole.

No one there.

David opens the front door and looks around. Nothing but the usual chirp of crickets and the occasional far-off hoot of an owl. Somewhere in the distance, he can smell something burning, but he can't tell if it's a backyard barbecue or something else.

He closes the door and walks back over to the couch but stops in mid-step.

Click.

It's the sound of the glass door to the living room sliding shut.

David walks slowly toward the darkened living room. He peers through the darkness and sees nothing.

And then he hears the match strike.

David's eyes follow the sound of the match, over to the face of the man sitting on the couch. David hasn't seen him since Phil hosted those parties with people who wanted to talk about revolution while sitting in a comfortable living room, high up in the hills, away from anything unsafe.

"What you say, little man?" says Brother Louie.

He takes a long drag of his cigarette, but unlike Phil who usually looks off to the side when he does this, Brother Louie looks straight at David and narrows his eyes into slits. David also notices that Brother Louie's leg is shaking.

"Where's your old man?"

"He's out."

"You sure about that? He ain't hiding in his studio?"

Brother Louie stands up, walks over to the studio door, and jiggles the locked handle.

"He's not in there."

"What do you say we check and make sure?"

Brother Louie reaches into his waistband and pulls out a gun. He points it at the lock on the door and fires. There's a loud *pop*, unlike any gunshot David has ever heard in the movies or on TV, and a flash, then the door opens slightly and Brother Louie pushes it open and looks inside.

"What do you know. Little man don't lie."

Brother Louie puts the gun back into his waistband, then walks over to the couch and sits down next to David. He reaches his hand into his pocket and takes out a little glass vial, then reaches his pinky inside, scoops out some white powder, and sniffs loudly.

David watches as he rears his head back, closes his eyes and smiles. "You want some?"

"No, thanks."

"Nice manners. Your old man taught you good. Gotta say though, he'd be wantin' some of this if he was here."

Brother Louie picks up the remote and aims it at the television set.

"Mind?"

Brother Louie doesn't wait for an answer as he changes the channel back to the burning house, which is now little more than some smoking embers on a flat, charred lot.

"Mother…" Brother Louie's eyes narrow and his nostrils flare. He stands up and throws the remote control at the television set, but it misses and crashes into a fireplace poker instead. "You see that? You see that?"

Suddenly, with a sinking feeling, David realizes that Brother Louie smells like smoke. Not cigarette smoke, either.

"Pigs," says Brother Louie. "Might makes right, huh? Well, wait'll we regroup."

Brother Louie takes his gun out and walks over to David.

"Now you listen to me. You gonna tell me where your old man is. 'Cause he got a plan for me. He and I talked about it. Gonna go to Cuba and find a whole new set of troops. Bring the revolution back to the people. Dig?"

David nods slowly.

Brother Louie places the gun an inch away from David's face. "No. Dig?"

"Excuse me, but I could not help overhearing your conversation."

Vladimir is standing in the kitchen doorway, holding a peanut butter sandwich. "Did you actually say you were going to look for new revolutionary troops in Cuba?" he asks calmly.

Brother Louie points the gun at Vladimir. "Who are you?"

"Forgive me. My name is Vladimir."

"You Russian?"

"I speak Russian. But now I am American."

Vladimir takes a bite of his sandwich and walks into the living room. "As far as Cuba is concerned, perhaps I can save you trip. Revolution is over."

"There, maybe."

"Everywhere. Some ideas won, but all people lost. Why do you think all community-minded societies also have most strictly enforced borders? Are you not intelligent enough to see that?"

David wants to close his eyes. He wants to brace for the gunshot that he senses is coming, the one that will tear into this weird Russian kid and put him out of David's misery. He wants to shake Vladimir for being too stupid to know a dangerous situation when he sees one, for deserving that episode in the bathroom. He wants to pick up the phone and call Carole and scream at her for bringing these people here in the first place, but there's no way to reach her, by phone or otherwise. But he doesn't do anything except stare at Vladimir, who is staring at Brother Louie with the same strange, sad look he had on his face when Tim and Robbie were going at him in the bathroom. David turns back to the television, to the house now surrounded by fire trucks and police sirens. Only something doesn't seem right. The sirens are louder than they should be on television.

Almost as though they're coming up the street outside.

Brother Louie's eyes flare. He jabs the gun excitedly at Vladimir.

"You call the cops on me, Russian boy?"

"I took liberty, as extended to me by this country's rights, of dialing new nine-one-one number. Quite handy, I must say. Real numbers that lead to real outcome even David here could calculate."

Vladimir smiles at David, who is in no mood to smile back.

Brother Louie's hand starts to shake. "Just like Russia, huh? The police come to take away the revolutionaries?"

"Not at all. In this country, good guys get to call police. And you are no revolutionary. Just bad guy who needs to go."

The sirens grow louder. Brother Louie tucks the gun back into his pants and runs over to the sliding glass door. He pauses for a moment and turns back to face David and Vladimir, the gun still quivering in his hand. Then he slides the door open and disappears outside into the canyon with its sweet, sagebrush smells and endless darkness.

✦

LATER, AFTER THE POLICE have taken their report and Phil and Carole have finished blaming each other for what happened at the house, David is standing by Carole's car, allowing her to give him a good long hug for the first time in what feels like years. He wants to push her away, but doesn't because he's too tired. Also because it feels nice right now, even though he would never share this with her.

"I don't ever want to lose you," she whispers.

David wonders if she will feel this way once she stops feeling scared, but he lets her hug him all the same.

"Okay," he says in return.

Carole climbs into the car where Svetlana and Mikhail sit in the back seat with the sleeping baby in their arms. Vladimir stands by the front door of the car with David, who is shivering in the cool night air and probably from what's left of his nerves as well.

"Thank you for hosting me this evening," says Vladimir, opening the car door.

"Vladimir?"

Vladimir pauses by the open door.

"How did you know he wasn't going to shoot us?"

Vladimir strokes the imaginary beard on his chin. "People may seem strange to others at times, but they always make sense to themselves. This is what I would have told you about constants. Had you asked me."

Vladimir climbs into the car as Carole starts the engine. Svetlana and Mikhail take the baby's hand and wave to David, and David, despite himself, waves back as the car pulls away. He watches until it disappears around the bend, then he realizes that there's a peanut butter sandwich waiting for him in the kitchen and suddenly his stomach feels much, much better.

DIASPORA

THE FLAG IS EVERYWHERE David looks these days: on the seats of bus stops, the fronts of postage stamps, and the backs of coins. And especially on TV. The United States is turning two-hundred-star-spangled-years-old next month and nowhere is it more in the mood to celebrate than on TV.

David should be studying for the Haftarah part of his Bar Mitzvah, which is scheduled for the day before the Bicentennial, but he's had enough of the tired, thirsty Israelites wandering around in the desert. Instead, he's preparing for the party part of his Bar Mitzvah by watching a dance show, doing his best to copy the dancers. He's half-hoping it will translate into success a month from now and half-hoping it will distract him from the noise Carole and Phil are making in the kitchen where, for the past few weeks, they've been planning the Bar Mitzvah. Or trying to plan; they don't seem to disagree about many things so much as they seem to disagree about everything. Phil wants a traditional service with a bearded rabbi; Carole wants the service led by a woman who spells the word "woman" with a "y" and plays guitar. Phil wants some of the music to be played by an Eastern European klezmer band from New York; Carole wants a deejay who plays pop music and physical games with the kids that involve a lot of screaming and the occasional, inevitable physical injury. Sometimes Phil and Carole keep the arguing to a seething whisper, but sometimes it gets so loud that David isn't sure who is more unhappy: the bickering Jews in the desert or the bickering Jew and Jewish convert in the kitchen.

David is about to turn off the TV and go back to his Haftarah when the lights on the dance floor go down and a song comes on with no one singing, but something that sounds like the voice of God telling the dancers to do something called "The Hustle." The dancers form a line, take a few steps forward and a few steps back, then spin to the right and to the left. They clap at the end of each successful set of steps, all in sync with the music, which, like the soft, dreamy-sounding voices cooing away in the background, manages to be both soothing and bouncy at the same time. Best of all, there doesn't seem to be anything hard about it; no tricky hand or arm gestures or complicated steps that would keep anyone, even someone as uncoordinated as David fears he might be, from being able to do the entire thing in front of other people on the most important day of his life.

The song ends. David turns off the TV, grabs his backpack, places his Haftarah inside, and heads down the hallway toward the front door. Out of respect to Carole, even though she no longer lives there, Phil has taken down the charcoal sketches of the naked women that used to line the hallway and replaced them with watercolors of sailboats and beaches. Sailboats and beaches do not offend people, especially women, and especially women who spell the word with a "y."

Phil is on the phone and Carole, arms folded and lips pursed, is standing at the kitchen counter. Phil is talking about a reunion concert Ben will be playing with his brothers in Washington,

D.C. on the day of the Bicentennial. The Sandmen's biggest hits from their early days have just been released on a compilation album, and the United States is in the mood to think about how much better things were back when Ben, his brothers, their music, and the country were squeaky and clean cut.

"You're gonna be onstage. Anyone who could possibly help you is gonna be backstage, too far away to help if things get hairy," says Phil.

"Hairy sounds about right. Last time I saw him he looked downright prehistoric," mutters Carole under her breath, but not so far under her breath that Phil can't make out what she's saying.

Phil glares at Carole and holds his hand over the receiver. "For Chrissake, Carole. He's having a major family crisis."

"Tell him he can swing by here if that one gets too tame for him."

David clears his throat. "I'm going out."

Phil and Carole look up.

"Where?" asks Phil.

"To the record store."

Phil tells Ben to stay put and hangs up the phone.

"What for?" asks Phil.

"I want to buy a record."

"I've got three thousand of them in my studio."

"This isn't something we have already. It just came out a few weeks ago."

"What's it called?" asks Carole, perking up.

"'The Hustle.'"

"Oh, sure," says Carole.

Phil turns and stares at Carole. "You've heard of it?"

"For the record, so to speak, I've heard of lots of things that you haven't."

Phil lights a cigarette. He's smoking a lot more since he and Carole started planning the Bar Mitzvah. Sometimes David hears him coughing in the middle of the night, even through the thick walls of the studio where he spends every waking minute, and even several non-waking minutes, working on Ben's almost-finished solo album, the one he's calling *The Golden State*, about California and childhood and everything between.

Phil has been begging Ben not to go to Washington, not to compromise his newfound independence, and not to dig his heels in the sand on this issue. But even though Ben and his brothers don't get along, and haven't in years, Ben seems to find the sand to his liking and his heels perfectly comfortable there.

"Any particular reason you want to buy this particular record at this particular point in time?" Phil asks David, flicking ash into the sink. Even though he always washes it down, even though this isn't where Carole lives anymore, David knows that this habit used to drive her crazy. Out of the corner of his eye, he sees Carole's arms fold right back over her chest.

"I kinda want to play it at my Bar Mitzvah."

Phil winces. He hates disco records even more than he hates that new record about California from that band made up of people who aren't even from here, as he likes to point out. Not a single one of them, but that still didn't stop them from putting out a record that seems to cover the same territory Ben's record is covering. And the other band's record is covering that territory all over the radio to boot, and when millions of people aren't listening to that, they're listening to disco music, according to Phil.

Carole finally unfolds her arms. "Whatever you want, honey," she says.

Phil stubs out his cigarette, then reaches into his pocket, pulls out a five-dollar bill and puts it on the kitchen counter. "What the hey. Long as we're having a female rabbi and an American Bandstand competition, why don't you go ahead and buy anything else you think the deejay would approve of, too?"

David feels like he should forget it and head back into his bedroom, but Carole and Phil's fighting makes him want to dig his own heels into his own patch of sand.

"I only want that one. And I have enough money from my allowance to pay for it, plus bus fare to and from the record store."

"You sure?" asks Carole.

"What, like you're gonna give him the money?" snorts Phil.

Carole glares at Phil, then grabs a stack of envelopes from the kitchen counter and hands them to David.

"Oh, honey? On your way over to the record store, would you pop these invitations in the mailbox?"

As David walks over to the door, he hears them arguing again. Carole is saying that Phil's comment about money was a low blow and Phil is saying something about Carole giving tradition the middle finger right up until it's the man's turn to pay for something.

David closes the front door and thumbs through the stack of envelopes as he walks down the block. The addresses are in fancy calligraphy he can barely read and most are going to people he doesn't know. One of the ones he does know is Harris, so he decides to deliver that one in person. David hasn't seen much of Harris lately, not since the night of the Rustler's Moon when Harris injured his leg and hung up his cleats for good. Sometimes David's and Harris's carpools pass each other on the way to school, but Harris usually just slouches in the back seat and stares straight ahead.

When Harris opens the door, David barely recognizes the hollow-eyed teenager standing less than a foot away from him.

"Been a while," says David.

Harris nods at the envelope in David's hand. "What's that?"

"An invitation. To my Bar Mitzvah."

David hands the envelope to Harris, who holds it the way a guy in a spacesuit would hold an alien space rock. David has the feeling Harris hasn't been invited to too much of anything lately.

"It's okay if you don't want to come."

Harris doesn't say anything, but he doesn't close the door either. David isn't sure if this means he wants to come, if he wants David to stay, or if he's getting ready to punch David for having the gall to drop by unannounced. Even back when David thought he knew Harris pretty well, he felt that people like Harris only let you know them pretty well at best, and that if you knew them any better than pretty well, you'd realize there wasn't much in them that was pretty or well.

"Cool hat," says David, nodding at the black cap on Harris's head. Harris always used to wear a Cat Diesel cap, but this one has a picture of something blood-splattered and some letters in a language David's never seen before.

"They're a British band. Not exactly the kind of stuff your old man does."

Harris pulls out a cigarette and lights it. He and David stand there, shifting their feet back and forth as if it's the ground beneath them that's unstable; something physical they could blame for the discomfort between them, and not just the simple fact that they've known each other for years, but it took them all of five minutes to run out of things to talk about.

"Who's there?"

Harris steps aside and David sees Keith standing behind him. Sort of standing, actually; he's holding on to two cane-like objects strapped to his hands to help him balance on two plastic objects where his legs used to be.

"Hey, man! Good to see you!" says Keith. He wobbles over to the front door and almost slips, but Harris grabs him and keeps him steady as he reaches out and grips David's hand.

"Prosthetics. My feet are finally planted firmly on the ground again," says Keith, proudly gesturing down to the plastic objects.

"Yeah, you're a whole new person now," mumbles Harris.

"Well, I'm a whole person now. Working on the new part, thanks to my new friends at the Center."

"Keith's a Scientologist," says Harris. Even under the pulled-down hat, David can see Harris's eyes roll a bit, and he is grateful for at least one familiar sight.

"So how come you two don't hang out anymore?" asks Keith. Harris shrugs.

"Probably 'cause you quit baseball," continues Keith. "Like my friends at the Center say—quitters never win."

"Remind me to tell you that next time you're up my ass to quit smoking," says Harris.

"I will. Because I did."

"Only after we stopped stealing your smokes for you."

"I feel for you, brother," says Keith, shaking his head sadly. "So lost in the wilderness."

Harris turns back to David. "What's the date?"

"July third," says David.

"Day before the Bicentennial," says Keith, beaming. For a guy who used to wear a black armband on the Fourth of July, he seems unusually excited about America's birthday this year.

Harris hands the invitation to David. "Save a tree. I'll be there."

On his way back down the hill, David passes the old baseball markings on the cul-de-sac. Even though it's been only two years, even though David can hear faint echoes and shouts and the occasional smashing of glass signifying yet another home run off Harris's bat, it somehow feels like it all happened to another group of kids on another block in another neighborhood, somewhere far away from this one.

✳

DAVID IS SITTING ON the bus, staring at his Haftarah. He can recite the Hebrew part pretty much from memory at this point, so he's reading on the English side of the page. David's Haftarah portion includes the part where the Israelites, fed up with their directionless wandering through the desert, make a gold calf out of their jewelry. David finds the story fascinating no matter how many times he reads it, but today his eyes keep straying from the page to the other passengers on the bus.

Four Mexican women dressed in housekeeper uniforms are sitting across from him, their eyes closed as they lean back in their seats. Two teenagers are making out a few rows behind David, underneath an advertisement with a picture of George Washington eating a taco. A long-haired man with a floppy hat sits at the back of the bus, playing a guitar and singing a song about Uncle Sam and the United States Blues. A homeless man who smells like week-old garbage bobs back and forth in rhythm to the song, even though David suspects he probably doesn't mean to.

The bus stops at a red light across the street from the pony rides where David used to go when he was little. Phil still has a picture he took of David posing on a pony in full cowboy gear, and on the back of the picture Phil had written the words "Half pint in a ten gallon hat." A two-story billboard above the riding ring has a painting of an indoor shopping mall that promises to replace the pony rides with everything from movie theaters to restaurants and clothing shops. Standing underneath the billboard are a pony and a man in boots and chaps, and even though it's been years, David recognizes the wide-shouldered cowboy who smelled like hay and helped him up onto the saddle. The cowboy is a dead ringer for the one on a different set of billboards, which advertised a brand of tough guy cigarettes and used to be all over the city. Then people decided that billboards for cigarettes were unhealthy and replaced them with billboards like this one.

The cowboy meets David's eyes, and for a moment, David wonders if the cowboy recognizes him. David remembers how scared he always felt, right up until the moment when the pony started walking, and how the cowboy trotted right alongside and reminded David that he hadn't lost a riding partner yet. David wants to smile at the memory, but it's like most happy memories from when you're younger; whenever you conjure them, they only make you feel kind of sad instead.

The bus groans and belches out some exhaust as David takes one last look at the cowboy in the riding ring, his pony swatting away some flies with its tail, both of them waiting for the kids who will never again show, who now only want to go someplace to eat, see movies, and dress in the kind of clothing that doesn't belong at pony rides.

David's stop is coming up on the right. He stands up to pull the cord but as he does, Harris's invitation falls out of his pocket. The letters that spell out Harris's name and address don't look right in loops of fancy calligraphy, and David wonders if Harris felt that way, too, if that was why he gave the invitation back to David.

He reaches into his backpack, and when he does he spots the corner of his Haftarah book peeking out. He thinks about the

Israelites walking around with sand in their eyes and throats, their jewelry fed to them without so much as a glass of water to wash it down, and before he knows it he's sitting back down in his seat, watching the record store pass by the window.

✦

WHEN DAVID STEPS OFF the bus, he doesn't recognize anything at first. There's a cluster of houses with pillars and marble, which don't seem to belong on a bluff that overlooks the ocean.

He reaches into his backpack and runs his fingers over the ring that he still carries around with him most of the time. He likes the feeling of it against his skin, but he's also trying to convince himself that giving a Bar Mitzvah invitation to a girl he met one night seven years ago, and hasn't seen since, isn't the craziest idea he's ever had.

The sky is darker now, and he's pretty sure Carole and Phil will be plenty angry when he gets home, provided they haven't used up all their anger on each other. He thinks about the looks on their faces on that night at the beach, then about the looks on their faces a couple of hours ago. Then about the fact that he's weeks away from the biggest rite of passage in his life and he's not sure how much actual passage there has been in his life, or in life in general, for that matter.

Then he spots Topanga's house and sucks in his breath. Unlike the other nearby structures, her house looks exactly the same as it did the night he met her. His insides swell with excitement as he runs over to the front door, practically tripping over his feet and a few broken pieces of sidewalk he doesn't see too well in the dark.

He takes a deep breath, raises the big metal knocker on the door, and lets it fall with a loud thud. The lights are off and

David can hear the sound from the knocker echoing inside. Then David hears another sound—the *clack-clack-clack* of heels against hard floor—and he suddenly realizes he has no idea what his thirteen-year-old version of himself should say to her thirteen-year-old version of herself. Back then, it seemed like they just spoke, and whatever they said felt natural and good. He thinks maybe he should tell her that, but he wonders if it will sound like a pickup line guys with sideburns and feathery hair use on TV.

"Who is there?"

It's a woman's voice, speaking with an accent he's never heard before. Then the door opens and both the woman and her accent are standing three feet away from him. The woman wears lots of makeup and is dressed in a sparkly dress with wide shoulders. Her eyes are almond colored and shaped, her hair is the darkest shade of black David has ever seen, and her skin is as deep a brown as her hair is black. Down the hallway, David hears what sounds like flying carpet music, and plates and glasses clinking, and several people laughing. The house smells like chicken and spices and baking bread, which makes David realize how hungry he is. He's about to ask what's cooking when two young children come sliding down the marble-floored hallway in their socks, screaming with delight as they're chased by a short, dark-haired man. He grabs them, then puts one under his arm and hoists the other on his shoulders.

"*Mitoonam ke komaketoon konam?*" says the man as he staggers over to the front door, the squealing kids squirming and climbing all over him.

The woman turns to David. "My husband is asking if he can help you."

"Sorry. My name is David."

The woman smiles. "It is very nice to meet you, David. Are you hungry?"

David's curiosity overcomes the gnawing pangs in his stomach as he stares at the children in their father's arms. He fumbles in his backpack for the invitation with Harris's name crossed out and the word Topanga written in its place and thrusts it into the woman's hands.

"For me?"

"No, for her. The girl...the girl who used to live here, I mean," stammers David. "I thought she still lived here."

The woman gives David a puzzled look. "We live here now. For six months."

Six months, thinks David as his stomach feels like it's going over the cliff behind the house. "Are you happy here?" is all he says.

"We are very happy. The people who were here before us were not so happy. But we are very happy here."

"Indeed. Much better here than in Iran," says the woman's husband. He places the children down on the marble floor, then yells and beats his chest. They scream and scatter and their father chases them back down the hall as the woman takes another look at the invitation.

"The writing on this envelope. It is so beautiful."

David nods, then gestures to the bluffs. "Your kids, do they like to play down there?"

"On the beach?"

"Yes, on the beach."

"Yes," she says, with a smile that makes mincemeat of cultural barriers. "Are you sure you will not have something to eat?"

David shakes his head and swallows, the lump in his throat preventing him from saying anything else. He hoists his backpack over his shoulder, turns and runs down the block, back over to the bus stop. He hears the woman's voice calling out to him, but he doesn't turn around. Instead, he jams one of his hands into the pocket with the ring in it, and as he runs his fingers around its cool circular shape, he thinks that it makes perfect sense that his Haftarah includes the Israelites getting their jewelry shoved down their throats before they've even had a chance to hear the voice of God.

✦

DAVID IS LEANING OVER the railing, his stomach turning and twisting itself into knots. His Bar Mitzvah party is going on inside, without him, and as far as he's concerned it can continue to do so right up until it's time to pack it up and go home.

The trouble began almost immediately. Somehow, both Carole and Phil assumed that the traditional rabbi knew about the guitar playing womyn rabbi, but he took one look at her and promptly announced that no self-respecting rabbi would lead a service that had an agenda.

The womyn rabbi, insulted, stormed off, and a traditional service went on with the loudly sobbing womyn (apparently she'd flown all the way in from Seattle to be part of something groundbreaking) in the lobby, despite Carole leaving the service several times to try to calm her down. One of Carole's respites coincided with David's Haftarah, which David flubbed at times because his eyes kept scanning the rear of the temple to see if Carole had returned.

His speech went smoothly enough, but he wasn't able to concentrate fully because his friends gathered in front of the stage, holding handfuls of sourball candy to throw at him, a tradition he'd learned of all of a few minutes before the speech began. Most of the candy missed him, but Harris, despite his mangled leg, still possessed the arm of a world-class athlete and managed to nail David on the right temple with a grape sucker. So David stood in the lobby after the service, greeting the guests, some of whom looked like science fiction creatures on account of his temporary double vision.

Just as everything seemed to settle down, Phil's mother marched over to Phil and announced they'd run out of herring at the buffet. Then she complained about all the green fungus stuff (alfalfa sprouts, one of Phil's favorites) people were putting in their mouths without first testing for bacteria. That, however, was a picnic compared with the real food, where Carole and Phil had compromised by hiring a long-haired caterer who came from an Orthodox family, but specialized in organic fare. It turned out that all his food came from farms that were under siege from striking migrant workers, so the food had arrived in drips and drabs. When the salad finally did make it to the buffet table, Robbie and Tim decided to see if lettuce could be set on fire by candle flame. That caught on so well that within minutes even Vlad the Inhaler was making salad flambé, but Phil and Carole didn't notice because they were too busy arguing about which music should go on first. While they argued, the klezmer band, hired for a twenty-minute session only—Phil's concession in exchange for getting his way on the tofu appetizers—informed Phil that their time was up, which made Phil's mother start to cry and Phil even angrier, which made Carole frantically tell the deejay to get something, anything, playing, to drown out the sound of that woman's voice.

And yet all of it would have ultimately been fine by David—the jittery Haftarah, the crying womyn, the shrieking grandma, the double vision and candy-pelting, lettuce-burning teenagers—if it hadn't been for one small detail that David counted on at least one of his parents to handle.

"The Hustle."

The record store had closed by the time David left the beach that night, so he'd asked Phil and Carole to buy it for him. Carole had said, "She'd take care of it," which meant that Phil had insisted he'd take care of it, but then Ben had changed his mind a dozen times the week before the Bicentennial concert and was arrested in the Washington airport for charging up the baggage chute in his underwear. David had been so busy writing his speech and trying to keep Carole and Phil from killing each other, he'd forgotten to remind them about the record—until fifteen minutes ago when David asked the deejay to play "The Hustle" and the deejay gave him a blank look. David glanced over at Phil, who was talking to some record company executives he'd invited, then over at Carole, who finally calmed down the womyn rabbi and was drinking wine with her over by the bar. Phil was laughing and Carole was laughing, and some of the grownups were dancing, but they looked nothing like the people on the dance show, and there was lettuce on fire at the table where he was supposed to be sitting with his friends and nobody was going to be doing "The Hustle"—the one grown-up decision he'd wanted to make on his first day as an adult.

He turned and ran out.

That was ten minutes ago, and no one had come to look for him. Not Carole, not Phil, not Phil's mother who'd flown all the way out from the East Coast, along with the long-gone klezmer band. Not the no-longer-crying-now-drinking womyn, not his friends; not even the deejay who was supposed to do some announcements with a microphone and a synthesizer and whose job it was to make sure everyone was busy paying attention to David.

And certainly not Topanga.

A tear fights its way through David's clamped-shut eyelids, another rite of passage he'd thought he'd left behind, along with the baseball games and pony rides and bluffs overlooking beaches where families ended and children played circle games in the sand.

A few premature fireworks are going off in the sky, celebrating two hundred years of independence, of leaving the British behind. David finds himself wondering if any of the Pilgrims, sick from choppy seas and dysentery, ever complained about how much better off they were back in England, or ever looked back at the disappearing mainland and wondered if it was maybe worth a little religious persecution in exchange for some firm ground under their feet.

"How's the party?" asks a vaguely familiar voice.

David looks up to see Ben hovering over him, dressed in a sweat suit and sandals. "Aren't you supposed to be in Washington?"

"Huh." Ben sits down next to David and pulls out a bottle of some green liquid, takes a long sip, then holds the bottle out to David. "Wheatgrass?"

"No, thanks."

Ben takes another sip and makes a face. "Don't blame you. This stuff tastes pretty bad."

"So why do you drink it?"

"People tell me to."

"Do you always do what people tell you to?"

Ben stares at the bottle, then tosses it toward the trash can nearby, where it banks off the side and lands on the lawn. "I'm not in Washington. People told me to go there."

"Why'd you come back early?"

"I missed the beach."

"Don't they have beaches over there?"

"Couldn't find any of them. So I came here. But I can't find them here anymore, either. Like my old man used to say, high tide always catches up with you sooner or later."

Ben leans back until he's flat on the ground and stares up at the sky. Years ago, Carole and Phil used to lie in the backyard and do the same thing. Carole only saw smog where Phil claimed he saw stars, but David remembers how nice it was to see them seeing the different things they saw together.

"So what are you looking for?" asks Ben.

"Nothing really."

"Then how come you're out here?"

David tells Ben about "The Hustle," and if Ben thinks dance music is the same existential threat Phil thinks it is, David can't tell from his expression.

Ben sits up and leans forward, then remains like that for a moment before he starts humming. It's a few seconds before David realizes he's humming "The Hustle," note for note.

"That sound about right?"

"Actually, yes."

"Anyone got a keyboard in there?"

"I think the deejay has a synthesizer."

Ben stands up and disappears inside. David hears a few murmurs, then some cheers, then applause. Then, a few seconds later, "The Hustle" starts to play, just as it would sound on the record, only instead of the voice of God, it's the voice of Ben commanding everyone to dance. Then David hears the deejay get in on it, too, relishing this chance to perform alongside someone who is supposed to be in the nation's capital, celebrating America's birthday as part of America's band, but is somehow here instead to mark the Israelites' passage out of Egypt en route to the promised land.

David stands up and is about to go inside when he stops. Right by the front entrance is a small patch of sand, which is funny because the temple is nowhere near the ocean. And if his spirit had been bruised, nearly broken tonight, right now it's soaring, proving itself to be every bit as resilient as the spirit of '76. Because right in the center of the sand, drawn crudely, maybe hurriedly, but most definitely clearly, is a circle.

All of a sudden, he's somewhere else—in time, in space, older perhaps, looking back on this, trying to find a patch of sand on a beach he can wrap his arms around to keep it from slowly washing away. And even though he knows he can't, any more than an hourglass can keep its own grains of sand from disappearing through the tiny bottleneck in the middle, even though he used to think it was strange how people always got sad when they looked back on happy moments, now he thinks he understands.

He thinks, he hopes, that it might work the other way around too, that Ben and his father were wrong about not being able to outrun high tide. And for the first time in his life, a grown-up smile, a perfect half-circle, creeps across David's face as he heads back inside to join the Jews and gentiles, rabbis and womyn, divorced parents and other Americans, line-dancing together in an unbroken, united state.

DISCO INFERNO

THE HEAT IS EVERYWHERE.

It's in the physical space all around David, both inside and outside the house, thanks to the winds that have blown through the canyon every night this week. They curl the leaves on the trees into a pointy brown crisp and make the inside of David's nose tickle.

The weather forecasters talk about how the winds come from south of here and, combined with the heat, turn the whole area into a tinderbox this time of year. Usually it's worse outside the city, but because conditions are so bad this year, the city dwellers—especially the canyon residents—need to be on high alert. They use that word, conditions, as if they're diagnosing a medical ailment that hasn't happened yet but is pretty much guaranteed.

The heat is also there in other, invisible hotspots that pop up in the way David feels and in the language people are using around him. A few sprouts of hair here and there and a change in the curvature inside his neck, which makes oxygen flow a little tight and leads to some uncomfortable moments, and suddenly everyone's behaving differently, as though David's physical discomfort is now suddenly theirs, too. The situation has only grown worse in the last forty-eight hours, starting with the hot seat David found himself on yesterday when he told Phil that Father Adams, his new Religious Studies teacher, had made a comment that David had found, if not exactly anti-Semitic, not exactly pro-Semitic either.

"We were discussing Ramadan," said Father Adams when Phil and David went to his office to see him.

"So how did Yom Kippur come up?" asked Phil.

Father Adams stared calmly at David through a pair of round eyeglasses that seemed barely big enough for his eyes to see through. "It didn't."

David's seat suddenly felt hotter. He waited for Father Adams to explain his comment about Arabs who fasted during the days of Ramadan and only permitted themselves the slightest amount of bread and water at sundown. Which, as he'd put it, was far different from the Jews who couldn't wait to stuff their faces the minute Yom (he'd pronounced it 'yahm,' which he might or might not have meant to rhyme with yawn) Kippur was over.

"So you didn't say anything about Yom Kippur?" asked Phil.

"Not as I recall," said Father Adams. If his eyes blinked, his orb-constricting glasses weren't giving anything away.

"Because David was pretty sure you did," said Phil, but David saw him turn his attention away from Father Adams and over to David.

"Were you?" asked Father Adams.

The inside of David's nose tickled again and he shifted in his seat a little. "I thought I was."

David's voice cracked when he said this, and Father Adams stared at David until David looked away. Then he turned back to Phil.

"Our class is a study of comparative religions. Sometimes we compare the tenets of one religion with those of another. I can assure you, however, that there is no judgment or preference shown toward or against any one faith."

"Little hard to believe with that big cross you got hanging right over the front driveway to this place."

Father Adams smiled again. "Our boys are among the finest in the city, and the good Lord loves them all equally. As do we. But they are still boys. It is our job to try to preserve all that is good inside them and keep their souls free from guilt."

Phil didn't say much on the way home, other than something about how he'd heard that Muslims during Ramadan not only stuffed their faces come sundown, but even went up in hot air balloons so they could see the sunset earlier. But David was barely listening because Phil was barely talking. He was mumbling in that way he had when his mind was on something else, which in this case proved to be a phone call. A phone call going on right now, in the kitchen, where Phil used to receive phone calls from executives begging him for a chance to listen to the hot new tracks coming out of his studio. But now, in the much hotter, more tense present, Phil seems to be the one doing all the talking.

"The thing is, Jeff, you can't dance to this kind of music. You actually have to sit still and think about it."

Phil puts down the phone and takes a drag of his cigarette, then he picks up the phone and exhales loudly into the receiver while the other man is still saying something about disco record sales.

"Okay, let's try this another way. You've seen the Sandmen's numbers lately? Yeah? Well, fuck that. That's a baby Kahuna— this is a goddamn tsunami."

David wonders if he should be worried about Phil—his increased cursing, smoking, and overall irritability, not to mention the fact that Phil seems more worried about Phil these days too—but right now David is worried about the event that's consuming his immediate future. Namely, that night's mixer at a nearby Catholic girls' school, which Robbie, who claims to have eyes and ears in all the right places, insists is home to some of the hottest female specimens on the planet.

"Fucking square," Phil mutters after hanging up the phone.

"I've heard Ben's album," says David. "It isn't anything like the Sandmen's music."

Phil turns and notices David standing by the open front door. "Where are you going?"

"The dance. Remember? I told you?"

David can tell from Phil's expression that he doesn't. "What time will you be home?"

"Probably around ten. Will you be here?"

"Maybe. There's a neighborhood meeting tonight."

This is another reason for Phil's increased smoking and swearing: his role organizing the people protesting the widening of the main road, which will supposedly allow traffic to flow more freely through the canyon. The protestors claim that this will lead to a procession of trucks to and from the Valley, and even though their protests are blanketed in concerns about increased noise and pollution, it's clear Phil and the protestors also feel the Valley and its strip mall sprawl should not be too easily accessible to any place they call home. So far, they have managed to postpone construction by a year, but they're meeting again tonight to discuss their not-too-distant future prospects.

"Hell, that's progress," one resident said during a meeting one night at the house.

"Hell *is* progress, more often than not," Phil responded, lighting another cigarette from the stub of the last one. That night, he pledged to quit smoking for good if he and the others won their battle. Tonight, however, he stubs his cigarette out in the ashtray and exits into the studio where Ben is putting the finishing touches on one last mixing session.

A horn honks outside. David takes one last look at the embers of Phil's cigarette, glowing hot and hellish from the winds outside, before heading out and closing the door tightly behind him.

✦

"THE HELL DOES THAT even mean anyway?"

Tim is sitting in the backseat of Robbie's mother's station wagon. They're driving past the sheikh's estate, the one with the classic Greek statues on which the sheikh painted pubic hair. David has been by this place on more occasions than he can count, but he still feels the need to turn his head away every time he passes by.

"Means I got recon," says Robbie, who's sitting in the front. Robbie's mother always makes Robbie watch the road while she drives so he can learn.

"More like he's got an older sister whose yearbooks he snoops through," whispers Tim to David.

Without taking his eyes off the road, Robbie leans back and slams a perfect charley horse right down onto Tim's thigh.

"Well, it's true," says Tim, rubbing his leg.

"What is true?" asks Robbie's mother, but she doesn't pursue it because another car screeches around from behind them. Its driver barely avoids a head-on collision as he passes, yet he still manages to give Robbie's mother the finger as he zooms away.

"Terrible," says Robbie's mother.

"They really should make the road wider," says Robbie.

When they arrive at the girls' school, Robbie, Tim, and David get out and mix in with their classmates, many of whom look like they're in some kind of disco-Halloween mode with open shirts, wide collars, platform shoes, and chains. One kid is even dressed in a white suit with a silk black shirt underneath, like the star of that movie Phil blames for pumping the airwaves full of disco in the first place.

David suddenly feels self-conscious and wonders if he should have spent more time in the mirror, making sure his hair wasn't too poofy and his plaid shirt wasn't too goofy. But Robbie, who hates that they go to a boys' school and uses the word "fag" the way some people use punctuation, would probably call David out on it if he sensed that David spent too much time getting himself ready.

David is relieved when he feels the rush of cool air as the three of them step inside the lobby, filled with a thick, white mist that makes his nose tickle. He wonders if this is what it feels like to smoke, to suck a poison into your body that fools your brain by making your body feel good. He makes a mental note to ask Phil, provided Phil hasn't quit by the time David gets home.

"Smokin' cee-oh-two," says Tim, nodding at the mist. "Better known as dry ice."

"Save it for chem class, fag," says Robbie.

A few girls are standing around the lobby, watching the boys as they make their way inside. Robbie takes out a comb from his back pocket and runs it slowly through his hair as Tim pauses by a large stained-glass window of the poet Dante, positioned over the entrance to the school's Great Room.

But David isn't paying attention to Robbie or Tim, or the girls in the lobby, or the stained-glass window for that matter, because his eyes are on one girl in particular who's standing on the staircase that winds down into the lobby. She's leaning over the balustrade, elbows propped against the carved wood, eyeing the cavalcade of uncoolness as it passes below her unwavering gaze. Even through the darkness, David can see that she has black hair and blue eyes, colors that look like pain on a bruised arm, but pure pleasure on this girl's heavenly head.

"'Abandon hope all ye who enter here,'" says Tim, staring at the stained glass window.

"Speak for yourself, fag," says Robbie.

Robbie puts the comb back in his pocket and jerks his head toward the door. David takes one last look at the girl on the staircase, then follows his friends inside, where he is immediately bombarded by an auditory blast that's equal parts disco beat and screaming girl. He can't see anything because a flashing strobe light hits him square in the corneas no matter where he looks. It's not until he's jostled around a few dozen times in half as many seconds that he realizes he's standing in the middle of the dance floor. He lowers his head and fumbles his way over to a group of boys plastered against one of the room's walls, looking like they're holding on for dear life.

David wiggles in between two smaller kids and lets his eyes adjust to the strobe-lit darkness. He lost Tim and Robbie somewhere in the entry surge, and the dry ice is making his eyes and sinuses tickle, but at least no one's bumping into him anymore. He looks over at the dance floor, where several couples are dancing, looking more relaxed and comfortable in their skin than David suspects he'll ever look or be in his.

That expression, "comfortable in your skin," is something he finds himself thinking about a lot, as though whatever it is right beneath the surface has to wriggle around and see if it's compatible with all the gestures you show the outside world. Sometimes he wonders what it would be like if he could keep his outside self—which, even in his most self-conscious moments, doesn't strike him as all that bad—and trade it in for a completely different, far more comfortable, inside self.

David looks across the dance floor where the less intrepid girls have lined up against their part of the wall. Unlike the boys, they aren't squirming or moving around. But looking comfortable is not the same thing as looking approachable, and neither David nor anyone else on the boys' wall seems ready or willing to trek across the pulsating no-man's land to find out firsthand. The deejay must sense this because the minute the song ends, his voice explodes through the crackling loudspeakers.

"Okay, people, this one's ladies' choice. Which means it's time for you fine ladies to make your move on, then make some moves with, those handsome fellas across the floor!"

A loud scream erupts from the other side of the room, followed by what sounds like a stampede of high heels, then David is pulled onto the dance floor by a force unseen but, from the angle involved, one much taller than he is. The inside of his torso is doing flip-flops, so he closes his eyes and tries to let the outside of his torso flip-flop right along—up and down, back and forth, the way he's watched people do it on the dance shows he watches when Phil isn't looking.

"Where did you learn how to dance?"

He opens his eyes and finally takes a good look at the girl he's dancing with. She has brown frizzy hair and big round glasses, and when she smiles the strobe lights bounce red and blue reflections off her shiny braces.

"I watch a lot of TV!" he yells.

"What?" yells the girl.

"Dance shows! On TV!" yells David, as loud as he can.

The girl bobs her head back and forth. She's at least a head taller than he is, and between that and all the clunky-looking metal in her mouth, it's as though her center of gravity is so top-heavy that she's doing everything she can just to keep from toppling over.

"I like your hair."

"My what?"

"Your hair," he yells, pointing to her head.

"Thanks. I just got it permed. Does it smell?"

"I can't tell. It's too hot in here."

The girl gives David a strange look and they don't exchange another word. She continues to bob her head back and forth, giving David a few shy smiles as she does. Suddenly David's arms and legs don't feel so clunky, and soon a few other girls are watching, which only makes David feel warmer inside.

"Wow! Look at you!" yells the girl.

David looks up and realizes he's so low to the ground that he's practically on the floor. He wipes some sweat from his forehead and slides back upright as the song comes to an end.

"I'm Gloria," says the girl, extending her hand.

A slow song comes on. Before David can say a word, Gloria turns and runs, giggling, back to her friends. Back at the wall, Robbie and Tim are waiting for David, holding three cups of punch.

"Smooth moves," says Tim, handing a cup to David.

"Yeah, you looked like one of those dudes in that fag disco group, only without the construction worker costume," says Robbie, running his comb through his hair.

"I didn't exactly see you out there," says David. He doesn't bother to point out that Robbie just called him a fag while talking about how another guy would look without his costume on.

"I was scoping the punch bowl. I'm not here to shake my booty like you and the rest of the butt pirates. I'm just here for the babes."

"How's that working out so far?"

"Taking the slow and steady approach. Hare and the tortoise."

"Yeah, the minute the girls see he's got the face of a tortoise, they run away as fast as a hare," says Tim.

"Least my head's in the game, not in my pants with my hand stroking it," says Robbie, dead-arming Tim with an elbow to Tim's bicep. Tim rubs his arm, and is about to say or do something back to Robbie when he spots something on the dance floor.

"Whoa. Disco Pat."

David and Robbie turn to see the floor filled with kids, but none are concentrating on anything their partners are doing because they're busy staring at a couple in the middle of the floor. The girl is tall and wearing a beaded dress that is up to the considerable challenge of clinging to her advanced curves, but even David isn't really looking at her. He, along with everyone else, including his male classmates, is watching her partner who, at a full head shorter than the girl, is putting on a show for which even Robbie can't quite muster any insults.

Pat Pattinson, aka Disco Pat, is a seventh grader—short, squat, and unmemorable-looking, who barely cracks Cs on his report card. Then he cut school one day, talked his way onto a dance show, and wound up in the front row, two feet in front of the camera, dancing with a woman twice his age, who was caught on camera looking flushed by the time the show was over.

Suddenly, the warmth that was flowing through David's insides drains down his legs, through his feet, and into the grooves between the wood planks of the dance floor as he watches this kid, who is clearly more comfortable in his skin than David suspects he will ever be.

The song ends and the deejay's voice booms and crackles through the loudspeakers.

"Okay, ladies and gents, it's dance contest time! Grab a partner, show us your stuff, and our judges will tap you on the shoulder if you're disqualified. And if you're the last couple standing? Each one of you gets a twenty-five dollar gift certificate for Power Records!"

A big cheer goes up from the crowd as the kids scramble to pair up. Disco Pat launches into a new array of physical impossibilities while David stands in place, mulling over his options. Suddenly there's a hand on his shoulder and he turns around, fully expecting to explain to the judge that he can't be out of a dance contest he hasn't even entered yet.

But he isn't greeted by the sight of a judge.

This isn't supposed to be happening, is his first thought when he sees the black-haired, blue-eyed girl from the lobby. She isn't supposed to be standing right behind him, to be smiling, to be asking him to dance—none of it is supposed to be happening, but somehow she is, it is, and they are.

The blood in his veins isn't supposed to be this hot if it's expected to calm his nervous brain, his entire nervous system for that matter. She isn't supposed to be watching him in his goofy shirt with his poofy hair—poofing up higher now from all the heat and hairspray floating around in the room—and still be smiling, not because she's laughing at him but because she's not only enjoying herself, but maybe even a bit awed.

For that matter, he isn't supposed to be enjoying himself so much either; he can hear, not over the music so much as under it, Phil's voice, whispering how mindless this is, how stupid it all looks. But the one thing that more than anything isn't supposed to be happening somehow is—one by one, the other couples are tapped on the shoulder and make their way off the dance floor until there are just four couples remaining.

And David is one half of one of them.

The song ends and the room erupts in cheers, with the boys enthusiastically shouting their support for Disco Pat while the girls scream for the female contestants. As the judges take down the names of the remaining dancers, David's partner turns to him.

"Any of that noise for you?"

Her voice is low and raspy and sounds like it should be selling cigarettes on TV.

David shakes his head. "You?" he asks.

She nods at a few girls, who are screaming and jumping up and down and waving their hands.

"Nice," says David, sneaking a quick look at the boys' side of the room, where Robbie's back is to the dance floor while he devises new methods of physical abuse to heap on Tim.

"You're nicer," she says with a smile. For a second it looks like she's actually winking at him too, but David can't be sure because it's dark and her face seems like the kind of place that could easily hide a gesture like that. Everything about her—her smile, her forwardness, the fact that she hasn't even told him her name yet—suggests a coolness that makes her seem much older than he is. He's almost relieved that the music is about to go on again and he won't be forced to make conversation, which would not only make him sound his age, but most likely include a few inopportune voice cracks to boot.

The judge approaches them with his notepad.

"Lynne. With an E at the end," she says, after David gives the judge his name. The judge nods, writes it down, and walks back over to the deejay's table.

David and Lynne turn to face each other.

"Hi, David," she says softly.

"Hi, Lynne," he says back.

The music starts up again. The other couples immediately start to move.

David closes his eyes.

Hands, he thinks.

Without opening his eyes, his hands reach out for hers. She takes them, and now he opens his eyes, and her eyes are on his and they're off—spinning, twirling, finishing off a sequence with a pretzel move he watched an especially limber couple perform one night, late, when he shouldn't have been up watching TV but is now glad he was. The temperature is getting hotter and the kids around the dance floor are stomping their feet to go along with the cheering. Out of the corner of his eye, David sees the judge tap one of the remaining couples on the shoulder.

Feet, thinks David.

He lets go of her hands and backs up a few steps, then moves left, right, back and forth, making sure the balls of his feet are turned in just enough to allow his knees to flex outward from side to side. Again he closes his eyes, and again when he opens them, Lynne is right there next to him, matching him step for step.

Tap. Another couple out.

David finally musters up the courage to sneak a look at Disco Pat, who, along with his partner, is the only competition remaining. There's no more smiling, no more winking and playing to the crowd, nothing but bloodshed in his opponent's eyes, which are doing everything in their power to silently remind David that nobody out-discos Disco Pat.

Sure enough, Disco Pat has saved his best for last. He and his date break into a routine that involves him shimmying like a wall of jelly in a circle around her while she runs her hands up and down her body and shakes her hips. David sees a few of the proctoring Sisters cast sideways glances at each other, but no one steps forward; even they seem too transfixed to do anything.

Disco Pat finishes by jumping up into the air and landing in the splits on the floor, then sliding slowly back up and into a pose with his partner that's timed perfectly with a break in the song. The crowd bursts out into applause as Disco Pat, not even sweating, sneers at David and Lynne.

Lynne turns to David. "Dip me," she says.

David places his hand around her waist and they're off again. There's a bongo solo in the song that's smooth and swively-sounding, and David spins Lynne over to the center of the room and slides one of his hands around the lower part of her back. Then, praying that what he's about to do looks more like a Friday night dance show than a Saturday morning kiddie cartoon, he swings her around in a one-eighty and drops her down so that her back arches over the floor. Her black hair gently grazes the tiles as she sways back and forth. Then the music starts back up, washing over their bodies with an increasingly up-tempo beat that's half-salsa, half-disco, and all business.

Slowly, he pulls her off the floor and into his arms. He isn't even thinking anymore; any thought process he'd once had has become something elemental, a thing that just is, that exists well beyond any realm of shoulds or shouldn'ts.

And then she kisses him.

David knows his arms are still technically present somewhere, probably still wrapped around Lynne's back, one probably up somewhere around her shoulder blades, the other probably a little lower in that small part of the back Cosmo (another benefit of Robbie having an older sister) claims women love so much. But he isn't registering anything other than how hot and sticky her lips feel on his, and the simultaneously soothing and tickling sensation of her tongue as it does its own dance in his mouth.

The next sensation David feels is the tap of a finger on his shoulder.

"You're out," says the judge.

David opens his eyes to the sight of teenage pandemonium. Screaming, cheering, foot-stomping kids on both sides of the dance floor. Robbie and Tim staring at David, their jaws dropped almost as low as Lynne's hair was a minute ago. Disco Pat and his date with their hands raised in victory, shooting a second-place-in-the-hearts-of-the-crowd scowl at David and Lynne. And David sensing, as the sensation he'd lost fifteen minutes ago surges off the floor, through his toes, and back up his legs, that as comfortable as the two dance champions might feel in their skins, it isn't anything close to what he's feeling inside his right now.

＊

DAVID THINKS HE MIGHT never come up for air.

He and Lynne are in an abandoned storage closet somewhere upstairs from the auditorium. There's no circulation and it's so hot he can barely breathe, but as he makes sure every square millimeter of Lynne's lips are covered with his, he finds himself wondering if breathing might be just a bit overrated.

Tim and Robbie were somewhere behind David and Lynne when they'd fled the dance, one step ahead of the Sisters, but David lost track of them when Lynne suggested a special tour of the campus. Which consisted of her showing David where her locker was, then telling him about a special place she snuck off to when she wanted to be alone, followed by a beeline up to this place.

On their way up, David thought he heard Robbie say something to Tim about taking care of some business in the foyer, but right now Robbie and Tim are a dead-arming, charley-horsing memory who can go fag each other all they want as far as David is concerned. Whatever this elemental thing—this thing that just is—is, it has taken over. He knows he's supposed to be finding out all kinds of tidbits and factoids about her, aside from the bubblegum lipstick she seems to favor, but the two of them have clearly skipped that part and have gone straight to this part instead. He has half a mind to slow things down right now, but he also has half a mind right now, period, and every inch of it is screaming full speed ahead.

The wind has died down outside, but it doesn't seem to have gone for good; rather, like all evil spirits, it feels more like it's gone into hiding for the time being, resting up for a bigger battle yet to come.

Lynne slides her lips up David's right cheek and over his temple. Her breath is coming in short, hot spurts into his ear, which he suspects he should find annoying but doesn't because he doesn't find anything about her even remotely annoying. Even the sound of her name—Lynne, one short, perfect syllable—makes him sigh inside. He's scared to say it aloud, scared he'll gargle it around in his malformed, language-mangling throat, and it'll come out sounding like the word limb, which might make her think he's trying to put the idea of sex into her head.

"That was pretty amazing out there," she whispers, her tongue now licking a spot under his earlobe, again tickling, again in a good way.

David nods and moves his head so their lips are locking again. He hopes they'll stay locked, the same way the lock on that TV commercial does, the one that stays shut no matter how hard they try to blast it off with a rifle.

She takes her hand and runs it up and down the back of his head and unlocks her lips from his. "Know what I thought when I saw you that first time? In the lobby?"

Kiss.

Unlock.

"No, what?"

"That you had the face of an angel."

Kiss.

Unlock.

"It was the sweetest thing. There were all those other jerks, strutting around, trying to act all hot, and then there you were. An angel."

"Mmm. Thanks."

"Mmm. That wasn't all."

Her hand slides down the front of his chest and inside his shirt. David feels a stirring inside his jeans and shifts his position so he's not rubbing against her so directly.

Lynne, he thinks to himself. Lynne, Lynne, Lynne,

"You had the face of an angel, but you looked like you had the devil inside you, too."

Her hand slips out of his shirt and slides down his chest. "And when I danced with you, I knew I was right."

Farther down now...

Kiss.

Unlock.

"And I thought maybe that devil inside you needed a little help..."

David fees his belt unbuckle, feels her hand slip inside, feels the sensation of cold against warm. His breath immediately goes from exhale to inhale and his hand shoots instinctively halfway down his side, but no farther.

LynneLynneLynneLynneLynne...

He wants her to stop and he doesn't want her to stop. He wants her to move faster, harder, and the harder and faster she moves, the harder and faster he finds himself breathing, and the harder and faster he finds himself breathing, the harder it is to breathe. Then something inside of him, something that feels really, really good and a twinge of bad at the same time is coming up...

"...a little help getting it out and away from all that pent-up heat," she whispers.

...and gone.

He's exhausted and overheated and at the same time feels a little cold inside, as if the dry ice from the dance has replaced the air in his windpipe. And even though her head is on his chest, even though every part of her body is touching his, it somehow feels as though she's completely detached from him. Then she sighs, and the bubblegum smell of her lipstick wafts into his nose, practically suffocating him, and before he knows it, he's fixing his belt and out of the stuffy, airless room, headed back to the loud, pulsating music and the sweet, cool taste of oxygen filling his lungs.

✶

DAVID IS TRYING HIS best to ignore Tim and Robbie who are squeezed into the backseat next to him, each of them too busy pointing out how badly the other one struck out to mention David's disappearance from the dance.

He's trying not to think about Lynne, but the more he doesn't think about her the more he thinks about her. The one thing he's not thinking about, in the small favors department, is the noise coming out of the mouths of his two friends; they sound like the adults in that cartoon he loves so much, the one where the kid never gets to kick the football or make contact with the little red-haired girl. David is doing such a good job of not thinking about everything around him that he doesn't realize something's wrong until the car turns onto David's block.

The fire trucks are blocking their way, and the fire captain doesn't seem like he's in the mood to deal with Robbie's mother until David explains that his house is up the hill. The fire captain finally lets the car through, but the road is filled with cars and news vans and they get only halfway up.

"Road too narrow. We turn around, go call your daddy," says Robbie's mother.

Before she can put the car in reverse, David jumps out and runs up the hill, his chest heaving as he dodges through the crowds of people. The air is filled with smoke, and most of the people have their shirts or jackets over their faces. David's breath is coming in short, hard gasps, which become shorter and harder as he reaches the cul-de-sac and sees the burnt trees, the torched carcass of Phil's car, and the smoking remains of his house.

He looks around at his neighbors, gathered on the street. He feels lightheaded and his knees feel wobbly, and he sits down on the curb and puts his head down between his legs, trying to bury what he's feeling so deep inside that he never again has to come up for air .

"Coulda got three more trucks up here on a wider road," says a voice nearby.

David looks up to see two firemen leaning against their truck, about ten feet away.

"In time, too," says the other, shaking his head. "Damn shame."

The first fireman points over to the driveway, where Ben is standing, wrapped in a blanket and shivering, even though it's nearly eighty degrees out.

"Ain't that the guy from the Sandmen?"

"Sure looks like him. The hell's he been up to all these years?"

"From the look of things? Hiding up here in this freak zone," says the first one.

David stands up, wobbly, and walks over to Ben, who is now talking to a policeman with a notepad.

"So you were mixing a record in the studio?" asks the policeman.

Ben nods.

"And where was the cigarette?"

Ben doesn't budge. He is staring at the spot where the studio used to be—now a heap of rubble and melted wax. There's some movement from behind the couch where David used to play, back before Phil used to sleep in the studio more often than he slept in his own bedroom. As David looks closer, he realizes that the movement is coming from Phil himself, who is on his hands and knees, frantically crawling around on what is left of the studio floor.

The policeman walks over to Phil and taps him on the shoulder. "Sir," he says.

Phil doesn't turn around.

The policeman taps him on the shoulder again. "Sir, whatever you're looking for, it's gone."

David's insides fill up with nausea and dizziness, and before everything goes black, he realizes that this must be what it feels like to fill your body with something toxic. Only it's all pain, no pleasure at all, and there's no way to get it all out of you no matter how hard you try.

✦

LATER THAT NIGHT, DAVID wakes to the sound of disco music. He looks over at the alarm clock on the table in the hotel bedroom.

Three-thirty in the morning.

He blinks his eyes and tries to swallow, but his throat is dry and he wants some water. He stands up and lets his head and eyes adjust to the hotel room, then he tiptoes over to the bedroom door and opens it a crack.

Phil is sitting in the living room of the suite, watching a dance show on the television's fuzzy screen. The wind is howling outside, making the windows rattle, but Phil's eyes are expressionless as they focus on the TV, looking through it rather than at it.

David wants to explain to him what had seemed so clear just a few hours ago—that sometimes people just want to dance, to feel happy without having to think about it, but the remnants of the smoke and the lump in his throat are blocking the air flow and he can't get the words out.

✦

THAT MONDAY, FATHER ADAMS calls a school assembly before P.E. class. David sits next to Robbie and Tim and listens to Father Adams praise the boys for being so well behaved during the dance and for conducting themselves like fine young men.

"With one exception," says Father Adams.

He pauses. The lights go off and a slide projector displays a picture of the stained-glass window from the girls' school.

"This is a beautiful stained-glass window, featuring an image of the Italian poet and writer, Dante," continues Father Adams. "It is located in the foyer of the school that was kind enough to host you last Saturday night."

The lights go down for a moment, then another slide is displayed, this time featuring the stained glass window with a Magic Marker image of a penis in Dante's outstretched hand.

"This is the same stained glass window at the end of the night," he continues.

David hears the sound of stifled chuckling throughout the assembly. He turns to Robbie and Tim, and remembers them discussing some business they were going to take care of in the foyer.

"There were sightings of certain boys who were seen in the foyer at times that would coincide with when this was done. Please understand that we will get to the bottom of this, and that the perpetrators would be well served by coming forth and owning up to their actions."

The assembly dismissed, Robbie and Tim stand up and sling their backpacks over their shoulders.

"Coming?" they ask David.

"In a minute."

David waits for Robbie and Tim and the rest of the boys to make their way out of the assembly hall before walking over to Father Adams.

"Father?" he asks.

Father Adams looks down at him through his inscrutable glasses, but says nothing.

"I just wanted to apologize for what happened. I had a really bad week. I…I guess I didn't know what I was doing."

Father Adams takes a handkerchief out of his pocket, then takes off his glasses and wipes them.

"Next time you'll think before you act."

"Yes, Father."

Father Adams holds his glasses up, inspects them, then puts them back on his face. "I heard what happened to your home."

David waits for him to continue, but instead Father Adams just looks at the clock.

"Please make sure to see Mrs. Hitchens in the lobby for your disciplinary assignment when physical education class is over."

"Yes, Father."

"Do you feel better now?"

There's no more tickling in David's nose, no more oxygen trying to force its way through his constricted windpipe. But the emptiness he feels inside feels lighter than before, and his voice hasn't cracked once during this entire conversation, so he nods, and before he knows it he's back outside, back under the hot sun and the swirling winds that suddenly don't feel so hidden or dangerous anymore.

COWBOYS AND INDIAN TRIBES

S IX MONTHS AGO A model had her face slashed up.
It was all over the news because her live-in boyfriend, the guy who woke up every morning and gazed at the glorious, man-made view splayed out beside him, was the one who took a razor to it.

The model had plastic surgery, appeared on talk shows and at nightclub openings, and even starred in a movie about vice cops on a mission to take down a pimp. She eventually married, but appeared on one more talk show years later, after she'd had twin babies. The host asked her what toll the experience had taken on her, and she said that even years later, she still had nightmares that her kids would wake up one day, open their eyes, and see only the scarred face of a monster who used to be their mother.

David is standing in Rich's study, staring at a wall-sized aerial photograph of a mountain. There are long, curved strips of thick white masking tape with scribbled names like Chippewa Place, Hiawatha Terrace, and Comanche Court that slice their way into the base of a pristine mountain. The location is currently home to an old Western movie set, but Rich, David's new stepfather, will soon be replacing it with a housing development. The strips of tape on the photograph will be streets filled with shopping plazas, an elementary school, and hundreds of model homes. They will run right through the rock formations that look like God-scaled versions of the structures David used to make out of the dripping, hardening sand at the beach. David is amazed that developers can plop a ready-made town right down onto a place as untouched as this, that a community full of people and institutions can be created practically overnight and hit the once-unspoiled ground running.

Carole and Rich married nine months ago, after meeting five months before that on a cross-country flight. Rich is nine years older than Carole and has never been married, but a local monthly magazine once profiled him as one of the Valley's most eligible bachelors. He still has a framed copy of the article on his office wall.

David has been living with Rich and Carole for a little over a year, since it became clear that Phil's situation wasn't going to work out for the two of them. Right after the fire, he and Phil alternated between hotels and the spare rooms in Phil's friends' homes. David had loved the hotels; the combination of room service and TV made him understand why some of Phil's rock star clients never bothered to buy houses, but Phil's budget had grown tight after years of diminishing royalties. And most of Phil's friends were divorced or never married to begin with, which made David feel about as welcome in their houses as the women with smeared makeup who were always leaving in the mornings.

"Whaddaya think?"

David turns around to see Rich standing in the doorway of the study, smiling. Rich smiles a lot, but his smiles are nothing like the ones that used to fascinate David when he was younger because they seem to begin and end on Rich's face instead of disappearing somewhere mysterious inside his head. But David doesn't see all that much of Rich or his smiling face, because Rich doesn't spend very much time at home; he's usually at one of his local developments or at one in another town. And when he's not dealing with his developments, he's out raising money, which he also calls development, for political candidates at private homes and businesses.

Rich's candidates are the same ones Phil and his friends used to meet about, only Phil's meetings were always against those candidates and always seemed to involve more anger than money. Judging from the frequency of Rich's smiles, it seems the money side is beating the anger side.

"Why are all the streets named after Indians?"

"What's that?" Rich asks David to repeat himself a lot. At first David thought Rich was hard of hearing, but then he realized that whenever Rich talked about business on the phone he always seemed to be able to hear just fine.

"The streets. They're all named after Indians."

"That's because the development is right below the mountains where the local Indian tribes used to live," says Rich, waddling over to where David is standing. He's not chubby, but he walks like one of those toys David used to play with when he was younger, the ones that wobbled but always stayed on their feet no matter how hard you pushed them.

"Here you got Chumash Lane. That's our main artery," says Rich, pointing to a street on the map that branches off from the existing road. "And that one's Geronimo Court. Everyone should know who he was," Rich adds, running his finger over a street off Chumash Lane that dead-ends right up against the mountain.

"Geronimo was an Apache, not a Chumash," says David, who reads the U.S. History textbook in the library during free periods when he doesn't feel like listening to Tim and Robbie argue about geometry or girls, or the geometry of girls.

Rich stares at the poster a little closer, as though he's seeing it for the first time. "Oh. Well, it's a pretty small street."

"It's connecting with Chumash, which is a pretty big street. Not to mention the name of a pretty big tribe, which probably wouldn't have done any connecting with any of the Apaches, let alone their fiercest warrior. For all the Mexicans and Americans these guys killed, most of them were every bit as happy to go around deep-sixing their fellow Indians, too."

"Huh," says Rich.

"You'd think they would have made it their business to get along. That they would have made a truce so they could fight the bigger enemies. But in all the reading I did, it never seemed they were able to figure any of that out."

Rich waddles over to his desk, pulls out a magic marker, then returns to the map and writes something on one of the strips.

"I just figured you might want to know a little about Indian tribes," continues David. "Seeing as how you're having one of them over for Thanksgiving."

"Not a whole tribe, just a family," says Rich. "And they're just like us."

"How?"

"Dad works in public relations. Mother's on her second marriage. Boy's around your age, maybe a year or two older. Like I said, just like us."

"Only they live on a reservation."

"Exactly." Rich snaps the cap back on the marker. "Hey, is there any way I could get you to run over to the market?"

"Sure."

"Thanks. Mom needs a few supplies before dinner tomorrow night."

As Rich hands David some money and starts rattling off a list of supplies, David thinks about how he has never heard Rich call Carole anything other than "mom," even though David has never called her anything but "Carole" in front of Rich.

Thanksgiving guests at Phil's place always involved the "riffraff" as Phil proudly called the people who had no place else to go, and who used to drink and argue so spiritedly that Phil would sometimes physically step in between them. These days, David wonders if Phil feels strongly enough to argue about anything, or if he even knows it's Thanksgiving in the first place.

"Anything else?" asks David when Rich finishes his list.

"Only whatever else you can think of. As the natives would have said, '*mi casa es su casa.*'"

David flirts with the idea of telling Rich that the Mexican natives might have said that, but the Indian natives would have given you whatever version they spoke. Only they weren't too big on the idea of home, because they spent most of their time being chased around by the Mexican natives and the white settlers. By the time David can muster up the required energy, he's already halfway over to the winding staircase below the pointed rafters, a feature Rich's salespeople refer to as a "cathedral ceiling." It makes the house look bigger, but since Rich's house and every other house in this development are well over five thousand square feet, David doesn't see why anyone would need more space. Rich says that very little of what he sells has anything to do with need; he's reminded David more times than David can count that people in the frontier days went to the store to buy necessities. Then department stores invented display windows to replace need with want, and from that point on, life on the frontier became a seller's market.

David trots down the circular staircase, wishing his sneakers made more noise. The wedge-shaped steps seem like they were practically designed for disruptive echoes, but between the cathedral ceiling and wall-to-wall carpeting that seems to run floor to ceiling as well, it's a pretty quiet experience. The entire house, for that matter, is a pretty quiet experience; it seems to suck up sound the way the newly installed central vacuuming system (no more bags or cords!) sucks up bits of fiber from the carpet. Phil's house was always filled with musical sounds and cacophonic voices, but Rich's house is so quiet that on the few occasions when they do eat together, David can actually hear Rich and Carole chewing their food. So quiet that, as he reaches the bottom of the staircase, David startles Carole, who is polishing some china by a tall brown cabinet and who always seems to be surprised any time she turns around and sees David standing anywhere near her.

"Goodness! I didn't see you."

"Want me to leave?"

"Not unless you've got somewhere you need to be," says Carole, recovering quickly and shooting a fleeting smile at David. Her smile comes easier these days and there is a new glow to it, but it's more fluorescent than luminescent, an externalized, industrial light, the purpose of which seems rooted more in self-deflection than illumination.

"Rich asked me to go to the market," says David. "Do you need anything?"

"I'm sure whatever he told you will be okay. Unless there's anything else you can think of."

"That's what Rich said. He also said '*mi casa es su casa*.'"

"He means it too. You know that, right?" says Carole without looking up.

"I guess," says David, quietly thinking about how his first week here, he told Carole that he was having a hard time sleeping because his room's ceiling looked like the surface of the moon. Carole told him he'd get used to it, and yet he still woke up groggy for school most mornings because he'd been up late the night before.

"He also had a bunch of streets up on a posterboard," says David, "with all kinds of incorrect details about Indian tribes."

Carole holds up the plate. The china belonged to Rich's mother and Rich likes for it to be spotless and on display in the cabinet by the foyer, even though they rarely have company. As Carole examines the plate, David can make out her faint reflection in its dull sheen.

"I'm sure Rich knows everything he needs to know about Indian tribes," she says.

"Including the one tomorrow night?"

"They're not a tribe, they're just a family."

"Just like us," says David.

"That's right," says Carole, "just like us."

She puts the plate back in the cabinet, positioning its face at the perfect angle to reflect the light shining down from the cathedral ceiling, and fastens the antique clasp.

✦

ABOUT FIVE YEARS AGO, a tornado in the Valley ripped the roof off a big discount store, the one where Carole used to take David years ago to buy household supplies. She would saunter down the aisles in her beaded shirt and oval-shaped sunglasses, oblivious to the stares from the other shoppers in pantsuits and polyester, her delight evident as she picked up anything that caught her eye.

Then the tornado, a freak collision of two weather fronts that had never hit the Valley before, flung the store's roof onto a family in a station wagon. The irony, that a family-friendly discount store, in the Valley of all places, had killed a family was not lost on the media and the store had eventually closed. Now there's a bank where the store used to be because that's what always seems to happen whenever a business closes down. It also seems like the kind of place where Rich would be more comfortable than Carole.

David passes the bank as he rides down the Valley's main boulevard, the insides of his legs chafing from the unseasonal heat as he does. The heat in the canyon is different, like a piece of classical music that swells and dips with a mind and moods of its own. But the Valley heat is thudding and oppressive and sticks to you like wet clothing after you've been thrown in a pool. Even at this time of year when the winds have died down in the canyon, there's a hazy residue in the Valley that feels like the filmy aura from the soap at a cheap motel.

The market is between a pizza place and a tropical fish shop in one of the Valley's many "nondestrip malls," as Phil calls them. All the stores face a parking lot filled with kids riding around on skateboards. As David pulls in, one of the skateboarders glides up a ramp made out of a discarded door, tucks his hand under the board and flips the skateboard around as he goes airborne, then lands neatly on the ground. Two other skateboarders follow, making David feel as though his Schwinn ten-speed, a "welcome to the neighborhood" gift from Rich, has a flowered basket on it.

"Dude…"

David turns around to see two skateboarders standing behind him. Both have ropy, streaked blond hair and wear beige shorts with drawstrings hanging from the waist.

"Haven't seen you around," says the taller one.

"I'm kinda new to the neighborhood."

"No shit," says the shorter one. He kicks his skateboard up and snatches it out of mid-air without taking his eyes off David. "What brings you to these parts?"

"I just need to get a few things from the market."

The taller one steps forward. "How much money you got?" he asks.

David slides his hand into his pocket. Even though Rich would never miss the money, would probably express only his concern for David's well-being were David to be beaten and robbed, David still finds his hand closing around the five twenty-dollar bills Rich gave him.

"You gonna answer him?" asks the shorter one, taking a step forward. They're not exactly surrounding David, but they don't look too concerned about him making a run for it, either.

David unclenches his fist and slowly pulls out the money.

The taller one leans in. "You're not buying shit from that market, bike boy." he says.

David swallows.

"Cause there's a better one a few blocks away," he continues with a smile. "Everything's straight from the farm, too, no DDT."

He removes one of the bills from David's hand and puts it in the pocket of his tee shirt. "I'm Greg," he says, then he nods at the shorter one. "That's my cousin Craig."

"Dude," says Craig, who elongates the word's syllable so it sounds as if there is more than one "u." Both Greg and Craig are roughly David's age, but the creases in their necks and T-shaped torsos make them look more advanced, like they've had prolonged physical exposure to the elements and have matured accordingly.

"We're full-on Vals," says Greg. "Third generation. Anything sold, told, played, or laid on this side of the hill—we're all over it like stink on a burrito."

"What's your *nombre, hombre?*" asks Craig.

"David."

"Cool if we call you Dave from now on?" asks Greg. David doesn't like the nickname Dave for most people, and he especially doesn't think it fits with what he sees in the mirror every morning. But he's either too scared to buck them, or too eager to be accepted by them, or a little of both.

"Sure."

"Bitchin," says Greg. "Say we blow this taco stand and go spark a doob?"

David is still working through the absence of an actual taco stand before the second part of the question hits him.

"Don't worry, we'll have you back in time for dinner with mommy," says Greg.

Craig smiles and pulls a thin white cigarette out of his pocket, and finally there's some language here that David might not speak, but definitely understands.

✦

LATER THAT NIGHT, LYING on his bed and staring at a ceiling that still looks like the surface of the moon, all David can think about are the marijuana health films he'd seen in school. In the end, it all boiled down to a shrug and a feeling that peer pressure was the epitome of the banality of evil. Or, as Phil used to say about the squares in the record business, "the evil of banality," which, like a lot of things, is first starting to make sense to David long after it came out of Phil's mouth.

He'd coughed a lot and hadn't had any idea how much to inhale, but after a few puffs he'd felt a little lighter and everything he said made Greg and Craig laugh. He thought about a screenwriter friend of Phil's who'd once left a script at the house, and remembered that a lot of the scenes ended with the words "dissolve to" before the script went right to the next scene. Now, as David thinks back on the rest of his day, he finds his memory dissolving from one scene to another, much in the same way the screenwriter's scenes did on the page, and with the same kind of in-the-dark delight as a weekday afternoon at the movies.

As in…

Dissolve to…

David on his ten-speed, Greg and Craig next to him on their skateboards, holding on to the back of David's bike as he pulls them through a neighborhood filled with ranch houses and riding rings. Greg and Craig volleying the word "dude" around, the word itself as pliable as a Hawaiian "*aloha*" or an Israeli "*shalom*," host to a wide variety of meanings that changed, depending on context and setting. A few people on horseback riding by, smiling and waving at the bike and skateboard procession as though it's an everyday sight. David recognizing the names of the streets and identifying several of the topographical landmarks from Rich's wall map, two-story houses giving way to one-story strip malls giving way to zero-story patches of dirt and grass with history no man-made replacements could match. Everything around them remaining flat and surrounded by mountains, another difference from the canyon where the architecture was odd and diverse and, if you were going off-road, the trees and overgrowth made you think in vertical, not horizontal, terms. Unlike this place, where all the houses look similar, if not identical, and it feels as though you can ride flat out for hours while staying put the entire time.

Dissolve to…

David and Greg and Craig pulling up to an empty reservoir bed lined with concrete, inside of which is a group of Mexicans on bikes that look too small for them.

"*Frijoles*, twelve o'clock," says Greg.

One of the Mexicans at the bottom of the reservoir looks up at Greg, Craig, and David. Then he starts riding in a circle around the concrete bed—slowly at first, then pumping his pedals harder, riding faster and closer to the top until he pops out and lands with a rubbery skid right in front of David. His head is shaved and he sports tattoos up and down his arms.

"Hey, *vato*. What you lookin' to do?"

His breath smells of alcohol and smoke and he's shorter and looks a little older than David, but it's hard to tell. Unlike Greg and Craig, whose physical appearances look more developed than David's, this guy has a hardened look in his eyes that seems years beyond anything his body has experienced chronologically.

"Keep moving, Fonzie. Nothing to see over there," says Greg.

A few more bikes pop out of the reservoir and land near David. He remembers those nature shows he used to watch about pack animals and how their leader always sat higher than the others. David's bike is about a foot taller than the others, but he's never felt more hunted or exposed in his entire life.

"Fonzie. Hear that? *Gabacho* thinks I'm some joker on TV, wears a leather jacket and makes all the girlies laugh," says the guy on the bike, nodding over at Greg.

"Sounds about right. Only you can't afford no leather jacket," says Craig.

The guy on the bike curls his lip and turns to David. "Name's Alfonso. I was named for *mi abuelito*. Everything you and these two clowns ridin' on out here? Used to be his land."

"So how come everyone you know cleans toilets for a living?" asks Craig.

"Don't forget the fancy ones who mow lawns," adds Greg.

Alfonso reaches into his pocket. David flinches when he sees a glint of silver in the sunlight, but relaxes when he spots the curved side of a flask.

"My people don't expect shit," says Alfonso, unscrewing the cap and taking a sip. "Mexicans know once the *gringos* come, we ain't in charge no more. We're like the dirt in the land—you can pack us tight, kick us around, but a hundred years from now we still gonna be right here."

Alfonso hands the flask to one of the other riders and turns to Greg and Craig.

"But you? Ain't you seen that big freeway they're building? Those houses going up? You think those shiny new neighborhoods want a pack of stray dogs roaming around, don't know their time's up? Wake up, *homes*, your own *skin* don't even want you."

The guy next to Alfonso says something that sounds like "orally, *homes.*"

"So I'm gonna ask you one more time," says Alfonso, his face about an inch away from Greg's. "What you lookin' to do?"

Craig cracks his knuckles and casts a sideways glance at Greg. David wonders if this is what a fight looks like, if this is what groups of people do when they feel that someone has insulted one of them and, if so, the entirety of them. But Greg just reaches inside his tee shirt pocket and removes David's twenty-dollar bill.

"Eighth. Humboldt red-hair. No shake."

The top of Alfonso's lip curls up again. "Sure you can handle it? Shit ain't *typico* white boy."

"You got it or not?" snaps Craig, his foot twiddling the tail of his skateboard.

Alfonso whistles through his front teeth. One of the other Mexicans takes a small baggie filled with green shrubs out of his pocket and tosses it to Alfonso. Alfonso flips the baggie to Greg, who hands David's twenty to Alfonso.

"This better not be that backyard garbage you sold those greasers at the garage over on Nordhoff."

"Nah, this is the goods, *homes*," says Alfonso. "Swear on my moms."

He pulls up his shirt to reveal his bicep, where there's actually a tattoo that reads MOM. Then he nods at Craig. "And next time, keep that runt chihuahua on a leash."

All the Mexicans laugh, except one who makes a clucking noise with his tongue as he spots something by the other end of the reservoir.

"Check it out, *homes*. Lucy's out again."

David follows Alfonso's gaze over to where a young girl is walking by the edge of the concrete basin, holding her arms out as if she's on a tightrope. She's maybe ten or eleven, but David isn't sure, because she has Down syndrome, and because his brain still feels like it's floating underwater in a pickle jar.

"Hey, Lucy, where you off to?" shouts Alfonso.

Lucy stops and looks at everyone as though she's first registering their presence. Then she waves and continues her tightrope dance around the reservoir.

"Better get her home so your aunt don't go off on you, eh?" says one of the Mexicans.

Alfonso rides his bike over to Lucy. "You wearin' your dog tags, *mamacita*?"

Lucy reaches inside her tee shirt and pulls out the bottom of a necklace, where David can make out two military-looking bronze tags dangling at the end of a chain.

"Good girl," says Alfonso softly, scooping her up and plopping her down on his handlebars. The other bikers follow Alfonso around the reservoir, over to the chain gate. They're almost out when Craig turns to David.

"Hey, Dave, you know that show with Lucy Ricardo?" he says loudly. "Well, this chick's Lucy Retardo. Only this chick's a lot funnier than the one on TV."

Alfonso stops riding and turns his bike around so that he and Lucy are facing Craig.

"You just crossed a line, *homes*," he says.

"Maybe you wanna shove me back over to where you think my side should be, Fonzie?"

Alfonso narrows his eyes at Craig, but Lucy starts squirming on the handlebars.

"Tomorrow night. Ten o'clock," says Alfonso, turning his bike back toward the gate.

"Good," says Craig. "And make sure you bring your girlie's dog tags 'cause this chihuahua's gonna wrap 'em around your kidneys so hard you're gonna be peeing on three legs."

"*A donde?*" says Greg.

"Old town. Over by the new freeway," sneers Alfonso.

David's ears prick up. He's pretty sure Rich's development is by the new freeway, which makes him pretty sure Rich's development is going up where the gauntlet is being thrown down tomorrow night.

Dissolve to…

Craig, standing on a rock formation, staring out at a sheer wall of red stone, while Greg and David lie on the ground, passing a joint back and forth, staring at the taillights of a row of planes through the velvet gray haze blanketing the sky.

"So the first guy's pounding away at the door," says Greg, "and he keeps saying, 'It's Dave, I got the stuff, open up,' right? And the second guy keeps saying, 'Dave's not here, man.'"

"Are you really gonna fight those guys?" asks David.

"Yeah, yeah…but wait, I'm not finished. So the second guy… no wait, the first guy…yeah, the first guy keeps trying to explain to the second guy that he's actually Dave, and the second guy—"

"He doesn't get it," mutters Craig, not turning around.

"Right," says Greg. "No matter what the first guy says, the second guy just doesn't get it."

"Wasn't what I meant," says Craig. He walks over to Greg, snatches the joint out of his hand, and takes a puff.

"What don't I get?" asks David.

Craig slowly opens his mouth into a crooked smile that looks like a Jack O' Lantern with tendrils of smoke pouring out.

"That we're gonna rumble. Ain't that what you city boys heard we crackers do out here?"

"You wanna see it up close?" asks Greg.

"Maybe," says David.

"Why?" sneers Craig. "You thinking of joining in?"

"Maybe."

Greg snaps his head up. Then he chuckles, then Craig chortles, then the two of them start laughing so hard they're actually holding on to each other.

"Dude, that is without a doubt the funniest thing I've heard all day," says Greg.

"All week," says Craig.

"All fuckin' year," says Greg.

"I'm serious," says David, the tips of his ears burning. "I want to get it."

"Get what?" asks Greg.

"Whatever you said it was I didn't get."

Craig pulls out a small piece of paper, then flicks in some of the baggie's contents and starts to roll a joint.

"You practically shit your pants back there in the parking lot. Didn't look like you wanted any part of a fight, back then."

"What do you care if he wants to come?" asks Greg. "Fonzie's beaner mom's gonna pop out five more cousins by tomorrow night. We'll need all the numbers we can get."

Craig finishes rolling the joint and stuffs it into David's shirt pocket.

"All right then. Tomorrow. You know where to find us."

They hop onto their skateboards and ride off. David is excited and stoned and more scared than he's ever been, but come tomorrow night he'll be damned if anyone in this neck of the woods—or dirt, or wherever it is the Mexicans live—is going to be saying, "Dave's not here, man."

✦

A GROUP OF PEOPLE decided to create their own utopia last year, down in one of those countries in South America no one ever hears about unless something bad happens. Their leader was a man in sunglasses who spoke to them through loudspeakers while they cultivated the land, which was surrounded by a big fence. The people worked together and ate their meals together, all lined up in rows, men and women sitting right next to their children.

But some of the people weren't quite feeling the utopian vibe, so a few days ago, a Congressman flew down to their compound to look around. When the Congressman tried to leave and take some of the people back with him, some men with guns showed up at the airport and killed everyone except the Congressman's young aide. Back at the compound, the leader assembled his followers and told them their utopia had been destroyed and that it was time for them to go. One by one, the people came up to the front and drank poisoned fruit punch, and when the last one was dead, the leader put a gun to his head and pulled the trigger.

But a few people had escaped into the jungle, and one of the survivors is on the news, saying that most of the people died against their will. But the television keeps showing the peoples' bodies lined up in neat, obedient rows, all together, the way they were in the fields and at the dinner tables as they sang their songs and watched their children dance. All David can think about is how the people had settled on the land and built their fences, but hadn't been killed by any of the natives from whom they'd taken such pains to protect themselves.

David hears the doorbell ring from his TV viewing post in the sunken living room, a feature that used to be called a conversation pit until, as Rich proudly explained, he realized that the word "pit" wasn't usually associated with anything positive.

As David hears the front door open and some unrecognizable voices come floating into the foyer, he wishes Phil was here to make fun of sunken living rooms, to make sense of the rows and rows of dead bodies lying on the ground, to make noise that might echo off the cathedral ceilings. But every time David called any of the numbers Phil gave him, the person on the other end of the line told David that no one had seen Phil in weeks.

David turns off the TV and heads out to the foyer, where an Indian family is introducing themselves to Rich, Carole, and a few of Rich's guests whose names David has already forgotten.

"I am Joseph," says the father. His eyes are set deep inside his sun-hardened leathery face, and they crinkle more than twinkle when he speaks. Joseph points to the woman and the boy, who looks about two years older than David but is easily six inches shorter. "This is Muriel and Brandon."

David's eyes follow Carole's over to Muriel's frock. It looks like what Carole used to wear back when she lived with Phil. David also notices that Muriel's hair is long, the way Carole's used to be, and is not dyed to add any new colors or to escape the "gray weeds," as Carole's hairdresser, who comes to the house, calls the kinds of stringy ropes that cascade freely down Muriel's back.

Muriel smiles and holds out a tinfoil-wrapped plate. "Dried dates and figs. May they be sweetness where they see sweetness."

"Thank you," says Carole, taking the platter from Muriel. One of the housekeepers steps forward to take the platter, but Carole shoos her away quickly.

"What a beautiful home," says Muriel, pointing to the roof. "Is that a cathedral ceiling?"

"Why, yes it is," says Rich with a wide smile. "One of the company's standard features in all the new homes."

"Don't forget, we're teepee people," says Brandon. "We're big on pointy roofs."

"You'll have to forgive my son," says Muriel. "He wants to be a standup comedian."

"And at this size that's what the audience will be asking me to do—stand up. Good night folks, and don't forget to tip your waitress."

"David? Why don't you show Brandon around a little?" asks Rich.

"Looks like a little goes a long way around here," Brandon mutters, his eyes following the adults into the sunken living room, where dishes of cheese and other delicacies sit on Rich's mother's china.

David had plundered some of the appetizers the night after his afternoon with Greg and Craig, and Carole had come into the kitchen and caught him eating from the items marked "DO NOT EAT." But she hadn't said a word about his late-night munchies or squinty red eyes; she'd simply returned to her room and ordered replacements the next day.

"Want to see the central vacuuming system?" asks David.

"This house vacuums itself?"

"Kinda."

"Cause it's too big a job for any one person to do alone? Well, that's definitely one feature missing from the model homes on the res."

David steers Brandon away from Rich and Carole's room, with the his-and-hers toilets, two-person bathtub, and rain shower with rock walls. They go into David's room instead, where Brandon takes in David's few belongings—a couple of music posters, a baseball he kept from one of the pickup games on the block. And an unframed picture of Phil who, with his untamed hair that hadn't been outside in days, looked the way David liked to remember him looking: like "a guy with a care or two in the world…but only one or two," as one of Phil's friends had once put it.

"Nice," says Brandon, looking around. He picks up the baseball on David's desk and starts tossing it up and down. "Stepdad did you right, *kemo sabe.*"

"I guess."

"What's he like?"

"What do you mean?"

"You guys get along?"

"I don't know."

Brandon stops tossing the ball. "How can you not know something like that?"

"I mean, I guess so. We don't fight or anything."

"Shit, that's not getting along. That's just keeping quiet," says Brandon.

"Maybe we just don't have anything to fight about."

Brandon puts the ball back on the desk and plops himself onto an overstuffed beanbag chair.

"People always have something to fight about. And when they don't, they find something. That's just what people do."

"Says who?" asks David.

"Says history. People fight over territory, for the right to be themselves. To keep other assholes from destroying their culture. Hell, the only reason we're even here tonight is 'cause Big Joe's trying to get your stepdad to push some casino through the Legislature."

"I thought you guys were here 'cause it's Thanksgiving."

Brandon laughs. "Damn, that's about as whitewashed as the shit they teach us in school."

Brandon's eyes spot the picture of Phil. His expression changes and his tone softens.

"Look, I'd rather go and live with my old man, too. But hey, that's just family…"

Brandon doesn't finish. He wrinkles his nose in the direction of David's open sock drawer where David stashed what's left of the joint he got from Craig and Greg. David had lit it up earlier that afternoon when the housekeepers were preparing dinner and Carole was overseeing, and Rich was overseeing her overseeing, and it was bustling and, finally, a little noisy. He'd only smoked part of the joint, but apparently there's still enough stink left on it to attract Brandon's attention.

"Am I smelling what I think I'm smelling?" asks Brandon.

"Which might be what?"

Brandon smiles. "The flavor saver spirit of Thanksgiving. Now what say you and I go smoke the peace pipe, paleface?"

✦

BY THE TIME DAVID and Brandon make their way to the dinner table, the guests are already seated. The staff—all of whom, David realizes, are Mexican—bring out plate after plate of food, "themed," as Carole proudly explains, to invoke the First Thanksgiving: duck, venison, and mussels, along with several varieties of baked and steamed squash and dried fruits. Rich is holding a wine glass aloft, standing by the wall mural, set up by the table.

"After the initial phase, we'll be breaking ground on a second development, allotted specifically for lower-to-middle income residents, with special consideration given to Indian families, who will enjoy some of the finest homes in the Southland."

David notices that Rich says the word "homes" differently from how Alfonso says it, and even though the next time David will hear that word will probably be over the sound of fist against bone, he still likes the way Alfonso's version sounds much better.

Everyone raises glasses and drinks. Brandon takes a healthy gulp of wine, then nods at the poster.

"Which ones?" he asks.

"Which ones what?" asks Rich.

"Those finest homes in the Southland. Which ones are you putting aside?"

Rich points to an area near the bottom of the mountain, by a wide strip of tape that appears to be getting the boulevard treatment.

"Right here."

"Ah," says Brandon. "And will the homes in that area have cathedral ceilings? And sunken living rooms?"

Joseph glares at Brandon, but if Rich notices, his smile doesn't give him away.

"We haven't actually worked out all the features yet. But all the homes will enjoy some of the perks that make all of our communities so special."

Before Brandon can open his mouth again, Rich turns to David.

"David actually taught me a fair amount about how I was misusing the street names. Turns out he's pretty well schooled in some of the local tribal history."

"Just a little," says David who, even in his compromised state, knows his cue.

"Brandon and I are Chumash, David. What did they teach you about our tribe?" asks Muriel, leaning in partially because she's interested in his response and partially because she's trying to block Brandon from making eye contact with David.

"They're a matriarchal society," says David. It's the only thing he can think of and yet the words seem to float involuntarily out of him, practically evaporating the instant they do.

"Know what that really means? We're the only tribe without any federally recognized land," chortles Brandon. "Which means we gotta go cozy up to some guy. A guy with some pull at the res, who knows a good deal when he sees one. Right, Joe?"

Muriel puts her hand on Brandon's shoulder and squeezes it.

"Honey, remember those talks we had? About what is and isn't funny?"

"I wasn't trying to be funny, least not 'til white boy here busted out the wacky tobacky."

David's stomach drops. He doesn't have the nerve to look around, and even if he did, he's not sure he'd be able to read anyone's expression because the only expression he'd expect—the only one that should be present and that he'd know how to read for sure—would be anger. And what angers him is that he's pretty sure no one on his side would be angry; they would look down, or stare straight ahead, or blush and be embarrassed, but not be angry enough to fight about it.

"He keeps the goodies in his sock drawer," Brandon continues. "Go look if you don't believe me."

Joseph leans forward in his chair. "Perhaps your father should have named you Chief Running Mouth," he says.

"My father wouldn't have sold his people down the river. And if he had, he would have gotten a much better deal than a few crappy apartments."

Joseph smacks Brandon across the mouth. Brandon stands up, clutching his jaw, his eyes wide with fear and rage. Then he, Muriel, and Joseph are all talking at once and gesturing wildly while the other guests sit in shock, staring ahead, or averting their eyes.

Brandon slams something down on the table and storms out the front door, but not before shooting David the slightest hint of a smirk. Muriel follows him out, saying something about how their family is still going through an adjustment period while glaring at Joseph, who is right on her heels as the door closes behind them.

Carole stares down at the table and Rich nods at one of the housekeepers. As they clear the table, all that's going through David's mind is that the whole scene looks just like the ceiling of his bedroom, like the surface of the moon.

✦

THE BOGEYMAN HAD A family, which was made up of a bunch of people who'd run away from their real families. Before they ruined the lives of others, they camped out here, in an old Western movie set with fake facades, setting up a family complete with a father and leader, all from scratch, all in the middle of nowhere.

David is leaning against a rock, trying not to check his watch again because it will only remind him that it's all of five minutes later and no one is here yet. He's sure he's got the location right, although there's a slight chance that he heard incorrectly, especially given his frame of mind that night. Which was only slightly more fragmented than his frame of mind right now.

He can't shake the image of Brandon storming out, smirking as his family fought, while Rich and Carole sat in silence, staring down at their laps and giving the housekeeping staff quiet orders to clear the table. As David expected, no one reprimanded him—no one so much as spoke to him; they finished eating and David excused himself, went back to his room, and waited an hour before sneaking out. Which, he was also sure, he wouldn't be reprimanded for, provided anyone even checked on him in the first place.

Clop…clop…clop…

David looks up and sees what appears to be a cowboy riding down the main drag on a horse. It's so unexpectedly perfect that it's a few seconds before David gets a closer look at the man's face and recognizes the cowboy who used to work at the pony rides, back before the brown shopping mall and billboards replaced them.

"Bunch of us used to work those rides," says the cowboy when David asks him about it. "They used to have 'em all over the city. Ain't many left."

"So do you run this place now?"

"Parks Department pays me to check up on it. Make sure it ain't bein' vandalized, or the locals ain't booby-trappin' it for the developers. So on that note, mind if I ask what a fella your age might be doin' out here this time of night?"

David tells him about Greg and Craig and the Mexicans.

"But I'm the only one who showed up," he says.

"Don't surprise me. Things like that happen all the time out here. People talk big, then do business together and marry each other's sisters. Bigger question is, you don't strike me bein' part of any of that, so what is it exactly you were lookin' to do here?"

"I wanted to know why people fight."

"Good question. I mean, this land's been here forever. It's gonna outlive me, you, and everyone we know. But people forget that, think they actually own it. So I guess I can't tell you why people fight. But I know why they should."

David thinks about the noisy debates Phil and his guests used to have at Thanksgiving, the arguments with Ben and other musicians around the pool, the screaming matches on the phone with the squares at the record companies. How musical all the voices sounded, even without harmony.

"People should fight for what they love," David finally says, but the cowboy isn't there when he looks up. It's a full minute before David registers the tears that are making his eyes redder than anything he's smoked the past few days.

"Boo hoo hoo."

David turns around to see Lucy a few yards away, teetering atop a row of rocks lining the main drag.

"Cry baby cry," she says.

She walks up to David, pulls out a small handkerchief, and hands it to him. "Lucky hanky. Make the tears go bye-bye."

David takes the handkerchief and wipes his face. Then he hands it back to her. "Thanks," he says.

"*De nada*," she says. "Look."

She pulls out her necklace and shows it to David. He glances at the dog tags and recognizes the address from Rich's land map, which he's memorized by now but also now realizes he has no clue of ever truly knowing.

He walks Lucy over to his bike and puts her on the handlebars, the way the cowboy did on the ponies that rode around the doomed Western riding ring, the way Harris did in the cul-de-sac back when David didn't have his own wheels. Slowly at first, then gaining confidence and balance, he pedals the two of them down the bumpy dirt road of the fake Western town until it leads to something that feels smooth and paved and very much on the way home.

A TRIANGLE IS NOT A CIRCLE

"**B**INARY…"

"Right."

"As in, the entire scale is made up of two numbers," says Robbie.

"That would be the definition of binary," replies Tim.

"Don't tell me the definition of binary, you manfucker."

"Did you just call me a manfucker?"

"That's right. You're a fucker of men."

David is sitting in the backseat, trying his best to ignore Robbie, who's driving, and Tim, who's riding shotgun. Tim's long legs are forcing the front seat back so far it's practically crushing David, whose backseat space seems better suited for an overnight bag.

"How is that any different from being gay?" asks Tim.

"Forget it," says Robbie. "Just explain how this scale of yours works."

"The conventional rating scale is completely uneconomical. Whether some chick's an eight, a nine, or even a ten overlooks the only true reason for making a judgment."

"Which is?"

"Whether or not you'd bone her," says Tim with the casual shrug of someone who's actually made this decision before.

"So a one if you'd do her, a zero if not," says Robbie. "Any modifications?"

"Like what?"

"Like say, a one if you're drunk, a zero if you're sober. Shit, I can name five chicks right off the top of my head who'd require at least a six-pack."

"A, you don't drink," scoffs Tim. "And B, my mom says booze is an excuse. And she uses that excuse better than anyone."

"Do you realize you're the only person I know who makes 'your mother' jokes about his own mother?" says Robbie, who will gleefully sink his orthodontically-enhanced teeth into any profane topic, with the sole exception being the woman who brought him onto the planet.

"Any other modifications?" asks David.

"Like what?" asks Robbie.

"Dude, you don't get to ask 'like what?'" says Tim. "It's my theorem. I'll decide what is and is not 'like what.'"

"That doesn't even make sense," mutters Robbie.

"Makes sense to me," responds Tim.

Robbie glances in the rearview mirror. "Make sense to you, Pluto?"

Ever since David mentioned that he was becoming more interested in quantum mechanics than straight math, Robbie has been calling him Pluto, in honor of the solar system's weirdest planet. And David's performances at their last two math meets, including the one this morning, have done nothing to dispel Robbie's and Tim's concerns. Neither of them said anything to him about it, but David saw the way their eyes kept flickering toward each other, all the while calculating precisely what lopsided percentage of problems the two of them were solving with little to no help from David.

"Our math skills are gonna take us all the way back to the point of origin," Robbie said after the meet. "The Big Bang one *and* the one every member of our gender spends his whole life trying to get back inside."

"And yet you'd rather treat them both as unquantifiable mysteries," Tim added.

David thought about telling them that they'd have an easier time solving the mystery of the Big Bang than the mystery of how to get themselves banged, but they'd just won the state math meet and were determined to settle all vestigial matters pertaining to earth-based banging tonight.

"Fine," says Robbie. "Your theorem. Go for it."

"So what other factors would there possibly be?" Tim asks David.

"I just asked that!"

"No, you implied 'could.' I expressly stated 'would.' There's a difference."

"An infinitesimal one, fag."

"What, no more manfucker?"

"Consider yourself upgraded."

"I guess what I wanted to know is, what if there are non-concrete factors?" asks David.

"Like what?" asks Tim.

"Like what if you actually like her?"

Tim and Robbie look at each other the same way they did during the math meet, then Tim turns to face David.

"The scale is tailored to accommodate boning, not liking," he says, again with a shrug that again suggests firsthand knowledge of the distinction. "It's built to quantify a simple, utilitarian function, not some incalculable, emotional non-matter."

"Why can't it be tailored for both?"

The traffic light turns red. Robbie puts the car in park, because apparently it's his turn to turn around. "Do not tell me you're still carrying that ring around in your pocket."

David runs his hand over the smooth ring that is indeed lying at the bottom of his front pocket. He says nothing, but Robbie sits with David at too many math meets and knows everything about how David stores and conveys information.

"Okay, Pluto, you want my position on quantum mechanics? Out there, in the universe somewhere, on some fagtastic plane of fagterrestrial fagdom, there exists a planet whose sole inhabitant is some cosmically lovestruck..."

Robbie pauses and searches for the word.

"...fag," he finally spits out, "who met some chick on some beach ten years ago and still—still carries around some trinket that reminds him of her."

"Duly logged," says David.

"Good."

"Just a quick question: How is it that every negative quality I have is somehow covered by the word 'fag'?"

"Yeah, and can you finally explain the difference between that and a manfucker?" adds Tim.

Robbie sighs, the way David imagines a nun would, right before bringing down a ruler on a schoolboy's knuckles.

"What is clearly lost on our backseat, backdoor, butt pirate here, is that the word 'fag' covers everything on the spectrum from an English cigarette to a man who has sex with other men—make a note of this, Timmy, that manfucking is a subset of fagdom, not vice-versa. Pluto's negative attributes, while obvious and colossal, are not permutable. Ergo, it only makes sense that they would fit somewhere in the aforementioned spectrum."

"Well put," says Tim, nodding.

"Now, Pluto, when you finally realize this chick—this whole ring thing of yours—is just a concept, nothing computable, merely another cosmic theory that won't ever lead you anywhere or to anything, much less the sweet pudenda-lined trail o' tail, you, too, will be on the path to mathematical enlighten...whoa..."

David follows Robbie's redirected focus out onto the street, where two girls in tight clothing are cutting through the traffic next to their car. Without taking his eyes off the girls, Robbie dangles his right middle finger limply away from the rest of the hand, then whips the digit forward, smacking Tim in the left earlobe.

"Quick, where's the trophy?" snaps Robbie.

"In the back," says Tim, rubbing his ear. "And no more one-finger limpies. That one got more cartilage than lobe."

Robbie reaches into the back seat and fumbles around. "Little help?" he says to David.

"Gonna need a lot of help if you think a math trophy will help," mutters David as Robbie's hand grabs the trophy and hoists it out the window.

"Check it out!" yells Robbie at the girls. "First place, California State Varsity Mathalon!"

"And we're only sophomores!" adds Tim.

The girls, who look about twenty-five, give Robbie and Tim strange looks, then disappear behind the cars in the next lane.

Robbie tosses the trophy in the back seat, narrowly missing David's ribcage, then turns and glares at Tim.

"'We're only sophomores?!' Way to annihilate us the second you open your mouth!" yells Robbie, flicking a limp middle finger into Tim's forehead.

"I said cut it with the one-finger limpies!"

"Next time it's gonna be a five-finger firmie!"

"Green light," says Tim, now rubbing his forehead in addition to his earlobe.

Robbie puts the car into gear and they lurch onto the Strip. It's chilly out, but the women on the Strip are wearing next-to-nothing—or, as Robbie had put it, "next to godliness."

"Gorgeous, isn't it?" says Tim as Robbie passes through a three-way intersection.

"Isn't what?" asks Robbie.

"The triangle," says Tim, pointing to the yellow yield sign. "It's nature's perfect shape."

"Agreed," says Robbie with an approving nod. "Speaking of which, that was some killer Pythagorean sword-wielding you busted out back at the meet."

"Thank you."

"Unlike Pluto here," adds Robbie.

"A triangle isn't a perfect shape," says David.

"Then what is? Oh, let me guess—what was that game you played with your little friend all those years ago? Something involving a circle?"

I quit, thinks David. The words erupt through his head, as sudden as they are firm. But he's worried that if he shares this with Tim and Robbie now, he'll find himself alone on the Strip, which looks much more forbidding these days than it did years ago when he was much younger and much more scared of everything.

"A triangle is the perfect shape because it's the strongest," says Tim. "And it's the strongest because you can't just change one of the angles or one of the side lengths without breaking the triangle itself. All the angles and sides reinforce each other."

"I thought you were gonna say it's perfect 'cause it's shaped like an upside-down girlie part," says Robbie.

"And I thought you thought I was gonna say it's perfect 'cause it's one dude, two chicks," says Tim.

"Now those are some mysteries of the universe worth solving," says Robbie, nodding in the rearview mirror at David. "Just like in that song, the one your old man produced."

"What song?"

"The one about that perfect beach. You know, where there's two chicks for every dude."

"There's infinite wisdom in that tuneage," says Tim. "Double selection possibilities translate into exponential breeding opportunities."

"I don't think that's what they were talking about," says David.

"Oh no?"

"No."

"Then why don't you ask your old man next time you see him what they were talking about?"

"Better yet, let us ask him," offers Tim.

Sometimes the universe presents its logic in its own mysterious ways, thinks David as he runs his hand over the ring in his pocket again, then darts his pinky over to the folded-up, handwritten letter that came in yesterday's mail. Phil had always hated typewriters and computers, but David had the feeling that he wrote this letter in long form less out of principle than from a lack of access to any other form of communication.

"…twenty-four hour orgy," Tim is saying. "At least, according to the guy who was boning my mom last week. And he didn't hang around my mom for too long, so my feeling is we can trust his judgment."

"And what did he say this place was called again?" asks Robbie.

"The Halfway House."

David's ears perk up, the same way the hair on his arms perks up whenever he feels cold or scared or both. He takes the letter out and opens it, gives it a quick scan, just to make sure he had Phil's address right, then folds it back up and jams it into his pocket.

"So where'd this dude say this place was?" asks Robbie.

"Up in the canyon somewhere. Claims it's not too hard to find 'cause there's usually a steady stream of people headed there any weekend night."

Robbie slows the car and makes a U-turn.

"You're not seriously thinking of trying to find some orgy house," says David.

"Actually, that's exactly what I'm thinking of doing. I'm also thinking we're gonna ask one of those women over there for directions."

Tim blinks through the windshield at two women dressed in spandex pants and fluorescent tube tops. "You mean one of those hookers?"

"Well, it does make sense, probability-wise." Robbie pulls up to the corner where the two women, whose vocations Tim seems to have correctly identified, are watching the traffic through heavily painted, barely open eyes.

"Excuse me, girls?" asks Robbie.

One of the women, who's black and older-looking and whose figure looks misshapen, squeezed as it is, too tightly into her clothing, steps forward.

"Do I look like a girl to you?"

"She's a he. I knew it," says Tim, with a shudder.

The woman stares at Tim, then lifts up her skirt to reveal that not only is she not a he, she is also not wearing underwear.

"Got two boys roughly same age as y'all, came right outta there," says the woman, pointing at her exposed nether region before pulling her skirt back down. "So don't be callin' me no girl. Now what can I do for you?"

"Would you happen to know where the Halfway House is?" asks Robbie.

The woman does a quick scan up and down Tim's, Robbie's, and David's arms. "Y'all don't strike me as the skin-poppin' types."

"Not *a* halfway house. *The* Halfway House," says Robbie.

The woman laughs, a deep belly laugh that sounds like a genie liberated from its bottle for the first time in a thousand years.

"Now what would a bunch of nice boys want with a place like that?"

"I'm sorry, but was that a rhetorical question?" asks Tim.

"A what?"

"A rhetorical question. One that has no—*ow!*" Tim now rubs his temple, where Robbie has just one-finger limpied him with a *thwack* so hard, the woman can hear it outside the car.

"Tell you what," says the woman, leaning back in through the window. "Why don't you tell me what you think you're gonna find there, and if you're right I'll tell you where it is. Maybe even throw in a little something extra," she adds with a wink.

Tim and Robbie raise their eyebrows at each other, but David is busy watching the woman's companion approach a pickup truck idling by the corner.

"My mom's boyfriend said it's this nonstop orgy house where there's lots of drugs and women," says Tim.

"But we're only interested in the women part," adds Robbie.

"Y'all think you'd know what to do with some women once you got your hands on 'em?"

The other woman opens the door of the pickup truck and climbs in. The pickup truck drives off with a stammering backfire noise and a cloud of grey-black exhaust, leaving David to ponder how quickly, cheaply, and noisily sex comes and goes around here.

"We've got serious mathematical knowledge," Robbie counters. "We can evaluate the angles and lines on a woman's body in ways most people can only dream of. We can calculate immeasurable ways to physically pleasure a woman."

"You've heard of multiples? We're talking exponentials," says Tim.

"There you go," adds Robbie, shooting Tim an impressed sideways glance. "So yeah, I'm thinking maybe a triangle would be nice."

The woman raises an eyebrow. "You talkin' a three-way now?"

"There's a difference?"

"Honey, a triangle usually got the word 'love' in front of it. And ain't no math skills on earth can make a three-way have anything to do with love."

She shifts her gaze to the backseat. "Your boy here knows that," she says. "He's all about that. I can see it in his eyes."

"He prefers penis. We're gonna drop him off in Boy Town after you give us what we came for," says Robbie.

"Fair enough," says the woman. "Twenty bucks."

"You want me to pay you twenty bucks for an address? That's halfway to all the way around here."

"Actually it's two-thirds, math genius," says the woman. "Times are hard, but then again, so are y'all."

"But you said you'd tell us where it was," whines Tim.

"That was me havin' fun. So y'all can have some of your own."

Robbie hands the woman a twenty-dollar bill. She folds the money into a square and stuffs it into the front of her tube top.

"Wait here."

She scurries off down a side street, away from the lights of the main drag. Robbie sticks his head out the window.

"Hey, where you going?" he yells.

"Get you some information," she calls, without turning around.

"What the…?" says Tim.

"Go after her!" says Robbie.

"You kidding?"

"Do I look like I'm kidding?"

"Well, you must be kidding because I'm not chasing some hooker around this neighborhood."

"No need. She's gone," says David.

They turn to where they last saw the prostitute, but her loud, clattering heels have disappeared somewhere in the overgrown shadows of the darkened block.

"Goddammit!" yells Robbie, banging his hands against the steering wheel. "Bitch took my last twenty bucks!"

"Bitch took your only twenty bucks," snickers Tim.

Karma, thinks David, as the universe finally makes one of its mysteries clear.

✦

"WHY DO YOU THINK they call that place the Halfway House anyway?" asks Tim, between slurps of a chocolate milkshake.

They're in a diner where the big selling point is hot food at hours when people are typically not eating hot food, or any food for that matter. David suggested the diner when it became clear that treating his friends to a meal was the best combination of redirection and resolution for the evening.

When David was younger, Phil had never been good about stocking food in the house. So on nights when Phil forgot about dinner until it was late, he would put David in the convertible and drive to this place. They never went in to sit down, but Phil was always kind to the prostitutes outside, some of whom he knew by name. David is pretty sure that Phil's behavior back then had nothing to do with information, but whatever it did involve probably cost way more than twenty bucks.

"Dunno," says Robbie.

"Think it means drugs? That's what the hooker seemed to think."

"You know what I think?" asks Robbie. "I think we're not getting laid tonight, and I think Pluto here couldn't be happier about it."

David remains silent, but the truth is he's not unhappy that, while Tim's mathematical breakthrough might someday revolutionize bar talk and construction sites, for the three of them it remains a theoretical exercise. It was as though the prostitute could look inside David and immediately sense that he was in no hurry to get inside her.

"Maybe it's all for the best," says Tim. "Maybe the universe has other plans for us."

David is about to break the news about his decision to quit the math team—he's even come up with a short list of serviceable replacements at school—when he catches a glimpse of a girl through the window. She stands out from the other denizens of the Strip because she's not wearing any jewelry or other adornments except for an old, threaded necklace.

"Are you kidding?" asks Robbie. "'Us' is exactly who the universe put that place on this earth for!"

"Maybe not," says Tim. "If the name is any indication."

The girl draws closer. She tilts her head as she turns around and scans the traffic.

"What does the name have to do with anything?" asks Robbie.

"Halfway House. Means you're halfway to where you need to be. Exactly like the midpoint formula—one of the most basic tools in mathematics. Useful for figuring other things out, but answers very little in and of itself."

A yellow convertible with three girls inside pulls up in front of the girl. As she walks over to open the door, David gets a closer look at her necklace…

…and sees the round, smoke-stained, shiny object hanging on the end of it.

"Hard to love indeed," concurs Robbie. "No secrets of the universe lurking in the midpoint formula."

David reaches into his pocket and tosses some money on the table, then he jumps out of his chair so quickly it tips over backward and lands with a loud clang on the linoleum floor.

"What the…?" says Robbie.

But David is already out the door, over the protestations of Tim and Robbie, whose voices subside when they realize that he's left enough money not for his third and not for half, but for their entire meal.

✢

It can't be, thinks David, even as the kinetic energy generated by his legs churns his barely masticated meal into a greasy, esophagus-blocking blob. The convertible weaves around a creeping bus, then, in peals of burnt rubber and girlish screams, cuts across two more lanes.

David gulps, trying to force the surging reflux down his throat and back into his stomach, but it gets stuck midway as his lungs expand and contract in a vain quest to muster a few smog-choked, oxygenated particles. He's so focused on the backs of the girls' heads, on the eruptions of the acid sloshing around in his chest, on the fact that the car has just come to a stop at a red light fifty yards ahead, that the fat woman in spandex seems to appear out of thin air.

"The hell you in such a rush for?"

David hits the brakes, just in time to keep from slamming into the woman's considerable mass.

"Sorry," he says. He double-takes when he realizes it's the prostitute who took Robbie's money.

"You," she says. "The different one. Hey, I got that address for you—"

Without a word, David sprints off, back down the Strip, thirty yards from the convertible. Now twenty. Now ten.

The light turns green.

David's lungs, maxed-out about a hundred yards ago, are shutting down. He lunges for more air at the same time he lunges for the car, his hand feebly outstretched…

…just as it makes a right and speeds off.

David stands at the corner of the intersection, gasping, his breath returning to him in dribs and drabs. He looks down and realizes three things: one, he's holding the antenna from the yellow convertible, which has snapped off in his hand; two, he's standing right by the main road that leads up to the canyon.

Ergo, three: the universe has made the night's objective abundantly clear.

✦

THE CANYON'S MAIN THOROUGHFARE has at last been widened, and much of the landscaping and architecture is new, but David chooses instead to focus on the things that look familiar—the store where he got Keith's cigarettes, the rickety telephone poles that sometimes disrupted phone service for the canyon residents, the stilt houses on one hillside that seemed to pop up all by themselves one year—the same way an Indian scout or wolf cub would, no matter what season it was or how many moons it had been since he'd last set foot or paw to turf.

David turns up a street and hears a few shouts and the sound of shattering glass coming from around a corner. He stops, pulls out the letter from his pocket, and gives it another look.

Dear David,

I'm sorry I haven't been able to see you in a while; things are pretty tight, and I had to sell my car. If you ever make it out to the old neighborhood, swing by. I'm staying with some friends down the canyon from the old house, at 3678 Kirkland Place.

Phil

PS: in case you can't find the address, ask around. Everyone refers to this place as the Halfway House.

David puts the letter back in his pocket, then turns the corner and is engulfed by an olfactory haze of alcohol, cigarettes, marijuana, and garbage hovering above a laughing, smoking and, in the case of someone off to the side, vomiting crowd. The people and their smells and noises are gathered around a rectangular-shaped, dung-colored, two-story house that is indistinguishable from the other houses on the block, except for the metal grate on the front door and the intercom where the doorbell should be.

David presses the button on the intercom. He hears a click, which he takes as his sign to open the metal grate. Once inside, he finds himself climbing a dark staircase covered with darker shag carpeting and cigarette burns. David turns around a hallway bend and practically collides with a mass of dancing, drinking, topless flesh. The more David looks around, the more he senses that none of the major questions about this place— who, what, why, and how—are clear, the way at least one of them should be when you visit the house where your father lives. No one seems to notice David, which makes it easier for him to stumble over to where logic tells him the kitchen should be. He is suddenly aware that he had no way to call ahead of time to tell Phil he was coming.

The kitchen has bodies on virtually every plane—the floor, the table, the counter by the sink, even, David realizes, the sink itself. David clutches the ring in his pocket. His heart is pounding, and his normally docile sweat glands feel like a fire hydrant someone cracked open to give an inner city block a summer shower.

"Yeah, they were a great band. 'Til you got 'em offstage. Their idea of a business meeting was sitting around in a circle and sucking on a tank of nitrous oxide until they passed out."

Phil's familiar alpha growl is coming from an adjacent alcove that's a step down and has a built-in dining table. David nudges his way inside where he gets his first good look at Phil in almost a year.

Phil's cheeks and forehead are splotchy red, the same color as his eyes. He stands at the head of a table covered with bottles and powders, surrounded by a group of people who look like they can relate to the nitrous oxide part of Phil's story, but not the successful rock band part.

Phil looks up.

"David," is all he croaks.

He raises his glass and the group around him hushes. Then he hurls his glass against the wall, sending shards and brown liquid all over the dining alcove, before running over and wrapping David in a hug that feels as though it doesn't know where to begin or end.

Phil leans back and stares at David, his already red eyes even redder as they fill with the beginnings of some moisture.

"Jesus fucking Christ, look at you! You're a bona fide teenager!"

"I was this time last year too," says David.

A guy with a scar on his cheek sidles up to them. "You gonna work with me on that shipment in the basement?" he asks. "'Cause if your boy in Lynwood is ready, I got a fence that'll—"

"*This* is my boy," says Phil, shooting the man a look. "His name is David."

The guy stares blankly at David. "This is the guy from Lynwood?"

Phil escorts David out of the living room, up a sagging staircase, and into a tiny room that looks like a closet, where he sits down on a mattress with his legs crossed, the way David and the other kids used to sit at the cooperative. David looks at the ceiling, which angles upward into an ambivalent patch of extra space, as if someone thought about adding an attic but changed course halfway into the building process. A few pairs of jeans and some shirts are peeking out of a stack of milk crates, and several stacks of envelopes and official looking papers with red print cover practically every inch of the floor.

"Hand me that letter. The one right by your foot," says Phil.

David reaches down and hands Phil a letter, written in the loopy cursive of a grade-school student.

"Some guy, a big fan of my early stuff, asked me what he should do to get into the music business. I told him to cheat, steal, do whatever he had to, but that the soul of rock and roll should always come first. Now he's in prison."

Phil takes out a cigarette and looks around for a lighter. "So what's eating you these days? Any parental advice I can offer?"

"I'm quitting the math team."

"How come?"

"You know that old saying 'three's a crowd?'"

"Yeah. Unless you're talking about that beach my guys wrote about that one time, the one with two girls for every boy."

Phil spots a lighter under a pair of non-matching socks and reaches for it.

"You mind if I ask you not to smoke?" asks David.

"You telling me not to smoke in my own room?"

"I'm asking you, and I'm even asking you if you mind if I ask you."

Two mostly undressed girls stumble by outside, giggling and holding each other up as they make their way over to an open door, behind which several naked bodies are splayed out on the floor. Phil's eyes follow David's gaze over to the room down the hallway.

"Interested?" he asks.

David shakes his head.

"I went to a hooker for my maiden voyage, but that's what we did back in my day. Sure wasn't anything like this place."

"Which is what, exactly?"

Phil uncrosses his legs, then leans over and pokes his head out into the hallway. "You mind closing the door?" he calls out.

David hears a few muffled laughs and some muted voices, then the door closes. Phil rummages through the pile on the floor, then holds up a taped-together piece of paper. "I found this a few weeks ago."

David looks at the piece of paper. At the top of the page are the names Carole and Phil. Below them, in the middle of the page, is David's name.

"What's this?"

"Our family crest. I drew it the night you came home from the hospital," he says, tracing his finger back and forth between his name and Carole's. "There were the two of us, and you. We'd gone from two dimensions to three dimensions. And the point was…well, you were the point," he says softly as his finger makes its way from their names to David's and stops there.

"How is Carole these days?" he finally asks.

"She likes to be called 'mom' now."

"Huh. Well, she always was more of a lover than a fighter."

Phil stares blankly ahead, as though looking for those invisible shapes in the universe he used to tell David about—the connective tissue between creative vectors that, for many of his artists, was the only thing that gave their chaos a center, a place in the middle they could hold onto. But it looks like all Phil can see there anymore is a bunch of gaping black holes of unstitched-together universal matter, filled with a whole lot of dark nothing.

"You shouldn't pity me," he finally says. "Everything we were fighting for, all the squares we were trying to take down? It's all still going on…still…out there…"

Phil's eyes start to droop, then David hears a light snoring sound and realizes Phil has fallen asleep.

David pulls the small gray blanket over Phil, trying to ignore the hotel logo at the bottom. Then he reaches into his pocket and takes out the ring, the one he'd kept for himself after he'd given Topanga the other ring that he thought he'd seen tonight, but now figures he will most likely never see again. Then he takes Phil's letter out of his pocket and places the ring on top of it, right next to where he has written the phone number of the jeweler he visited a few weeks ago, making sure the ring is right next to the jeweler's estimate and signature.

He looks around the room and sees nowhere to put them, then realizes he's still holding the metal antenna from the yellow convertible. He slides the ring onto the antenna, followed by the piece of paper with the jeweler's valuation and phone number, then he twists the antenna into a circle and hangs it on the back of Phil's doorknob.

On his way out, he passes the family crest lying on the floor, and it isn't until after he's out the door, down the stairs, through the crowd and on the canyon's main thoroughfare that he registers the position of the crest on the page and acknowledges what a sharp, pointy shape a triangle truly is.

THE END OF ME

A BANDLEADER IS SINGING A song about happy days in the ballroom of a hotel whose exterior appears covered in black. Black limousines line the hotel's circular driveway, black tint lines the hotel's windows, and black-suited security guards escort the tuxedoed and evening-gowned guests up the stairs and through the revolving doors. All under a black sky, the starlessness of which provides the perfect cover for the dimly-lit road leading from the main boulevard to the hotel.

Inside, however, it's a completely different story. Color abounds in the pink and green streamers wrapped around the hotel's interior columns, in the lavender and maroon be-ribboned champagne flutes, and, most of all, in the fifty-foot American flag—"Biggest damn one in the Southland," David overhears someone say—hanging from the ceiling. But it is the carpet which reflects the night's most prevailing color, which seems to be the perfect complement to the mood tonight: it's the kind of rich-looking, traditional white that sits well in the background, while also pulling the room together with its quiet, understated power.

Which, thinks David, the more he looks around at the crowd, seems to be a fitting description for practically every single person here.

The country has a new president—the actor who used to play a cowboy, then, according to Phil, used to play governor. Rich is smiling and shaking hands and either knows, or knows how to acquaint himself with, most of the people here. Carole stands next to Rich, also smiling, somehow looking both younger and older at the same time. She waves in a downward motion at David whenever she spots him, even though he's actually five inches taller than she is. David feels a general loftiness—high cheekbones, upturned chins, tall heels on already tall women—whose elevation and gap seem to grow with every step he takes. But he likes the way the men slide their arms into the crooks of the women's elbows, and he likes the way everyone seems to glide over the surface when they walk. And he really likes the music, which feels like it has one arm wrapped around his waist and the other massaging the soles of his feet, making him want to dance and hold someone at the same time.

"Isn't this divine?"

David turns around to see Carole standing next to him. David has noticed that Carole is using words like "divine" and "ungodly" a lot lately. He's also noticed that she usually uses them to mean the same thing, which he doesn't understand and isn't sure she does, either.

"Yes, divine," says David.

"Your bow tie is crooked," says Carole, eyeing his tie's crisscrossing plaids.

Two weeks earlier, Rich took David tuxedo shopping and David had decided on a dinner jacket with a red and green checkered bowtie and cummerbund. Now, as he steals a look at himself in one of the lobby's six-foot mirrors, he can't help but think that the combination looked better on the mannequin in the store and is probably more appropriate for a Christmas formal than a political victory party. Rich probably knew this at the time, but kept silent because Rich is big on accountability. What any of this might have to do with poor choices in formal wear is lost on David, but Rich has also said that he might let David take his Mercedes out for a spin, should David prove himself responsible with Carole's Volvo. So David is more than willing to put up with the gray areas of Rich's life lessons, especially where black-tie-related matters are concerned.

Carole finishes fixing David's tie and shoots a look over at a group of younger women in dresses that show off their bony clavicles. Carole has lost a lot of weight in the last couple of years, enough to make David wonder if the older generations of nobles weren't right: that wealth and privilege were like butter, a lot more appealing when a little fat was involved. The ads on TV are featuring more and more products for jogging, and a lot of David's friends' mothers are on diets that come from conversation-dominating health books. David wonders if they're missing the point, if all the attention they're paying to themselves is actually unhealthy, but he's afraid Carole will tell him he sounds like Phil.

"Let's go inside the ballroom," she says. "There's someone I'd like you to see."

Carole and David make their way past the main stage area and over to what looks like a small pulpit, where about a hundred people are listening to a tall, wiry young man in a slim black suit. The young man speaks with a strong Russian accent, and David recognizes him immediately.

"Where I came from, leadership was small and absolute," Vladimir is saying. "Everyone outside this tight circle knew and accepted their low stations in life, and any attempt to rise above that station ended badly. The West, however, introduced the concept of the sovereign individual, the leader whose leadership was formed not as a tool of an absolutist government, but rather for the purposes of his own selfish interests."

There are enthusiastic nods from the listeners, even from those whose glazed expressions suggest that they had understood only a few words Vladimir had said, and only barely at that.

"Still, despite this philosophy, most people are more comfortable living in a static hierarchy where they know their places. This creates the opportunity for the government to take advantage of its disempowered subjects, and to overregulate and encroach upon their individual freedoms. This is very much what has been happening during the past ten years, which some have incorrectly referred to as the 'Me Decade.' What, pray tell, was so 'me' about it? Inflation? Government-impeded trade?"

More people are making their way over to Vladimir now, and David hears a few rummy, fuzzy-sounding rumblings of approval.

"As for the 'me' before you," Vladimir continues, "when this so-called 'Me Decade' began, I was living under communist rule, eating state-issued beans out of a state-issued can. Now, five years later, I am honored to have been part of the election of a president who will bring about a true 'Me Decade.'"

As the group applauds, Carole leans over to David. "He's donating an ungodly sum to the Party," she says, rubbing her hands together quickly, the way she always does whenever she's proud of someone.

"How?"

"He created some computer program that's going to revolutionize financial trading. Something involving synthetic derivations, or along those lines. Your father absolutely loves him."

"*Rich* loves him," says David.

Carole turns and stares at him. "Of course. Rich loves him. That's what I said."

David suddenly feels thirsty. Without waiting to see if Carole notices or cares, he goes over to the bar area where he orders a ginger ale. He doesn't love the way ginger ale tastes, and the carbonation tickles the back of his throat, but he figures the soda more closely resembles a libation than his customary apple juice.

"One-fifty," says the bartender.

"For a ginger ale?"

"Sure," says a girl's voice from somewhere. "Where else do you think our new president is gonna get the money to lower taxes?"

David turns to see a girl about his age sitting on the floor against one of the floor-to-ceiling windows. Her hair is blonde and her eyes are brown, a color that, conventional wisdom be damned, David finds a more attractive complement than its blue-orbed counterpart. Her eyes are also behind glasses and are peering half-above, half-through, a book she's holding upside down.

David walks over to her while stirring his drink, which he hopes looks more suave than he feels doing it.

"*The Origin of Species*," says David, turning his head sideways to read the spine of the book.

"It's for school."

"You always read your school books upside down?"

She shrugs and turns a page. "I like the challenge."

"Is that why you're sitting on the floor instead of at a table?"

The girl slides her glasses to the edge of her nose and looks at David, who realizes she's both dorkier and prettier than he'd initially thought.

"I guess that's probably going overboard on the whole proletariat rebel daughter number, huh?" she says.

David swallows and offers her his hand. She stares at his hand, then bites her lip and smiles, a non-committal smile that gives his insides the flutterflies feeling he used to get when he was younger and somersaulted down a hill, as though he was going to throw up but unable to resist another trip down—then another and another after that. Right as David feels as though he's going to tip over, the girl takes his hand and hoists herself up, her weight shifting into his as she does, the bigness and brownness of her eyes now simultaneously in the middle of her glasses and in David's line of vision. Just like that, David is right back on top of the hill, feeling strong and confident and ready for another chaotic, stomach-rumbling tumble back down.

"I'm David," he says, holding her hand an extra second to shake it, but also because she seems to be in no rush to let go.

"Seven," says the girl, linking her arm through his and guiding him over to the bar area.

"Your name is Seven?"

"Actually, my real name is Ivy."

"Ivy's a nice name."

"Ivy's a plant where rats build their nests, or a drip-line that nurses put into the arms of sick people, or a league of colleges filled with pretentious twits. I'm not sure which is worse."

"How'd you come up with Seven?"

"My family has a tradition. Anyone who doesn't like his or her name can use a number instead, as long as it's in sequence. My great-aunt Six was a nurse in World War II."

"So you're one of those kinds of families?"

"One of what kinds of families?"

"The kind that has traditions."

She shrugs. "Don't all families have traditions?"

"Not mine."

"We have another tradition where my parents host cocktail hours for the neighbors. I've been running everything from sidecars to Shirley Temples since I was ten."

"Sounds fun."

"I've also been puked on and groped at since I was that age. Alcohol does funny things to people," she says, nodding at his glass. "Speaking of which, if you want to make it look like you're holding a real drink, skip the ginger ale next time and go with a bitters and soda. Puckers the nose a little, but it's easy on the stomach and doesn't look like a fizzy urine sample."

David looks down at his ginger ale, which is indeed starting to look like a fizzy urine sample. He places the glass on the bar as Seven tries to get the bartender's attention.

"So what kinds of traditions does your family not have?" asks Seven.

"Well, for starters, they split up."

"Oh." She puts her hand on his forearm. He wants to tell her it's okay, it was a long time ago, but he's scared she might move her hand. "Who do you live with?"

"My mom and stepdad. But I lived with my dad at first."

"What's he like?"

"He wouldn't have been caught dead at one of these things. Sidecars *are* Shirley Temples compared with what he was running."

Seven throws her head back and laughs, clapping her hands together as she does. David relaxes and starts telling her stories about Phil and his friends, and she keeps smiling and putting her hand on his forearm, which makes him feel floaty and safe inside. It's not what he felt with Lynne, not what he can remember feeling with Topanga, but something right in the middle. Something that'd be a-okay with Goldilocks, as Phil used to say, but he said it more theoretically because nothing in Phil's world was ever right in the middle. Nor is it—was it ever really—that way with Carole, as David is starting to realize the more time he spends not getting to know her.

"Pardon me, sir?" Seven says to the bartender. "Two Greyhounds, easy ice, light lime spritz. Scandinavian vodka, if you please. The Russian brands are hangover city."

As the bartender fixes their drinks, David finds himself wondering whether the president and his donors will experience Russian hangovers from their association with Vlad the former Inhaler.

"God, I'm thirsty," says Seven.

"I thought you said alcohol makes people do funny things."

"Funny things. Not necessarily bad ones."

The bartender returns and places two glasses down in front of them. "Nine dollars," he says, looking at David, who reaches into his pocket and pulls out a ten-dollar bill, the only money he has left.

David takes a sip and tries not to gag, especially because Seven has downed most of her drink by the time he musters the courage for a second sip. He tosses the rest of the liquid down his throat and conjures up images of frozen tundras to offset the burning feeling trickling down his chest. Seven signals the bartender for another round, which David isn't thrilled about because the burning feeling is slowly being replaced by a weird, woozy dizziness. That, plus he's out of money.

"Don't worry, this one's on me," says Seven. She puts her hand on his forearm again and the weird, woozy dizziness is replaced by a nerve-coating warmth that makes him feel strong and brave and happy.

"Let's get some fresh air."

The balcony outside the bar area overlooks the most perfect garden David has ever seen. Swans glide on a moon-kissed pond, surrounded by trees filled with dewdrop-shaped sparkling lights that seem to line the hillside all the way up to the sky.

"It's beautiful," he says.

"Like a fairy tale?" she scoffs.

"I thought girls loved fairy tales."

"They're for kids."

"Not the real ones. They all end badly in ways only grownups understand."

Seven giggles.

"What?" asks David.

"The way you say 'grownups.' It's sweet."

"What should I say?"

"'Adult.' Sounds much more grown up." Seven wrinkles her nose when she says this, and David finds himself thinking there isn't a single look on this girl's face that isn't worth a dozen in return.

"So what was it like?" she asks. "Being in the middle?"

"Of a divorce?"

"No, of that whole scene. A kid surrounded by all those amazing people trying to change the world."

David doesn't know how to tell her that being in pajamas didn't exactly put him at the epicenter of the new world order, but he doesn't want to shy away from a golden opportunity, either.

"It was scary," he finally says.

"Just scary?"

"And exciting."

Seven moves in closer. "How exciting?"

David swallows. "Very."

"Tell me."

"Tell you what?"

"All about your scary, exciting life, about your intense, wonderful father, and about how all of it led to this place. Which, if you ask me, is a lot scarier."

Her eyes start to close—a little at first, then a lot, but just as their heads are slowly gravitating toward each other, he hears a loud rustling in the bushes below.

His eyes open, just enough to regret settling on the sight that greets them: a man whose eyes are bloodshot and whose hair pokes up and out at every angle. The man looks like a vagrant, looks like he's been camping outdoors in his clothing, and right now, and worst of all, looks right up at David and Seven on the balcony.

"There the hell you are!" bellows Phil.

✦

"WHAT ARE YOU DOING here?" hisses David.

They're standing in the garden, five minutes after David asked Seven if they could continue their conversation in ten minutes. Maybe she was feeling sorry for David, or maybe that was just how that Goldilocks sweet spot worked, but Seven smiled and went back inside to her drinks, proletariat rebellion, and upside-down reading.

"It's a fundraiser. Figured I'd donate a kidney to the cause, but they already got my spleen. Seems the bastards have a soft spot for all things painful and evolutionarily unnecessary. Who's the girl?"

David doesn't answer.

"Give me a break, all right?" sighs Phil. "I've been looking all over for you."

"Tonight? Or in general? Because I haven't exactly been too hard to find these past, say, eleven months."

Phil leans in and sniffs. "Have you been drinking?"

"Have you?"

"Shut up," says Phil, taking out a cigarette and lighting it. He takes a long drag and tilts his head back, then blows a long stream of purple smoke through his nose and into the night air, the same way he used to when David was younger. Now, like then, David wonders how a person can do something so wrong but look so right doing it.

"You wouldn't happen to have access to a car, would you?" asks Phil.

"I can call a taxi if you need a lift home."

"I can *call* the same taxi you can call. What I *need* is for you to come somewhere with me."

"Why?"

"Because I haven't seen you in…"

Phil trails off.

"Eleven—"

"Eleven months. Because I'm the grown-up here, even if in title only. And at the end of the day? Just because."

David hates it when people answer a question with "just because," because it isn't a real answer. But Rich did hint at access to the Mercedes, and given how well lubricated everyone inside must be by now, David figures that maybe it's time for a question that doesn't really have room for an answer.

✛

"So tell me all about my replacement," says Phil, looking around the spotless car as he turns down the hill.

Rich, who was usually hard to faze, looked shocked when David asked him for the valet ticket. But he was also standing with a bunch of red-faced guys who'd all been in fraternities in college and didn't strike David as being all that different now.

"We just elected a guy who's gonna stick it to the liberals on this end and the commies on that end," one of them said. "And you're not gonna let the kid get laid in your fifty-thousand dollar car?"

Everyone laughed at this, and Rich, who never needed a second reminder that he was in public, handed David the valet ticket.

"His name is Rich," says David, trying not to wince from the grinding sound as Phil downshifts. "You sure you know what you're doing?"

"I drove a stick shift for years."

"Years ago," David reminds him, wondering if Phil's logic—that he had a lot more experience driving under the influence than did David, who's definitely feeling the effects of those two drinks—was as solid as it had seemed ten minutes earlier.

"So I know his name," says Phil. "And I'm sure it's richly appropriate. Other than being a complete square, what else can you tell me about him?"

"What else do you want to know?"

"What you're all doing at that hotel, for starters."

"He says we're on the ground floor of a revolution."

"He's got the revolting part right." Phil lights a cigarette.

"No smoking in the car," says David. "He's pretty anal."

"You do know that word isn't just a synonym for clean, right?"

"Yeah, but—"

"For example, it speaks of a kind of probe that a doctor can give you. Or that a new president can give the country."

"Phil—"

"It can also speak of a sexual act, practiced by gay people, that the aforementioned new president would just as soon see abolished. And that includes the aforementioned gay people as well as their aforementioned preferred sexual act. And yet here you are in a fucking dinner jacket, celebrating an ostensible revolution."

"Please. I'm asking you."

Phil sighs, then tosses the cigarette and whatever else he was thinking out the window. David follows the cigarette as it flies into the air and lands on the sidewalk, right in front of the brown shopping center where the cowboy used to give pony rides. Then David realizes that they're passing the main road up to the canyon without slowing down.

"I thought you said we were going by the old house. That you had something to show me."

Phil keeps driving, right through a red light.

"Phil—"

"Relax," says Phil in a low voice, the hint of a smile creeping up his face. "Everything's gonna be just fine."

David wants to throw up, only partially from the alcohol sloshing around in his stomach.

"Are you…kidnapping me?"

"Call it whatever you want," says Phil. "Far as I'm concerned, I'm doing you a favor."

Phil makes another turn down a steep hill that feels like they're falling off the side of the earth, the way the explorers, pre-Columbus, feared they would when they reached the end of the sea.

"Look…Rich…he isn't big on this kind of stuff. You might think you're making some larger point, but he'll have the cops looking for us if this thing isn't back at the valet stand in an hour."

"Sad, isn't it? That he'd call them over this thing's disappearance, but not over yours. Nice replacement."

Phil turns into a driveway on the left side of the street that leads into a darkened alley.

"What are you doing?"

"Making a left turn."

"I can see that. But…into an alley?"

"Yeah. We're gonna park behind the club."

"What club?"

"The club I'm taking you to."

"Don't you have to be twenty-one to go to a club?"

"Don't you have to be twenty-one to drink overpriced cocktails with girls? She was cute, by the way."

David squints through the windshield at the spot Phil is easing into. "You're gonna park Rich's brand new Mercedes next to a dumpster?"

"They know me here," says Phil, opening his door. "We're going in through the band entrance."

David follows Phil past several piles of broken glass and over to a large door, which is guarded by a large black grate and an even larger black man whose arms are folded across his chest.

"I'm here for Dilweed," says Phil, handing the man a twenty-dollar bill.

"Right this way," says the man, swinging open the metal grate.

Phil leads David down a vertiginous staircase that feels as though it actually sinks an inch or two with every step. It's hot, the kind of hot that comes from a combination of little ventilation and lots of body heat, or from an extra layer of grandmother-advocated clothing. It's too dark for David to be able to see anything at first, but he hears a dull, thudding bass line followed by a screaming, scraping guitar, and a gut-churning roar. Then a door opens, and they're inside a small room filled with a writhing, herky-jerky mass of spiked hair, safety-pin-pierced limbs, army fatigues, and studded leather jackets.

On the stage is a drummer whose face David can barely see, a guitarist whose back is to the audience, a dead-eyed bassist, and a lead screamer clutching the microphone. David looks around at the slam-dancing audience and suddenly his white dinner jacket and plaid bow tie feel even more out of place than they did at the victory party.

Phil scans the room. "Great," he yells. "She's here."

"Who's here?"

"You'll see," he says. He leads David over to a small table, which is little more than a metal pole with a Frisbee-sized piece of plastic on top. Sitting behind the table, on a plastic folding chair, is a young woman who, like David, is too well dressed for this place, and glances at her watch more than she does at the band.

Phil pulls two chairs up next to her and plops himself down on one of them. "Hey," he says.

"Hey, yourself," she fires back as David sits down.

"Remember your old babysitter?" Phil says to David, nodding at the young woman. "Katie?"

"Actually, it's Kate now," says the young woman, turning back to Phil. "So what's this big surprise you played every guilt card to get me here to see?"

"Kate's moving to New York to work for some new music channel that's going to be airing live performances twenty-four seven," says Phil.

"Not live performances, Phil. Videos. Music videos. And that didn't exactly answer my question."

"All right, all right," replies Phil with a smile. "The surprise isn't a what. It's a who. Check out the lead singer."

Kate and David turn to face the stage, where the screamer is on his knees, the microphone pressed so closely to his anguished mouth that it looks like he's swallowing the thing.

"Recognize him?" asks Phil with a slight twinkle in his eye.

The screamer raises the microphone over his head, and David immediately has a flashback to his baseball games on the cul-de-sac.

"So I'm out scouting the clubs like I always used to," says Phil. "And I keep hearing about this act that's unlike anything out there. I come here and listen to them last night and lo and behold—the people have spoken."

Phil leans in, the way he used to whenever he was talking to the suits, back when they used to make the homage trip up the canyon to see his bands.

"And on my way home, I'm flipping radio stations and the instant I pause the dial, I hear one of the deejays talking about how their programmer is heading to New York for this music video venture. He also called you 'Katie', by the way. On the air."

Phil leans back and puts his hands behind his head. "So, as we say in Yiddish, I figure this is *b'shert*. My son just up the hill from here. His baseball buddy up on stage. And the girl who used to babysit, in a position to put our block on the map again."

They turn to the stage in time to see Harris close his eyes. Then, to the immense pleasure or disgust—David isn't too sure which—of the hooting crowd, Harris takes a shiny instrument out of his pocket and plunges it into his thigh. He howls into the microphone as blood spurts all over the thrashing audience.

"Okay, I've seen enough," says Kate. She stands up and walks briskly over to the staircase, pushing her way through the surging crowd, some of whom misinterpret her navigational attempts as a cue to include her in their slam dancing and push her right back.

Phil follows Kate across the crowded floor. David takes one last look at the stage where the kid he used to play ball with, used to sneak out and ride bikes with, is writhing around, his blood still spurting up into the air and all over the crowd, who are now starting to spit in the direction of the stage. David ducks under the various airborne bodily fluids and pushes his way over to the staircase, where Phil has caught up with Kate and is holding her arm.

"Don't talk to me about programming for some fad. I was booking stadiums when you were still in utero," yells Phil over the guitar solo.

"Yeah, well, the umbilical cord is in the rearview mirror, Phil. Along with your version of the music business," says Kate, wresting her arm free. "Silent film stars said talkies were a fad, too."

"Years ago, Ben tossed some buddies a country rock knockoff and they rode it all the way to a career. You telling me that kind of collaborative spirit's gonna happen with someone risking keeping his own mug off millions of TV screens?"

"Collaborative spirit? Did you forget that Ben's buddies paid him back by putting out a more radio-friendly version of the album you two were working on together?"

Kate turns to David. "Nice seeing you again. Hope you enjoyed looking at my tits back in the day."

"I've seen better," says David. Even though it's not true, he feels it's the least he can do for Phil at this point.

Back on stage, Harris tosses the microphone down and storms off to a chorus of cheers, boos, and more flying spittle.

"And this music, this whatever the hell this is? *This* is a fad," says Kate with a shudder as she dashes up the staircase.

Phil watches until she's out of view, then turns to David. "Wanna go say 'hi' to your old buddy?"

David shakes his head. He wants to get back to the victory ball, to the nicely dressed people and music that feels like you're floating, to Carole and Rich who, for all their Carole-and-Richness, at least feel like they're on a playing field he can feel under his feet. He's thinking this loudly and clearly, if silently, but if he was thinking of sharing any of it with Phil, it all evaporates the minute the door to the alley opens.

✦

"HE WAS SUPPOSED TO fend off the tow truck guys," says Phil.

"Tow truck guys don't take your car when you park in front and go in through the front," replies David. He is leaning against the dumpster, trying not to be sick from a combination of alley scents, non-complacent alcohol, and the fact that according to Phil, the twenty dollars he gave the guy by the door was his last money on the planet.

"I don't suppose you have any dough for a taxi?"

"Blew it buying drinks for that girl," says David. "The way I'm supposed to at my age."

Phil shakes out a bent cigarette butt and lights it while David leans over and coughs up what he hopes isn't stomach lining.

"Some night, huh?"

The nausea in David's stomach clears immediately. He stands up as straight as he can and turns around. "What do you mean 'some night'??? My night was going fine until you became part of it."

"Okay, so maybe you got a point there. Still, look at you. I barely recognize you."

"You haven't seen me in a while."

"You haven't grown."

"You're one to talk."

"Don't talk to your old man like that."

"Old man? A couple hours ago, Mom—that's what she goes by now—referred to Rich as my old man. Freudian slip on about a million levels, wouldn't you say?"

"I was actually kidding about him being my replacement."

"You made yourself replaceable!"

"Why, because I drink? Because I don't check in with you right and left? Because I hang out in dive clubs where you shouldn't park a Mercedes?"

"No," says David. "Just because."

"Touché," says Phil. "But you still look like an asshole."

They stand in silence, facing each other like two battered heavyweights who have just gone fifteen rounds, but only if each round was a year long and the boxing ring was a dark alley that smelled of vomit and rotten fish. David is so busy glaring at Phil that he doesn't hear the garage door open, then a van that's covered with cockeyed UK flags and a circled letter "A" rumbles out and screeches to a stop.

"David? Phil?"

The voice belongs to Harris, who is sitting in the driver's seat with his drummer in the front seat next to him. Harris's voice is soft and incredulous and sounds nothing like it did inside the club.

"You guys need anything?" he asks.

"No thanks," says Phil. "We're good."

"You sure?"

David gives Phil one last glare, then turns back to Harris.

"Actually," says David. "I wouldn't mind one last lift on your handlebars."

✴

ON THEIR WAY BACK up the hill, Phil and the drummer sit in the back, swapping stories about gigs where roadies are too stoned to set up the stage and club owners try to stiff you when it's time to pay. David sits next to Harris up front, neither of them saying a word. David isn't sure whether this is because Harris feels uncomfortable, or is just even more taciturn than he used to be.

"So how long have you been…doing this?" David finally asks.

"'Bout a year."

"And how's it going?"

"What do you mean?"

David shifts uncomfortably in his seat, not wanting to admit that he wasn't exactly expecting more than a one-word answer. "I mean…have you reached any of your goals?"

"We don't really have any."

Phil is laughing at a joke the drummer has just made about groupies and a certain kind of fish.

"So how about you?" asks Harris. "What are your…goals?"

"College."

"What for?"

"I used to think math, but now I might be leaning toward quantum physics. Figure out how the universe works."

"Well, let me know how that goes."

They pull up to the hotel and David steps out of the van, catching a glimpse of himself in the side mirror as he does. The white dinner jacket and Christmas-colored plaid bowtie look even sillier as a small reflection than a large one, but they're not without a certain dignity either, a dignity he'd like to think he's still going to feel even after Rich gets the bad news about his car. Rich, who thinks the world of Vladimir, the Russian kid who loved Westerns and is now teammates with a fake cowboy who plans to take down the bad guys in the Eastern bloc. The former godless communist with an affinity for imaginary numbers and a system that involves derivatives, a system that gave him the freedom to donate an ungodly sum of cold, hard cash to the Me people.

David turns his attention back to Harris and catches a brief glimpse of the boy whose athletic skills used to rule their cul-de-sac. Then he blinks and sees the same guy plunging a blade into his thigh, the one he'd ruined all those years ago when baseball became something more than a game played by children. It makes David wonder if becoming a grownup isn't really a slippery-slopey evolutionary thing but rather, like those animated flip-cards he used to play with, a series of "me," where one "me" is replaced by a new "me" in a similar pose, but is moving in a different direction away from the "me" in the last frame.

Phil slides into the front seat and leans out the open window. "Rich gonna kick your ass over this?"

"Doubt it. But he'll probably find a way to use it for leverage at some point."

"Sounds healthy."

The band in the hotel starts up again as a big cheer rattles the windows, through which David can see the new president take the stage and wave to his supporters. Phil is watching too, but he looks as though he's looking through the whole thing, as though he can see all the way to the other side to an ending that hasn't yet been determined, but that he's sure he won't like.

"Doesn't matter," says Phil, his still-red eyes focused on an unlit cigarette in his hand. "The grownups always win in the end."

"No smoking in the van," says Harris.

Phil sighs and tosses the cigarette out the window, then turns to David. "Do me a favor?" he asks. "Tell my replacement he did a hell of a job with you."

Harris puts the car into gear, and the van lurches forward and chugs slowly around the circular driveway.

David watches the van until it disappears onto the main drag. Then he hears the band launch into another verse, and it reminds him that there are swans and tuxedoes inside, as well as a girl who's waiting for him, and that Goldilocks is just a fairy tale for kids.

SEVEN IN HEAVEN

"**R**ED LIGHT," SAYS SEVEN.

David's hand stops halfway down her side. He waits for her to say "green light," but she lowers her head and stares straight ahead without saying another word.

She does this sometimes, turning their make-out sessions into playground games with rules and customs only she understands. He goes along with it because she's a girl, and that's what you're supposed to do with girls when they don't make sense to you, and also because he likes it.

"Penny for your thoughts," he finally says.

She closes her eyes.

"What are you doing?" he asks.

"Making a wish."

"Why?"

"If I tell you…" she trails off.

"It won't come true?"

"No. I'll have to kill you."

She opens her eyes. "Green light."

She smells like suntan lotion and her body feels warm and summery against his as he leans down to kiss her. He opens his mouth and guides her tongue inside, still feeling the same shivery prickles he felt the first time they kissed in a bumper car at a nighttime carnival. The idea had been to team up and take on all comers, but they'd instead found themselves parked in the middle of the action and with their mouths immediately upon each other's. Later, he'd marveled that their car hadn't been hit once, which, given the proximity of tongues to teeth, might have landed one or both of them in the emergency room. Now, however, unlike then, her lips seem to pause as if to regroup between kisses, and her breathing is coming in halting spurts and with more hesitation than usual.

"You okay?" he whispers.

"Aces," she whispers back.

"Because we don't have to stay in here the full time if you don't—"

"Red light," she says, placing a finger over his lips, first vertically, then horizontally, then back and forth, as his eyes follow its movement before closing again.

✦

IN A FEW HOURS David will be eighteen, old enough to die for his country, a fact Rich was only too happy to point out two or three times this week—once or twice more than was necessary to make the point. Rich did offer to take David to the country club for one of its famous midsummer clam bakes, but David had already made plans to celebrate with Seven, whose parents are either working out or drying out at a spa in Mexico.

David's last day as a child in the eyes of the law began with a short, mostly wordless breakfast with Carole, their last remaining ritual together. Years ago, when David was at the cooperative, the two of them would spend hours at the breakfast table by the bay window—David delaying bites of the strange, mostly inedible morsels placed before him, Carole turning her defeats at the stove into something that resembled structured time, neither in any rush to leave the lazy comfort of the sun-splashed kitchen. But Carole seems decades older now, and while she might not be in any major hurry to see David die for his country, she might be in a bit of one to see him off to college, if the brevity of their breakfasts together these days is any indication.

✦

"It's so far away," was the first thing Seven had said when David's thick packet had arrived in the mail. She was still a junior, with the topic of college mostly a distant consideration, but the early returns were leaning west, not east, and largely adjacent to her current zip code to boot.

"You can visit."

"I don't like to travel."

"You just got back from Europe."

"That's different." But she hadn't said how, and she hadn't said anything else, and she hadn't brought it up again.

✦

When he arrived at her house that morning, she was asleep on the couch, a few loose strands of hair hanging over the top half of her face, a polka-dot bikini covering just enough, but not too much, of her body.

He stayed in the doorway, fully aware of how much he loved looking at her when she was like this, her upstream-flowing river of thoughts run temporarily dry inside the otherworldly ecosystem that housed it. He ran his eyes over her miraculous curvature, finding his own thoughts vacated, save for the one about the musical instrument all female bodies supposedly resemble. He found it both wondrous and unfair that a simple visual could stifle his typically overactive neurology while rendering the complete opposite effect on the rest of him. He wondered if there was some way to explain it quantitatively, something more than just the obvious part about blood flow, which would have explained his supercharged, red-celled nether regions, but not the gray area blackout upstairs. Maybe there was some God-particle-loaded energy that, with one prompt, could be massively rerouted for hours at a time so that when things downstairs finally settled back down, it still felt as though he was experiencing the residual effects of a stroke or a baby seizure.

Or maybe, just maybe, he thought, as he sidled over to the couch, this is what it's like when you find yourself in uncharted territory, in the celestial heavens—over-explored yet unknown by scientists, theologians, and romantics alike.

✦

"BASICALLY, SHE TURNS YOU on at the same time as she turns you off."

Robbie had pointed this out one day in the lunch area. But he had done so in a way and, uncharacteristically without Tim around (the two of them were heading north next year, had signed up to room together, and were thus inseparable these days), that it felt like he was actually interested, not just calculating something he could use against David later. David had come away from it thinking that if people were mostly less than you thought they were, they were sometimes more too.

✛

SHE STIRRED, SHIFTED A bit, then wrinkled her nose and rubbed it. David bent down to wake her with an earlobe nibble when the phone rang.

And the answering machine picked it up.

He listened to the entire message, all the way until the answering machine clicked off, then he sat down on the couch across from her and watched her sleep as he processed what he'd just heard.

✛

"MMM," SAYS SEVEN, FEELING him against her. She pulls him down on top of her and the two of them stay like that, the way they just do sometimes, not caring if it's minutes, hours, or even days, during which nothing else seems to move other than their chests breathing up and down in harmony.

So why ruin it? he thinks. Why say anything?

Because, he thinks again.

Because what? One phone call that could have meant anything?

He goes back and forth another round or two before he's saved, if that's the right word for it, by his friends.

"Attention lovebirds, sexhounds, and all other indoor sports-loving creatures," says Tim from the other side of the door. "Twenty-eight-point-six percent of your time is elapsed."

"For those of you less mathematically-inclined—which would be you, birthday boy—that translates into two minutes gone by," adds Robbie.

There's snickering, then silence, then David looks back at Seven as Tim and Robbie and the voice on the answering machine fade away and everything goes blissfully still again.

✦

THAT TIM AND ROBBIE would be coming had been a given, but the immediate blank on David's face when Seven had pressed him for more invitees to his party had made him realize that he'd made few friends at school and had retained none from the years he'd lived with Phil.

Despite this, Seven had insisted that eighteen was one of life's few event birthdays and thus deserved a party worthy of the occasion. Which had surprised David because Seven was, for the most part, anti-party—both political and social, on account of her parents' gung-ho and frequently drunken participation in both—and he'd had a hard time convincing her that he preferred to keep things intimate.

✦

INTIMATE...

He'd spelled it out one night when they were playing Scrabble on her parents' frayed game board, the one on which someone had written, in indelible marker, "no four letter words allowed." They had just finished a heated argument about a word she'd sworn had come from her women's studies class, which had led to an overheated state of mutual half-undress—loose, but still-fastened underwear, and a light sheen of sweat and suntan lotion, the de facto uniform for all their summer games.

"Define the term," she'd said softly and without looking up.

He'd gazed at her smooth, caramel-colored leg pulled halfway up her other thigh, forming an isosceles triangle at her knee, and he'd done everything in his power to work through her question before realizing he didn't want to define the only word on the table that didn't feel like it was part of a game, something they could wipe the tiles away from and start all over again from the beginning.

"It's the opposite of infinite. The universe is infinite. It has no boundaries. Whereas something intimate has nothing *but* boundaries."

"Says who?"

"Science."

"What if I think it's the other way around? What if I think that the universe is intimate, because just like it had to begin somewhere, it has to end somewhere? And that if you're really and truly intimate, there aren't any boundaries?"

"The universe doesn't have to end somewhere. But maybe you're right about half of the boundaries part. Everything important in the Big Bang, the foundational boundaries of the universe, happened during the first three minutes."

"Which is exactly how long it takes for a woman to decide if she's going to be...intimate with a man," she'd said, unable to stifle a giggle.

"Your women's studies teacher said that too?"

"Actually, I read it in *Cosmo*. Mom's got a pile of them, waist-high."

"When I met you, you were waist-high in *The Origin of the Species*."

"Upside down, no less. And let me guess—now look at me?"

"Good guess. I am."

She had met his eyes and stayed like that, and she had allowed him to stare right back at her, too, and there had been no need to say or do or even think anything, but he had anyway. He'd thought about his school's library, about how Seven's school had reciprocal study privileges, and about the librarian who was known for walking noisy students over to a sign that read, SILENCE IS GOLDEN, then smiling and saying nothing while pointing to the sign, making sure to do it right in front of everyone. The librarian had done this to David the only time Seven had ever met him there, when the two of them had argued too audibly over a game of hangman in her notebook, and the librarian had smiled just a little wider when she'd realized the extent of David's humiliation. Coming up with just the right word to play in this game of Scrabble— and the bliss of Seven's resulting wordlessness—had made him want to find that librarian and tell her as loud as he pleased that this silence, this wordless, infinite space in the cosmos, *this* was golden.

This was how their arguments ended these days: with a mutually acknowledged, electromagnetic tug from somewhere in the realm of the physical, and an unspoken agreement to disagree about everything else.

KIRA AND NICOLE REPRESENTED Seven's delegation to the party, mostly because they knew Robbie and Tim the way most of the girls at Seven's school knew most of the boys at David's school: more as mixer partners or potential off-campus pairings than as friends. Robbie had gone so far as to take Kira, an Asian girl who was known for pushing her own highly sexualized version of boundaries, to their senior prom a few months ago, only to realize after the fact that she drew the line on pushing those boundaries when it came to Asian boys. Nicole, who played field hockey, gave famous shoulder and neck massages and wanted to go to a women's college, even after spending six years at an all-girls school. She had once played a game of strip poker with Tim at a party where everyone else had passed out. They'd wound up completely naked but, according to both, hadn't laid a hand on each other.

When the girls arrived, David sensed that they were coming out of equal parts obligation, curiosity, and opportunity. Because, as it turned out, David wasn't the only party celebrating a birthday: the new all-music video channel, whose ubiquitous billboards featured a white-suited astronaut flying through space and holding a flag with the channel's logo, was set to debut that night at 11:59 p.m. That its birthday was slated for one minute before David's would officially be history, that David's girlfriend had figured out a way to pirate the broadcast (which was only available to people who had cable, and the rabbit ears on Seven's parents' TV antenna looked like Van Gogh after his famed act of self-mutilation), was the kind of sad irony that wouldn't have been lost on one-half of David's own point of origin, back when Phil was loud and chaotic and full of points of his own.

✦

"IT'S THE END."

Phil had proclaimed this during one of his last coherent visits, sometime between the victory party at the hotel he'd crashed and the graduation party at Rich and Carole's he'd missed.

"It's gonna shorten—nah, fuck that—decimate—attention spans. If," he'd added, "that's even biologically possible. So put that one under the category of 'science permitting.'"

David had wanted to remind him that shortened attention spans were science's way of being permissive, that the need to adapt to a faster, ever-expanding rate and volume of external stimuli was just evolution's way of keeping its younger members on their toes. But he could see that by the time his thoughts had crystallized, Phil had already moved past—and likely forgotten—the subject at hand.

✦

"So they're just gonna like, play music all day? Like concert clips and stuff?"

Kira was having a hard time grasping the concept behind the music video channel, partly because she was four wine coolers into the night and partly, David suspected, because she wasn't very bright.

"No. They're more like short films," said David.

"How do you know for sure?"

"I don't, but my dad—"

"Cucumber liqueur anyone?" Seven entered with a tray filled with shot glasses and passed them around.

"Your dad what?" asked Kira.

"Yeah," said Seven, not looking at David as she handed a shot glass to Nicole, "your dad what?"

"Nothing," said David, watching Seven as she avoided his eyes, trying to remember the last time she'd shown any interest in Phil, and drawing the same empty set he'd drawn when mulling over the party's guest list.

"Well, I can't wait," said Nicole. "It's like, kids are finally gonna be seen as well as heard."

"Where'd you read that?" Tim snorted.

"I didn't. Made it up myself," Nicole shot back.

"I'm still not sure what this thing even is," said Kira.

"And yet you still want to watch?" said Robbie.

"Well, duh. Everyone else does. Why shouldn't I?"

"What if it's just not for you?" said Robbie, a bit softer than before.

"Who even knows how to decide that? I mean, you guys are going to college next year, right? What if one of you comes back next summer all New Wave or Euro? Or gay? Life's just too uncertain to be so final about things."

Children of the Canyon

"Maybe no one will watch," offers David.

"No way," scoffs Nicole. "I've already read, like, three magazine pieces about it. They're gonna wind up cutting down a rainforest full of trees writing about it. Mark my words, this is one thing people are definitely gonna be watching."

"I'd rather be watching two things," said Seven, as she wobbled to her feet and held up her glass. "A, you guys downing that liquid I chilled to the perfect temperature before running it through fresh cucumber and lime. And B, my boyfriend being feted the way an eighteen-year-old…"

She trailed off because, as far as David could tell, she didn't like where that was heading.

"Because," she continued, "it's his last birthday…"

Her voice cracked, just a little, barely noticeable, but enough that it warranted a slight clearing of her throat. "So, to eighteen. To the end of immaturity. And the beginning of eternity."

They drank, then Seven refilled everyone's shot glass and they drank again, which was followed by a few more concoctions that Seven pulled out of her bag of tricks. By ten o'clock, they were past the drinking and socializing part of their night, but still two hours away from the part that was supposedly going to reshape the teenage universe as they knew it.

Which was when Seven suggested that they all play a game.

✦

WHEN DAVID WAS IN first grade, the boys had taken on the girls in a relay race. One of the boys had slipped on a wet patch of grass on the final lap, and by the time he'd risen to his feet, the girls were celebrating and taunting the boys.

David, who hadn't shed one tear over the baseball games on the cul-de-sac—not even the ones in which Lon had berated him for missing the cutoff man, or striking out with the bases loaded—had come home that night, locked himself in his room, and cried for hours.

✢

THE FIRST FEW SPINS yielded nothing but truths, which divulged Kira's crush on her seventh grade math teacher and David's queasiness from the odors in AP Bio lab. Then Tim decided to push the evening's danger ceiling up a notch with a dare and ended up mooning the group. It was as though any potential flab in his beanpole physique had melted and followed gravity, then coagulated and formed a pair of oversized buttocks that he shook back and forth so rigorously they made a slapping sound that repulsed everyone, except Robbie. Not to be outdone, Nicole dared Kira to make out with someone. After slowly eyeing her three realistic options, she stared right at Robbie before choosing Nicole.

The kiss outlasted the obligatory whoops and hollers, and Kira gave them a long, exaggerated curtsy when they finished— mostly, it seemed, for Robbie's sake—but Nicole looked straight down and immediately spun the bottle as hard as she could. A fair amount of suspense, given Nicole's athletic talent and palpable adrenaline, fermented before the bottle wound down its last few wobbles and pointed right between David and Seven.

✢

"HOW MUCH TIME DO we have left?" asks Seven.

David glances at the grandfather clock in the corner of the room. "According to gramps over there, three minutes."

"Ah," she says, her eyes twinkling with a mixture of sarcasm and delight. "The time it took for the Big Bang to form the universe."

"It wasn't three minutes the same way you and I experience three minutes," says David. "Time at that point was measured in one billion-billion-billion-billionth slivers called Plancks. So in the time we've been in here right now, entire galaxies would have been formed back then."

"Sounds...intimate."

"Like I said before, more like the opposite."

Seven props her head up on her elbow and stares at David. "Is something on your mind?" she asks, but her knee is bobbing up and down.

It's not that David doesn't want to say what he's been wanting to say, it's that he's back in that unchartered territory where he actually can't.

"Jesus," says Seven. She rolls her eyes, then she sits up and slips out of her bra and underwear. "Do you need a triple word score to spell it out?"

+

SEX WAS ALWAYS THE first thing everyone wanted to talk about. Until it was the only thing left to talk about, and then nobody seemed to want to talk about it at all. And Seven, for all her high-volume political, or gender-based, or politically gender-based discourse, had been completely mum when it came to intercourse discourse. There had been a fair amount of tactile tentativity on both ends, even the slightest hint of some oral exploration, but everything had stopped just short of crossing any irrevocable thresholds. Which had made David realize that he didn't even know what to ask—or, for that matter, whom to ask—if he had any questions about the subject, which, of course, he had nothing but questions about. He couldn't pin down Phil, of course, and Tim and Robbie were entertaining but unhelpful, of course, and Rich, who should have been the most of course of all, was…well, Rich, of course.

And so David and Seven had ruminated endlessly about nothing in particular, and had said nothing in particular during their endless rumination, but at the end of the day, they'd obeyed the rules and had allowed no four-letter words on the board.

UNTIL NOW.

THEY'D HAD DINNER WITH Seven's parents once, at a lobster restaurant, after Seven's father had made a point to ask David if "his people" ate at places like that. Once there, Seven's father had excused himself to talk with a group of men at another table, where he'd stayed for nearly forty-five minutes.

Seven's mother had reeked of gin in the car on the way over and had argued with the waiter about the freshness of her appetizer, then had spent the rest of the night casting sideways looks at David that had progressed from seeming disgust to open curiosity, then finally to something that resembled a leer. On the way home, Seven had sat next to David and rested her head against his shoulder, and all David had thought about was that he'd never seen her look so happy with him before.

DAVID OPENS HIS EYES long enough to glance up at the clock.

Two minutes…

Beep…

"Hello, Ivy? This is Vance Bergen. We met a couple of weeks ago, at the club, when our moms played in that doubles tournament? Anyway, I really loved sitting by the fire with you that night and thought it would be a good idea if we went out for dinner together, maybe met for tennis at the club, or took our boat out for a sail on the water. Your mom has my number, so give me a call."

Beep…

✦

The facts, the science; it was all starting to congeal as quickly as it was rushing at him.

She hadn't told him about meeting some guy named Vance…she hadn't asked about Phil…she was unsure about coming to visit him…she'd met some guy named Vance at her parents' tennis club, where they'd never asked David to join them…either because of "his people," or for some other reason, maybe because they didn't expect him to stick around the big picture for long…his "people," who probably weren't even allowed in their "intimate" club…where she'd met some guy named Vance…and hadn't told him, either because it was unimportant, or because it was too important.

Sometimes he wishes there just weren't so many games involved.

✦

She puts her head on his shoulder and runs her hand down his chest and around his navel in a loop-de-loop before finally coming to a stop.

"You don't seem happy," she whispers.

David stays silent.

"Is it just that you weren't ready?"

David wants to remind her that the grownups think he's old enough to die for his country, but he's moving forward—faster, now faster, and for the first time in his life, he understands how Plancks work, how things move so quickly that sometimes they can only be felt in residual, elemental terms, in billion-billion-billion-billionths, and how little time it takes under the right circumstances for entire universes to form.

✦

IT HAD TAKEN NEARLY a month before they'd seen each other for the second time. She and her parents had left the election party by the time he'd finally returned, but he'd learned her family's name from one of Rich's friends.

They were listed, and the first night he'd called, he'd practically hung up in between every ring—and there had been at least five of them, or maybe it had been more like fifteen—but it had been her voice he'd heard when the phone was finally picked up. And when her voice had recognized his on the other end, it had risen just a bit, and with a quiver to boot. They'd gone on like that for hours, for weeks, for any and every length of time that time had had available to throw their way.

This, he'd always known, was what he would miss the most about her: that point of origin, when everything was only energy and not mass, when everything was possible and nothing was finite.

✦

"Everything has to come to an end," whispers a little voice from somewhere in his waking brain. "Even the universe. That's the whole point of the Big Bang Theory."

He opens his eyes and looks over at Seven, but she's fast asleep.

✦

David opens the door just after midnight, and the only two people in the living room are Tim, who has passed out on the floor, and Nicole, who's watching the launch of the music video channel.

"Where are Robbie and Kira?" he asks.

"Upstairs in Seven's room," says Nicole, staring straight ahead.

"He really does like her," says David. For some reason, he feels like he owes her that.

Nicole looks at the staircase, her eyes following it up into the space where the steps disappear. "Well, goody gumdrops for him," she says.

She turns back to the TV, and she and David watch the ancient tube's fuzzy broadcast of the astronaut forging his way through the darkness to the big, bright light looming at the end of the cosmos.

✦

David had almost taken her to the old neighborhood one night, after a movie (he didn't remember what it was, because he never remembered what movies they saw, because they never found themselves facing the screen once the lights went down) when, on their way home, she'd started asking about Phil even more than usual. No matter how many times he'd spun life in the canyon into folkloric gold—even the smallest items, like the places in his house where he'd found sleeping bodies— she'd always wanted more. He'd driven up the canyon road but at the turn to the cul-de-sac, his palms had gone clammy and he'd had that heartskippy feeling between his stomach and his chest he'd stopped having since he'd met Seven. He'd ended up driving her around the neighborhood instead, feigning surprise and disappointment when he hadn't been able to locate a street he was confident that, blindfolded, he could have hit with a dart while standing on the Goodyear Blimp.

Then he'd dropped her off, and just like the other conversation about college and traveling, she'd never brought it up again.

+

ON HIS WAY HOME, he turns off the main drag, onto the canyon road that snakes up the hill. He notices a few new streetlights, but it feels as though they aren't responsible for the increased visibility, a thought that's confirmed when he looks up into the sky and sees the big, orange orb looming over the neighborhood.

A Rustler's Moon.

He passes the block where they'd once played baseball, but the only games he's thinking about right now are the ones he played with Seven, everything from word games to board games, to word games they played when bored, all of which he's pretty sure have come to an end.

He pulls the car onto his block, about ten yards away from a new house that sits on the property where he used to live. He's exhausted and empty inside, and as the light from the moon washes over him and the car, he wonders if somewhere, someone is trying to steal the childhoods from a bunch of kids who love everything about who and what they are, but are completely unaware that it can't last forever.

✦

"YOU ALL RIGHT?"

David opens his eyes to see a shape, covered in fluorescent yellow, right outside his window. When he rubs his eyes and looks closer, David realizes it's a man, maybe in his early thirties, with one hand against the window and the other on a baby stroller.

"You all right?" asks the man again.

David nods and rolls down the window. "Fine. I used to live here. On this block."

"Oh yeah? Which house?"

David looks over at the nice, new house, and sees the door open and, in the dawn of the sunlight peeking over the mountains, the baby toys strewn all over the new lawn.

"You know something?" he says. "It was too long ago to remember."

✦

HE'S ON HIS WAY back to Rich and Carole's. The radio is on, and he's taking the canyon road extra slowly because the new smoothness is unfamiliar to him. He's concentrating so intently on the road, that he almost doesn't hear the radio voice announcing a gruesome crime scene last night in a seedy house up at the top of the canyon.

Seven bodies. All the residents with the life beaten out of them, in what appeared to be a drug-related revenge killing.

It isn't until the announcer mentions that the location of the crime scene was also known as the Halfway House that David's stomach falls, and he looks up, sees the traces of the Rustler's Moon disappearing from the sky, and senses that the grownups have won again, this time for good.

THE CIRCLE GAME REPRISE

THINGS ARE SUPPOSED TO come around full circle.

David used to love circles, but he's not sure that things come around in them, full or otherwise. Sometimes things just move forward and stay that way until they land at their destinations.

Like the airplane he's on right now.

He's sitting near the front of the coach section, watching the first class passengers as they settle in. Several rows behind him is the smoking section, where even before the plane has closed its doors and begun its flight, several passengers have already lit up. The sight and smell floods David's head with stories from the funeral about Phil's smoking. In meetings, during sex (apparently), and on flights—especially on flights—where he would smoke, even if he wasn't in the designated section, and remind anyone who objected that they were in a floating tube and that the smoke would catch up with them sooner or later.

When they were finished, someone threw a pack of Phil's favorite cigarettes into the open grave, right along with the shovels of dirt that were being scooped on top of his casket.

*

THE POLICE HAD ASKED David a few questions until it became clear that they knew more about Phil's habits in his last days than David did. Either they'd felt sorry for David or they'd felt the need to scare the old man's DNA out of him, because they had provided David with more details than he'd felt were necessary.

"Body parts and paraphernalia everywhere," one of the cops had said. "Looked like someone dynamited Hell."

"Worst crime scene I've ever seen," one of the other cops had agreed, and David knew that as strange as it would have seemed to someone who didn't know him, Phil would have felt a small sense of pride in knowing that.

✦

DURING THE FUNERAL, BEN, who'd lost weight but had somehow become even more stooped, spoke of how sorry he was about Phil's death. Then, in the same breath, he added that he was also sorry he'd never finished *The Golden State*.

"But now," he said, "in Phil's honor, I never will."

It had been Ben's third funeral that year. The other two had been for his brothers.

✦

THE PLANE'S DOORS ARE still open, even though the last boarding call was supposedly twenty minutes ago.

David sits next to the window, and the seat next to him is empty, but practically every other seat in his section seems occupied by young parents and little kids. He waved to a few of the kids when he first sat down, but they all hid behind some piece of parental appendage and averted their eyes. He tries to remember if anyone had ever told him anything about safety around strangers, but can't, which means that either he's forgotten it or no one ever thought it important enough to share with him.

✦

SEVEN CAME TO THE funeral. She sat in the back, and even though David didn't turn around once to look at her, he sensed her tears, heard her quiet, choked sobs, all for a man she'd never met and had only known in secondhand anecdotes that excluded any behavior David deemed too Phil-like to include.

After the funeral, he and Seven talked—awkwardly, briefly—her wishing him luck and telling him to have a good flight, him nodding and promising to call her, knowing full well that he wouldn't, and under the circumstances, that he didn't have to cross his fingers and hope to die.

✦

HIS EYES STUDY THE plane's concave ceiling. It's not a circle, and not even a halfway-decent semi-circle, but a perfect, aerodynamic shape that will permit this beast of machinery to bend physics to meet its needs. He hopes college will give him the chance to study the physics of all those shapes in the universe, the ones Phil and his artists always claimed they saw. He tries not to think about the very real possibility that by the time he reaches that point, he'll realize that everything he's looking for is gone for good or, worse yet, never existed in the first place.

The stewardesses signal to each other, and the doors to the plane close, even though there are still people storing their luggage and trying to find their seats. David has a peanut butter sandwich in his bag in case he doesn't like what they're serving for lunch. He's already feeling clammy thanks to the recirculated air, and he can't understand why everyone won't sit down and fasten their seat belts already, and all of those factors plus the closed off-ness of the plane's cabin are starting to make him sweat.

He's leaving, just like Carole had all those years ago, off to a place where he hopes the smiles disappear inside the head so he never has to feel like he's stuck somewhere in the void between two pieces of a broken circle again.

✦

ONCE UPON A TIME, in a temporary clearing in the middle of the woods, two coyotes came together and created a third. One of the coyotes was unable to adapt to a changing habitat, and the other became a domesticated pet, and now their cub is trying to find his way in the world, leaving behind memories that, even back then, he realized were worth holding on to: memories of cowboys and Indians, of desperados and baseball, of constants and revolutionaries, of pointy triangles, suited squares, and elusive circles—the swirling, confusing, and, in just the right light, he realizes, beautiful universal shapes and music that formed and defined the children of the canyon.

✦

"MOMMY…"

David turns to see a boy, maybe four or five years old, sitting across the aisle from him. The boy's mother is on one side of the aisle and his father is on the other side, each one trying to fit a bag into a space that is clearly too small. The boy reaches out and tugs on his mother's arm, then does the same with his father's.

David closes his eyes, but instead of families on airplanes, there's just a six-year-old boy on a beach, thinking his life from this point on will be a struggle from inside a circle to pull everything back in, and an eighteen-year-old college student who wants to go back in time and tell him that it's never going to be possible because he's finally figured out the part of the brain where the smiles disappear. It's the part that's been holding in all these images, and feelings, and memories that, with each passing day, are at last making more and more sense, and are allowing him to grow up, yet still retain the same him he hopes he will always be. And he has the feeling that, no matter what lies in front of him, he can connect it to everything behind him and somehow it will all work out. That the grownups might always win in the end, but the children will somehow always find their way.

"Please fasten your seat belts," says the faraway voice over the speakers, and as the plane starts to move, David closes his eyes, peacefully, for the first time in what feels like forever.

✛

DAVID OPENS HIS EYES.

They're in the air, surrounded by clouds on both sides of the plane, but they're still on the way up so the "fasten seat belt" sign is on.

David goes to stretch, but there's a girl sitting next to him.

"Sorry," she says. "I couldn't stand the smoke."

She smiles, which makes her look even prettier than she already is.

"No problem," says David.

"So where are you headed?" she asks.

"School. You?"

"*Same.*"

Before David can ask her where, the plane starts to shake and he tightens his grip on his armrest.

She puts her hand over his and smiles at him. "*Don't be afraid,*" *she says.* "*There's nothing to be afraid of.*"

He turns to face her and as he does, the light from somewhere above the clouds shines in through the window, creating a kaleidoscopic image with sun-kissed, golden-flecked rays dancing around the edges of the universe. Where a girl once told him she lived everywhere, but he couldn't always see her.

Until now.

"*Topanga,*" *he whispers.*

She lifts her necklace out from under her blouse, and David catches a glimpse of something that is no longer gold, not shiny and perfect anymore, but somehow stronger and better.

He clasps his hand in hers, and the plane disappears above the clouds, and the circle, long broken, is at last whole again.

ACKNOWLEDGMENTS

FOR PEOPLE WHO LIVED there during its heyday, the Canyon was said to be populated by fairies—magical entities that turned life in those parts into something elevated. I, too, have been blessed with many such beings, who are listed below in no particular order.

Matt Roshkow, my great screenwriting partner and even greater friend. Thank you for the read, the advice, and above all else, the perfect title.

Barnaby Harris and the Norman Place Gang/Azure Stadium All Stars. Thank you for allowing a strange interloper like me to be part of your childhood adventures.

Rebel, my publisher, and Jayne Southern, my editor and hand-holder, throughout this wonderful journey. Your faith in this work would require a volume of equal length for me to express sufficient gratitude.

Tyson Cornell, Alice Marsh-Elmer, Julia Callahan, and Mariel De La Garza: I will forever believe that it was a higher entity that sent Rare Bird from the sky and into my personal stratosphere. Thank you, thank you, thank you.

Alexandra, my beautiful junior editor and novelist soulmate. Your otherworldly literary gifts, precocious insights, and unerring sense of humor are a daily revelation.

Zachary, my child of inspiration, both in print and in life. Your formidable genius is matched only by your unyielding kindness, grace, and sensitivity.

Ilana, my Gibraltar in what has at times been a Black Sea, my eternal forgiver and life guide extraordinaire. This book, simply put, would not be if not for you.

ABOUT THE AUTHOR

A NATIVE ANGELENO AND GRADUATE of Columbia University and UCLA Film School, David Kukoff has eleven produced film and television credits to his name. He has published two books on film and television writing, has been the subject of features in Variety, Entertainment Weekly, and The Hollywood Reporter, and has taught writing at Northwestern University.

Though he does not currently reside in Laurel Canyon, he has spent the better part of his adult life trying to get himself, as Joni Mitchell put it, "back to the garden."

Children of the Canyon is his first novel.

INTERVIEWS WITH THE AUTHOR

DAVID ULIN

David Kukoff: In *The Myth of Solid Ground*, you describe the journey you went on following the earthquake of '94. Could you talk a little bit about that book?

David Ulin: I'd lived here before, and I'd spent a lot of time visiting, and I had what I consider to be a healthy fear of the earth shaking. It was something I felt I had to deal with when I decided to move here in 1991, about two and a half years before the Northridge quake, but that whole period from Spring of '91 up through January of '94 was fairly seismically active. So I started thinking about how we dealt with the uncertainty of earthquakes. I was really kicked into overdrive with Northridge, which was obviously a big quake, but more so was a psychologically big quake. It was disruptive and it was scary. So I just stumbled onto a small piece in The *Los Angeles Times* talking about a set of files that were known colloquially as the "X-Files." They were essentially the prediction files kept by a woman named Linda Curtis, who worked at the US Geological Survey in Pasadena. I was originally going to write about the predictors and who they were, whether there was any validity to their theories, and where their theories were coming from. When I finally got a hold of the X-Files and read through it, it was like a long, multi-author, speculative novel. I realized fairly quickly that I wasn't grounded enough in the science, and I needed to talk to geologists and seismologists about time, and deep time, and human time, and what I would almost call the metaphysics of seismology. You know, it is a way of thinking about eternity in a physical way, as opposed to a celestial way. It seemed like there was a lot that could continue to be explored, and that was how it grew into a book.

DK: I think it's one thing to be a good writer, and quite another entirely to be able to break down the principles of writing into digestible, learnable bits. Could you talk about some of the principles that you feel strongest about sharing with your students?

DU: I actually feel like my work as a critic has been very helpful in terms of teaching. It's also been very helpful in terms of my own writing, because I think it has taught me, as a necessity, how to break down a work critically—to look at how a book or a piece of writing operates in succinct language and structure, and how to verbalize those things. I've always really liked the back and forth between the creative and the critical, and I think there's a lot of creativity in criticism, as I think there is in teaching.

But I've always liked the relationship between thinking critically and thinking creatively, between writing and, after the act of writing, being able to think critically about what it is you're doing and what you want to be doing. It helps a lot in terms of revisions, for one thing. As an instructor, I'm very anecdotal and honest about the experience of being a working writer. The other part of it is that there's a community that gets built in a classroom. It encourages writers to take risks. It reminds them that they're not alone in their fears and frustrations. I think we all, even the most practiced writer, have the occasional resistance to writing. It's lonely, and difficult, and can make you feel like you're Sisyphus.

The other thing I'll say, too, is that I spent a long time working as an editor, which also helps. I often, when I'm teaching writing, think that the workshop room is a kind of heightened editorial meeting, or editorial conference space. And I think that the notes that I'm making are kind of editorial notes. The process is not dissimilar, let's say, to how I would approach something due for publication.

DK: You edited a book called *Writing Los Angeles*, and another called *Los Angeles: Portrait of a City*, which you co-edited with Jim Heimann and Kevin Starr. How did those projects come about, and do you have any plans for follow-up volumes for either?

DU: *Writing Los Angeles* came first. I think the Starr and Heimann book came out because of *Writing Los Angeles*. It was one of those projects that, it's a weird thing to say, but it just kind of dropped into my lap. I knew some of the people at the Library of America from various things over the years. From having written some pieces over the years, from writing books, from meeting them over the years at various functions. I was also on the Board of Directors for a long time with the National Book Critics Circle, and I knew them through that. So I was at Book Expo in the 1990s, I was walking down the aisles, and I stopped by to say hello. I ended up in a conversation with them, and they had just done *Writing New York* at that point, and by the end of the conversation, one of the editors said that they were thinking of doing an LA book. The editor asked if I would be interested in talking to them about it, and I said, yes, absolutely.

Then the convention ended, they went back to New York and I went back to my life, but we started e-mailing back and forth about it.

I suggested that we start with the twentieth century, with a little bit of nineteenth century just to set the table. Culturally, and as an American city, Los Angeles is really a twentieth century city—twenty-first, too, but at the time, twentieth century. There's so much, so how do you define the city? You need to find a frame that works. We talked about whether it should be Hollywood focused, or should we leave Hollywood out. In the end, I think we decided on essentially the shape the book had, which was to have Hollywood be a part of it, but also to really capture the full range of the city, and in some ways, its history. So I signed on, and then we started gathering materials.

Gradually, it became clear to us that the book was going to be a sort of narrative of Los Angeles. In some ways, the really interesting early writing is non-fiction journalism, so we wanted to have a bunch of that stuff in. Certainly novels, but we didn't want to excerpt too heavily because it's always hard to build a book out of excerpts. You want as much stand-alone material as you can possibly get. The great challenge and frustration of that book was that even at roughly 880 pages, it was still too short. There's tons of material I wish we could have gotten in that we couldn't for space reasons, or copyright reasons, or in some cases, there were terrific book-length works that we simply couldn't excerpt. So, I always think of that book as—and it really is comprehensive, and that was the intent—but it's just the tip of the iceberg. One of the great revelations for that book, for me, too, and I hope for others as well, is just how rich the literary heritage of the city really is.

DK: I really appreciate, as a native Angeleno, the scope you just mentioned. Hollywood is just a part of this city, even though it's seen by the outside world as being very much akin to what politics is to DC. It's not an apt comparison; Hollywood is just one of this city's many faces, one of its many vital identities. It's an important one, and it might be the shiniest face that we show to the world, but by no means does it solely define what the city is. The fact that your book clocked in at almost 1,000 pages speaks to your point.

I'd love to wrap up with a question about *The Lost Art of Reading*. I'm sure I'm not the only one who's quoted this magnificent line back at you, but when you called reading "an act of resistance in a landscape of distraction," I almost stood up and cheered. Like you, I'm a Kindle owner, but I find that certain works, most notably *A Visit from the Goon Squad*, don't scale properly on an e-reader. That work in particular needs to be gone back through and perused, and you can't quite plow through it in as linear a fashion as you would other pieces. It would almost be like watching *Star Wars* on an iPhone screen. How have you found, since you're such a reader and a writer's reader, that your relationship to reading changing in the face of technology? If in fact, it's changed at all?

DU: I think we do live in a culture of profound distraction, and we're all susceptible to it. It doesn't matter whether we embrace it or not. I don't think it's as simple as just embracing it or not, in general. I am a great lover of technology and browsing the Internet. For me, it just comes down to trying to be conscious as much as possible. When I'm reading or concentrating, I want to be focused on that to the extent that I'm able. And when I'm messing around, I want to be conscious of that. I need to consciously procrastinate for a while, or consciously amuse myself for a while, and then I'm going to go work. That way, those two things are not in conflict with one another. Does it always work? No. Can you still fall down the black hole of serial linkage? Absolutely. I think, for me, the only difference is consciousness.

The actual process of reading is not so different. It's not as effortless as it was when I was younger, but I'm not sure if it's fully because of distraction. I think it's also partly because I read in different ways and with different goals now, even when I read for pleasure. I don't read as innocently or unconsciously as I once did. I can't, because I am wired from 25 years of reading as a writer to read as a writer. So, even when I'm reading a book on vacation, I'm taking that book apart in my head: I'm thinking about what the writer is doing. I'm noticing the phrases that really speak to me, or the parts that I think are clunky. I'm noticing where the writer is speeding up the plot too much and I want them to slow down, or when their pacing is good. But I don't think that's a function of technology. I think that's a function of being a writer. The other thing is that I read mostly on paper, which isn't a knock on e-readers. I think the more available venues for reading, the better. I love that we can get things digitally that I can't find. I love that I can get public domain books downloaded for free. My phone and my iPad are both loaded with books, but I like having a book in my hand, I like turning the pages, I like the physical experience of reading, and I like page design. I like that 3-dimensional experience of reading, where it's not just the story on the page, it's the way that story is presented. I read on screens when I have to, or even recently when I went on a trip, I didn't want to bring a whole bunch of books, so I just brought my iPad. But, my preferred mode is, and will presumably remain, ink on paper.

David Ulin is book critic for the Los Angeles Times. *He is the author or editor of eight books, including* The Lost Art of Reading: Why Books Matter in a Distracted Time *and the novella* Labyrinth, *as well as the* Library of America's Writing Los Angeles: A Literary Anthology, *which won a 2002 California Book Award.*

DAN FANTE

David Kukoff: I want to start with a quote from your memoir. You wrote that, "My father was an artist, win, lose, or draw. He avoided his passion for long periods but never denied it. Throughout a life of near obscurity, he clung to his gift. Most of his novels were written for nothing. Not fame. Not recognition. He wrote because a writer was what he was. For me, his second son, a ne'er-do-well, a whackjob, and an alcoholic, this enduring example made me love him with all my heart." I was really taken with that quote, Dan. Could you tell us a little bit about the context in which you wrote that?

Dan Fante: People often say to me, "Oh, you're the son of John Fante. What was it like to be the son of John Fante?" And John Fante wasn't John Fante until just before I became a writer in my early forties. My father was an out-of-work screenwriter—kind of cynical and embittered by the movie business—but toward the early-seventies, when he could no longer work in the studios and he was ill, he began to write again, and he was a true artist. His craft was the novel, and he was no longer mitigated and was pulled away by a fat paycheck, and he really concentrated on his work. Just watching his process was an honor.

DK: You pointed out that everyone from Faulkner to Fitzgerald traveled in Hollywood at points when the fiction world wasn't quite as easy or lucrative for them. It seemed as though about twenty or thirty years ago, there was a preoccupation among writers to write the great American screenplay instead of the great American novel. I noticed that you, for example, have written fiction predominantly. Do you think that there might be kind of a return to the art that your father still clung to amidst the turmoil of his Hollywood years, or do you still see people holding on to this shiny new brass ring of the great American screenplay?

DF: Well, I don't want to be unkind here. I'll just say that screenplays are at best a collaborative effort. Whatever the screenwriter writes is, by definition, semi-final depending on the director and the actors attached and their influence. I've currently written a screenplay based on one of my books that I've changed at least three times based on some preferences and comments by the people involved. It's a medium that is essentially a collaborative medium, first off, between the director and the screenwriter. Which is not to say that there aren't some fine screenplays written. But it's a process, and it's a process done, at least in my experience, through consultation.

DK: Having worked as a screenwriter myself, I saw what you wrote about your dad, how he found the transformation from novelist to screenwriter somewhat frustrating, whereas I don't know if I could say the same of my experience in the reverse. I find the transformation from screenwriter to novelist absolutely enlightening. It strikes me that that's probably more likely going to be the case. Because, as you rightly point out—especially in a medium in which the director is referred to as the auteur, or the author of the work, which is already an insult to the person who actually wrote the language—it's so collaborative. At the end of the day, a screenplay is a blueprint; it denies the writer a chance to really witness his language and thoughts in as pure and unadulterated a fashion as possible. It seems that you've mostly sidestepped that, and mostly gone straight to turning out a number of of wonderful works. I'd like to ask you about the title of your memoir. You called it *Fante: A Family's Legacy of Writing, Drinking and Surviving*. It seems as though that title already addresses the junction where creativity meets addiction, which is very much in the public conversation these days. Can you speak a little bit about this from your own personal and familial experience, and maybe even from a societal perspective?

DF: You know, David, I'm from a family that has alcohol issues going back several generations. That is not to say that my father was an alcoholic; only he could define that, but he was a heavy drinker for a long time, and he had some of the by-products of what happens to heavy drinkers physically. I think many artists of this period had their issues somehow exacerbated by booze and drugs. We live in a culture where that's real common. It kind of comes and goes with the territory. That's not to say that it has to, but the screenwriters and writers I know, many of them have had issues with substances.

DK: I'm a native of Los Angeles as well, and a lot of us seem to share varying ideas about the city. One of the things I love about your work so much is that I notice a similarity to Joan Didion's debut novel *Play It as It Lays*. Didion's protagonist, in that book, aimlessly roams the highways, seemingly in search of connection as the city's rhythms ebb and flow all around her without truly impacting her. I notice that you've written a fair amount about your experiences as a cab driver, and it strikes me that, intentional or unintentional, transportation is a running theme through your work. I'm wondering if there's any connection, if that maybe speaks to some restlessness, or maybe if that somehow factors into your take on the city.

DF: I would say that I grew up in Los Angeles in the late-fifties, early-sixties, and it's a motor city, and it's a car culture. When I was a kid, it was all about cars. So when I went to New York, and began driving a cab, I had lived there for a year and hadn't driven a vehicle at all. The first time I got into a car after about fourteen months of living in New York was when I took a driver's test. So I took it and passed it, and then I became a cab driver and took a geography test, but had no knowledge of New York City whatsoever. I'll never forget the first passenger who got in my cab, and it was in the Bronx on the Grand Concourse, and he said, "Well, take me to 176th Street and Clay Avenue," and I said, "Can you direct me," and he said, "It's three blocks!" I didn't have a clue. For the next eighteen months, everybody who got in my cab, I said, "Can you direct me," and that's how I got to know New York City. That's a long answer, but the other answer is the wonderful thing about driving a cab is you don't have a boss, and when you're driving a limo, which I did as well, there's a lot of downtime for reading. It was an easy job, and the money was good, and I could sustain myself.

DK: When I first met you, I remember telling you that I had just finished the first Bruno book you'd written. What I loved so much is the presence of hard-boiledness that I felt was so absent in any contemporary Los Angeles fiction these days. Yet, when I was thinking about it, this noirish sensibility is such a vital part of our city's literary tradition. Are there any writers of this tradition who've influenced you in that regard? Who have really helped identify this great hard-boiled edge that you've brought to your own fiction?

DF: My inspiration as a writer was mainly Hubert Selby Jr., who wrote *Last Exit to Brooklyn*. I read that book in the mid-eighties, and after writing poetry for ten years, unpublished and unoffered I might add. When I read *Last Exit to Brooklyn*, it just spun my head. I said: Wow—if he can write that, so can I. Because my latest novel is detective fiction, I immersed myself, and I reread some Chandler, some Dashiell Hammett, and then all the way up to the current writers, so I probably read fifty or sixty novels in considering my detective novel, *Point Doom*. I think that the person who writes the best fiction in that genre today is Connelly. If you consider that these publishers want a new manuscript from you every nine months, their incomes depend on it, and this guy is coming out with—I don't know how many books he's written—thirty, thirty-five. I consider it an extraordinary achievement that he can continue to write good prose and sustain interest from the reader. I admire his work very much in that genre. In terms of local writers, there's also another writer who's quite good. His name is Mark SaFranko. He's written *Hating Olivia*, which is a terrific book. He's probably got four or five novels in print. He's also published in France, as I am. I look for a tone from a writer, and a personal experience that I can relate to. I can't help it as a reader. Kafka's line has always stuck with me as a great line—a good novel should have the same effect as a blow to the head. Unless you've got something to say, if it's an exercise for you, then maybe screenwriting is better.

Dan Fante was born and raised in Los Angeles. At twenty, he quit school and hit the road, eventually ending up as a New York City resident for twelve years. Fante has worked at dozens of crummy jobs including: door to door salesman, taxi driver, window washer, telemarketer, private investigator, night hotel manager, chauffeur, mailroom clerk, deck hand, dishwasher, carnival barker, envelope stuffer, dating service counselor, furniture salesman, and parking attendant. Fante is married and has a two year old son named Michaelangelo Giovanni Fante. He hopes eventually to learn to play the harmonica.

MICHAEL WALKER

David Kukoff: Laurel Canyon occupies a special place in the hearts and minds of a number of Angelenos. In your opinion, what do you think were the social, geographical, and historical factors that made the world of which you wrote about so memorable and such an important part of this city's history?

Michael Walker: For one, it's only five minutes from the Sunset Strip. It's astonishing—you feel like you're in a different world already. There's all these winding roads, eucalyptus trees, coyotes, deer, raccoons. I live there still, and it's like a nature preserve at night. But you have this beautiful canyon tucked into this incredibly unattractive city. It was a good place for musicians to congregate. The other thing that happened was that the area had declined and it became cheap to live there. Most of the people who came to Laurel Canyon were failed folk musicians who'd come up from New York and elsewhere. So, all of those factors were very important. It was a setting that was idyllic. It was very conducive to creativity.

DK: You made an interesting point, that this was sort of a last stand, that a lot of these folk musicians had washed out elsewhere. Some of them had been kicked out of their bands, or things had just generally not gone well for them in other outlets.

MW: Start with The Mamas and The Papas. John Phillips, Michelle Phillips, Denny Doherty, and Cass Elliot had gotten close to making it in the folk music scene in New York. If you saw the movie *Inside Llewyn Davis*, that was a pretty good example of that scene. There was no money, a few people did really well out of it, but basically they'd run out of steam in New York and come to LA. John Phillips came to Los Angeles with his suitcase and his guitar and the music in his head for "California Dreamin." Cass Elliot was already here, and she was staying with a guy named Jimi Hendrix, who had played with Denny Doherty earlier. There was all this incestuous activity going on. So, they're all broke, and when they finally get to play their songs for Lou Adler, owner of Dunhill Records, he kind of looked at these guys and couldn't believe they were good. He couldn't believe that no one had bought these songs or signed these people. He went to his sound engineer, Bones Howe, and said, "What do you think?" And Bones said, "If you don't sign them, I will."

The other thing was that at the time, technology was so primitive compared to what it is now. Most of these people didn't have phones. They didn't drive; they hitchhiked everywhere. So, you were constantly going out into the street and running into people. That's how a lot of these songs got written. You would wander into so-and-so's house, hang out on the deck with your guitar, and then hitchhike down to the Sunset Strip and Santa Monica Boulevard and go to the Troubadour. Everyone went down there on Monday nights, so the Troubadour was just packed. If you can imagine, Monday night: Glenn Frey, future member of The Eagles, John Phillips, Michelle Phillips,

Denny Doherty, all of The Mamas and The Papas, half of The Byrds. These people would all be in one room at one time. You can imagine the sparks that were going off.

DK: Activism seems so naturally compatible with music, and yet it's hard to think of any similar musical movements that left an indelible imprint on the social conscience of the country as the scene that existed in Laurel Canyon. What do you think was so different from, say, grunge in the early 1990s Seattle, or alternative or industrial music in early 2000s Williamsburg?

MW: You had a bunch of people coming of age all at the same time. That's very important for why this happened the way it happened. It's this huge bulge of 18-25 year olds hitting young adulthood at exactly the same time, and they spoke with a much more unified voice than later on. Janis Joplin said at one time, in response to someone saying that the 1950s weren't so bad, "Oh honey, you have no idea how boring it was."

This was a generation that was bored of it. They did not want to be like their parents and follow the same path, and where they happened to coalesce, for a lot of serendipitous reasons, was Laurel Canyon. They started writing the songs and making the music they did, but they already had the precursor of The Beatles coming in and unifying the future of rock and roll in a way that Chuck Berry and Elvis didn't really do. This was new. This was different. This was much sexier, and it was just for them. That's how you got a song like "For What It's Worth." Stephen Stills could watch the Sunset Boulevard riots—which were riots about a club, Pandora's Box, where the West Hollywood sheriff's deputies were just randomly harassing people because the business owners wanted them off the Strip. They should have welcomed them, because the Strip was dying without them. So, when Stephen Stills writes a song about this and they put it out as a Buffalo Springfield single, it speaks to a lot of people about issues that they all dealt with.

DK: Both of your books, *What You Want Is in the Limo,* and *Laurel Canyon,* address a seismic shift in the cultural landscape. How do you think some of that has manifested in the current social and political landscapes? Is there any residue that you see as dovetailing back to a similar point in the mid-seventies?

MW: The music had more influence then than it does now. Contemporary music just isn't as politically and culturally important as it was then. It's far more commoditized, it's far more star-driven, and moreover, all of that was pre-Internet, so the music business isn't as powerful as it used to be because the money isn't as big. The hits that the industry took; it's a staggering amount from pre-Napster to now. Thirty to forty percent decline across the board? It hit everyone really hard, so it just isn't the cultural force that it used to be. I should clarify: the commercial cultural force. It's very hard for musical trends to set the agenda as much as they did. They just don't anymore. Probably more people listen to music than they did then, because it's much more available, but it's not available in a viable business model anymore, or at least to the extent that it could support what came before. It's far more personal now. You don't buy an album as much as you make a playlist. You take albums apart and desynchronize the songs to fit your tastes. You customize everything now on your iPhone or iPad or any mp3 player. You can go to Spotify or Pandora, and have nothing but the music that you want to hear and like streamed to you. That was impossible back then. You had to listen more, and there weren't that many radio stations, so you had to go and see the bands and share with your friends little by little and hand by hand. It was a much slower progression, but I think that people were more devoted to the music and the musicians than they are now. I think it's more temporal now.

DK: I find it interesting that literary authors in the 1950s were viewed as rock stars. Norman Mailer sold millions of books and was world famous. Now, literary fiction is kind of a niche, which, along the lines of what you're talking about, seems to be similar to where serious musicians have gone as well. The types of bands in the days that you wrote about—especially in *What You Want Is in The Limo*—who sold ten or twenty million albums now sell hundreds of thousands and have to rely on concerts to generate revenue. They might have a loyal fanbase, but they would hardly be the worldwide phenomenon they were then. When I read *What You Want Is in the Limo*, I knew of course that The Who and Led Zeppelin were enormous touring bands in the 1970s, but I had forgotten how big Alice Cooper was. Can you talk about what they represented as far as the future of showmanship is concerned?

MW: Before Woodstock, the record industry was a very small industry. Then executives saw 350,000 people standing in the mud to hear this stuff, realized it was huge and started investing in it. The interesting thing about the Alice Cooper band is that they put that show out on a two hundred thousand dollar stage designed by Broadway set designers and it cost them a fortune; because of that, the tour didn't actually make much money. The overhead was too high, but that tour changed the game. Lady Gaga's tours would not exist if it weren't for that, because it brought the element of theatricality into the live performance of rock music, which had never been done before. Alice always bragged that, "We did it before David Bowie, who did it before everybody," and that's true. After 1974 or 1975, everyone went out with a big stage. Led Zeppelin in previous tours were essentially standing in a bare stage with roadies waiting in the wings and cables hanging everywhere. They got a lot flashier after that.

DK: When I was writing *Children of the Canyon*, I realized I had this unique opportunity to view Joan Didion's universe through the eyes of a child, which I didn't think had been done before. What were some of your personal reasons for your fascination with this time and place in music history?

MW: The seventies were important. Roe V. Wade was passed in 1973. In my introduction to *What You Want Is in the Limo*, I mention that there was a lot that happened that year, like the World Trade Center opening. The early seventies were a period of transition, and it's always fun to write about periods that are kind of astride two eras. The subtitle of the book could very well be *The Year the 60s Finally Died*. For a lot of the people I talked to, there was a kind of carryover from the hippie era. Robert Plant was still writing lyrics with a straight face in 1973, like "You are my flower, you are my power, you are my woman who knows." Even I thought that was a little bit much at the time. You could still get away with that then, but the window was closing fast, and the business really changed after that. It got much more muddy, much more cynical. It became the plodding dinosaur stuff that, years later, punk would kick out the door.

They were successful in what they were trying to do, which was to make something out of nothing, encourage people to try a different approach. There was just so much great music made that year: *Dark Side of the Moon* by Pink Floyd came out, *Innervisions* by Stevie Wonder came out. It really was the end of an era, and I felt like no one had really written about it with the affection that I had for it. I really liked it, and I wanted to pass that along as a very affectionate memoir of the bands that I was such a big fan of.

Michael Walker is the author of the national bestseller Laurel Canyon: The Inside Story of Rock-and-Roll's Legendary Neighborhood, *as well as* What You Want Is in the Limo. *His writing has appeared in* The New York Times, *the* Los Angeles Times, *The Washington Post, and* Rolling Stone, *among other publications. He lives in Los Angeles.*

EVELYN MCDONNELL

David Kukoff: *Queens of Noise* was one of my favorite reads this past year. What I was especially taken with, was how you began by talking about Reyner Banham's *Los Angeles: The Architecture of Four Ecologies*: the hills, the flatlands, the beaches, and the freeways. Can you talk a little bit about how you rooted some of The Runaways' development in this theory, and how that philosophy might be a little different in today's Los Angeles, if you think it is, in fact, different?

Evelyn McDonnell: Well, the Reyner Banham book *Four Ecologies*—which also became a BBC special documentary—I saw in an architecture class I was taking at USC, about basically the modern contemporary houses in LA, the mid-century Modernism movement. This book was written in the early seventies; Banham is a Brit who embraced some of the things that other people consider negatives about LA, including the freeway system, which most people think, "Oh LA, the freeways," and he's saying, "No, they're these works of beauty." He refers to the city as Autopia. He really just positions LA as the prototype of the modern city in a good way. He divides it into these four different ecologies as he calls them, different environments. Autopia being the urban parts. Surfurbia being the Golden Coast, Orange County, Huntington Beach areas, anywhere along the coast. The Plains of Id would be the lowlands, and the Highlands would be the Hollywood Hills and such, which I thought was an imaginative, kind of a playful, poetic way of defining the city. It was written just a few years before The Runaways started, so it's contemporary. I also talk about the response to his book, which was the art critic Peter Plagens writing an *Artforum* essay called "Los Angeles: The Ecology of Evil," which was really coming down on the other side of LA.

DK: In *Queens of Noise*, you discuss some of the original Runaways, their place in the Four Ecologies.

EM: One of the things that's interesting about The Runaways, is that it wasn't like they were all friends in Echo Park and they all played in their parents' garages. They were brought together from different parts of LA that really captured the different ecologies. Sandy [West] was living in Huntington Beach, and was born in Long Beach. Lita [Ford] was also from Long Beach, so they really represented Surfurbia, as he calls it, which is one of my favorite terms. Then, on the clear other side of LA, up in the Valley area, were Joan Jett, Cherie Currie, and Jackie Fox. Sort of representing the Plains of Id was the original lyricist, Kari Krome. So, the thing that's kind of missing from Banham's work is really a description of Hollywood itself. It's weird that he doesn't really address the LA that most people think of when they think of LA, which is Hollywood, where the band ultimately came together. I use his work more to describe the kind of suburban sprawl. Which is, what we would call it later, the exurbs of places like Orange County.

DK: As you mentioned, The Runaways' world really started at the Sunset Strip, which is geographically close to, but realistically worlds apart from, the area about which I wrote in my book, *Children of the Canyon.* Yet both these areas seem to be unified by this healthy disregard for authority. Could you discuss the ways in which you think the counterculture movement of the sixties and early seventies, but primarily the late sixties, might have affected the hard rock aesthetic of the Strip?

EM: I talk in the book about Hollywood, West Hollywood in particular, really being a Bohemian outpost. This was like the Greenwich Village of LA. It was where outcasts went to escape their nuclear family nightmares. The fact that the band is called The Runaways is important; they were completely tapping into both the mythology and the reality of people escaping abusive homes, or homes that were not accommodating to their sexual orientation, and coming to Hollywood. Hollywood was the place where they could be weirdos and experiment with sexuality, and experiment with drugs, and experiment with Rock and Roll. All of those things were happening, and all the Runaways, particularly Kari Krome, really speak about this eloquently. This is mostly her story, although I think it is all of their stories to a degree. But I think a lot of the young women who came into that scene also became sexually exploited and became groupies. What I think is really interesting about The Runaways, and I give Kim Fowley (their manager, producer, and songwriter) complete credit for, is that he put them on the stage. He didn't just have them service the rock stars—he wanted them to BE rock stars. To me, they created the blueprint for Los Angeles rock and roll. It transitioned from The Doors and Frank Zappa into punk rock and hair metal.

DK: I had the good fortune to be present for the panel you moderated with Exene Cervenka and Allison Wolfe. And I remember them talking about how they felt in both their worlds that—and Exene made this point quite nicely—there was such an opportunity for women to come in there and express themselves. Punk, unfortunately, got a bit of a bad rap in its later years, when it was consumed by the hardcore scene. People forgot that in its early days, really in its first and purest iteration, it was much more rooted in performance art and in questioning what music could be in so many ways. I had forgotten, until Exene brought it up in the panel, how strong the women were in the punk scene versus how little power they had elsewhere in the music industry. Could you discuss some of your takeaways from that night vis-à-vis The Runaways' lasting impact on the role of women in the music world?

EM: That was such an amazing night, a complete honor to share the stage with those two women and to moderate the discussion. There's a quote in my book that Exene gave to The Los Angeles Times around 1980 that was very dismissive of The Runaways. And it's funny, because I had tried to interview her for the book, so I was relieved to find her at the event and be able to ask her things. I know she, Joan Jett, and her then-husband John Doe all hung out. They were friends. So, to press her on that, she admitted that she was being very Exene when she said what she said about the Runaways. They—Joan Jett in particular—actually were a big influence on her. Certainly, Allison Wolfe represented the next generation of women musicians, the riot grrls of the early nineties. And, as singer of the band Bratmobile, she sang a cover of "Cherry Bomb." That was actually one of Bratmobile's signature tunes. Joan Jett was extremely supportive of Bratmobile in particular, and all the riot grrl bands in general, by getting on stage with them, co-writing songs, and producing records. There's a very clear lineage. Something Exene brought up actually, that Allison is very active in, is the Rock and Roll Camp for Girls that exists all around the world (including LA, Portland, and New York), and how it's passed the torch to a new generation of very young women.

DK: A quick question on a personal note: I like to tell people that the book I wrote is far more personal than strictly auto-biographical. Certainly when people look at me with concern after reading the book, I have to say, "Don't worry, it didn't happen exactly like that; it wasn't a thinly veiled memoir," but it certainly was highly personal. Could you talk about how, if applicable, *Queens of Noise* was prompted by your experiences growing up? How your own background might have led you to be so fascinated by the story of The Runaways?

EM: They're very much an LA band, and I was born in LA. I'm a third-generation Californian, and it's always been very import-ant to my identity, although I haven't lived most of my life here. I just moved back a few years ago, after leaving when I was a child. But, we always came back here. I always had family here, and I always thought I would come back here. I had older cous-ins that lived in LA whom I was very much enthralled by, and they were so tough, and worldly, and they snuck out at night. Although, I have to say, I wouldn't want a lot of the things that happened to The Runaways to have happened to me. Nonethe-less, my cousins led the life I wish I'd been able to lead, except I was in a small town in the Midwest, and there was no Sugar Shack or Rodney's to sneak away to.

I'm a few years younger than they are, and I don't remember knowing about The Runaways when they actually existed. I was probably just a little too young and a little too remote. I knew about Joan Jett, and I was into punk shortly after that, but it just didn't penetrate my small town Wisconsin consciousness. That is, until they were rediscovered by the riot grrrls, and I just started to pay more attention to women's rock history.

Evelyn McDonnell is assistant professor of journalism and new media at Loyola Marymount University. She has been writing about popular culture and society for more than 20 years. She is the author of Queens of Noise: The Real Story of the Runaways, Mamarama: A Memoir of Sex, Kids and Rock 'n' Roll, Army of She: Icelandic, Iconoclastic, Irrepressible Bjork *and most recently co-edited* Rock She Wrote: Women Write About Rock, Pop, and Rap.

CARL GOTTLIEB

David Kukoff: *Children of the Canyon* explores the Los Angeles music world of the 1970s, which was kind of the first cousin of the film world in which you came of age, professionally speaking. I say "first cousin" because it seems to me there was so much overlap between the two worlds. I read about parties where young Hollywood luminaries were doing a lot of elbow rubbing with Dennis Wilson, even a fair amount with the likes of Charles Manson and the Family. A lot of interesting walls were coming down. Can you talk a little bit about your perspective on the interplay between those two worlds?

Carl Gottlieb: Well there's always been, among creative artists, a sense of community. I mean, that's why there are bohemian enclaves everywhere around the world, and Los Angeles was no exception. It had a deep intellectual history that people forget about, mostly stimulated by the arrival of the German émigrés just before World War II, and as refugees afterwards. That was when Thomas Mann, Stravinsky, and a number of influential intellectuals were here working, mostly in the picture business. At the same time, there were artists who were painting on the

Westside. Barney's Beanery was a fine art hangout. Ed Ruscha and painters like him had studios in West Hollywood where they worked. Then of course, you had the world of rock and roll that had found Laurel Canyon. When I worked in variety television, there was a lot of crossover between musical acts, comedy acts, and writers of television who went on (like me) to write movies.

DK: Did you have much experience with the music world?

CG: Well, if you look at Barney Hoskyns' *Waiting for the Sun*, you'll see me in the index. My then-wife and I were very much a part of that world from both sides. She was in vaudeville movies, worked with contemporary artists, was a tour manager, and an accountant. I was a performer, and I came from an improvisational theater in San Francisco and then we performed live here. So we were a stage act, a comedy act in Los Angeles, and then I went on to write television. When I got married, our house was conveniently located halfway between Laurel Canyon and the studios in Hollywood where people recorded. It was equidistant between the rock and roll hotels up the Strip, and venues—the Hollywood Bowl, [Hollywood] Palladium, Greek Theater. It was kind of a nexus, and people would stop and meet from all avenues of the business.

DK: A lot of screenwriters came from theater or publishing, or more experiential angles. Screenwriting wasn't always viewed as a writing career in and of itself. It was seen more as a way station in which people found themselves. Can you talk a little more about how you ventured into long-form film writing?

CG: It was kind of a natural progression of events. I had been writing variety television and comedy. Then I started writing some episodes of comedy shows–the first *Bob Newhart Show, All in the Family*. So then, with a good agent and a presentable appearance, you made your rounds to the studios and movie executives. In those days, there was still a tradition of development of material, where you could pitch an idea and be commissioned to write a screenplay about that idea, without the pressure of it having to be a studio blockbuster in order to get made.

DK: Off that point, I'm going to move on to the 800 pound shark in the room.

CG: (laughing) The *Big Fish* Movie?

DK: So much has been written about [*Jaws*]. I've read about your take on it—all the great stories about the shark not working and the budget soaring. I wish someone like Coppola's wife had been around at the time to film a *Hearts of Darkness*-type documentary, like she did about *Apocalypse Now*, because the making of *Jaws* is in some ways as fascinating as the movie itself. You wrote the film that, along with *Star Wars*, most film historians consider to be the symbol of when the movie business really moved in a different direction. Do you have any thoughts that might differ from that conventional narrative?

CG: Major industries such as movies, which is now well over 100 years old, go through an evolutionary process. Corporations have a life of their own, and the movie business is no different then any other. It started as an exciting, new industry, then it progressed through the studio system, where the monetization was maximized, and they secured a global market. *Jaws* was not the first summer blockbuster, but it was the first studio summer organized release. There were a few before *Jaws*—the pattern was not revolutionary. *Jaws* opened on 450 screens or so, and that was considered a wide release, whereas a wide release now opens on 2,500 or 3,000 screens.

It wasn't the blockbusters that changed the business in the seventies. The seventies, as a time for making movies, were just fine. So were the eighties for that matter. Pictures were being made for modest budgets, they were well marketed, and they sold. Hollywood was hitting a lot of doubles and triples—they weren't swinging at the fences for a home run every time.

DK: It seems like there's been this tectonic shift toward this trend called "the head of the comet," in which there are a few big titles and tentpoles, and everything else is this niche-ified piece of dust in the tail. It wasn't like the minute *Jaws* and *Star Wars* came around, that the head of the comet immediately presented itself in 1975 and 1976 and that was the end of it. Where do you see the film business heading now? Do you see it dovetailing back to what happened in the sixties, or has it changed to the point where we can't ever revisit that type of filmmaking?

CG: Well, it's kind of in danger of becoming like the Broadway theater–every season is worse than the one before that, and yet somehow there's always a Broadway season. There will always be movies. There's too much of a global audience for it, and there are too many more delivery platforms where they can be viewed, and a variety of venues—people can watch them at home more—as screens get bigger and sound gets better. People will always want to go out to the movies, so you'll always have a generation that wants to leave the house and go somewhere.

The studio system has consolidated almost as much as they possibly could. Unless there's going to be one global, mega-corporation that makes exactly as many movies as they have to in order to keep their screens full, and we'll watch whatever they tell us because there will be no alternatives for distribution. That's the 2084 scenario, but more likely it will limp along. Eventually—if the top-heavy sequel reboot, graphic novel adaptation model continues—there will, I think, have to be more smaller budget films to fill the screens of the multiplexes. They can't all play the same fifteen blockbusters all year long. Perhaps it takes a spectacular failure, and maybe that will convince them that they should change. As long as this model is successful, in business terms, they'll keep doing it like they're doing it.

DK: I don't know what you're watching these days, but do you see any sprouts poking through the concrete?

CG: It's not subtle—the best dramatic writing in the pop arts is right now on cable television. There are thousands of television writers making WGA wages. Whether it's *Breaking Bad, Sons of Anarchy, Justified, The Americans, The Blacklist, Nurse Jackie, Orange is the New Black*—there's a whole range of high quality, popular television that addresses some very interesting themes. That's where the artists are migrating to, and that's where some of the commercial interests are migrating. There's just more money and more fun doing television then there is in doing movies.

DK: And the exhibition model seems to be supporting it as well. My concern in the past with television was that it would just become so diffuse, between the phones and the computer, that there wouldn't be any center holding it all together, but that doesn't seem to be the case. People seem to be finding it just fine and they seem to be perfectly happy. The networks and basic cable have even been able to factor DVR viewership into ratings. Whereas what we're seeing with the exhibition model in cinema might not ultimately be sustainable. I used to say that as long as dinner and a movie was still the fallback Saturday night date option, we'll always have movies. But so many more people seem to be happy to watch a movie on demand and don't necessarily seem to be craving the communal environment that the multiplex offers. Do you see that as being the case or do you see any promising signs coming out of independent cinema to change all that?

CG: When the multiplex became the standard model for exhibition, those of us who really like movies were hopeful that, out of sixteen screens, an exhibitor could find one screen in a smaller theater and devote that to alternative, foreign, or independent films. But it was not to be—if they have a vacant screen, they put up another print of "Pirates of Hogwarts," so they can show it every twenty-seven minutes, and that's discouraging.

What has to happen is that exhibitors have to figure out how to bring prices down a little bit, because I think the general population can't support the movies as being a $100 evening out if it's a family of four. There has to be some effort made—take the model of the Alamo Drafthouse down in Austin, Texas. They started with one little theater, and now they've got more than thirty screens in the Southwest, and it's a damn fine way to see a movie—they play good films. If there are enough Laemmles, Alamo Drafthouses, and New York art theaters, then there's a hope that in the urban centers, there will always be a public place where you can go see a good movie.

Carl Gottlieb is an author, screenwriter, director, actor, and occasional producer. Currently he's an officer of the Writers Guild of America, West (Secretary-Treasurer) and most recently co-authored with Toni Attell The Little Blue Book for Filmmakers: A Primer for Directors, Writers, Actors and Producers. He is best known for his work as co-writer for the movies Jaws and The Jerk.

MATTHEW SPECKTOR

David Kukoff: Like me, you're a second generation Angeleno, and so much of what we consider to be great Los Angeles literature is written from the first generation perspective—do you think there's a difference in coming from where you came from, versus the perspective of some of those other authors?

Matthew Specktor: My first inclination is to say, "hopefully," which is not any way to disparage my peers or our predecessors. I was having this conversation last night with the novelist David Grand, who also has a recently-published novel set in Los Angeles around the turn of the twentieth century. He's an LA native like you and I, and we were talking about the particular ways LA gets represented, not just in fiction, but in the culture. I think it's a place that, historically, has been maligned and disparaged in ways that may or may not have fit with what the city used to be about, but it certainly seems not really congruent with what this place is now. Any writer has to confront the place of making their experience and their geography real. I felt like the challenge I was facing with *American Dream Machine* is really not that different from the challenge that any writer does.

Which is to try to bypass the perceived understanding of their life and their landscape, and try and refresh it in some way.

DK: So many natives lay down roots and stay here. I wonder if you feel the same way I do, that somehow at the core of the city, there still exists an intact, small town, one full of second or third generation locals who all know and marry each other and send their kids to the same schools and camps as the ones they attended. I think this makes Los Angeles different from a lot of other big cities. Has that been your experience as well?

MS: It has been. That's certainly a large portion of it. You're describing something that, as you were talking, I was thinking that this seems to be the trajectory for shall we say, privileged, male, Los Angeles writers who grew up on the Westside in the eighties. By which I mean at least the two of us and Bret Easton Ellis. Bret grew up in the Valley, but I've had this conversation with him too. He had that, "I grew up here. I'm not comfortable with the culture of Los Angeles (as it existed). I'm going to go East to college. I've got to get to New York." Exactly the same thing—that sense that Los Angeles was something to get out of. I'd like to say it's not true of New York based novelists, but I think it's hard for me to think of. When I think of contemporary novelists writing about New York, not that many of them seem like natives to me. I mean, Jonathan Lethem writing about Brooklyn, but Jonathan left Brooklyn too. I think that's a fairly common path for writers, not just for writers, for people.

DK: You're a co-founder of the *Los Angeles Review of Books*. Who are some of your favorite Los Angeles authors? I feel like there are so many locals who are doing such great writing, with whom many of us might not be familiar.

MS: I've been rereading a lot of Eve Babitz lately. I just think Eve's work is wonderful, because on the one hand, it's situated in that Los Angeles that I was so afraid of when I was a kid and so terrorized by, that sort of seventies Hollywood, with everything that that carries with it, but I think her tone and her approach to that is just completely different. There's a lightness of touch on the one hand. There's real ease, and affection, and a comedy, while at the same time there still exists this stringent moral and aesthetic rigor.

Thinking of books and writers that people probably don't know that well: MacDonald Harris—there's a novel of his called *Screenplay* that I'm very fond of. *A Way of Life Like Any Other* by Darcy O'Brien. On the one hand, there's a very rich shadow canon of Los Angeles books and authors, besides the ones that everybody knows and thinks of already. In terms of contemporaries, there are so damn many, but I feel not enough people read Steve Erickson. I mean, a lot of people do, but I think of him as this major, towering American novelist. I think his peers know that. DeLillo knows that. Thomas Pynchon knows that.

DK: Do you think he gets unfairly regionalized?

MS: On some level, most writers are. I'm hovering over that idea of being unfairly regionalized. On the one hand I think, the way that we tag and ticket books, all of us do that in a way, and the industry is hungry to do it too. Of course, my shelves are groaning with books where I think, *Well, I don't want to read a book about blah*. I knew when I wrote *American Dream Machine*, I thought, it's interesting to me that there are going to be people out there who are just going to say, "I don't like books about Hollywood," and neither do I, actually. Oh, and I also should mention Kate Braverman, an absolutely surpassing Los Angeles novelist.

DK: An extraordinary Los Angeles novelist. Her story, *Tall Tales From the Mekong Delta*, is one of the most compelling pieces of short fiction I've ever read.

MS: And I'm sitting here looking at Antoine Wilson's *Panorama City*, a fantastic book that came out the year before. I'm seeing a novel over there by a woman named Katherine Taylor, *Rules for Saying Goodbye*, which I think came out in 2008, and I guess that book is set in New York, but she's a Los Angeles writer whose work I really, really love and admire. Of course, the city's been sucking up the expats too with Lethem taking a spot in Pomona, and Jeff Dyer just moved here.

DK: Isn't that amazing? Who would've thought that almost forty years ago, when Woody Allen made that right-turn-on-the-red-light crack—an argument that wasn't even really valid back then—that a lot of the New York writers would actually want to take residence here? It's a shift in the national literary landscape that I hope continues.

What I feel sometimes escapes the radar, when it comes to assessing the Los Angeles novel, is the wonderful Latino literary tradition: Héctor Tobar and his excellent book, *The Tattooed Soldier*; Brando Skyhorse's *The Madonnas of Echo Park* was one of my favorite books of the last few years. These books are every bit as important about the Los Angeles experience, only they're not from the Anglo perspective that sometimes gets a little more PR. For example, Junot Díaz gets all kinds of props for writing about the Dominican perspective in New York, but I don't know if we necessarily afford our Latino writers the same luxury.

MS: No, no we don't.

DK: Given how rich a part of the city's history it is, it feels like a bit an oversight, and one I hope, at least from the literary perspective, we're moving toward being more inclusive of.

MS: This is an acute symptom of a much wider literary problem, but I do find that curious. Whenever they decide: This is the great Chicago novel. This is the great New York novel. This is the great Los Angeles novel. Of course, they look at the white guys.

DK: I have one last question for you: I know you're adapting *American Dream Machine* for Showtime right now. Writers have all kinds of thoughts about adapting any work, let alone their own. Given that there's been no small amount of press written about how television is the new literary form, what has been your experience in adapting your own literary work for the small screen?

MS: You know, people have asked me for as long as I've been writing, "Oh, did you think about that as a movie, or did you think about that as a TV show?" The answer is, of course not. When you're writing a book, you're just trying to write the best book you can write. It would be sort of like trying to cook two dishes out of one ingredient at the same time. You can't really simultaneously make a roast chicken and a chicken Parmesan with the same thing. In many ways, it's been a fully separated process. I finish the book, and around the time the book was published was when we sold the book to Showtime, and that experience of adapting, I sat down to adapt it and the material was completely recalcitrant. It just wouldn't budge, and I thought, good God, it's just no help to me at all having written this book. I have to invent this story from scratch, again.

So I did, and the truth is, it's been a delight. Startling, as someone who's only ever been a reluctant writer of features. I find the sort of aesthetic features being offered, in this case, really exciting. The material obviously, the kind of emotional impulses behind the book and the show are close to me. So there's that, which is quite wonderful. As much as I am enough of a cynic about stuff to feel like, all this sort of golden age of TV blather, well how much really good TV is there? Because, I turn on *Walking Dead*, and it's popular, but it sucks. But, it's also true that I watch *Breaking Bad* or I watch *True Detective*, and I think this is a truly, literary art form at this point. *True Detective* in particular, I think is so like a novel. It's a show, but so many of its strategies seem to me to be novelistic strategies employed in a different medium. Much more explicitly than I've seen with any other show on TV. I look at that and I think it is a very rich medium, and I'm loving doing it. Absolutely loving it.

Matthew Specktor is the author of the novels American Dream Machine *and* That Summertime Sound, *as well as a nonfiction book about the motion picture* The Sting. *His writing has appeared in* The Paris Review, The Believer, Tin House, Black Clock, *and* Salon *among other publications. He is a senior editor and founding member of the* Los Angeles Review of Books.

BRANDO SKYHORSE

David Kukoff: Echo Park functions as a major character in your book. You've spoken extensively about its character, about the ability of a neighborhood like Echo Park to insulate its inhabitants at times. I remember you talking about how your grandmother had an account at the liquor store, at the market, and was able to walk around and speak Spanish pretty much to everybody and never really have to leave the neighborhood or use English if she didn't want to. My question to you is, do you think that the Echo Park of which you wrote is changing, and if so, what effect do you think that might have on the resident cultures there now?

Brando Skyhorse: I certainly feel a little apprehensive about talking about Echo Park now, because I realize that I have not lived in the neighborhood for a number of years, but our family was there for decades. My grandmother bought a house with my grandfather in 1952, and we stayed in the neighborhood until about 1999. That was when my grandmother passed away, and I ended up selling the house. We were there for about fifty years. That's an enormous time where you can see an area undergoing several transformations.

Thinking about the transformation that Echo Park has gone through just in the past few years, I feel like it's helpful for me to think back to what my grandmother used to tell me about how the neighborhood was back in the fifties and sixties. My grandmother actually did speak fluent English. I have a memoir that's coming out this June in which I talk about being raised as an American Indian, even though I'm Mexican-American and my family is Mexican. My mother on one hand, who really wanted to be American Indian, didn't want me speaking Spanish at all, and my grandmother who spoke Spanish, and basically talked with everybody in the neighborhood, would try to teach me Spanish on the fly, but it never really stuck because every time my mother was around, I couldn't learn it at all. So, I grew up knowing that Echo Park was this weird, anomaly of a neighborhood for Los Angeles. At least it seemed that way to me.

I know when my grandmother first moved here in the fifties, her next-door neighbor asked her to sign a petition to prevent a black mailman from taking over their route. Then in the sixties and seventies, that's when you had white flight; people who had been in the area, lots of Polish immigrants and other Europeans, left the neighborhood and Latinos and Vietnamese people came and took their place. The area in which I grew up, in the seventies and eighties, was largely Latino with Vietnamese and Filipinos as well. It was already this cultural stew in which you had all these different ethnic groups kind of just trying to find their own little piece of the American dream. I think as far as what's going on today, again, I feel a little uncomfortable speaking to it directly, because I'm sure I would have a very different opinion of it if I were actually living in Echo Park now.

I did a reading at Stories Bookstore, I think it was last year or something, and it was a very special moment for me, because I'd always loved the idea of bookstores in Echo Park. My grandmother raised me to be an avid reader, but there were no bookstores in Echo Park. In order to get books, we either had to go to the public library downtown, because she felt that the selection at the Echo Park Library was too small, or we had to go to Glendale, to the old Crown Books over by the Glendale Galleria. It was like a forty-minute trip to get books. As far as the changes for minorities and younger kids in the area, the fact that there are bookstores now is a great, positive thing. At the same time, at least what I've seen from a distance, the area is changing, because people who could not afford other places to live in Los Angeles moved to Echo Park, and those people—largely minorities, largely poor, working-class—they're going to be squeezed out of the neighborhood. So what happens to them? It's a complicated issue. It's a complicated question, and I try to wrestle with this through my writing. I think just addressing the question is more important than actually coming up with any specific answers, because as far as the idea of gentrification goes, I don't think anybody really has a specific, pat answer that works for every single demographic or every single group.

DK: You've mentioned in other interviews that there is nothing harder to grow virally than literary fiction. I feel like there are these three growth circles that determine how a piece of material gets out there. Pretend you're looking at a model of the earth; you have the core, the mantle and crust, and the stratosphere. The core is friends and family, the people close to you who would support you no matter what. Beyond that, if you've addressed something of regional or cultural interest, maybe you can spread to the mantle and crust. Then, if there's something either truly universal or zeitgeist, it can explode out into the stratosphere. You have worked as both an editor and as a writer. What kinds of elements do you see at play from your vantage points? What would you advise a writer who's first getting going to try and incorporate in order to give his or her work the best chance of getting out there?

BS: I think it's a fantastic analogy, and the idea of spreading literary fiction virally, I didn't use those exact words, but that's a far more intelligent a way to look at it than I actually said it, so again, I'll be happy to take credit for that.

I've seen, working as an editor, a number of seismic changes to the publishing industry. The changes that have affected the music industry and the movie industry have basically affected the publishing industry in the same way. Publishing was always a much smaller business than music or movies in the sense that if you want to try to convince somebody to make a movie, you have to get a lot of people on board committed to spending a lot of money. In order to convince somebody to publish a book, you only have to really convince maybe five or six people. It's a much smaller area, a much smaller group of people that you basically are trying to connect with.

I think that publishing has always been catered to people who perhaps have more specific, singular visions in mind. I know that people in LA, who are thinking about trying to get their books published, are a little skeptical of New York publishing. They feel the publishing world sees LA only being virtuous for creating screenwriters who have books in their back pockets. Which, of course, is completely inaccurate, but I could understand how somebody who doesn't have any publishing contacts might believe that. I've never worked for a large publishing house. I've been published by Simon & Schuster for both of my books, but I only worked in independent publishing. Publishing any book is relatively small-scale, but publishing through independent publishers…now that's really small-scale.

You need basically three or four things in order to get attention for your book from an editor or an agent: You need a really sound idea. You need a really well-written manuscript. You need patience and time. And, the most important thing—which is something I tell everybody every time I have this kind of conversation—you need to not be insane. What I mean by that is that you have to be a responsible person and treat this like a profession. Treat this like a business, and treat the people that you're working with as businesspeople.

DK: I read more than my fair share of literary fiction that's perfectly observed, nicely written, and well-mannered enough, but there's no real cultural or zeitgeisty reason why this book, other than it having some pretty prose, would stick around for ten, twenty, thirty years. Whereas with *The Madonnas of Echo Park*, not only are the bona fides there from the literary standpoint, but it also sticks with you because you're going to use it to ask yourself so many questions about the state of, for lack of a better term, indigenous cultures in America today. How are we interconnected, the way your characters found themselves interconnected both literally in neighborhoods and sometimes spiritually in terms of how their paths would cross? How is this book a cultural piece of Los Angeles and California's history?

BS: I am by no means any sort of paragon of social media magnet, but somehow, the book has found its way. And two reasons the book has found its way is: 1) It was fortunate enough to win a couple of awards, and 2) colleges have started adopting the book in a really big way. Those two things coupled together kept its nose right above water; it's not like it's ever going to be like a Stephen King bestseller, but it probably won't ever go out of print, and that's enough for me. I think that hopefully this model is enough for other writers in that you want something to give the book attention, get it in peoples' hands, and continue slowly and steadily so that it becomes a part of a publisher's established backlist. That's something that really no author can predict. But if the book is solid and it can find its way to people, the book will stay in print.

Brando Skyhorse's debut novel, The Madonnas of Echo Park, *received the 2011 PEN/Hemingway Award and the Sue Kaufman Award for First Fiction from the American Academy of Arts and Letters. The book was also a Barnes & Noble Discover Great New Writers pick. He has been awarded fellowships at Ucross and Can Serrat, Spain. Skyhorse is a graduate of Stanford University and the MFA Writers' Workshop program at UC Irvine. He is the 2014 Jenny McKean Moore Writer-In-Washington at George Washington University.*

DEANNE STILLMAN

David Kukoff: You're very much a writer of the West. Your books address a lot of very Western themes and motifs, some of which I'd like to talk about a little later. How did you first become fascinated with the region, and who, if any, were some of the literary influences that might have led you here?

Deanne Stillman: Well, I grew up on the mostly frozen shores of Northeastern Ohio, so that explains it, right? I never felt at home there, really. It never resonated with me, or I with it. And I don't like ice fishing, I don't much like winter sports. I just never felt comfortable there, but beyond that, there were a couple of other things going on. My father used to read a lot to me when I was a kid, and one of the writers he loved was Edgar Allan Poe. He used to read the poem El Dorado a lot, and that just opened up this escape hatch for me. It conjured up this notion of the "open road," and you know the refrain from it:

> *Gaily bedight*
> *A gallant knight*
> *In sunshine and in shadow*

Had journeyed long
Singing a song
In search of El Dorado

I loved that poem, and the idea of heading to El Dorado, which was the promised land—lined with sage, and cactus, and all these great imaginary figures, conquistadors and Indians, and so on. Also, my mother had horses, and she taught my sister and me how to ride. And that's kind of fueled my wanderlust, and so when I would go riding, I was also living in the West in my imagination and running with all of these characters across the open plain into El Dorado.

DK: Your specific milieu is the high desert, at least in the books I've read. Do you see the worlds of which you write, especially in *Twentynine Palms* and *Desert Reckoning*, as being places that contain any of the run-off of Los Angeles? I know some of the characters are either gang castoffs or people who have kind of fled the city, but could you speak a little more about how Los Angeles specifically touches and affects the high desert?

DS: Again, a really good question. LA, for sure, touches everyone, but for people who live in the immediate outback here, the wilderness around LA, they are very much affected by being so near the Emerald City because they know they can never truly be part of it. These are America's outcasts, unwanted figures to a great degree. They've come West and moved to the desert, many of them, to start over. And the West is every American's birthright. "Go West, young man," or woman, or whoever you are, and invent yourself, crank it up one more time, have it your way. But the flip side of that is that it doesn't really work for a lot of people, and especially for the figures I write about. In *Twen-*

tynine Palms, which is about two girls killed by a Marine after the Gulf War, I traced their family histories back through decades, in one case to the Donner party, and the other to a shack in the Philippines. They know that the desert, two hours east of LA, is as close as they're getting to the actual dream itself, and they know they count for nothing in this country. They put on their game faces like everybody, but it's pretty urgent out there.

DK: It seems as though there's this spiritual component to the high desert, something that makes it so much more than just a refuge, a place for people looking to hide out in the margins. You mentioned the Native American component; could you speak a little more to that, as well as how that affects your, if you'll excuse me saying it, high-brow/low-brow literature? High as in high desert, and low as in the culture that you're writing about?

DS: Well, first of all, there's all this great Old Testament scenery of the desert I am really steeped in, mostly because of El Dorado. That's kind of my heritage as a member of the Hebrew persuasion. Also, we're a country that's jacked on freedom. I really believe that our wide open spaces fuel all of that. You don't even need to have been there. We've heard this since we were school kids: "It's a free country, I can do what I want." That's kind of true, in a lot of ways, but must we? That's the flip side, and that's what I get into with *Desert Reckoning* in a certain way, because that's about the fatal collision between a hermit and a sheriff, set in latter-day LA in the Antelope Valley. In the desert, there's all this Native American history. There's this part of our past that we ignore and pretend isn't there that kind of underlies everything. When you start exploring that area, and even LA proper, you find that there are tunnels under the LA [Central] Library, which may have been constructed by the ancient Hopis, who were apparently traveling between the Southwest and the Coast. So, there are a lot of things going on that we tend not to know about or talk about, but they're burbling under the surface. Place really drives narrative in a lot of ways, and is kind of a character itself in my work, and I think it informs all of our lives, which is something I like to look at too.

DK: Something you mentioned about Donald Kueck [the protagonist of *Desert Reckoning*] and the two girls in *Twentynine Palms* struck me. On one hand, what these two narratives have in common is that they're both sad stories of demise on the fringe of the Emerald City. And yet, they're very different. The girls struck me as very different. They were trying to move toward something that was tethering them, trying to create this home, this community, whereas Donald Kueck had done the complete opposite.

DS: Kueck walked out on his marriage, after being married for a couple of years and having two kids. He knew he was not cut out for the conventional life; he was more of the classic hippie character when he came of age. I think he was born in 1950, 1952, or something. Just hit the hippie trail in the seventies. He tried to fit in; he came from a family of law enforcement, his father was in the air force, and he had relatives who were state troopers. But he went the opposite direction. He was the rebel in a lot of ways. He just dropped out totally. He cut himself off from civilization, headed for the outback. But later on, he tried to reach a rapprochement with his son, who was a real chip off the old block. Donald's son became a junkie and followed in his father's footsteps in a lot of ways. There's a thread running through all my books, which is, "Where's Dad?" The fathers have vanished from the lives of a lot of the people I write about.

It's very palpable. Here's Donald Kueck, who was this really dedicated hermit, living off the land up in the Antelope Valley. His best friends were animals. When he would have breakfast, he would set places at the table for jackrabbits. He had a raven living in his trailer, and he had a rattlesnake living in the bucket by his front door. These were his allies.

DK: Like a twisted Dr. Dolittle.

DS: Yeah. He was a Dr. Dolittle with an assault rifle.

DK: And a stash of crystal meth.

DS: Really demented man, but sad, because you know it was obviously some deep wound in his family that was never reconciled. That, and the failed rapprochement with his son, who did at some point come to live with him in what they called the "anarchy van" that was parked on Kueck's property in the Mojave. Things just didn't really work out, as I get into in my book, but that failed connection, that failure to get back with his son fueled his descent into the abyss. He was pretty far-gone anyway, but it just shows how essential these connections are, because that's when he really started to lose it. Telling family he was going to kill himself; he even dug his own grave and sent them a map of where it was. Then with Mandy and Rosa in *Twentynine Palms*, there was a series of father figures in and out of their lives, basically absentee dads. Mandy was the town babysitter; these girls tried very hard to form their own community, and did. They had Debie McMaster, Mandy's mother, who was this amazing ex-biker chick mom. A lot of these families had military history, their brothers and fathers had served in all of our wars, and then they come home and they're not treated well.

They know they count for nothing, but they would literally give their blood for this country. They're not welcomed back for a whole range of reasons, and then they fall into a whole host of trouble. Debie called Mandy and the girls who were kind of in her orbit the "Lunchbox Gang," and that was in response to all these other tribes in town: Marines, Crips, Bikers. It's very tribal, and everyone has their own crew.

DK: Like the people who lived on the land hundreds of years before.

DS: Like the original inhabitants of the land, exactly.

Deanne Stillman is a widely published, critically acclaimed writer. Her books include Mustang: The Saga of the Wild Horse in the American West, *a Los Angeles Times "Best Book 2008," and winner of the California Book Award silver medal for nonfiction, and* Twentynine Palms: A True Story of Murder, Marines, and the Mojave, *a Los Angeles Times "Best Book 2001." Her latest book,* Desert Reckoning *is based on her Rolling Stone article, "Mojave Manhunt," a finalist for a PEN journalism award.*

JERRY STAHL

David Kukoff: When you came out with *I, Fatty* a few years back, what attracted you to the story of Roscoe Arbuckle? What made you want to write a book about him?

Jerry Stahl: Well, Bloomsbury was doing a nonfiction series about various characters, and my friend Anthony (who's now huge, Anthony Bourdain) was doing one on Typhoid Mary, and he asked me if I wanted to do one on a character out here. So I picked Roscoe Arbuckle, but when I started writing it as nonfiction, it just came out as a term paper. It was just dry, and other people had done it better. So I figured, what I can do is just give him a voice. So, without telling them, I wrote it as a novel, sort of by default.

DK: I'd read a lot about Roscoe Arbuckle from other journalists, but you really got inside his skin, his ample skin, and did such a marvelous job of capturing that sense of self-loathing without self-pity. For a guy who had a rough go of it, he was really kind of a triumph too. I've got to tell you, it's one of my favorites.

JS: Thanks, man. It's easy when you have a plot. I remember, for about a minute, Philip Seymour Hoffman was going to play Fatty. Johnny Depp owns the property, and he said it was "your autobiography under the guise of this fat man." Which is just what you're talking about; a lot of the self-loathing and all the stuff we all go through, me just sort of projecting my emotions in his corpus. In fact, he wanted to use the actual fat suit he had to wear as a character in the movie, so that the guy's front, in effect, was also a character as well as his reality, essentially. Kind of brilliant.

DK: Did anyone you know actually go the other way, kind of the way you went, from less-challenging Hollywood fare to more personal fiction? From *Alf* and *Moonlighting* and an episode with Mark Frost in *Twin Peaks* to writing *Bad Sex On Speed*?

JS: Well, I was always writing this stuff. You do what you have to do to pay for what you have to pay for. So, for me, there's not that much difference between *Bad Sex On Speed* and *Alf.*

DK: Really?

JS: Ah, different costume. I only wrote maybe two of them, and maybe eight of my words survived. I got that gig because the woman I ended up marrying for a green card knew Tom Patchett, who would go on to found Track 16. He'd known my stuff in *Playboy,* so he brought me in. I'd never seen a script before, I didn't know how to indent, or know about Final Draft, or any of that shit. I didn't have an office or anything. I just sort of bumbled in and bumbled out.

DK: What's your writing process now? Obviously, you're incredibly prolific. You wrote a lot of material, like you said, even when you weren't in the best frame of mind.

JS: Do you wait until you're in a good frame of mind to write?

DK: No, not always.

JS: Do you get up every morning and write?

DK: No, I write at three in the morning sometimes when I can't sleep. I think you quoted Voltaire in your first book; he said "Self-delusion is the key to happiness."

JS: I've been known to quote Voltaire only because I keep a lot of quotation books by the toilet, so I can muster quotes from books I've never heard of and authors I've never read.

DK: I was actually asked to leave my school.

JS: There you go bragging! You were asked to leave your school?

DK: When I was in first grade.

JS: You got expelled in first grade? What did you do? Were you a biter?

DK: No! I tried to check a book out of the library. That's a true story. I went to this über crunchy school that was, quote, "not into pushing reading onto the kids," and they decided that I was a bad apple.

JS: You were too crunchy for them!

DK: No, I was too straight for them. I was the kid who wanted to read, you know?

JS: I'm impressed you could read in first grade. God bless.

DK: Yeah, I was reading from a young age.

JS: Wow, early bloomer. So, when did you write your first book?

DK: After college.

JS: And where can we get that one?

DK: You can't. It never got published. It's still in my library somewhere.

JS: You know what I like about you? A lot of people, when they get asked what they've done, they only include things that have been produced or published. You're not afraid to march out stuff that never got published. People don't like to talk about that stuff.

DK: Really?

JS: Yeah! Who cares if it got made or published? You wrote it.

DK: My first five scripts were so bad that no record of them exists on the planet. It's almost like they biodegraded.

JS: That's almost like my entire journalism career. See, I never wrote a spec script. To this day, I haven't written anything on spec. I'm lucky. Actually, I'm working on some stuff with Larry Charles, so I'm lying, but I've always had the inclination to write a book. Even now, you can make much more money doing film. But I just don't think…screenplay-icly

DK: It's kind of a weird 'tween step.

JS: Oh, not at all.

DK: It wasn't when I first started writing features, because you could actually get work as a screenwriter. It was a great job. You had the novelist's hours and the novelist's lifestyle but you got paid and you got to see some end result for things.

JS: Oh, I never thought about it like that for the novel. For me, writing a screenplay, the difference between that and writing a novel is that when you're writing a screenplay, it's like people are yelling in your ear and smacking you in the back of the head while you're writing. When you're writing a novel, it's pretty much just you. At least, that's my experience.

DK: Anything you want to tell us about *Bad Sex On Speed*? I want to hear more of your thoughts on it.

JS: Ask me anything, man. You can hear my thoughts.

DK: Did it just pour out of you? Did you have structured ideas at the time, individual stories?

JS: Do I look like the kind of guy who has structure to anything?

DK: Probably not. Yeah, that's probably the wrong question to ask. So how'd you end up writing it?

JS: Well, I was asked to write a book of poetry by a French publisher. Failed abysmally. You know, because "Roses are red…" just doesn't translate, it doesn't rhyme as much in French. What're you gonna do? Rouge is not a good word.

I wrote a crazy version, sort of an early version of that. Then I revised and expanded it and polished it up. Made it the gem it is. And I was on a strange drug when I wrote it. I was on a trial drug to cure Hepatitis C, which I got from being a dope fiend, that wasn't yet approved. And one of the side effects, the main side effect, although there were other kinds of heinous side effects…I didn't want to do Interferon, as you may know. So, they came up with this thing, you know, I had been sort of dying for the last few years, not to brag. And the side effect was basically like being on bad acid, and it was really just a kind of fractured way of thinking. It's hard to explain. It's like my brain was itchy, you know? And I thought I could fight that, and fight against it.

We have the great good fortune to be artistic types. You can actually use that kind of shit. So I basically wrote in the grips of, and in the voice of, someone who's just so mentally twisted up and kind of significantly crippled in an ability to think rationally. And that was very reminiscent. It was like an echo. Because I've done some research into the world of hard narcotics including methedrine, and the pills, and the powders, and the needles, and the nose, and all that shit you can do.

DK: What was it like writing *Bad Sex On Speed* for a smaller publisher, versus some of the other work you've done for other publishers? Can you speak to that?

JS: Hey man, writing's writing, you know? The difference is that I actually know my publisher. The actual publisher. I haven't met Mr. Harcourt or Mr. Harper or Mr. Collins or Ms. Harper or Ms. Collins. I don't know what gender my corporation was. Whereas Tyson Cornell (Stahl's publisher) and I are good friends, and it was great. Total freedom.

Jerry Stahl, *a Pushcart Prize-winning author, has written six books,* *including the memoir* Permanent Midnight *(made into a film with Ben Stiller and Owen Wilson), and the novels* Happy Mutant Baby Pills, Pain Killers, Bad Sex On Speed *and* I, Fatty *(optioned by Johnny Depp).* *Former Culture Columnist for* Details, *Stahl's widely anthologized fiction and journalism have appeared in a variety of places, including* Esquire, The New York Times, Playboy, The Rumpus, *and* The Believer.

TONI ANN JOHNSON

David Kukoff: Can you talk about how you wound up adapting *Ruby Bridges* for Disney?

Toni Ann Johnson: That came about because of a play I had written, called *Gramercy Park is Closed to the Public*, which was a stage play about a biracial woman coming to terms with where she fit in society. It took place in New York, and there were children in it, which I think is part of why Leah Keith (the Disney executive on the project) realized I knew how to write a child's voice authentically. The other was that I was writing about race and examining race, and also writing about race equally from white and African American perspectives, so it wasn't just a black perspective or a white perspective. I think elements of that play were particularly right for the material for *Ruby Bridges*.

I had to learn so much. I had to basically be a historian. I got this job in '95 or '96, and we had the Internet, or we were just getting it, but I didn't know how to use it for research then. I went to fiche, and looked up articles from *The New York Times* at the time, the *New Orleans Times-Picayune*, and all of the journalistic perspectives for what was going on. Disney did send me on a research trip, so I went to New Orleans and met with Ruby, and then I went to Boston and met with Dr. Robert Coles and with Barbara Henry, who was her teacher. I met all of those people, and taped interviews, and then I think I transcribed them too. I read a book called *The Second Battle of New Orleans.* I just immersed myself in that time to learn everything. I went to all of the locations, the ones that still existed anyway, just to see and feel how the walk was for her. She showed me her neighborhood. So, I really just saw everything that I possibly could, and read everything that I possibly could, and talked to everyone—anything that could give me a look at that world.

DK: Can you talk about some of your other theatrical and feature work–in particular, *Crown Heights*, for Showtime? What kind of research did you do for that movie? I want to tread lightly with regard to the tensions between different cultures sharing neighborhoods, but I'd also love to hear if you've seen any similar situations here, or in New York.

TAJ: In my research, first I read a book by Dr. Laz, who wrote a memoir about the experience. Then I went to New York. I got on the subway by myself to meet one of the kids who one of the characters is based on, somewhere past Crown Heights actually, and when I got off the train, something was going on–there were police cars everywhere and I was terrified. I talked to this kid, TJ, and I had a great conversation with him and learned a lot about his perspective. He and Yehudi, another person that a character in the book is based on, are still friends. Yehudi was away, studying I believe, so I didn't meet the other kid. The movie, for those who don't know, is about how after the Crown Heights riots, there were a series of summits that brought together boys from the Hasidic community and boys from the African American community to talk, and out of that came a musical group that did rap. They sang and rapped, and all of their songs were about peace and bringing people together, building bridges. They would travel around the city presenting it, and they did a couple of events in their neighborhood in the park. These boys became friends through that, but they fought a lot throughout the process. I think they met when they were fifteen, and when I met TJ, I think he was twenty-one or twenty-two, but they were still friends and they had overcome their differences. They had things they would tussle about, but they were always able to work it out. I think a sincere, genuine friendship came out of that.

DK: Like you, I chose to make music a significant thematic motif in *Children of the Canyon*. In my book's circumstances, the music is reflective of a childlike set of ideals, as it becomes clear that the literal and figurative children in my book must stop playing. The kids grow up, and the adults in the music industry, many of whom were behaving like children, finally have to realize that the country is moving on, away from their ideals. And their music, the non-corporate music made for art's sake, actually stops playing too. How was it that you came to factor music so significantly into the thematic fabric of *Remedy for a Broken Angel*?

TAJ: I'm an actress by training. I started at twelve, in upstate New York, and at fourteen, I was going to the Lee Strasberg Institute. At the time, it was the *Fame* time, so you did acting, dancing, and singing. I started singing, and a couple of my voice teachers thought that I'd be appropriate for jazz, so I was kind of steered toward jazz. I studied with one significant teacher of jazz, Hal Schaefer, in New York. He worked with Marilyn Monroe, he worked with Robert De Niro on *New York, New York*. Diahnne Abbott, who sang "Honeysuckle Rose," he coached her in that. He was awesome. So, I sang jazz, and because of that, I was trying to see it a lot. I was in New York, I was going to a lot of jazz clubs, I had a boyfriend who worked at one and would take me in, so I was going every weekend. Then, I dated a jazz musician after that, and I was going to jazz several times a week, so I was just in that world, trying to sing better. There's a character in the book who is a jazz singer, and I kind of knew about what she did and what her life was like. Her husband is a jazz musician, and the girl's husband is also a jazz musician, so it was familiar to me because I was in that world at the particular time that the book takes place in New York, 1990.

DK: As you mentioned, you've written about your neighborhood for the *LA Times*, about your pocket of South LA, and its resilience during the recession. You've also written about the greening of its streets. Can you talk a little more about your neighborhood's sociological make-up, how it reflects Los Angeles, and if you see that as being where LA is headed now?

TAJ: I live near the Forum, and you may know, the Forum has been revitalized. That may expand east to some of the other neighborhoods, I really don't know. I've been there long enough to see the property values go up and down. My property's value doubled, and then it went all the way down, and when it doubled, there were new people who moved in. Certainly, those people were doing better financially than the people who were living there before. But those people didn't all last, because when the value of their houses plummeted, a few of them lost their houses, and new people now occupy them. A lot has happened, even since 2007; there's been a lot of change. But as I mentioned in that piece, the core of the neighborhood has always been families that have been there for generations and have lived within their means.

There are people who, like me, come from the middle class and want to own rather than rent and are buying homes in those neighborhoods and fixing them up. I'm not saying I want to gentrify the neighborhood, but I am trying to make it more like a place where other people could be comfortable to live. It doesn't have to be a working-class environment. But it's definitely different types of people, which is a good thing for neighborhoods. That's one of the reasons I wanted to plant trees, too. I feel like having more green space and trees in a community, whether a kid is conscious of it or not, they're growing up in a place where something is growing—something is thriving and being nurtured. Even though they're not my children, I don't want to be in a community and have it be all concrete, and let the kids think they have nothing alive around them.

DK: There's no question that artists are always good for neighborhoods, because they bring a sense of aesthetics. There's a children's book that came out a while ago called *Frederick the Mouse*, about this little mouse who, while all the other mice are gathering food for the winter, is just collecting colors and pretty little things. And everyone's asking him what he's doing and telling him he's going to starve. Of course, the winter comes, and the mice are in this bleak chamber underground, and Frederick's colors give them something to look forward to, a distraction that lifts their souls and their spirits. It's why totalitarian regimes are always so colorless and monochromatic, because the whole point is to crush the soul. The slightest touches that you're speaking of, work immeasurably to create these intangibles in people that aspire to something they maybe never would have realized otherwise. Having an artist in the neighborhood is like having trees or flowers where, before, there was just a fence and a sidewalk.

Toni Ann Johnson *won the Humanitas Prize and the Christopher Award for her teleplay* Ruby Bridges, *the ABC movie and true story of the young girl who integrated the New Orleans public school system. Johnson won a second Humanitas Prize for her Showtime teleplay* Crown Heights, *about the 1991 Crown Heights Riots. Her stage play* Gramercy Park is Closed to the Public, *was produced in Los Angeles by The Fountainhead Theater Company and in New York by The New York Stage and Film Company. Her essays have been published in the* Los Angeles Times *and her short fiction has appeared in* The Elohi Gadugi Journal, Sprout Magazine, *and and* The Emerson Review.